The Gatekeepers of Elements

Awakening: The Meaning of Life

According to Strong Interaction

A. S. Dyrhon

ISBN: 979-8-8717-6642-2

THE GATEKEEPERS OF ELEMENTS

CONTENTS

THE GATEKEEPERS OF ELEMENTS

1

Far out in the dodgy end of the city, a slight clang marked a dark sight from the kitchen as Alex gasped for air. It should have been a simple nightly routine, casually sipping the last drop from his glass before he goes to bed, leaving the empty glass carelessly on the countertop.

But tonight, as the cool liquid slid down his throat, an inexplicable thirst gripped him and forced a sharp sound out from his throat. In his head, he heard loud voices screaming from the deepest ocean and felt a sudden pressure on his legs, making his sturdy knees weaken like playdough. This thirst and force seemed to reach beyond his body, but the voices whispered to him in a familiar voice.

As he set down the glass and stared into the abyss, he tried to stay focused and find a logical way to make sense of this feeling, but after all, it was just a quick, sharp sense. A couple of split seconds, so it could be just the long day, he thought and moved on without further worries. But what he didn't know was that this thirst was not his alone. And this very moment marked the change of his entire life forever.

The next morning, he had already forgotten this episode as his workday monotonously started with the same routines, but he did notice one thing. The office seemed a little too quiet for a regular Wednesday.

"What happened? Do we have a new virus? Where is everyone?" Alex asked the bald, sweaty guy sitting at the table next to him, who looked surprisingly fresh and less stinky today, for a change.

"Not sure," the guy replied as he turned towards Alex. "I'm always the last one to know about anything here, but if you want to know, in my opinion, something is definitely going around." He replied anxiously, eager to have someone who was finally listening to him.

"Jenny, my wife took the witch to the hospital two days ago. You know my mother-in-law," he added casually, "But when she came back, she was devastated, crying that her mom was left on the corridor, lying on a stretcher. All rooms are taken, and the hospitals are full. It's all like 2020 again, but now it's pretty weird. People are quiet, no screaming or yelling, just deathly silence. From my point, I am happy," he smiled contentedly, "Quiet and peace. That's all I want. Finally!" Then he turned back to his desk, opened his drawer to take out his half-eaten sandwich, probably from yesterday, and continued munching on it. "Gross…"

Alex felt a bit puzzled and cloudy since the morning, and frankly too tired to even just wonder any further about the guy's weird story, so he quickly put his worry aside. "Maybe I'm just thirsty," he concluded and made his way to the water cooler, which annoyingly was always squeezed out till the last drop by his colleagues and left there empty for someone to replace the heavy water bottle on the top. "Lazy buggers," he thought, but always felt like a good Samaritan after changing it. This performance was his daily amount of charity contribution for the common good, on the altar of the office Gods.

As days turned into weeks and months, the mysterious thirst grew more pervasive, and rumours began to spread. In office cubicles, on street corners, in hushed conversations over tea and lunch breaks. Headlines on every news channel on the TV, people shared their stories of weird lethargy and unstoppable need for water. A need that defied medical explanations, a need that seemed to weaken everyone deep down into their core level.

To be honest, it did not affect too much Alex. His life was all about his routine, and as long as every day after work he could catch the same car in the tube, he felt that his day was complete and fulfilled with productivity. Only one thing made him smile, the first time maybe in months. As Alex opened his home-built monstrous PC, he found the long-awaited email with a ticket to the GameCon. Just a casual weekend, where finally he can put his hands on the old relics of the gaming history, and he can be himself again. To relive his long-lost childhood memories, where he felt comfort in winning and being the best in every game he played. It was something he really missed, the feeling of completion and accomplishment.

And that was the moment he felt a sudden urge to dive into his old carton box, which was kept in his closet of shame. Where all the precious toys and memories were smashed into one container in a random, messy order, so only he could recognize the content. He quickly grabbed out a black console with the cable and looked around for the nearest plugin to fire up his Lynx. It was Alex's first toy, the first game, which he saved his money for months and played for hours, hiding after bedtime with a small torch light.

This Atari Lynx was the sole reason he had memories of his grandfather. The kind, old man, who often shared his enthusiasm and fascination for this game and bonded with him before he passed away so suddenly. It was everything he needed at this moment, but when he set down on the floor, he felt a sharp pulsating poke on his leg. "Erm, what is this thing doing here?" Alex mumbled quietly. "It must've stuck with the cable when I pulled it out from the box."

He picked up the little metal amulet from the carpet, covered with decades of dust and patina, and started to examine it more closely. Vaguely he remembered when his grandfather Aron brought it for his seventh birthday as a present. While his grandfather was taking out the medal from a shiny velvet pouch, he was murmuring something odd. Then he placed the thick, heavy necklace with the amulet in Alex's tiny hand, and he said: "The whole universe is in your hand now." Alex couldn't really make much sense of the story at that time, plus wearing something like that necklace was way too long and heavy for a little kid, so his mom safely put it in a box. Out of sight, out of mind; more than 30 years have passed, and Alex has totally forgotten about it.

"Gosh, how this ended up here? I can't remember seeing it. Mom or Dad must have thrown everything into this messy box when I moved out," Alex concluded.

The even stranger thing was how he actually felt at this point. It was not about the fact that this medal was traveling with him unnoticed for so many years from one college room to another apartment, over a dozen times, but the warm cozy feeling he felt when he held it. It was familiar, magnificent, and empowering. Like he had suddenly travelled back in time and space for a hug from his grandfather.

This little hollow object, with rectangular facets, looked like a misshaped dice cube. Alex vaguely remembered that some years ago he was reading about an ancient artifact, the Roman dodecahedron, and its mysterious use. For centuries, nobody could solve the enigma of how and why it was created. So, he quickly searched the internet, and there it was, exactly like his medal. The same shape and form, but in a smaller, walnut-size amulet on a chain.

"How cool, I have an ancient toy, wow!" He thought while he placed the necklace with the dodecahedron around his neck. And surprisingly, he totally forgot about his precious Lynx, laying just next to him, waiting to start the game. Without even placing it back in the box, he just went straight to bed thinking about his new lucky charm.

2

The next morning when Alex woke up, he felt a tingling sensation in his chest. For him, it was a bit unusual and a slightly uncommon feeling. He was happy. As he walked on the street, people smiled at him and even said good morning. A young guy went out of his way to hold the door, just to let him step into the car on the tube.

"Wow, I should shave more often," he thought to himself, concluding why everyone seemed to be so nice to him. But it felt rather good and flattered his ego, so he just nodded and enjoyed the ride.

As time passed, Alex started to get used to this nice feeling of having everyone praising him and his work. Things went pretty smoothly, besides the continuing terrible news and announcements from the media about the mysterious illness, claiming countless lives and spiralling out of control. Nobody was able to come up with any solid theory about what could cause this change in people with all the same symptoms at the same time around the world.

Just one common point was mentioned over and over in the news: "Drink lots of water! It's essential! Patients seem to be dehydrated, which can cause these serious problems, especially with elderly and sick people."

Only one notable thing happened in Alex's life, which was actually pretty annoying. The water malarky obviously resulted in Alex having to change the water bottles now twice every day, yet half of the office was already empty, as everyone was either on sick leave or worked from home.

"How on Earth does the water disappear so quickly? Seriously, nobody is here!" He looked around, trying to tell someone that enough is enough, but even the bald, sweaty guy's chair was empty. "Ha, I never actually got to ask him what his name is. We might never know…" Alex thought and smiled devilishly.

On the way home, he decided to run into the half-decent off-licence store, just around the corner. He figured out that if he makes a couple of ham and cheese sandwiches for the trip to the GameCon, from all the leftovers he still has in his fridge, he doesn't need to place a yellow biological hazard crime scene tape around his door when he comes home after 3 days. So, although it was not the usual and, more importantly, preferred place where he goes for shopping, it was on the way home.

When he stepped into the tiny store, a quite scary scene awaited him. The flickering neon light started buzzing, and as all the heads slowly turned, everyone in the shop sharply looked at him, like they saw a ghost.

"Hi. Hello," Alex said timidly, "Could you tell me where I am going to find the sliced bread?"

Silence, only the buzzing from the neon. No answer, just slowly and meticulously each hand raised and pointed in the same direction to the corner. As Alex was walking further, he felt suddenly a terribly strong, extremely pungent, foul, and overwhelmingly unpleasant smell. Like a dark age sewage ditch in the middle of the street between two pubs, collecting urine from both sides of the street, filled with hundreds of rotten eggs during an extremely hot summer day, at noon. In three words: it was bad.

Alex kind of stopped and looked again at the standing people in the store, but nobody seemed to care or stress, just watching. So, he stepped one more ahead and looked behind the bread aisle, where he saw a huge splash on the floor. The longer he was staring, the more it started to form a human body, in a flowery-print oversized dress, which was already soaked through with the blood and the fluids from the decomposing body.

"I... I... am... sorry, but... I... think this is... I mean, she is, or ..." stuttered and gasped for air from the stinking smell, and then from the sudden rising fear from inside him, he started yelling. "What the hell is going on here??? Call the police!" He screamed, while his body was shaking, hyperventilating as he was looking around, and locking eye contact with everyone, one by one. He couldn't tell if seconds or moments passed at this point, but it felt like hours. His whole life flashed down before his eyes like a film reel, and suddenly he was definitely, positively sure that this was his last day. He would never step out from this filthy store alive or see daylight again. And finally, but most importantly, he will miss the GameCon again, the third year in a row. "Bugger!" He thought and looked again, but still nothing happened.

Nobody moved or said anything, just slowly turned their back, continued with their shopping, and made their way in a calm and relaxed manner to the cashier to pay for their chips and beer, like nothing was wrong with the picture. "This... this is madness. I call the police. I call them now!" Alex uttered in a trembling voice as he reached into his pocket with a shaking hand for his phone, but there was still no reaction.

By the time the cops arrived, 40 minutes later, a new set of customers lingered in the store, paid, and also left, but nobody seemed to notice what happened. Only Alex was still there, holding his phone in his shaking hand, like his life depends on it. But even the cops seemed pretty chilled.

"Yeah. It happens," said the young officer to Alex, looking pretty bored as he was scribbling something on his paper. "Actually, we have more and more accidents, and we try our best, but you know... It happens, so life... Anyway, thanks for calling, and we will take it from here."

"And do you need my number or my name?" Alex asked, "Somebody will contact me, for the record? Or how does it work?"

"Hm, no. It's okay. Just try to relax, go home, and enjoy the rest of your day."

"What? What do you mean, enjoy the rest of your day? What's this? No investigation, or crime scene marking, like in the movies?" Alex asked, with obvious frustration in his voice.

"Calm down, this is probably just an accident, plus we are quite overwhelmed at this point. This seems like a pretty common case, so we just take it from here. Go home. That is the best you can do."

Alex was confused, tired, and felt that although it didn't make any sense, but he did his part, the police is here to handle everything, so it was time for him to leave. He had one last quick glance at the splash on the floor, grabbed angrily a pack of sliced bread, and slammed a fiver on the counter, in front of the cashier guy.

"Keep the change, you filthy animal!" Alex grumbled at him indignantly and left with the overwhelming feeling of emptiness, but also a dash of unexpected complacence with a subtle grin on his face, that he finally had a chance to say this epic line out loud.

That night only one thing kept his sanity and mind in a straight line after this terrible encounter in the shop. He imagined the next day with the lovely, warm feeling of entering the slightly overcrowded buzz of the huge convention centre, with its dozens of vintage arcade games, and the countless welcome taps on his shoulder and handshakes from the weirdos, who Alex dearly considered as his friends. Even though he never met those guys more often than once a year in the best-case scenario.

Nevertheless, it was something to look forward to, and as he walked home along the empty street, with the sliced bread in hand swinging around from his pace, he thought about this and felt at ease, with a glimmer of hope.

3

The morning came quickly, and as Alex put his luggage into the trunk of the Uber, he glanced at the corner, towards the off-license store. He was curious and wondered if it would still be open. To his surprise, he only saw two guys inside in white overalls scrubbing the floor, while customers were still casually walking in and out as if nothing unusual had happened. "Wow! This is definitely not normal," he thought as he jumped into the car, feeling that the place was like Sodom and Gomorrah, and most probably ready to be wiped off from the face of the Earth.

On the other hand, the Uber driver was a delightful experience for Alex after last night's encounter with those zombies. The guy instantly started to talk to him, and although half of what he said Alex didn't hear due to the loud Asian music from the radio, it made him feel relaxed, and he just kindly nodded to everything he understood as a type of question from the driver. Alex felt content and happy. Normally, he would actually promise a tip to the driver as soon as he sits in the car, just to shut his piehole, but now it was different. Surprisingly, he enjoyed this scenario. When they arrived at the station, the guy even helped Alex take out his luggage and wished him a pleasant journey. Then he added: "Whatever your destination would be..." It kind of made Alex feel like he could share something so personal, something he would never bring up in a normal conversation, but knowing he would likely never see him again, Alex felt safe and opened up to him.

"It is strange," Alex said, "I pass near this station so many times, but I never connected in my mind what this place means to me."

"Really? Why?" the guy stopped and looked at him with a kind smile.

"My grandfather lost his parents during the Second World War and escaped from Greece in 1942. Somehow, he managed to hide and spent weeks in train wagons to random destinations. After French soldiers found him and sent him here with other kids to Paddington station. You know, to find new parents. I can literally thank this place that I exist today."

"Oh, this is a beautiful story. You are a blessed man, can you see? They are taking care of you from up there," he smiled at Alex and hopped into his car, just before the bus behind him started honking for stopping in the wrong line.

His train trip was pretty standard, nothing extraordinary, but it allowed him to contemplate and put his ducks in a row in his head. Wondering about destiny, and how a nuanced minor change could alter someone's life and direct it to a different path. Like the train rails.

Who arranges the path of our life? Who is the traffic controller, sitting in a mighty room, and arranging the rails to go left, not to the right?

It was a one in a million chance that his grandfather didn't end up in the hands of Nazis and he managed to survive. He arrived with only one coat, no papers, but found a smiling face at the station and ran to her. All so random yet seems so perfectly aligned.

He was only twelve, didn't speak any English, but after changing his name and finding some random jobs here and there he managed to learn the language, the foreign country, and grew to love his new home. He always talked so kindly about the people here. To be honest, until now Alex never even thought to find his original roots in Greece or learn about his ancestors. He never considered himself anything but 100% English. But I guess you already kind of know where I am going with this, don't you?

But finally, after the long journey, there he was. Standing in front of the big door with a small sign: GameCon -left entrance. He was so excited; he wouldn't even notice if the taxi driver would've just driven off with his luggage. But the guy actually left it on the side of the pedestrian, after Alex jumped out and ran to the building. So, it was pretty much available for anyone fancying a blue Samsonite 'cat in a bag.' Alex eventually realized that it was almost ten meters away from him, and now fully armed with his trolley, he was ready for the adventure and made his way to the door.

As he was approaching, Alex saw a guy in a wheelchair, looking pretty annoyed while fighting with the entrance door. It didn't open wide enough for him to go through with the wheelchair, so as a good Samaritan, he stepped in and tried to hold the door for the guy, bless him. But instead of a thank, Alex just got a nasty look.

To be fair, at this point he couldn't care less. He was finally in the building, breathing the same air that he shared with the most important games of his life. Plus, in his book, he already made his daily humanitarian donation by opening the door, and if he finally finds the Holy Grail of the games, what he has been searching for in the last 30 years, he doesn't need to be gallant anymore.

Finding that treasure would most probably play out in a nasty fight with some random bloke, but now he doesn't need to hold himself back. After a quick calculation that takes into account charitable human interactions, it would easily break even for the entire day.

"You're in my way," Alex heard a voice from behind him. "Step away or I just run you over."

"What the..?!?" Alex turned back and with that second, he felt a nudge on his legs. The same guy with the wheelchair deliberately bumped into him and tried to push him away. "What is your problem, man?"

"We don't have all day; you are in my way, the corridor is narrow, so move out from my way. I won't say it again," the guy replied in a frustrating tone.

But Alex didn't even have a chance to prepare an appropriate response to this weirdo. With a quick bump, the wheelchair just ran over his feet.

"Whaaat the…!" Alex shouted with a surge of anger. "Wait, you miserable, little piece of…" but he couldn't finish the sentence as the guy quickly turned around, rolled back, and started to stare at him.

"God! Now what? Do you want my insurance and registration number? Or what?" But Alex stopped before the worst thought could even leave his lips. He noticed that it was the same zombie stare like in the store the day before.

"Where did you get that medal?" The guy blurted at Alex with an astonished face.

"Hm?" Alex mumbled still in pain.

"The medal with the dodecahedron, how did you get that?" the wheelchair guy pointed to the amulet, which somehow during the trip just made its way out and now it was clearly visible over Alex's NASA t-shirt.

"Piss off! Why would I bother to talk to you? You are practically the best example of why people shouldn't drive just because they can."

"I am sorry. I was a little…."

"A little??? You almost broke my pinkie!" Alex yelled at him.

"Yes, I apologize. I hope you can forgive me. But I do have a rather good reason! Although you probably wouldn't understand."

"Try me," Alex replied while he put his hand across his chest, which almost always gave him the feeling to get the moral high ground.

"Look, the medal, what you wear means a lot to me, so I am happy to buy it from you. How much did you get it for? 50, 100? I pay double," and he started to reach for his backpack.

"No, it's not for sale. It was a present from my grandfather." Alex replied with determination in his voice.

The guy gasped and stopped as he turned. "It's yours?"

"Yes. Any problem?"

"No, no, on the contrary," the guy smiled at Alex. "If it's true, you just made me the luckiest man on this planet."

"Ha, big words, but I still don't get it."

The guy seemed really determined. "Okay, look. As I said, I am sorry, we started on the wrong foot."

"No, actually, you started on my good foot."

"Yeah, you're right. So let me introduce myself, I am Daniel Morse."

"NO!!! Noooo waaay. Are you joking?" Alex looked at him stunned.

"The. Daniel. Morse. From Atari? You can't be, it's impossible. You look so different; you changed a lot. No offence though!"

"Look, I'm late, I have no time to explain everything, but you need to trust me. I will explain everything later. But if I just say: The whole universe is in your hand now." Daniel said slowly. "Does that mean anything to you?"

Alex froze and got goosebumps instantly. It sounded so familiar and magical, like words of chimes. "What did you say?"

"Yes, you heard it correctly. Now I see that you told me the truth. This medal is yours." Daniel replied.

"These were the exact words my grandfather told me when he gave it to me," Alex explained with utter confusion on his face.

"I can explain it to you later, but now we have to go, or I won't make a penny if I don't sign those stupid cards. Probably I lost already £300 since we talked. Now, let's go." Daniel turned around and started to roll quickly towards the crowd.

They both went straight to the middle aisle in the hall but kept eye contact all the time, looking where to find each other even after they separated.

The convention was exactly what Alex needed, a well-deserved siesta, an oasis with exotic treats and unique toys. The building was a little island, locked away from the surrounding outside world of empty, heartless, and boring reality. He was so excited; he didn't even realize the noise. Or to be exact, the total absence of noise from the crowd.

Hundreds of people, where normally you couldn't hear a word from a two-meter distance, it was now dead quiet. All walked in a nice, calm, and organized manner, no fights, screaming, or yelling. But Alex didn't care, didn't notice. He was just running around, stumbling on everything like a 4-week-old husky puppy seeing grass and a tree for the first time.

Alex often checked on Daniel while he was giving lectures, spoke on forums, and signed hundreds of cards. By the end of the day, they were both beyond exhaustion. Yet as they made their way out, they started laughing and telling all the stories they had during the day, and no power on this planet could stop them for sure. Or maybe one.

Daniel started to feel weak and looked really pale, so Alex offered him a taxi ride to his hotel, which allowed him to share a couple more minutes with this gaming legend.

"So, what are you doing here? You were with Atari in California, as far as I know. When did you come to England?" Alex asked with fascination in his voice. "You made my favourite game, my first Atari Lynx. I had all the games, I bought everything. You are my hero, man."

"I moved here about 20 years ago. I had to change, so I left." Daniel said with bitter sadness on his face.

"I still can't believe that we are sitting here, and we talk. But to be fair," and Alex slowed down, "You disappeared, nobody ever heard of you since. I thought that you already died or something."

"Yeah, you are right, I did. I actually did." Daniel sighed.

"Ha, that's not funny. How would that be possible?"

"I had another life before Atari, a different life. But things caught up on me again, so it was better to leave. Now, this is all I have left," and as Daniel looked down on his lifeless legs, he said, "What you see now is my carcass, only a shell to show and hide behind from the world."

"No, I don't get it. Carcass? It's a bit harsh, don't you think?"

"I know, you don't believe me now, but when I show you what I see, you will realize how many ways you can see reality." Daniel continued, looking really serious, "When did you start to hear the voices?"

"Voices? Erm, I'm not mental, I don't hear voices." Alex laughed.

"But you are wearing the medal."

"I just found it a couple of days ago. For more than 30 years it was in a box."

"God! I was not expecting this," Daniel turned away and looked a bit troubled as he continued slowly, "Ok, we can work on it, you just need to be extra patient and open. I mean open. To everything. All the possibilities," then he turned back and looked straight into Alex's eye. "If I tell you that you don't live without the medal, you would probably say that I am crazy, loco, and you'd put me in a straitjacket, right?"

"Hm, probably! Unless you show me some solid evidence that I can believe."

Daniel glanced at Alex, "Okay, tell me. What has changed since you started wearing the medal?"

"Nothing really. Same work, still no girlfriend, playing games every night, and…. that's it, same old."

"No, around you. Of course, you only feel slight changes from inside," Daniel added "But the real difference is visible from the outside. People around you will notice it and see you differently because you become someone else. A version of you."

"Well, yeah, maybe a bit," Alex raised his brows, looking like he was searching in his mind, "I did feel that people were suddenly kind to me, and surprisingly I even got a couple of pretty nice looks from gorgeous ladies lately, but I don't mean to brag about it." he smiled with confidence, then he added on a more pragmatic tone. "To be true, I know that I am a pretty average Joe. Not bad, maybe a solid six, but with girls, I never had any luck. Hm, but other than that, nothing major really happened."

"Okay, I show you something, but don't freak out." Daniel glanced at him very seriously.

"What? Are you going to take off your skin like the Edgar suit from Man in Black? Hahaha." Alex laughed.

"I didn't tell you, but I have a medal as well. But unlike yours, it's an icosahedron. The 20-sided version of your medal. I wear it here, on my belt," and Daniel leaned back on the car seat, opened his cardigan, and grabbed Alex's hand, who looked at him seriously hesitant but morbidly curious. "Touch it and you will see me. The real me. If you experience it yourself, you will believe me."

"Wowowo! Wait, no, it's really bizarre. We are sitting in the back of the taxi; I will not touch you." Alex tried to pull back and looked really puzzled.

"Just shut up and do it whingy boy." and Daniel strongly pulled Alex's hand to touch his belt buckle.

"AAAAAAHHH!! What the hell man, what was that?" Alex screamed out extremely loud.

The terrifying scream hit the taxi driver so unexpectedly that he had to jump on the steering wheel to jerk it back and keep the taxi on the road after the shock. But now he was just keep turning back and looking with shear panic on his face.

"Just drive the car, nothing to see here." Daniel shouted to the driver, who was now finally pulling back in the line, although he was still anxiously checking them from the corner of his eye in the mirror.

"That's impossible, I don't understand, how could this be possible?" Alex gasped.

"This is us, all of us on this planet. As long as I am wearing the medal you see me as now. Without it, what was left from my other life. But if you want to understand you need to be open."

Alex looked at the taxi driver, but he was now even more concerned, his veins visibly bumped out on his forehead and practically ready to jump out from the moving car any second, jolted and scared to death about what kind of crazy nonsense they were doing on the backseat.

"Okay, you need to tell me everything, I want to understand," Alex exclaimed still in a tense tone and with piqued determination in his eyes.

But at this moment the tires loudly squealed, and the taxi stopped suddenly at the hotel entrance. Alex hurried to get out the wheelchair from the back and gently helped Daniel to sit in it, while trying to avoid super carefully not to touch the belt at all costs. But as he slammed the door behind Daniel, the driver took his chance and floored the gas pedal, leaving them behind with a palpable sense of abandonment.

Alex and Daniel exchanged glances, their faces a canvas of astonishment and surprise, looking at each other speechless. Then Daniel's eyes shifted up, and his gaze fixated on the hotel's darkened windows, while slowly tilted his head, and he said, "I have a sofa. You can sleep in my room, but no funny business."

"Well, I should say that no funny business, and I have one condition," Alex smirked.

"What?" Daniel looked baffled.

"That bloody belt stays on!" Alex pointed to the belt with a dead serious expression.

"Haha, okay. It's a deal." Daniel giggled, while Alex slowly started to push him in the wheelchair towards the hotel entrance.

The weight of the unspoken words settled in the space between them, wrapping their faith together with anticipation, hinting at unknown revelations that seemed to hang in the air, just like the profound journey that lay ahead.

4

The long day and overwhelming excitement overran their curiosity, and both of them fell asleep as soon as their heads hit the pillow. Even though countless questions were still buzzing in their heads, it was just an in-vain battle to stay awake. But as soon as they woke up the next morning, still fully dressed and in the same exact position, with a stingy taste from the morning breath in their mouths, they slowly started to reboot their thoughts, like an old, temperamental Commodore PC. Blinking, twitching, and searching for memory.

After a long silence, Daniel broke the silence first. "Shall we start with the inevitable, or do you want to spare your questions until we're done with GameCon?"

"Man, I need a shower and change first, before I can deal with this," Alex replied in a sleepy voice. "Is it okay if I meet you later? I just try to prepare myself a bit more mentally."

"Of course, just don't forget. We met for a reason. It's not just coincidental. There are probably many of us out there; maybe you've even met someone already, you were just not aware. Think about it."

Daniel's last words sounded almost begging, trying to convince Alex. But it was not only his words; this whole new experience was beyond crazy and made him think all the way in the taxi. Questioning in his head: What is actually real? Is everything just a mirror of our expectations? A glitch of our imagination? What could we find if we could see the truth without a strong filter of our own judgment?

No matrix, just to take the red pill and see how deep the rabbit hole goes. And would it be worth it? After all, we all want to be superheroes, admired, and appreciated by others. We want to belong to that circle, in a tribe where we are welcomed. But what if we find the truth, the ugly truth, and we don't like it?

We all got so used to having the free money-back guarantee option that making a decision for a lifetime seems like a life-threatening death sentence. Being brave is kind of foolish. Sitting in front of the computer and sending messages and food orders seems so harmless. You can delete or recall everything. Even in this digital era, you will forget about an unsolicited picture, but you're scared to commit to a relationship. But why are we so scared?

Our great parents had not much choice in life. Most women married at 18 and had one husband for the rest of their lives, in good and bad. But they didn't file for divorce after a rough patch. Did men really become so violent, unbearable, or useless in the past one hundred years that we can't keep our vows to go through tough times?

And on the other side, men had to go to war, got wounded, died. All through their life, they had to struggle, fight against nature's all forms and elements to provide for their offspring. But now, it feels like a waste of money to even buy a drink on a first date because we can just swipe again, and by next day, we could get a better option. Why did everything become so cheap and replaceable? You throw away your car, your phone, your clothes, even your feelings. Why did our own life become so replaceable?

It's us; we've become cheap. We like to have a bargain, to have a way with rules, and find an escape back to our own little comfort zone. We cheat in the game of life for the same exact reason dogs lick their balls.

Because we can.

Alex was never a particularly brave type. All the past 42 years of his life everything was well organised, a carefully planned sequence of choices. This encounter with Daniel held a great significance in his life but seemed unreasonably dangerous. His curiosity was struggling to sink into the fear of becoming an outsider.

The fear and the look on the face of the taxi driver from last night haunted him. He doesn't want to be that person. What if he will become like Daniel? That's just not something he would be able to cope with for sure.

After all these questions were still racing in Alex's mind, no wonder when he saw Daniel, he was a bit aloof and just dropped a quick wave at him and walked away to the opposite direction. The mental picture of that creature from last night was not letting him rest and every time he interacted with someone that day, Alex seemed to be extra careful to keep a distance.

But later Daniel found him off guard while he was playing on an age-old Asteroids arcade game, just on the far end of the hall's quiet part. "I got one of this at home. Nolan sent it to me," and he rolled closer to Alex. "He thinks it's funny to leave an over one hundred kilograms arcade game gift-wrapped in front of your entrance door when you are stuck in a wheelchair. He'll never grow up."

"Do you mean Nolan? Nolan Bushnell, the founder of Atari?" Alex's face lit up after hearing the name. "That's crazy. Are you still in touch?"

"Well, kind of. Not officially. We had some project we worked on after he left Atari but not everything went as planned," and Daniel looked around if somebody hears the conversation. "But you know probably the story."

"What story?" Alex replied with curiosity in his eyes.

"That was the age of computer revolution. We often met, argued, and planned about innovative ideas. Me, Wozniak, Jobs. And Nolan was like a link between us. I miss that vibe a lot, but we all had our own path. Nolan had his Chuck E. Cheese's, and Wozniak and Jobs started Apple, you know for sure." Daniel stopped and slowly sighed, "Mine was the Polybius."

"The what?" Alex looked at Daniel with amazement. "You must be joking. The Polybius arcade game is just a hoax, an urban legend."

"Is it? That's why you are searching for a hoax like a Holy Grail in the past 30 years?" Daniel smiled suspiciously.

"How could you possibly know about that?"

"I had a quick look on you after you left. I still have some connections and I know how obsessed you are with that game." Daniel replied with a hint of uncanny confidence.

"Look, if it would be real, I would've found it, or someone, but there is just nothing," Alex turned back to the arcade game with an annoyed scowl on his face, then added, "People just seem to have amnesia or hallucinations, whoever got near to it. There's no solid evidence as soon as you get closer to any relevant information. Like everyone got brainwashed. The only thing I know is that after just a month from the release, all of the machines disappeared from the market, wiped off from the face of the Earth by some Men in Black, like it never existed. It's impossible to find any clues."

Alex seemed really pissed off but after a little while he continued. "And what do you mean it's your path? What do you know about it?"

"I created it. It was my quest." Daniel replied with sudden sadness on his face.

"Your quest? For what?" Alex turned back and raised his voice angrily. "To create zombies?"

"Well, not everything went as planned. I just started testing it in Oregon for a couple of weeks, and later I wanted to expand and find people like you. Who owns these medals and ability." Daniel explained with honest hope on his face, and then he looked down almost like he was ashamed, "But it all turned out very wrong. Black suits showed up, they hunted me, so I had to disappear, and start with a new name and a new life. My game was pure and only programmed to train you, to awaken your ability. But they threatened me and destroyed everything and everyone who ever contacted the machine." Daniel seemed really emotional and sad when finally continued. "Why do you think I picked the name Polybius?"

"Erm, sounds intriguing, maybe?" Alex replied in a phlegmatic voice.

"I would've name it Enigma dumbass," Daniel snapped back, "For your information, Polybius was the first person who wrote about The Gatekeepers in his work The Histories. From Greece he raised his fame to Rome, where he became the main figure of the Scipionic Circle. The famous group of the biggest philosophers, poets, and politicians of the era, to discuss culture, literature, and humanism. Everything what makes us human. He gained great recognition everywhere in the Roman Empire and with his power he had a chance to search for and unite the Gatekeepers, once again after thousands of years. Of course, in time most of his work had been lost, but even in the remaining ones, it was only partially discovered to carry these cryptic messages for centuries, due to the steganography he used. But I decoded them." Daniel exclaimed with a proud smile on his face.

"Wait. A steno what? You need to slow down." Alex stopped him, "This just doesn't make sense. What cryptic messages?"

"It's not a simple cryptic message, not just a code," Daniel explained with enthusiasm, "It was designed to conceal both the fact that a secret message is being sent and its contents. Think, have you ever felt in the movie theatre that suddenly you want to drink a coke or crave popcorn? You see, all the ads at the beginning of the movies are packed with hidden commercials."

"Actually, I heard about this," Alex seemed intrigued, "Inserting extremely brief images or frames into a film or video at a speed that is too fast for the conscious mind to perceive, but the subconscious mind can still process. But the effectiveness and ethical implications of subliminal messaging is not even proven, it's all just theory."

"Bingo!" Daniel laughed out loud, "They stole my work and used it everywhere to make people like zombies. Every time when you feel addicted to a movie or feel some unexplainable crave for something it's their work. They use steganography on you, not for you. This technique is used now for psychological and emotional effects, and it's intended to influence you and your decisions without your conscious awareness. To create obedient consumers."

"But if you know this, why don't you do something about it?" Alex looked baffled.

"Ha, you are living in a fantasy world little Padawan. It's not that easy," Daniel got very morose as he continued, "I escaped once from their experiment. What you see now it's their work. They tortured me for months, to get the secret out of me, and in that sense, they succeeded. Taking a part of me is how they created this shadow of what I was once, and now stuck in a wheelchair."

"CIA, FBI, MI6? Who done this?" Alex asked with a concerned face.

"They are all the same, one group. It's not even important for us. We are not fighting against human forces," and Daniel took a long breath as he continued. "What we need to do is to protect the world and everything in it, with good and bad. No exception. If we die not just the good guys will die, but everything."

Alex looked surprised. "But if you tell them they will help, no? I don't get it."

"Until the world won't reach the point of absolute no return, nobody will believe me. Trust me I tried many times. Humans delay making difficult changes or adjustments until they are faced with dire consequences." Daniel stopped and looked deep into Alex's eyes as he leaned forward, "You are the best example! You tried to walk away from the biggest opportunity of your life just because it requires some changes in your pathetic little life."

"You have no right to talk about my life this way, you know nothing about me! Look at yourself, old man. Like you all made it work, and figured it out, right? I guess no. You are the pathetic!" Alex replied with anger in his voice.

"Am I too harsh, little flower? Yes. Am I telling you the truth? Yes! You wanted to walk away." Daniel retorted in a really upset tone.

"I need time," Alex snapped back at Daniel. "It's not like you just casually ask me for a sunny ride in a park. But you want me to believe that my life will change, and I will become like you. I'm sorry buddy, but it's not what I have signed up for or planned for this weekend. So, thank you, but no thank you."

"Got it, you just freaked out and act like a little wuss."

"Well, you should learn that you can catch more flies with honey than with vinegar. You are just a bitter old man with a horrible manner is what I see," and Alex turned away with anger.

"Okay, so what do you want?" Daniel's voice was mordant.

"Just leave me alone."

Daniel looked really determined. "You just don't get it, do you?"

"Get what?" replied Alex with an annoyed sigh.

"This whole epidemic which goes on with the water, it will get worse. If we don't do something, that's it. Armageddon."

"Oh, come 'on! That's not fair!" Alex rolled his eyes at Daniel. "You try to make me feel like the whole universe's future is on my shoulder now. That's rubbish. There are millions, way more equipped and trained people are out there. Organisations, police, armies, witches, and self-proclaimed televangelists who can save the world. Not me."

Daniel contemplated for a bit and continued, "Maybe. There are thousands like us, but I met you. I know that you have a medal. This is already a miracle. So, name your price. Tell me what you want?"

Alex stopped and looked surprised. "There are thousands? Do you mean like us? You and me?"

"Yes, there must be, but I need help to find them. My game failed; I couldn't recruit anyone with the Polybius. They wiped off everything too quickly. So, I have to work in secret. In 30 years, you are the first one I found, who actually physically has the original medal," Daniel seemed really emotional and disappointed when he slowly continued. "But I am sure there are many more out there. There must be more, we had thousands of these medals..."

"But how can you be so sure?"

"I've seen it," Daniel said with cloudy eyes, almost ready to cry, his face filled with remorse, which made Alex kind of soften up, feeling a sense of hopelessness in him.

"Where have you seen it?" Alex asked.

"I heard their voices and saw them in the water as they screamed for help."

"Wait, I think that's what I saw. As crazy as it sounds, but couple of months ago when I was drinking, I saw this. It was terrifying," Alex added.

"So, you know that I am not making this up."

"Okay, I want to understand what this is and why it's happening to me. I help you recruit more people if I can, but you need to promise me that you don't turn me into some zombie."

"I told you already, it was not me. I could never do that, even if I would want to," Daniel replied. Alex slowly turned his body towards Daniel, and with a settling hand wave he continued, "So, what about this Polybius guy? How is he coming into this?"

Daniel nodded with a slight smile, "Let's have dinner and I tell you about him and the Gatekeepers' medals."

Alex looked surprised, "He made them?!?"

"Yes genius," Daniel laughed out loud.

"You seriously have to stop calling me names old man. I'm warning you."

"I try but can't promise," Daniel said on a funny and relived voice, as they were going out, side by side, leaving the GameCon behind, just when the securities were starting to shut the doors.

5

Finding a half-decent place should be an easy pick, but not for these two oddballs. Too crowded, too fancy, too spicy, not enough options, too low score on Yelp, the list goes on. Of course, they ended up just around the corner in the non-stop kebab place. The only restaurant which was still open after 50 minutes of pointless searching on the phone for a better option.

While they were waiting for the orders, Alex was still desperately Googling to find something on Polybius, just to look less uncivilized in front of Daniel.

"You could just ask me," Daniel smiled. "What you are looking for is probably not even on the internet."

"I just try to get this whole context," Alex said as he put his phone down on the table. "How is this guy so important to you?"

"Polybius?" Daniel raised his eyebrows as he continued, "This 'guy,' as you refer to him, became the advisor of the first big Roman general, Scipio Africanus. Later he rose up to Scipio's right hand, acting as his military advisor and led him to become one of the greatest military leaders in Roman history. Due to his work, Rome conquered North Africa, half of the Mediterranean, and became the great empire as we know it. This is how important Polybius was; he helped to win his battles."

"That's not really noble," Alex added in a sceptical voice, "He only helped to slaughter thousands of men and to enslave whole nations."

"He was also held as a hostage himself after being taken from Greece. He had not much of a choice, but he aimed to make Scipio win every battle with the least casualties possible," Daniel explained. "That's why he helped him. With his family's legacy, he was able to offer something invaluable: knowledge of the past, healing of the future, and wisdom of the present. He gave the first Roman Dodecahedron to Scipio. Later, these medals were quite common in Rome, used by leaders, senators, influential people, even Caesar. Polybius' family in Greece descended from one of the ancient Gatekeepers, the guards of this knowledge. Many believed that they came from the lost civilization of Atlantis. But it's way more profound than just a story about a sunken island."

Alex looked intrigued, so Daniel continued, "What do you know about water? What do you think, how is it possible that we are the only planet in this solar system, near and far probably the only place in the galaxy where we have life?"

Alex raised his eyebrows, "We are in the right distance from the Sun, we have a Moon. God knows, where you are going with this?"

"In our world, water is just an economic commodity, which is owned, collected, and distributed according to needs and profitability. But this shift in modern perception has come only since the dark ages, where purposefully knowledge was made to believe it's a sin. So religion could become the only source of wisdom," Daniel explained and lifted up the glass from the table and pointed at the water inside. "For thousands of years, ancient civilizations considered water the source of life, not God. If you look at Egyptian, Sumerian, and all the most ancient creation epochs, the eternal symbol of the beginning is always the water. They believed that everything in existence was birthed from, and ultimately returns to one element, often portrayed as a shape-shifting dragon or snake. Forming a serpentine, like a river or the circular snake eating its own tail. Water has always played a fundamental role in the creation and maintenance of the physical world and, in particular, biological life. But not as one of the elements, but as the 'one and only' creator above all."

"Yes, yes, I know that, but what makes it so important in this story?" Alex interjected with a puzzled face.

"Water is alien to this planet, at least what we see on the surface," Daniel replied with excitement. "Water is the most unique element. The only naturally occurring substance on Earth that can be found in three physical forms: solid, liquid, and gas. Don't you think it's really weird? The ice floats in a glass of water, instead of sinking, and it's capable of carrying nutrition to the top of the tree due to capillary action. Cohesion, thermal-heat capacity, I could go on, against all odds, and physics of nature. Don't you see? Nothing like on Earth! She is an alien, arrived to bring life within and give the ultimate knowledge for us to survive."

"She? Do you mean alien, like an actual alien lifeform? You are out of your mind, seriously," Alex said in disbelief. "Why have we never seen or met a talking river or a pregnant Evian bottle? How do you expect me to believe this?"

"I know it's a lot to take in, but you better dig in and start to eat your kebab before it walks off from your plate," Daniel whispered quietly as he looked around after touching the sticky table from the grease, "I don't trust this place with their questionable four stars on that door."

"Okay, I am listening, but I am still not sure how this alien water woman comes into the picture with Polybius and the epidemic. This is just very messy," Alex muffled as he was stuffing his kebab in one big bite to his face.

"Let's start with what we learned from the Greeks. They called these aliens Hydrons," and Daniel put down his fork to use both his hands to explain his story with big hand gestures, "It was known that they came from another galaxy, to escape from a terrible genocide, and the only chance they had was to send interstellar comets to every other solar system to find a suitable planet. And when they found our Sun, they sent their first colony. The Hydrons first settled on Venus and tried to adapt, but their bodies evolved from silicate, nothing like our carbon-based lifeform. They were accustomed to vastly different laws of physics and nature. Yet they still managed to battle with the elements to survive and lived there for thousands of years."

"Hold on. On Venus?" Alex smiled, "This is getting interesting. It's like an episode from the local version of Star Trek Deep Space Nine."

"I am just saying what we know from Polybius, and it's not that funny actually," Daniel continued, "When their arch-enemy, the Ouron, who already killed and enslaved most of the Hydrons on their home planet, found their trace in space, he sent the plasma waves to destroy them."

"Plasma? Seriously, how can you not laugh when you tell this story?"

"Oh, just shut up and eat!" Daniel snapped, "So, they had no other choice but to transform into a new shape, a vessel if you want to imagine, to store their knowledge, wisdom, and spirit, and one by one transformed into water. Each molecule, one life, with the full capacity to carry millions of years of power and information."

"Daniel, this is the point where you lost me. How could they transform and store knowledge in water? This just doesn't make any sense," Alex shook his head doubtfully.

"If I have a chance to finally talk to them, this will be one of the first questions I will ask. And thank you for interrupting me again. So where was I?"

"The vessel, they transformed," Alex continued with a smile like a child.

"So, by the time when the plasma arrived, most of them were already transformed and moved to Theia, another planet close to Venus."

"Come on man! Theia? This must be from Star Trek. There is no planet called Theia in our solar system."

"As a matter of fact, it is proven that it was. Maybe you should educate yourself with some more updated science journals, other than Playboy magazines," Daniel rolled his eyes with annoyance. "But anyway, the only way to transport to the new planet and hide there was to lose their original physical body and to become invisible. The planet Theia was the perfect choice at first, but what happened then, changed everything. Ouron was mad and blasted the plasma to destroy life on Venus with such force that Theia was pushed to spin away and crash into Earth. The impact was so powerful that even the cores of the two planets collided, while the strike ejected millions of pieces into space around them, that eventually merged to form our Moon."

"Wow, that is a hell of a fairy tale, but I don't think that only the dinos would disappear after an impact like that. This would wipe out all life forms, everything from Earth."

"I am talking about 4.5 billion years ago!" Daniel added with a dead serious expression, "The beginning of life, not the asteroids and meteoroids which came regularly in the millions of years to follow."

"Okay, but how did they survive the impact? Didn't they die?"

"This is the beauty of it, the perfect plot twist. They transformed into something so pure, durable, and basic, that not even this impact could destroy all of them," Daniel smiled, "And Ouron left Venus after he found the remaining bodies of their original form laying around everywhere. He thought everyone got wiped out. Those carcasses left on Venus were just like the one you saw yesterday..."

"You?" Alex gasped, as the image flashed through his mind, he almost choked on the last chips from the shocking revelation.

"We all…" Daniel said very slowly and firmly. "We are all over 60 percent water; we are built from them. In everything and around us, water has been here from the beginning and lived in us for billions of years. Through dinosaurs, mammoths, apes, and humans. Regulating our body temperature, transporting nutrients, removing waste products, and supporting every single functioning cell and organ in our body. They created life."

Alex looked puzzled. "But why is she? You said they were a whole lifeform, a species. Hydrons, they must come in pairs."

"No, it's only our limited capability to understand the universe that makes us believe that two sexes are needed to survive," Daniel leaned closer to the table and added. "They had five tribes; divided and functioned different roles to create a whole," Daniel looked up and almost smiled as he continued. "It's kind of entertaining sometimes to think about how much more knowledge ancient people had about everything. Even Plato was able to describe these tribes with the five solids so precisely, and we fail to acknowledge even their existence. Life needs no shape, sex, or form to exist. Only energy. Remember what Nikola Tesla said: 'If you want to find the secrets of the universe, think in terms of energy, frequency, and vibration.' Everything is balanced between the two opposite positive and negative energies, like Ying and Yang. Never equal, and never lost. It's always there; energy cannot be created or destroyed; it can only be transferred or converted from one form to another. This whole is She, as ancient people could imagine the energy."

"Well, I am sorry, but I profoundly disagree. I can't just eat Duracell or charge myself with sunshine like a sunflower without photosynthesis," Alex laughed, "This is just utter bollox. We need to eat and multiply to survive."

"You talk with the arrogance of humankind," Daniel snapped at him. "Do you think that you matter in terms of the universe? No, let's narrow it down, even in this country. One more or less, who cares? Do you really think that you would make any difference if you disappear? You die and become humus; bugs eat you, chickens eat the bugs, and humans eat the chicken. Circle closed and back on the loop again. Bumm. If all humans disappear, do you know what would happen with life? Nothing! Eureka! That's right, nothing changes!" Daniel smiled smugly.

"Gosh, you are the most depressing prophet I've ever heard! I hope you are not planning to have this speech when you recruit the rest of the team because you will be the first to go extinct in a minute," Alex laughed so loud that even the half-asleep kebab guy lifted his head from the table at the entrance to check what's happening.

"You are right; I need to work on the approach, but it's getting late now, and we have a long day tomorrow, we should go," Daniel said with a hint of a smile on his lips. "But I hope that you finally start to understand how important this quest is. Not only for me but for us. We're on the verge of discovering forgotten truths about ourselves, and it could reshape our understanding of the whole universe."

"Look, what I actually start to understand is that you either have a very serious mental problem, which needs lots of attention from an expert psychiatrist, or I just heard the most detailed evolution lecture ever took place in a kebab shop. I am not sure yet, but I guess I will find out soon," Alex continued laughing with a sudden determination in his eyes. Although the journey ahead was uncertain, he finally felt ready to see where it would lead him. "Okay, let's go home," he added on a kind tone.

Alex waited a bit for Daniel to pass next to him while he was manoeuvring his wheelchair through the tables. And as he watched this bald, little, weak guy in the chair who seemed so lamentable, he couldn't help but feel a pang of sympathy for him. A brilliant mind, obviously a genius, in the body of a broken, bitter man.

Many unanswered questions were still lingering in his mind though. What does the Polybius game have to do with the Gatekeepers? How did water cause an epidemic? Why does this guy seem so convincing when the whole story is just so bizarre? The truth is that Daniel's words had stirred something within him. He felt more and more alive and drawn into this world with magical Hydrons, interstellar comets, and Roman dodecahedrons.

After two days with this obsessed game developer, and he already started to question everything he ever considered real. Life and evolution, humans, and emotions—all were unravelling in a new aspect in front of him. Could it be true that everything we believe and hold precious in our lives is just a mirage? Well, there's only one way to find out.

As they stepped out of the store, the door swung shut behind them with a resonant slam, and a subtle yet distinct chime filled the air— "ding-dong." The sound seemed to linger for a moment, then faded into the background. The juxtaposition of the forceful door and the delicate "ding-dong" painted a vivid picture with the kebab shop's fluorescent lights casting an odd glow on the scene, creating a surreal aftermath of their conversation.

Brilliant minds delving into planetary mysteries over late-night kebabs — it was almost like a scene from a Tarantino movie.

6

Not much else left to see for Sunday on GameCon, but without the crowd, it gave the opportunity to explore the unique vintage pieces and to try out iconic games without hours of waiting in line. Alex felt empowered, like a secret agent or superhero on a mission while playing with his favourites, armed with the hidden knowledge gained from Daniel.

The feeling that he had when he was with his grandfather, Aron. The guy was invincible, like a Hellenic ninja, and often called himself Arion while they were playing. Although Alex didn't know much about his ancestors, Aron often told him stories about his life as a child in Greece before the war, and the journey and life with the new parents after they changed his name.

The more time he was spending with Daniel, the more fragments of these memories popped up from the shadow of his mind, like after a corny school reunion, as conversations with old schoolmates rekindle anecdotes, stirs up forgotten narratives. Things that seemed long lost in the past now suddenly reminded Alex of his roots, and all seemed to connect. It was as if the random, jumbled letters of a crossword's finish line converged to create an intricate sentence to solve the puzzle.

One thing in particular stuck in his head. While it never really seemed an important detail before, he became curious about his grandfather's previous name. The only thing he remembered was Arion, and Alex was trying to figure out a way, how could he find out his original family name. Davis didn't seem particularly Greek, so it must've changed as well.

Alex's only hope was his mother, a woman whose serious OCD problem now appeared as a divine blessing. Despite his childhood torture of growing up in a house akin to living within a clinically impeccable sterile petri dish or the unrelenting banter he got from his mates, particularly about those crisply pressed jeans he was wearing, with the sharp faded creases running down the front and back. Alex's mom had a habit of meticulously folding and even bleaching his clothes before putting them in the washing machine, creating well-defined fading lines on the denim like suit trousers. Alex hated it, but now, as he looked back, these idiosyncratic details brought a fond smile to his face.

He already planned to be a little sneaky and take advantage of the whole water malarkey, just to call the boss Monday and start working from home. They can probably manage to change the water bottles in the office anyway, even without his personal contribution. To be honest, other than that, he didn't really find any particular use for his work. He just got a pile of invoices in the morning with some scanned documents to pair within the system and entered random numbers and percentages in spreadsheet cells for the managers' big and important meetings. Even better software could probably do his job, but as an accountant, he had not much of a choice but to act super important and mysterious, sit on everything which he already finished in 10 minutes for the next 5 hours, so everybody believed it was like rocket science, to come up with the figures.

He occasionally pushed the boundaries to the extreme, testing whether he could still successfully get away with it, and without fail, he always did. Each day, he would gather a stack of papers from his cluttered desk, stride confidently to his boss' office, and casually stick his head in, throwing some random question about the boss' personal life—his wife, his dog, or whatever came to mind. Then, with an air of diligence, he'd exit the room and head straight for the elevator. To anyone observing, it appeared as though he was briefly catching up with the boss, exchanging information or discussing his tasks for the day. But once outside the office, he simply pressed a button in the elevator, selecting to visit one of the other floors' office toilets.

His strategy seemed meticulous; even if a colleague from that department tried to engage him in conversation, he had a ready excuse—something about cleaning or if the pipe in the toilet was broken on his own floor. Slipping into a vacant cubicle, he comfortably settled in, playing a leisurely game session on his phone, watching funny videos, or idly coiling toilet paper rolls around his invoice papers, and using it as a pillow on the walls like a makeshift headrest for moments of rest.

His personal record was over five hours, a feat achieved mostly as he fell asleep and woke up around seven in the evening, when the entire building was already empty, and the cleaning lady came in to wash the floor. Even Alex couldn't believe when the following weekly meeting his boss commended on his extraordinary dedication for working so hard and staying overtime for free and offered him compensatory lieu time for the morning.

However, this unexpected recognition didn't really boost his motivation to be honest, if anything just made him feel even more useless with an odd blend of resentment and a growing feeling of insignificance. No wonder that this weekend with Daniel was like stepping up on a pedestal for his ego, and he couldn't wait to find out more about his heritage and the history of his original family.

When finally, Daniel finished with his last lecture about the 'Golden age of game consoles,' Alex rushed there first, to steal him with his wheelchair, even before anyone could start on the questions.

"So, what's next? What are we going to do now?" Alex blurted out as he was speeding out with Daniel on the chair.

"What's happening, what's suddenly become so urgent?" Daniel giggled. "We still have a half day."

"I know, but I want to understand, why are we so important? How are we going to do it? What's your plan?"

"Okay, just slow down, slow down. One thing at a time." Daniel said as tried to calm him down. "Look, you can call me or visit me anytime. The first thing is that we have to do is to find the others. Everything else, we just going to figure out on the way."

"What do you mean?" Alex stopped. "You have no plan? You're kidding me."

"How on Earth would I have a plan? Do you think I just pull out a detailed action plan from my sleeve to every possible scenario, on how to save the planet in case of Armageddon? Sorry buddy, that's not how it works."

"For God's sake, you were working on this for 30 years, and you have no plan?"

"Well, no! I was busy trying to stay alive, hiding from CIA, MI6 and you name all the other institutions with commercialised interrogation techniques for torturing. Sorry to disappoint you, but if I would know already everything, I could've done it myself, long ago! Don't you think?" Daniel seemed pretty upset and annoyed, but after a while he continued with a little more calmed tone. "Look, as I said we need the other elements."

"Do you mean the Gatekeepers?" Alex added.

"Yes. If my theory is correct as soon as we have all the five medals with the original owners, we will find the connection, how to work with the source. To find out why people get sick, what is happening with the water and makes everyone like zombies."

"Great! So, you have nothing. Any idea where to start?" Alex snapped with an annoyed expression.

"I told you. You have to be open. You are the last element, the connection between us! Your dodecahedron represents the universe, the space or spirit, however you want to call it. It's in your hand to find the others and unite them like a magician."

"And you? What is your belt supposed to do? Like transform or disguise?" Alex asked with curiosity.

"You have no idea about the Platonic solids, don't you?" Daniel looked at him and raised his brows.

"Of course, I do, I know, the cube and that tetra-thing and the other one, but how is it connects?"

"Okay, let's start from the beginning. There are a total of five Platonic solids, and there can only be five, never more. Mathematically impossible to create more. These sacred geometrical figures represent the fundamental building blocks of our universe and translate them into geometrical shapes that our human minds can comprehend and understand the five tribes. Each, let's call it a solid, is built from the same faces. Each edge has the same length, and all corners have the same angle. They were designed with spiritual and divine significance, to carry power and energy to create life."

Daniel pointed to his belt and started to explain. "Icosahedron, the one which I inherited from my family, represents water. It holds wisdom and symbolizes movement, flow, and change. Assisting others, instead of pursuing an active role. It allows for freedom of expression, creativity, and going with the flow, just as water runs through your fingers. Water is healing, emotional energy, transitioning or shifting through phases."

"So, what does it have to do with that thing I saw when I touched your buckle?" Alex asked with curiosity.

"That thing is my soul per se, or what's left of it, after they meticulously tortured me. Think about the Father, the Son, and the Holy spirit, remember? We all exist in three parallel forms: your mind, your body, and your psyche. The Hydrons gave you the shared reservoir of knowledge, your creativity, or the understanding of inherited symbols, just to name a few, by connecting you to the collective unconscious, your psyche. You can exist without it, but you will become just like now, the zombie people around us. Living dead."

"So, water, I mean the Hydrons are dying. Is that what you're saying?"

"Yes, that is the only logical explanation," Daniel replied.

"But you said that we can survive without our soul." Alex looked optimistically.

"Of course. We can live in a society without morals, without joy, or feelings. But not for too long before we lose our consciousness, and we all turn into cannibals, serial killers without remorse or empathy."

"So, you are a sociopath!" Alex laughed out loud. "It all makes sense now!"

"Not funny, and no. But if I turn into some monster, I will definitely come after you first if you don't stop making silly jokes about everything. And yes, I am sick," Daniel said with deep desperation in his voice. "My motivation, my drive, and creativity were all lost. But with time, I realized that if I'm constantly wearing the medal, it starts to heal me. Helps me somehow keep a balance, but that means the energy has to be taken from somewhere else. From my physical body."

"So that's the reason why I feel so alive and full of energy since I'm wearing it." Alex started wondering.

"Ha, more like since you met me, don't you think?"

"How do you know?" Alex looked really surprised that Daniel seems to read him like an open book.

"I believe that your medal and power work together to harness and combine the energy of the elements. You intuitively bring out the hidden strengths from people; that is your family heritage, but combined with the medal, you can create something new. Like I told you, a magician. This feeling of power is what makes you confident and surges you with energy since you are wearing it."

"Wow, true. I felt it with my grandfather and with you."

"Because we have the medal as well. I think that at the beginning of time we all had these abilities, and when Polybius needed to enhance these energies, to harness the power, he created the first medals."

"So, anyone can be a Gatekeeper?" Alex's eyes widened from astonishment.

"Not quite. The tribes chosen leaders, species, and forms to be trained and given extra skill sets to protect the knowledge. Not everyone could or should be a Gatekeeper. The medal in the wrong hands can be dangerous. Even fatal. But when Polybius was forced to bring out the strength, he created the tool to manifest it, even if you had no skill or knowledge to use it necessarily."

"So, he gave a fully loaded gun to people to play Russian roulette?" Alex was surprised.

"Kinda, but it worked. Well, most of the time."

"What do you mean most of the time?"

"It didn't help to save Cesar or Lincoln, to be fair. As I told you, the medal aims to harness power and energy, but it also brings out the negative as an opposite force, within and around the person who wears it. Only a trained master can be protected from the negative effects."

"Should I be worried? I mean, I had no training or such, and I'm wearing it." Alex asked and seemed a bit worried.

"If your grandfather gave it to you, he definitely trained you as well. You were just not aware. You only need some practice, and you can use it again."

"Could be, we played a lot when I was young, but I don't remember." Alex wondered and tried to think back.

"Kids are born with an imprint from their previous lives. Until the age of seven, their soul is pure, like a clear canvas. Much easier to teach and form their psyche. Think about Janissaries, the warriors in the Ottoman Empire, who often kidnapped young kids and trained them and converted to Islam, but only under the age of seven. Or the Spartans, where boys were with their mothers in the first 7 years to build their spirit and sense of belonging. Only after entering the agoge, a state-controlled education and training system for their mind and body, to become a warrior. This is the system that you see even nowadays in education."

"So, I need to find not only the medals but with the original owner, who had some form of training from their parents about how to use?"

"Correct! That's what makes you so unique; you have it all! It took me 30 years to find you." Daniel smiled with contentment.

"You don't help me by painting it like some sort of mission impossible quest! How do you expect me to find someone before we all start to eat each other? Any clue? Where shall I start?"

"Just think where you met people who were still open, caring, and friendly with you. Actually, it's much easier now when everyone is turning into vegetables. You look around, ask questions, and if you can, try to touch them if you see something. With your medal, you will see inside, the real person."

Alex grinned. "That's not much help; you just described how to meet on a dating app."

"Actually, it's not a bad idea." Daniel stopped and looked up at Alex wondering. "Why was I not thinking about this before?"

"You must be joking, right? Dating? That's your plan?" Alex laughed.

"Yes, imagine! Who is still looking to find love and emotions at this point? Only someone who's not affected by the epidemic, or even who's protected by the medal. The path is pretty much clear in front of you. There you go!" Daniel smiled; he was so happy, proud of finally finding the first step.

"Well, I have to admit, there is some logic in your madness. But I warn you, I had not much luck before, so we would need another miracle for me to find someone," Alex just rolled his eyes.

"Don't forget! Be open, tick both boxes, male and female! Hahaha."

"Yeah, right, it doubles up my options. Thanks for the tip!" Alex laughed and hugged Daniel as a farewell.

7

All the way home on the empty train, Alex buried himself in his phone, scrolling through contacts and memories, in search of old friends, distant relatives, and any hint or clue about his family. He sent countless messages to his pals, just checking in if anyone would reply. But it all seemed like an endless void of blank pages and faded images. Everything felt blurry and out of focus, as if he were looking through a foggy lens. He wasn't sure if it was the tiredness after the long weekend or the sudden absence of Daniel.

Although it was late, he decided to call his mother since nobody answered, hoping that she would remember something else about his grandfather. The phone rang repeatedly, what felt like an eternity. Was it too late to call? Did something happen to his mother? Thoughts of worst-case scenarios flickered across his mind. His worry only started to lift when finally, a faint and lifeless voice broke the silence on the other end. It was a voice he struggled to recognize at first, as if it had been ages since they last spoke.

"Mom? Hello? It's Alex. How are you? Sorry to call you so late, but I need to ask you about grandpa."

"Alex? Okay. How are you?" the woman replied slowly, in a quiet and painfully monotone voice.

"Is everything okay Mom? Shall I call you back tomorrow, are you sleeping already?"

"No. It's fine."

"So, about grandpa, do you know his original family name?" Alex asked.

"Who...? Aron...?" her voice was like gasping for air with her last breath.

"Yes, him. You sound very strange, are you sure you're okay?" Alex started to become really worried about his mom after imagining Daniel's vision for the future. "Mom, I'll come around. Is it okay if I pop in? I'll be there in an hour."

"Alex?... You okay. I'll be fine." she whispered slowly.

"Okay Mom, I'll be there soon, just don't leave the key in the door. See you soon!"

After hanging up the phone, thousands of horrifying pictures flooded through Alex's mind. The tone of his mother's voice had sent a shockwave of fear through him. He never heard his mom talk like this; it was scary. The woman who could engage in endless conversations, now a mere shadow of her usual self, reduced to uttering only a few words.

Alex couldn't wait even until the train fully stopped. Without wasting a moment, he jumped off and ran to the taxi stand and got into the first car. That 30 minutes seemed like an agonizing eternity, staring out the car's window, with a mixture of anxiety and dread. The passing scenery was a blur, each streetlight and passing building a mere backdrop to the whirlwind of emotions that consumed him. As the taxi navigated the streets, his imagination raced ahead, painting an ominous picture of what he might find when he finally arrived at his mother's doorstep.

The key was in the usual spot, under the stairs, so Alex quickly grabbed it and opened the front door. His gaze swept across the array of relics in the hall - each silently told the story of his past. The air was laden with the scent of old leather and aged paper, as if the very essence of history lingered within those weathered walls.

Only one thing was unusual. Piled-up clutter from the kitchen intruded into the hall, which was visible even from the entrance. As he stepped further into the semi-darkness, his eyes darted around the rooms, searching for any sign of his mother. His steps stopped abruptly as he reached the sofa.

There she was, sitting quietly on the worn cushions. Her usual vibrant energy was replaced by an unnerving stillness. The dim light cast shadows across her face, which wore an expression of both vulnerability and distress. In that moment, the room seemed to hold its breath, and a surge of worry tightened its grip around Alex's heart.

"Hello Mom." Alex's voice trembled. "What happened here?" he said slowly, his eyes sweeping the room and a puzzled frown forming, as his gaze fell on the scattered piles of boxes and bags that seemed to occupy the floor.

Her response was so gentle, a fragile smile that belied the chaos around them. She lifted her arms with an effort that spoke volumes, as if carrying a weight that extended beyond the physical realm.

"Alex! You are here," she whispered, the words carrying a mixture of relief and exhaustion.

Alex's emotions swirled, a torrent of worry and frustration mingling with his relief at finding her.

"Mom, why didn't you tell me? I should've known you needed help." Alex whispered as he fell on his knees, his eyes welling with tears that began to fall uncontrollably, like a cascade of emotion.

His mom looked at him with a mixture of tenderness and understanding, as Alex put his head on her knees, his tears dampening her lap, and cuddling tight her legs as a child grips to life on his mother's breast.

Her words were a balm to his wounded soul, reaching him through the haze of his feelings. "It's okay, Alex. You're here," she whispered softly, her fingers tracing soothing paths through his hair. "You came, that's all that matters."

He clung to her, seeking comfort in her touch, and in that embrace, he found solace amid the storm that had engulfed them both.

Alex couldn't tell how much time passed as they held each other, finding a fragile refuge in the middle of the chaos that surrounded them. Only the distant sounds of the street occasionally stopped the silence, serving as a reminder of the world beyond. Hours may have slipped by unnoticed when Alex finally felt enough strength to lift his head. He looked at his mother, and in that moment, unspoken understanding passed between them. Her face bore traces of pain, resilience, and the unbreakable bond that tied them together. In her eyes, he saw a deep, profound love that needed no words to convey its depth.

Gradually gathering his strength to stand up, his legs unsteady from the weight of emotions, Alex couldn't let go of his mother's embrace. He made the decision to lift her in his arms, carrying her to the bedroom—a gesture of care and support that mirrored the love he felt for her. As he cradled her fragile form, a sense of guilt gnawed at him. His mother seemed feather-light from losing so much weight. The realization struck him like a blow, and he could only think how selfish he was to abandon her all this time, consumed by his own concerns, while aware of the terrible pandemic, leaving her to struggle all alone.

His footsteps were deliberate and gentle as he carried her to the bedroom, his heart heavy with the weight of responsibility and remorse. Each step on the stairs seemed to echo the passing time, the distance he had unwittingly allowed to grow between them. The silence that hung in the air was heavy with unspoken words—apologies, regrets, and the yearning to bridge the gap that had formed.

The pandemic had created a world of isolation and uncertainty. But within that moment, as he carried his mother to her rest, Alex recognized the importance of being present for those who mattered most. It was a poignant lesson in the midst of adversity, a reminder that love and connection could withstand even the most challenging of times.

With utmost care, Alex gently placed his mother onto the bed, carefully arranging the duvet around her body. He laid down beside her, cuddling her fragile shoulder to feel the closeness to her, like when he was a child.

Morning came quickly, and as he opened his eyes, the light filtered through the curtains, awakening the room with a soft glow. He stretched slightly, and slowly rolled over very carefully, not to disturb his mother, to get out of bed and close the shade, giving her some more time to sleep.

A gentle voice pierced the quiet. "It's okay, I'm awake." His mother's voice, though weak, held a note of unexpected strength. "We can have breakfast; shall I make your favourite?"

Alex turned around and looked at her speechless, struggling to find words that could express the flood of emotions within him.

"Mom, you... you're, okay?" His voice trembled with a mix of astonishment and concern. "How do you feel? Shouldn't you rest a bit longer?"

"No, I feel much better. I just needed a good sleep. I had a strange dream about a little boy; he looked like you," and she slowly started to get up, looking for her slippers next to the bed. "But he was wearing some very unusual outfit. Couldn't really make any sense of it…"

As she continued with the story about her dream, Alex felt like a heavy stone rolled down from his chest. His mom was just talking and talking, the good old annoying way, which was once a source of frustration, and always made him mad and bored to his core, but in that moment, it was a reassuring confirmation and newfound appreciation for her.

"Mom, I'll go out and bring some food. Just take your time; I'll be back, and we can have breakfast, okay?"

His mother looked very peaceful and happy as she continued to get ready. Alex stepped towards the door and looked at her reflection in the mirror once more beside the door. Her peaceful demeanour and the simple act of carrying on with her morning routine gave a sense of comfort to him, knowing that, for now, his presence had brought a moment of solace to her. But as he glanced at his own image, he noticed the dark circles around his tired eyes and the prominent streaks of grey which suddenly appeared on both sides of his hair overnight.

A faint smile tugged at his lips as he muttered to himself, almost in placidity, "Ha, the energy has to be taken from somewhere else. I see now."

His observation carried a mix of amusement and realization, as if he had stumbled upon a small yet profound truth.

8

On the way to the shop, he tried to call the office with a quickly prepared speech in his head about why he didn't show up at work. But nobody picked up the phone, so he tried to call his boss, but the number was disconnected. It's not a good sign, he thought, but one less thing to worry about, he concluded.

One thing he remembered from every survival game and movie; he needed to get supplies. Food, money, and weapons. He was pretty much aware of what not to hoard, so the first thing he crossed from his list was the toilet paper, but about weapons he was kind of wondering. So, after emptying the first ATM machine, he headed to the only hardware store he knew about in the area, to get some ammo.

The salesguy seemed pretty chilled and happy to give away half of the store, no question asked why Alex needs ropes, shovel, industrial nail gun, axes, chains, goggles, and flashlights with three boxes of Duracell batteries. His only question was before he left if Alex wanted the receipt. Decent bloke, he thought and went straight to buy-up all the canned food and water supply from the Sainsbury's.

When he got home and entered the kitchen with dozens of heavy bags, hanging randomly around his arms, looking like a Christmas tree, he found his mom toddling around, and looking really confused.

"I can't believe, what happened here?" She was looking around on the floor, puzzled and desperate. "This is like a pig hole. It will take hours to clean up everything, but I feel so weak, I don't understand anything," she mumbled and as she sighed, she kept her hand delicately pressed against her face, a gesture that seemed to carry a hint of shame and vulnerability.

"Relax, I help you clean up everything, you just make the breakfast, okay?" Alex told her calmly to gently redirect her attention.

The rest of the day went on with the preparation: securing the doors and windows, tidying up the clutter, and stacking up the pantry, while Alex patiently listened to his mother talking, about the most random things he could ever imagine.

"So, what about grandpa?" Alex quickly added when he finally noticed a moment of opportunity. "Can you remember his original family name?"

His mother paused, her brow furrowing as she delved into her memories.

"I'm not sure," she stopped for a sec, her voice carrying a note of uncertainty. "Your Dad was always quite peculiar about his stuff."

"His stuff? Do you mean dad's stuff?"

"No! Aron's, your grandpa's. Everything was kept in a box, down in the basement," she added very obviously. "I promised your dad that I'd keep it for you, but after he passed away I kind of forgot about it."

"Could I see the box now? Where is it?"

"I'll show you; it's in the basement," she replied and slowly, still a bit trembling from weakness, started to walk towards the basement door.

"Let me help you." Alex hurried to open the door for her. As he reached to hold her hand, he felt the soft, fragile, skinny arm. He looked at her and realized how delicate this little woman became, who once was holding his hand so strong and been a steady force in his life. Alex tried to look back and find the time when the change happened but couldn't find the point when he lost touch with his mother.

"There, look," and she pointed towards the opposite corner of the basement from the stairs. "It should be there, but my knees just don't work as they used to. Can you go down and get it?"

"Of course, you go back. I'll get it in a sec."

As Alex walked down the stairs into the damp and musty space, the strong mouldy smell grew really intense, accompanied by the weight of heavy spider webs that clung to the corners. Despite the less than inviting atmosphere, he got closer to the wooden box with big water stains, and he suddenly noticed a unique symbol etched into the wood on the side, but it was way too dark to see it clearly. He carefully reached for the box, lifted it from the corner, and although it was quite heavy, Alex decided to bring it up so he could have a closer look. As he ascended the squeaky stairs with the box in his arms, he couldn't help but feel a sense of excitement mingled with curiosity. What secrets might this box hold? And what mysteries could he uncover about his family's history?

His mother looked at the box with a mixture of cautious interest and an air of scepticism, treating it almost like a potential time bomb carrying the bubonic plague. She took quick action, and after throwing an old blanket onto the kitchen floor, she started to spray everything super diligently, including the box, with sanitizer.

"Oh, leave it Mom!" Alex snapped at her. "Whatever is in this box will definitely not die from that spray after surviving 30 years in the basement."

"You just wash your hands when you finished with this... rotten crate," she responded with a determined tone.

After Alex wiped off the spiderwebs from his hand and hair, he turned his attention back to the wooden box, and with the towel in his hand, he gently cleaned the carving on the front. It looked like circles in the shape of a flower, connected with straight lines, all arranged in six directions in perfect symmetry. He didn't see any writing or other marks, no hinge or lock, just a simple cover. As he slowly started to lift the lid with gentle force, under his mother's close supervision of course, a very strange and bittersweet aroma started to flow out from the crate. He carefully placed the cover on the floor and looked deep inside the box and saw a ragged, old linen sheet wrapped around something.

As he glanced at his mother, who was already close to fainting from the vision of the filthy rug, Alex took a deep breath and pulled out the sizeable package. It felt solid, like a big and heavy metal object. He slowly started to unwrap the linen to reveal the same flower symbol on the top of a big metal cube. The heavy container showed no sign of a lid or opening, but as he held it in his hand, Alex felt some movement inside, like liquid sloshing when he tilted it on its side. He rushed to the table and placed it in the middle so he could take some pictures.

"Wait!" His mom screamed, "Let's just clean it first before you put that thing where we eat."

"Mom, I'll clean up everything after; you just go and watch the telly." Alex shushed her.

"Don't you even dare to think for a second that I will leave you with this whatchamacallit. Who knows what kind of exotic disease is inside that Pandora's box!"

"Erm, Pandora's box. That's not even a bad idea." Alex's face brightened up; he immediately swiped out his phone and started scrolling down in his contacts. The second he found the name, he just pressed the call button. Almost immediately, a familiar face popped up on the screen.

"Hello Alex, any luck with the dating apps?" Daniel chuckled.

"Hey, you must see what I found in Mom's basement," and he focused the camera on the large cube in the middle of the dinner table.

"Wow, that's quite the sight, but it's not even my birthday. What do I owe this pleasant surprise to?" Daniel's voice held a playful tone.

"Haha, very funny. Now, seriously, have you ever seen something like this?" Alex sounded with curiosity and eagerness.

"Show it to me a bit closer, what is that symbol on the top?"

"It's like a flower," Alex hovered the camera above it.

"Ahh, it's Metatron's cube." Daniel snapped in response. "It's about 18 inches wide on each side, correct?"

"Yes, about my arm."

"Uhm, one cubit," Daniel agreed. "The most ancient measurement, used by Babylonians and Egyptians."

"But what does that 'Metatron' mean?" Alex sounded very curious.

"An archangel from the Bible, and he was often mentioned by other ancient religions in their creation epochs as a mediator. A messianic figure per se, who brought knowledge to the world. The celestial scribe of the Book of Life." Daniel hesitated and then he continued. "The symbol on the top of the box is what is actually called Metatron's cube, but nobody ever discovered a physical item. There were only descriptions, but no evidence. It's kind of like the Ark of the Covenant."

"There's some liquid inside, but it's not opening. No lid or top anywhere." Alex tried to tilt it and show the sides.

"I wouldn't try to open it if I were you," Daniel warned him and quickly added, "You know! Indiana Jones? Thunders and melting people! Remember?"

"That's exactly what I told him!" Alex's mother interrupted the conversation suddenly. "It's Pandora's box!" She added, as she just couldn't contain her worry any longer.

"Hi, who is this lady?" Daniel asked politely.

"My Mom, Sophie." Alex introduced her and pointed the camera at his mother to show Daniel.

"Ah, my pleasure. What a beautiful, enigmatic name. I'm Daniel."

"Thank you. So very kind. That's exactly what Alex's father told me when we first met." Sophie smiled with a nostalgic glance in her eyes.

"Ahh, okay, sorry to interrupt the idyll, but what shall we do with the cube?" Alex continued tensely by pulling the camera back on the cube.

"Yeah, right, the box. When you lift it up, do you see any mark or script?" Daniel asked.

"No, just the flower on the top with some random lines carved on the sides," he pointed as he tilted the cube back on its bottom.

"Where was it exactly?" Daniel continued.

"In a wooden box, with the same symbol outside. Wrapped around with an old linen sheet, but nothing else."

"Are you sure?" Daniel sounded a bit surprised. "There should be some sort of warning, description, or manual on how to use it."

"No, nothing but let me check again," and he kneeled down next to the crate again, and started to investigate it, but it was totally empty. "No, just air!"

"Anything on the cloth?" Daniel asked, "There must be something!"

"Let me see!" Alex opened up the ragged linen sheet and spread it out on the table. Alex just saw from the corner of his eyes that his mother was already forming the words to burst out something, "I know Mom, I clean it later, promise!"

The cloth was torn, dirty from dozens, maybe hundreds of years of dust. Very fragile with no significant prints visible at first. Just faded, light-coloured strokes intertwined together.

"It looks a bit like the Delphic Epsilon symbol. Very pale, but I think that's it." Daniel commented on the view from the phone.

"Delphic? Like Delphos?" Alex wondered about the sudden feeling of bubbling up voices and stories in his mind, "Why does it sound so familiar?"

"This symbol is uniting three lines as a trinity and told to be originated from the Temple of Apollo in Delphi. Also, the home of Pythia, the Oracle of Delphi, which was considered the belly button or navel point of the world." Daniel explained.

"I remember!" Sophie interrupted them suddenly, forming a frown between her brows. "There were a couple of letters from Greece. Ages ago, but with the wrong name on it, like Delphos, Arion Delphos, I think."

"Delphos? Yes, that must be it, my grandfather's original name. It totally makes sense!" Alex shouted. "And where are those letters?"

"Well, I couldn't keep everything over the years, and it was written with some weird letters, so I think I threw them out."

"Oh no, Mom, why did you do that? Those letters could have been crucial in finding his connection to this symbol and the cube." Alex's frustration was evident in his voice.

"Don't be so hard on her, Alex. We're making progress already. We can research more about the Epsilon symbol and its significance. And perhaps somehow, we can research your grandfather's ties to Greece as well." Daniel's reassuring tone on the phone gave hope.

"Yes, you're right. Thanks for helping, Daniel. We'll figure this out together." Alex felt a renewed determination to carry on with the quest, especially now that he had more than enough evidence about his family legacy.

As they continued discussing the symbol, its ties to Delphi, and the potential clues hidden within Aron's past, a sense of purpose filled the room, driving them to connect with his mom even deeper than ever before.

9

After spending long hours the next morning searching for the perfect hiding spot for the box, as it was way too big to carry to his place, he finally succeeded. These couple of hours also gave him a chance to think through everything, and Alex made a somewhat seemingly immature but actually very responsible decision. Given the current situation with the water malarky, moving back to his mother's house was the most sensible choice. Besides, her house was much larger than his apartment, and it was already secured, making it an ideal base for a headquarters.

"Mom, I need you to lock the door from inside. Anyone comes or asks, you don't go out, don't answer, just call me immediately, okay?" Alex told her with concerned emphasis just before leaving.

"Yes, yes, don't worry dear. I will be fine!" his mother reassured him with a touch of indulgence. "But I need a few things. I'll make you a list for when you come back."

As he headed to the bus stop, Alex knew that it would take him way longer to get home, but it allowed him to use the internet. He couldn't tell how much time he had until everything collapsed, so just sitting around on the tube, dodging eye contact with strangers, seemed like a luxury.

When he sat down, Alex noticed a strange tiny object on the seat next to him, which seemed to be stuck in the cushion. An open safety pin was hastily attached to a frame, shaped like a double pyramid, made from very intricately intertwined wires. Alex recognized the form, the octahedron, one of the Platonic solids, but it was nothing like his own or Daniel's medal. The bus was almost empty, just a few strangers staring at their phones. He looked around but didn't see anyone near, so he decided to keep it safe in his backpack, and maybe he could check it out later.

His journey was actually quicker than expected; the streets were pretty empty, and while he was Googling all the things he needed to prepare for, according to every possible zombie scenario, he still had time to sign up for a few speed dating events. With no time for swiping through endless profiles, he figured it would be better to just meet and see what happens. Plus, it would provide an opportunity to engage in conversations with the guys as well. It was a win-win situation in his book.

The entrance to his building raised immediate suspicions; the glass door was shattered and left wide open. As he slowly stepped inside, Alex saw a couple of crows in the corridor, very casually strolling through, nonchalantly exploring, and walking in and out of open apartment doors.

"Where is everyone?" he wondered. But as he ventured further, he could see people still in their PJs sitting in armchairs and staring into the abyss. Alex couldn't help but wonder, how long will people stay in this nihil? How long before the pangs of hunger or the primal instinct to survive would kick in?

Alex knew that not everyone is affected, that some people will still be working, or at least taking care of the most essential things, but is it enough to provide and sustain a city for the millions? With no working public services, no running water, and no electricity, how long before the store shelves emptied without the workers? And then what? The prospect of looting, desperation, and ultimately, starvation. He didn't even want to think about it, but facing the grim reality seemed inevitable.

He pressed the button to call the elevator, but he almost immediately started to gag as the door slid open. A putrid odour wafted out, unmistakable and gut-wrenching, so he quickly covered his nose and opted for the stairs.

He rushed into his apartment and swiftly grabbed what he deemed most essential, knowing that he couldn't take everything with him. Alex carefully stashed away what he considered precious. Every moment counted, and he needed to be strategic about what he carried in his backpack.

The sight of the broken glass door downstairs already envisioned the near future that clearly reached his doorstep. Alex figured if he leaves his door open, as if someone had already been robbed, it would be better. He just threw a couple of things on the floor, opened the drawers, overturned a chair to create the illusion of a hasty break-in, and of course, with a marker, drew the picture of the solids on his front door and his number beneath it.

His logic was that if the zombies come here, they wouldn't bother to call the number, but if someone recognizes his doodle similar to their own medal, they might reach out to him. Or at least as long as the mobile line is working.

The city was slowly becoming a deserted and eerie place, and he knew that survival required making tough decisions. After waiting for 30 minutes for the bus, Alex slowly realized that without transportation, it would become more difficult to get through the city. As much as he felt that this drastic action should be his last resort, desperate times call for desperate measures. He had never stolen anything in his life and had always followed an extremely strict moral code. But now, as the world turned upside down, his principles were put to the test.

The idea of taking a car that had been abandoned by someone who might never return didn't really feel like stealing; it was more like a temporary borrowing to survive. A necessary action to ensure his safety so he could help save the world, like when they tell you on the plane that in an emergency, put the mask on yourself first.

Alex made his way to a nearby street in a residential area, where among rows of houses, he spotted a car parked at the curb. As the sun glanced at the window, he noticed it was cracked, so he decided to have a closer look. He carefully checked the door, half expecting it to be locked, but to his surprise, the driver's side door was open, and the car key was still in the ignition—a sign that whoever had driven it last had left in a hurry.

As he slipped inside, he felt a mix of excitement, guilt, and desperation. The feeling was surreal—almost as if he were in a Guy Ritchie movie scene. His heart raced as he pulled away from the curb, with only one thing in his mind. The irony of the situation: someone who had always lived by the rules now breaking them to save the world from falling into chaos, just to restore law and order.

Of course, he reassured himself over and over that this was only a temporary measure, but for now, survival was the priority. He didn't know that stealing a stranger's car was just one of many tough decisions he would have to make in the days to come as he navigated through the empty streets.

10

A lengthy list awaited Alex upon arrival from his mother.

"If I have to stay home, I need my medication and food that we can actually eat," his mom explained, presenting the extensive list.

"Mom, I already bought tons of food," Alex rolled his eyes, looking at the paper with a mishmash of groceries and items he never thought he'd have to hunt down.

"That's all garbage! You can't expect us to eat those horrible canned 'dog foods' for weeks," she snapped at him. "Here. I put everything down, so I can make proper meals and your favourites while you're here."

The magic word—favourites! Alex sighed, turned around, and headed back to the shop. "What is this Ashwa-naga-what?" Alex muttered in the doorway, trying to read the tongue-twisting word from the list.

"It's ashwagandha, dear. From the little shop across the post," his mom corrected him with a hint of amusement in her voice. "You won't find it at the pharmacy. There's a lovely little shop across the post office. Maybe you'll even meet that charming girl I've been wanting to introduce you to for ages."

"Ohh Mom! You should know that I won't fall for this," he shook his head with annoyance, a blend of frustration, and affection.

"Please, just get the pills for me and have a look," she smiled at Alex kindly, almost begging. "Here, take my card and take out as much money as you can. The pin is on the post-it note on the back."

"That's exactly where you shouldn't write your pin, Mom! Ahhh, okay, I'll take the pill for you, that's all." Alex snapped at her. "I can't even believe that we have this conversation again."

Alex sighed deeply with annoyed anger as he begrudgingly set out on yet another errand dictated by his mom's lengthy list. He couldn't help but be frustrated with his mom's naivety and careless action of keeping the pin on her card. And anyway, what the heck is this Ashwa-thing. So pointless...

After walking through the desolate aisles of the stores, gathering whatever he could find from the grocery list, Alex made his way to get his mother's medications while passing on the street next to the quaint little shop across the post office. It didn't seem like a big stretch, and despite his initial reluctance, a sense of curiosity got the better of him. He rolled his eyes and decided to step inside.

It looked like a vape shop from the 12th century, with cozy, dim lighting, an eclectic assortment of packages on the shelves, dried herbs in baskets on the counter, and an indescribable earthy aroma from the mingling musky and sweet scents. A gentle chime sounded as the door closed behind him, and within moments, a middle-aged, MILF-type woman stepped in with a broad welcoming smile. She had a ridiculous amount of makeup on, looking like a weird fusion of a chav and a '90s Russian prom queen.

"Hello there, what can I help you with today?" she said, in a distinct foreign accent.

Caught off guard by the peculiar harsh scents, Alex cleared his throat. "Hi, I need some Ashwa... Ashwanaga..." as he tried to stumble over the word.

The woman chuckled softly. "Ah, Ashwagandha. It's a wonderful herb known for its stress-relieving properties. Let me check for you. Is there anything else you're looking for?"

Alex glanced around at the suspicious products, feeling a bit out of his element. "No, it's for my mom. Sophie. You might remember her."

"Ah, of course. You're her son? She always tells lengthy stories about you; she's very sweet," she smiled politely. "Here, I found it. Let me get you the receipt. And please tell Sophie that I won't be able to join her for tea tomorrow. My boyfriend is unwell, so I need to stay by his side. Maybe I can visit her next week."

After Alex paid and left the shop, his lips curved into a bemused smile at the bizarre encounter. His mom's 'charming friend' couldn't be more far-fetched than his idea of a suitable mate. Never in a lifetime Alex would ever try to engage in a conversation with such an eccentric woman, plucked straight from a KGB movie. Even if the future of humankind would depend on it.

He couldn't wait to share his peculiar experience, but when Alex got closer to his mother's place, an unsettling sight greeted him. The entrance door was wide open. In a rush, he dropped the grocery bags and began searching the rooms when he suddenly heard loud noises coming from the kitchen. Alex sprinted in just to find his mother on the floor, locked in a struggle with a guy, fighting over her purse. Without hesitation, he leaped onto the stranger, grappling with him, twisting his arm, pushing him on the floor.

The scuffle resembled a chaotic clash, both fighting with fierce determination as they were wrestling around on the floor, like mad dogs. It was unreal; this guy seemed like a rabid animal, twisting, turning, shrieking, and hissing. When finally, Alex managed to restrain the man, he grabbed his arm and pushed his face on the floor, and it seemed to calm him down, panting, and looking around confused.

"Please, don't hurt him!" Sophie cried out. "He's Jason, Maggi's husband from next door," and she started to sob uncontrollably.

"What? Jason? Yeah, right! Sorry, I didn't recognize him. Especially," and Alex suddenly started to yell into Jason's ears, "Because I was busy bloody fighting with a rabid bastard while he was trying to rob my mother in her own house! What the hell is going on?"

Alex totally lost it, and from the adrenaline rush, he just kept pushing the man's face on the floor.

"Darling, let him go! Please let him go!" Sophie cried.

"I don't understand, do you try to defend him?" Alex was shocked at his mother's reaction.

"Nothing happened, I just gave him money, and we forget about this. Let him go!"

Alex slowly pulled him up and looked at the guy who was a minute ago a mad dog but was now a lifeless zombie, just hissing and blinking with utter confusion on his face.

"I take you out, but I promise if I ever see you again in a 5-meter distance from this house, I will hunt you down, break your arm and stick it up to your arse! Do you understand?" And Alex dragged the guy through the hall by his hand and tossed him out to the street. Slammed the door behind him and turned the latch and locks.

"Mom, what the hell was that?" Alex turned back and looked at his mother seriously pissed. "Why did you try to protect him? Why did you let him in? He was trying to hurt you!"

"I know, but he's a good guy, always helps with the work around the house, fixing things, so I give him money. He was standing in front of the door and begging me. He has two little children; Maggi is in the last trimester with the third child."

"Gosh. It's terrible," Alex collapsed to a chair as he heard the story.

"He just needs money," Sophie continued crying very emotionally while she slowly sat down next to Alex at the table.

They both sat in silence, only the rhythmic ticking of the kitchen clock marked the passing of the time. Alex's head was full of racing thoughts from the adrenaline—rage, fear, and fury—slowly brewing like a potent potion, but a new feeling began to blend into this weird mixture: sonder. He stole a car today; he too crossed his strict moral boundaries. This guy was trying to protect his family, getting money to survive, just like him.

Alex suddenly saw parallels between himself and Jason. Both were driven by a desire to protect their families and survive. He realized; he was not any better than Jason. His hands grew heavy, and his head buzzed from the endorphin. He just collapsed and buried his face in his hand on the table.

"I stole a car today, Mom. I had to do it, and I have no right to judge anyone. I can't harm people who are affected; they are not aware of their actions. Jason just wanted to survive," Alex was deeply embittered and ashamed of himself.

"My dear son. Don't be so hard on yourself. We all have our flaws, worries, and cross to carry. Life is complex, not just a straightforward march of victory, but a constant fight to find a balance while we struggle. You know, I read it somewhere that it's like you have two wolves living inside you. Both mighty and prideful, good, and evil, in a constant fight. And do you know which one will win?"

Alex lifted up his head, "Yes, the one who you feed," he replied softly. "I read that saying before. Very wise."

Sophie cuddled him. "You just have to feed the good thoughts, believe in yourself and the good wolf will win. As long as you don't hurt other people on purpose, you are doing the right thing."

"But Jason was hurting you," Alex snapped back.

"He doesn't know what he's doing, he's not himself, and we understand that. We need to help him."

"Ahh, no way, I will not help him," retorted Alex on the verge of anger.

"Just give him money to survive," Sophie replied. "Help in the way you can."

"Do you seriously expect me to go after him and help him after this?"

"Yes, or I will do it." Sophie said with determination in her fragile voice.

"Okay, okay, I'll go there tomorrow, but I have to calm down first. And you have to promise me that you won't override my rules. Nobody comes in without me, do you understand? I am serious!"

They looked at each other, with a shared understanding and peace in their eyes. This moment marked a significant turning point for both of them. For Alex, it was a newfound sense of responsibility and protectiveness toward someone. And for his mother, it was a deep acknowledgment that her life was now entrusted to her son's capable hands.

Like an exchange of their roles in each other's life.

11

The following morning, influenced by his mother's subtle hint, Alex gathered his mental strength, grabbed the money slipped inside his shoes, and went to visit Jason. He actually hoped to find out more about their condition, anything helpful about this illness and the epidemic. It was shocking witnessing firsthand the rage of a victim and the sudden change from madness to apathy. But how could the water affect people so much? He was already prepared for the worst, having seen two corpses already, so he kind of knew that whatever will wait for him won't be pretty.

He collected a few tins and food from the shops to take with him. The tins were mostly for self-defence, and he kept one in his hand while knocking on the door, but the good intention is what matters most. After a couple of minutes of waiting, since he didn't hear any movement, he just opened the front door and let himself in. It was devastating, as if a bomb exploded in the middle of the living room. Stuff everywhere, laying around in random places, and no sign of anyone. The only promising sign was the lack of stinge, I mean a tolerable level of stink. Alex decided to go up and check the rooms, but as he turned back, Jason was standing right behind him. Startled, he almost dropped the tin; he got so frightened, but they just locked eyes and looked at each other like deer stunned in the headlights. So, he slowly lowered the plastic bag down and held up the tin as a gesture of goodwill.

"Hi, Jason. I brought some food," Alex began, speaking slowly and segmented, in his hand holding the tin aloft like an offering. "I'm leaving it here for you, with some money. Do you need help? Where is everyone?"

Jason pondered, then turned slowly, and headed toward the staircase, with Alex cautiously following him, still stroking the tin like a birthday candle. In the bedroom, as Jason opened the door, he saw a couple of figures in the bed under the blanket, so he went closer and saw the kids as they were hanging on their mother, but her face was pale and lifeless. Alex checked her pulse; it was faint, barely imperceptible. A little girl and boy were skin and bone, looked like little angels just fallen into the hellish reality.

Alex tried to take the woman in his arms, but her lifeless body with the extra baby was way more than he could carry alone. "C'mon, Jason, help me move her. Lift her legs up; we need to get her to the hospital! I can't do it alone." But Jason didn't move. "Jesus, she's going to die!" Alex screamed with sheer horror. "Wake up, man! You need to help me!"

It suddenly dawned on Alex that it wouldn't help if he was yelling; Jason was paralyzed. No emotion, empathy, or remorse. So, he gently placed her back on the bed and rushed out to find his mother.

Sophie came immediately and quickly realized that she was seriously dehydrated, likely without water for days. "You need to go and get Maya! Tell her to bring her medicines!"

"Who's Maya? How should I know her?" Alex's frustration creased his brow. "I need a little more context, Mom!"

"Maya! You met her yesterday in the store!" Sophie retorted, puzzled. "How could you forget her name?"

"I didn't ask for her name, Mom! It wasn't exactly the topic of conversation! I was more focused on trying to pronounce that ungodly pill you wanted!"

"Oh, just stop arguing with me and go get her!" Sophie yelled at him.

"Okay, fine!" Alex grumbled annoyedly, rushing out of the house and sprinting all the way to the little herb dealer shop. Bursting in, he just kicked the door, and as he started stumbling over his hasty words, desperate to convey the urgency, the woman was looking at him like Alex would try to explain to her the word 'philanthropist' in a charade.

"Wait, wait! What are you talking about? Who and what?" Maya tried to stop him, to slow Alex down to understand what he was saying.

"My Mom sent me to get you," Alex gasped for breath. "A woman, pregnant, she's dying, we need you. Bring your medicines. Grab your supplies, the whole store if you have to!"

"Do you mean Maggi? Bozhe moy! I'm coming, wait!" Maya replied as she hastily dropped a couple of things in her tiny bag.

"NO! We need more than that!" Alex's frustration boiled over. "Take everything; she's not going to make it!"

"Calm down, I know what I am doing!" Maya replied in a very reassuring tone.

She snatched her cardigan, stormed out, and started running straight to the house on the other street. And suddenly it hit Alex, like a ton of bricks on his face.

"You are not affected! You are a Gatekeeper; you must be!" He shouted after her.

"A what?" Maya looked back at him, "Let's go, and you can explain it later!"

Alex felt so stupid, that he only just realized the obvious fact. She was smiling at him yesterday, and she's looking after her ill boyfriend. Argh, what a dumbass.

Maya set down on the bed, cradling Maggi's head, and put a couple of drops of tincture from a little bottle onto her tongue. Then nestled beside her and started cuddling and rocking her like a baby. Both little children climbed on her, like a merry-go-round.

Alex's voice held a note of concern as he started to talk to Maya. "I don't think it's a good idea..."

"My special herbal mix always helps," Maya replied in a caring and gentle tone with that weird, harsh accent.

"I know, but you help them! Not the mix! It's taking the energy from you! Look at you!" And Alex pointed to her arms, where it was almost visible when some faint, blue mist seemed to flow from Maya's veins straight into Maggi and the children. "You are killing yourself, Maya."

She looked at her arms with a startled realization and suddenly started clutching the children and Maggi tighter. "Good, this is how it should be," she stubbornly replied.

"Just please stop if you start to feel a little weak," Alex replied, his voice full of worry.

It lasted for another 15-20 minutes until Maggi suddenly opened her eyes and looked around. "Where am I?" Her voice trembled from weakness.

"You are at home," Sophie responded gently. "But we need to take you to the hospital."

"I can't. My children," Maggi's concern turned towards her little boy and girl.

"We'll look after them, but you need medical care. Your baby needs you," Sophie was very reassuring but firm.

"Oh, Maya. So nice to see you." Maggi turned her head, glancing at the almost sleeping Maya next to her.

"Are you okay?" Alex kneeled beside Maya and gently reached for her hand. Maya slowly lifted her head, and as she opened her beautiful luminous smaragd green eyes, their eyes locked.

It was like a lightning strike. Alex was taken aback, dropped his jaw, and looked at Maya like he saw the Virgin Mary herself. She was so beautiful, like an angel. Much younger, pure, no heavy makeup, just the natural glow radiating from within her.

"Alex, is everything okay?" Sophie asked in a concerned voice as her son was not breathing for almost a minute.

"I... I am sorry," Alex stuttered. "I've never been better," he smiled and looked at Maya again like an angel. "I get it now. All those pictures in the church, about angels and saints. I see it now! The glory around you, it's just so beautiful!"

Maya appeared puzzled and somewhat embarrassed, probably not accustomed to being viewed with such fervent astonishment. "Well," she replied and gently withdrew her hand from Alex's tight grip, who turned into stone again watching Maya, "I think, I better go slowly; I left the store open. I hope your son recovers soon and he can take Maggi to the hospital," she continued with little hesitation in her voice, looking back at

Alex, who was still speechless and not breathing at all.

After Maya left, Sophie took the kids to her place, and Alex forced Jason to sit in the car to wait until somehow slowly Maggi could walk down the stairs with Alex, holding her carefully. As they approached the hospital, it didn't look too bad. No crowd or angry mob, just normal people walking in and out. Surprisingly, the staff at the reception seemed competent and knew what they were doing.

It made Alex think. After all, people who are passionate about caring for others might belong to one of the tribes, like healers. Maya obviously is a natural healer. Or the others, passing on knowledge, like Daniel as a teacher could be another. It would totally make sense. And as Daniel said, Alex was the third, the magician. But what a magician is actually doing? Hmm, good question. But more importantly, two more Gatekeepers were still missing, and although I don't have a black belt in nitpicking, but I didn't see any medal on Maya either. Did you?

12

Alex couldn't wait to get home and instead left Jason with Maggi in the capable hands of the hospital, just in case he turns into a mad zombie again. At least there, he'd have someone who could manage him with sedatives, not just canned food. But his mind was entirely occupied by Maya, the thought of her tugging at his every step. With an almost childlike eagerness, he rushed back to her charming little shop, eager to see her once again.

"Hello! I hope you're feeling better," Maya greeted him, her tone tinged with a hint of sarcasm.

"I'm sorry for how I behaved earlier; I just never experienced someone like you before," Alex began, his tone polite and strategic, worried about scaring her off again. "I must admit, you have an amazing talent for healing. How long have you been doing this?"

"It's been in my family for generations," Maya explained. "Both my parents came from a long line of doctors, but for me, it took a different path. I chose to move to the UK and eventually opened this little shop.

"That's really interesting, and do you still keep in touch with your parents?" Alex inquired to find out more about her background.

"Not really, it's a long story, but anyway, how can I help you?" Maya replied, a hint of reticence in her voice after such a personal question. "Do you need something? How is Maggi? Will she and the baby be okay?"

"The doctors are taking care of them; her health is critical, but in a couple of days, they can tell more," Alex continued. "I will probably visit her tomorrow; would you like to join me?"

"Ah, that's very kind, maybe yes, I think I will." Maya said as she glanced around the empty shop. "Nobody comes to the store anyway since this thing started with the water."

"Ah, so you know about the water?" Alex jumped at the opportunity to find out what she knew. "And why do you think it's affecting people?"

"I started to see a couple of weeks ago, people were coming in, complaining about hallucinations and thirst. But I see on my boyfriend that it's more as if he lost interest in life, I mean he lost his feelings. But when I gave him my special mix, he seemed to get better by the next morning," Maya paused, then she looked down at her arms. "But perhaps you're right, maybe he's getting better because of me, not the herbal mix I've created."

"Maya, I have to ask something, but please don't be alarmed," and Alex pulled his medal from his T-shirt's neck, watching closely for her reaction to see if she can recognize it. "Have you ever seen this kind of medal before or something similar with a different symbol on it?"

"Oh, that's very nice, but we don't carry jewellery in the store."

"No, I mean, have you ever seen it on your father or someone in your family?" Alex explained.

"Hmm, no, it doesn't look familiar. This is nothing like our family brooch."

"Brooch?" Alex stopped her. "Where is that brooch?"

"Ah, I lost it a couple of days ago again." Maya looked really worried. "My boyfriend will kill me; he made it for me, it's shaped like a star."

"A star?" Alex seemed a little disappointed. "So, your family has a brooch shaped like a star? Not like a cube or pyramid?"

"Hmm, no. It's like a four-pointed star. I lost the one my father gave me a long time ago, and my boyfriend made me a new one, but a few days ago I realized that it was gone too. I've been so scattered in the past few weeks!"

Alex was devastated; he wanted so much to be her. To be the other Gatekeeper. But it seemed she only possessed unique skills, like the staff at the hospital, rather than being a true master of the element with a medal.

"Ah, I see," Alex tried to carefully hide his disappointment. "Thank you for your kind help, and if you're still up for the visit tomorrow, I can meet you here around ten. Okay?"

He was still hoping to see her, feel again the warmth she radiated. In his eyes, she had become like a glowing ray of sunshine, despite her thick layers of makeup, harsh accent, and little wrinkles. Even on his way home, he couldn't shake off the feeling of lost hope.

However, Alex noticed an invitation on his phone for a speed date event for that night, and to his surprise, a few friends had finally replied to his messages, breaking the recent silence. His gamer buddies from around the world, after all the years of three-word texts, were asking with genuine interest if he was doing okay.

Every little interaction seemed precious at this point because it meant that they were protected by their power. So, Daniel was right, there are millions in other countries too. He was also planning to explore further in the hospital. There had to be someone out there; he just had to look for the medal, not only the emotions.

The last thing Alex wanted to do was to attend the awful speed dating event after years of painfully awkward experiences, but he mustered the courage, put on his best Flash t-shirt (the Superman one seemed a tad too over-the-top), and generously applied Aqua Velva, thinking it might boost his self-confidence.

The bar was quiet when he arrived, with only a few people standing around looking bored and really lost. Alex knew he needed to break the ice, so he tried to act really goofy to lower the defence bar with the guys first. Behaving like a class clown had always worked because guys didn't see him as a threat. Although it also cut off all his chances instantly with the girls. Kinda like a double-edged sword, he was friend-zoned pretty much always since high school, but Alex didn't know how to sell himself when he felt embarrassed or shy.

"Hey, man. Tough crowd, yeah?" Alex started a conversation with a short, chubby guy at the bar counter, while stealing glances at the girls in the opposite corner.

"Ah, it's the same every week... Like fishing for a goldfish in a swamp," the guy replied, seemingly already gave up on his own life, even before he stepped in this place, but at least talking, so Alex continued.

"Ha, that's a good one, I'll be on the lookout for piranhas, then... My name is Alex. Nice to meet you," and he shucked the guy's hand, but nothing. He didn't feel much just the poor guy's sweaty palm. "Well, good luck, buddy. May the best one win!"

And he quickly escaped to find a napkin to soak up the dripping sweat from his hand before the guy could even reply or say his name. Quite rude, if you ask me, but time is essence so, Alex straight jumped on to the next contestant.

After ten handshakes and a desperate need for hand sanitiser, the host finally ended the foreplay, and Alex picked a cozy table with a goth girl. He figured, she had plenty jewellery, so it wouldn't be too strange to start the convo with the medal question. "Hey, that's a cool selection you've got there. Are those family heirlooms?"

"My piercings? Are you kidding?" The girl looked at him scornfully.

"Erm, I love unique and mystical pieces." Alex cleared his throat and looked for a way to bounce back smoothly.

"Well, this ring is from an auction, they said it's from the Victorian era's most famous serial killer." She pointed to the huge ring on her middle finger with a quirky smile.

After a troubled brow raise, Alex was ready to jump on the chance to show her the medal, "That's interesting. I have a unique piece too. Check this out," and he carefully took out his medal and rolled it around in his hand for her to get a good look.

The goth girl's eyes widened as she examined the unique relic, and it truly seemed to captivate her attention. "Oh, wow! This is interesting, my ex had a similar one, but more like a strange dice cube. Where did you get this?"

"Are you serious?" Alex couldn't hide his excitement. "Can you tell me where I can find him, maybe his number?"

The girl squinted and then shook her head. "Do you want my ex's number? What kind of sick, weird game are you into?"

Alex nodded, feeling a bit embarrassed, but he'd rather be a weirdo than end up as a dead zombie. "Yeah, well, I have a fetish and I'm looking for guys like me, to do weird things together... erm, but no luck so far," he replied timidly, desperately trying to sound mysterious. "Anyway, I'm Alex. Nice to meet you."

"You are sick man," the girl looked at him stunned but started chuckling. "I like you! The pleasure is mine, Alex. I'm Luna. So..., do you want to come to my place? We can just leave now. You really need to tell me all about this hobby of yours; I am intrigued," and she just stood up, as if she was ready to leave.

Alex couldn't believe his ears. He might have just stumbled upon the very person who could help him find someone with the medal. Plus, and this is the interesting part, actually, she seemed to be turned on by him, without bending over to please her.

"Luna, I'm starting to believe in anything these days," and with a big smile, Alex continued as he grabbed her hand. "Come with me if you want to live."

I know it sounds cheesy, but Alex seriously felt like The Terminator at this point.

As they continued their conversation on the way out, he couldn't help but think that maybe, just maybe, he was finally getting closer to finding another Gatekeeper.

13

With a bit of a limp and looking like he had just wrestled with a grizzly bear, Alex stumbled out of the front door, looked up at the beautiful morning sunshine, and took a deep breath. As the door shut behind him, he felt like the luckiest man alive, and not just metaphorically, mind you. To be honest, when the girl said that she's into spanking, at first, Alex kind of misunderstood the concept.

He fished out the crumpled post-it note from his pocket, still grinning like he had just won the lottery, and took a good look at the number. "Oliver, hm…" mumbled to himself, "Let's see what you know about the medal," and quickly dialled the number, fully expecting at this point that anything could be on the table. Especially after a total nutcase girl warned him about her 'mad' ex.

"Hi, good morning…" he began very shyly, "My name is Alex, sorry to disturb you so early, could I talk to you about…" Click. The line went dead. Alex raised an eyebrow. "Ha, that's rude! Did he just hang up? Let's try again." The mobile rang, and the moment Alex heard the connection, he burst out, "I know you have a medal! Please don't hang up! I need to speak with you!"

"What medal?" A deep masculine voice came from the other end.

"Hi, I'm Alex, and I have a dodecahedron medal. Your girlfriend, sorry, ex, gave me your number…"

"Luna? I told her to leave me alone," the voice replied, sounding really ticked off.

"No, it's not her," Alex added quickly, "I asked for your number! I need to speak to you. It's about… well, the Gatekeepers." And then, silence. A long silence. For seconds, no reply, just eerie quiet.

"Where are you?" The voice was really scary, sending shivers down Alex's spine.

"In London, Northeast. Where could we meet, what would suit you?"

"I come there. Meet me at the St Pancras, International Station Clock.

5pm."

"Great, ok. And at the corner of the station or the… beep-beep," and the line was cut off. "Ha, he is not a man of words. Just hangs up when he's finished. Wow. Okay…"

Alex felt the dignity of a spaceship captain, after crash-landing into a pond. Still in pain and limping, but with a mix of hope and determination, he decided to make his way straight to Maya. He really needed to feel a little TLC after the rough night. But hey, it was all worth it!

The little shop was empty, and Maya's face lit up as soon as Alex stepped in. "Hello, you are early," she greeted him with a warm smile, reaching for her cardigan quickly. "You look very handsome today, like a superhero," she giggled looking at Alex's t-shirt, "Is everything alright, Flash? You seem a bit tired."

"Ah, thanks! I'm fine; I just had a long night, had to deal with some stuff," Alex scratched his head.

"Oh no! Can I help you?" And Maya instantly started to look for something under the counter.

"I'm fine, 'tis but a scratch. A couple of Band-Aids, and I'll be back in business." Alex laughed mischievously.

"Let me see; I can just put some cream on it," Maya replied with caring gentleness.

"Oh, God no!" Alex looked down at his watch suddenly, desperately trying to change the subject and avoid embarrassment, "Let's just go if we want to get to the hospital in time." He simply wouldn't be able to explain his motivations if Maya saw the whip marks on his backside.

"Okay, if you change your mind, I can just give you the cream, no problem," Maya smiled kindly and continued, "I brought some homemade food for Maggi, but I'm not sure if they would be happy in the hospital if I bring it in. Could I just put the plastic containers in your backpack if you don't mind?"

"Of course, not a problem." Alex replied, placing his half-empty backpack on the counter in front of her.

Maya opened the backpack, and her eyes widened as she looked inside, and she instantly started to scream on a high pitch that could shatter glass, "Oh my God!… Where did you find it?"

"Find what?" Alex looked at her, not understanding what on Earth she could've seen in his bag.

"My brooch; I can't believe it, you found it!" Maya screamed almost in tears from the happiness.

"Your what?..." Alex asked back, and then, it suddenly hit him, "The medal." The one he found on the bus two days ago. So many things happened since then – he stole a car, the zombie attack, Maya's glowing halo, the speed date with Luna… It just totally skipped his mind. "Oh yes, I found it on a bus seat, but I didn't think it was yours. You said that your family brooch was star-shaped."

"Look! It closed when fell off! If you open the four little petals, it looks like a star. You attach it with the safety pin when the petals are open."

And there it was. The perfect octahedron with eight triangles. Four triangles' corners meeting in the middle at the top of the pyramid, while with little hinges opening up on the bottom, to create a four-pointed star, with the other four triangles. The third Platonic solid, opening towards the heart like a flower when worn as a brooch. Perfectly symbolizing the healing power of unconditional love.

Alex felt an overwhelming sense of relief as he watched Maya attaching the wire-woven medal to her cardigan and suddenly, as she looked at him with those emerald-green eyes – she became the most beautiful creature Alex had ever seen in his life. It felt like Christmas, his birthday, and his first kiss all rolled into one cosmic moment of happiness.

"Thank you, Alex! You have no idea how much it means to me," Maya said with a tearful smile. "I felt so lost without it. I know it sounds ridiculous, but it makes me feel at home, full of energy and love."

"I know exactly what you mean," Alex nodded, wearing the expression of someone who had just uncovered a hidden stash of cookies, "Maya, I am sure that what I am about to tell you will sound absurd, but please, believe me. You have something that could save millions of people. Your power, emanating from that brooch is what I've been searching for a long time."

"That's not funny, Alex," she said, raising her brows with a look that could crash steel beams.

Alex put on his most earnest expression. "Please let me show you something, give me a chance to explain." Alex implored her, seeing Maya's distant reaction. "Could I show you something? It's at my mother's place. Please! Give me five minutes, and after, we'll head to the hospital to check on Maggi, okay?"

Maya looked really sceptical, but somehow deep down, she had a hunch that Alex told the truth. Sometimes, even when things just don't make any sense, they feel like the right thing to do. So, she glanced around her little shop, in her mind waved goodbye to reality, and stepped out from behind the counter. "Alright, you've got yourself five minutes."

Alex rushed to open the door for her, standing there politely as if he were a footman from Downton Abbey, waiting politely until she passed next to him. Their eyes met, and in that brief moment, they silently found mutual agreement to join the rollercoaster.

As they entered the house, Sophie rushed to greet them in a whirlwind of joy, "Oh dear, I can't believe, you came. I'm absolutely thrilled you could make it," she beamed, embracing Maya with a warmth that could melt a glacier. "I thought you couldn't visit me this week. But I hope your boyfriend is doing just fine."

"Thank you, Sophie! It's so nice to see you too," Maya replied, her eyes betraying a hint of concern. "I am afraid he is not any better. I've been doing my best to help him, but it feels like I'm failing all the time. Maybe I need to spend more time with him; he really needs me," she admitted, glancing downward as if she carried the weight of the world on her shoulders.

"Darling, if you ever want to talk, please, just come here. You can even stay here if you want." Sophie said, her hands cradling Maya's like she held a fragile treasure.

"Mom, she just said that she wants to be with her boyfriend. Sorry, what's his name?" Alex inquired, turning to Maya for the answer.

"Boris. His name is Boris," Maya replied to Alex before turning back to Sophie. "Thank you; your kindness means the world to me. But I have to do this. You know, it's not just for him, but for me. I need to be sure I've done everything I can."

Sophie's eyes brimmed with protective love, her hand gently cupping Maya's face as though she could erase the shadows of her sadness. "Darling, I can't tell you what is right or wrong to do, but you need to know that we are here for you."

Alex began to sense that there was more behind Sophie's protectiveness. Don't misunderstand me, it's not like she was not really kind and caring with everyone, but he felt that something was missing from this picture. Like an unspoken secret hanging in the air, the elephant in the room, and they were carefully avoiding the obvious discussion in front of him. So, Alex, as ever the quintessential English gentleman, being the master of the stiff upper lip, tactfully brushed his curiosity under the carpet, deciding to mind his own business somewhere else.

14

After sipping on a warm cup of tea and going through a couple of used tissues, Alex decided that it was time for him to slip back into the room with them. He cleared his throat with the precision of a butler about to make an announcement, "So, ladies, perhaps we should consider heading to the hospital if we want to pay Maggi a visit."

"Oh, darling, I have to look after Maggi's little ones; they are still so weak and in poor health," Sophie replied with all her maternal wisdom. "But you go ahead, spend some time together, and I'll prepare a nice lunch for when you come back. How does that sound?" And she beamed with a hint of satisfaction, pleased that she had finally seen Alex and Maya together in the same room.

Maya stood up and approached Sophie. "That's truly kind of you, Sophie, maybe another time. I plan to head home after our visit. As I mentioned, it is important for me, and I need to do it. I am sure you understand," and she offered a heartfelt hug to bid her farewell. "Alex, we could have that conversation maybe another time if you don't mind. I just don't think it's a good time right now," she said apologetically, turning to

Alex.

"Of course, you take care, Darling. And please don't forget what I said." Sophie smiled, and her hands slowly started to tidy up the teacups from the table.

Alex knew that something must be going on with Maya's relationship, but he felt that it was more considerate to just keep a little distance and let her open up if she wanted to talk. So, he opted for a respectful distance, a silent presence that offered support but didn't demand answers. The car ride to the hospital visiting Maggi, and the journey back were filled with silence.

Alex treated Maya like a delicate, precious Fabergé egg, showing care and gentleness, feeling that she needed space, while he placed her on a pedestal, in a manner that showed his respect for her feelings. He didn't push any questions or further awkwardness into the quiet moments they shared.

When Maya stepped out of the car, he watched her for long minutes as she walked away, slowly searching in her bag for the keys. Alex just wanted to have one more glimpse of her face. Hoping to see that beautiful smile, a reassuring sign that she would be alright until they meet again.

He almost forgot about the time and his meeting with Oliver, so as soon as the door closed behind Maya, he just floored the car, determined to make it to the station on time. It wasn't so much the fear of missing the opportunity that concerned him, but more the prospect of facing Oliver's wrath if he arrived late. The guy's voice on the phone was like Thor from Ragnarök, so frankly the last thing Alex wanted was to provoke his anger.

Alex decided the easiest way was to park on the corner rather than search for a proper spot and risk running late. Anyway, he could just get another car if he gets a ticket on the windshield. But to his surprise, the entire square was empty, and he could effortlessly pull up next to the clock tower. As he closed the car door and quickly scanned the surroundings, he spotted a tall guy with a duffel bag emerging from a nearby building and headed towards him at a brisk pace.

Alex found it utterly fascinating how the duffel bag seemed to grow in size in mere seconds as he got closer, going from gym-bag proportions to easily fitting a smaller car and the tall guy transformed into a towering giant, dwarfing Alex's own six feet in height. He couldn't help but wonder, was this guy dining with the gods themselves? What he's eating? "Hey, you must be Oliver," Alex blurted out, feeling like he'd stumbled into a Marvel movie.

"Where is your medal?" Oliver rumbled like a thunderclap on a summer day, his voice so imposing that Alex couldn't help but shudder, feeling like he was caught in the midst of a celestial showdown.

Alex fumbled quickly to retrieve the medal, eager to show that he wasn't here to waste Oliver's precious time. "Here, I have it on a necklace," he stammered, holding the amulet as if it were the Holy Grail itself.

Oliver, clearly a man of few words and even less patience, examined the relic and grumbled, "Hm, okay, so you wanted to talk. You have two minutes."

"Are you in a hurry, or going somewhere?" Alex asked politely pointing toward Oliver's colossal bag.

"No, I just arrived from Bergen. And how should I know that you are really a Gatekeeper?" Oliver replied, his tone suggesting that he had zero time for idle chit-chat.

"Fair enough," Alex mumbled, racking his brain for something convincing. "I have a Megaron cube from my grandfather. I'll show you, but you need to come with me."

"Do you mean the Metatron's cube?" This seemed to pique Oliver's interest, and he dropped his bag on the floor, creating a smaller earthquake. "That would change everything," he declared, carefully scrutinizing Alex, every little detail, and then, slowly, he continued. "If this is true, I must see it."

Alex, emboldened by the turn of events, reached out to Oliver for a handshake, a symbolic gesture to seal the deal. But as their hands connected, something strange and extraordinary started to unfold. The air vanished with all noise like in a vacuum, and in that moment, time itself seemed to halt as if it never even existed, and just dissolved into a state of nothingness.

All around them, the buildings crumbled and began to melt down, brick by brick, to tiny particles. The entire city vanished in a matter of seconds like a mirage in a sandstorm. The light surrendered and transformed into darkness, leaving them in a cosmic expanse of the silent void, encircled only by the dark and boundless universe and its distant, shimmering stars.

Oliver instinctively knelt before Alex, bowing his head, and reaching toward his bag on the ground, as if he sought Alex's blessing or awaited a knightly accolade with the tap of a sword-blade. "I see now, you are the Magician; I am here to serve you!" His voice resonated with the profound echo of admiration and the very essence of nature's power. It was as if an ancient force emerged from the depths of the earth, a zesty, deep-red shield formed around them. Glowing like a crackling thunderbolt, protecting them in the boundless expanse of empty space.

Not quite sure what was supposed to happen next, Alex slowly looked around in the surreal surroundings, while he was trying to maintain his full composure. He waited in silence, contemplating if Oliver was expecting him to speak or if there was some specific action he was supposed to take. Frankly, at this point, he was so scared that no sound could come out of his throat, but eventually, Alex gently grasped Oliver's hand, as a silent indication for him to rise.

Oliver emerged and smiled like he understood his hesitant behaviour. "You've never met another Gatekeeper before, have you? Don't worry, you'll get used to this very quickly," and he put his massive hand on Alex's shoulder and patted his back, offering a comforting boost of courage. "Just breathe and let's go back."

"Back? What do you mean back?" Alex's eyes widened, blinking like a teenager on his first date, a mix of innocence and panic flickering on his face, "Where are we?"

"Out. In space, between dimensions." Oliver replied like it was just a casual everyday explanation back on his planet.

"Whaaat? No, no, no, nooo…! That's not possible, we couldn't. We'd just crash in space, no air, vacuum, and…" and Alex's voice trailed off into an incoherent stream of panicked muttering. His words came so fast that they blended together, reaching a high-pitched frequency that only dogs could understand.

"Slow down! Take a deep breath!" Oliver urged him, attempting to calm him down. "You brought us here; I just created the shield to protect us.

You can take us back, just the same way, let's go!" He looked at Alex like he was supposed to know what to do.

"Erm, I hate to break it to you, but I have no clue how we got here." Alex said and finally started to slow down a bit and breathe normally. "I've never been here or anywhere even remotely close to a place like this," he continued and braced himself for what he assumed would be Oliver's reaction, to twist him into a pretzel or some equally unsettling endings.

"Ha. Okay." Oliver muttered, looking around as he was just realizing that he was in a pickle. "So, what was the last thing that you were thinking? That was the way we got here. We just need to turn it back."

"The Metatron's cube! Yes, yes, we were talking about the cube!" Alex blurted out, his face lighting up with realization.

"Okay, so just try to concentrate on it again, and that's it." Oliver reassured him, maintaining an air of calm and helpfulness.

"Hm… hm… I'm trying. Hm… It's not working!" Alex looked genuinely frightened, fearing he might be stuck here for eternity with this scary guy, but he really didn't want to piss him off.

Surprisingly, Oliver remained still pretty chilled. "There must be something else. Was there anything else, maybe even just for a second, that you were thinking of?"

There was indeed something else, but Alex would have preferred to stick a rusty nail in his own eye than admit it to Oliver. So, he was just rolling his eyes, pretending like he was searching for some other option that would be helpful.

"Look, Alex, we have time; there's no need to worry about anything. I'm here now to help you. We can do this together," Oliver reassured him in such a comforting and convincing tone that Alex slowly started to give in.

"It's really embarrassing, I mean look at you! You are huge, looking like a half-god," Alex scratched his head, his embarrassment giving way to honesty. "I was just thinking about someone. If I would look like you, it would be so much easier. I really like her, but she has a boyfriend, and it's just so complicated."

Oliver erupted into laughter, a deep and hearty sound that resonated through the empty space around them, almost like a force of nature in itself. "Come on, man, we are in the same team now. I know we just met, but we're cut from the same cloth." and Oliver winked at him.

This idea struck Alex as oddly empowering. If it were true that he had brought them here and that they both possessed these incredible powers, then the possibilities were limitless. He now belonged to a chosen elite, an in-crowd of cosmic guards, and even a Colossus like Oliver could be on his team. "That's actually helpful, thank you Oliver. Let's go back," and with determination, Alex closed his eyes and focused on the image of Maya's beautiful emerald-green eyes, determined to return to the world they had left behind.

And just like if a massive electric shock surged through his body, when he opened his eyes, they were back in the same spot, right next to his parked car. "Wow, I made it! I thought of her, and it worked!" Alex screamed with a smug smile on his face. But then, a strong headache hit him, as if he'd just suffered a concussion from space travel. "Man, I don't understand. I didn't feel this nausea and terrible headache when we got there."

"Yeah, because I slapped you only on the way back!" Oliver's voice rumbled like a thunderstorm. "Don't ever mess around when we're out there! It took at least four years off my life just to keep us alive, you idiot!"

"What, the hell, man! You hit me?" Alex snapped when he finally realized that the shock he'd felt was Oliver's humongous hand smacking his face, which had sent them back to the ground. "Jesus, but you were so kind and understanding and patient! Why didn't you tell me anything? God, you're a psycho!"

"I doubt that if I panicked and fed your egoistic little meltdown would've helped us. I did what I had to do to protect us." Oliver explained as he grabbed his little arm bag and started to stuff it into the car's trunk.

Alex was still feeling a bit nauseous and seeing stars swirling around his head. Oliver glanced at him, slid over, and effortlessly lifted him as if he weighed nothing like a feather. With a swift motion, he placed Alex in the front passenger seat and climbed into the driver's seat. He pushed the front seat all the way back to create more space for his long legs. "So, what's the address?" he asked, looking back at Alex, who was still trying to process the situation and not entirely sure what had just happened.

"Erm, just give me a moment and I can drive home," Alex mumbled.

"I don't think that's an option. You'd better rest a bit now. So, tell me how to get there," Oliver replied, and he started to feel some sympathy for Alex. However, he couldn't resist adding, "You deserved it, but next time I'll be more gentle with you." He chuckled and slowly pulled off with the car from the sidewalk.

15

Oliver seemed to know his way around the city, though those who still held the firm belief that in the UK they should drive on the left side of the road were momentarily confused when they encountered Oliver's uncompromising, no-nonsense driving style heading towards them at full speed. May the stronger driver prevail. They arrived in one piece, with Alex stumbling on shaky legs as he made his way through the threshold into his mother's house.

"Oh my! Hello and welcome!" Sophie greeted Oliver with astonishment as her eyes widened when she looked up at the giant of a man. She didn't even notice how poorly Alex dragged himself in. "Alex, why didn't you tell me we were going to have a guest! Thank God I made some nice kidney pie. It'll be enough for all of us for dinner. Come in!" She kindly ushered them straight to the kitchen.

As Oliver entered the hallway, the picture frames on the wall swung away, unsure if it was the wind from his shoulder or the ground shaking from his steps. He grabbed a chair in the kitchen and sat down, looking like Gulliver in Lilliput. "Thank you kindly. My name is Oliver. I'm Alex's friend, and to be honest, I'd love to try that pie. I haven't had a chance to taste one in ages."

"Oh, Darling, I'm Sophie! Sorry for my son's rude behaviour, for not introducing me properly," she said with an apologetic smile. "He seems under the weather in the last couple of days, but let me quickly warm up everything. Just a couple of minutes, make yourself comfortable," she smiled, looking like she had just hit the jackpot with Oliver's appetite.

"Alex, are you going to join us?" She shouted to the next room, where Alex was making a loud noise, dropping, and banging something with great urgency.

"Here it is," Alex finally emerged, holding the metal cube in his hands.

Sophie yelled, "Gosh, wait! Let me put something under that ungodly thing before you place it on the table!" She continued, looking at the suspicious cube.

"Yeah, yeah, I know. I'll wait," Alex replied, rolling his eyes as he hobbled with the heavy box.

Sophie quickly laid down a tablecloth, and after Alex placed it carefully in the middle of the table, they all started staring at it with great devotion.

"I have to admit, I've never seen it before," Oliver blurted out. "My stepfather told me stories about it, but I never got a chance to see it up close. Did you open it?"

"God, no! Nobody opens this thing here!" Sophie exclaimed.

"Okay, Mom, we know," Alex reassured her. "Daniel told us that it's better if we don't open it," he added and sat down next to Oliver.

"Daniel?" Oliver asked. "Who is Daniel?"

"Yes, right, I didn't mention. I met him last week; he's also with us. He has the icosahedron. The water belt. I mean, belt. He has a belt," Alex explained with a slightly confused expression.

"A belt?" Oliver replied looking at him puzzled, "He has a belt?!?"

"Yes, I mean the buckle on his belt. He made a buckle from his medal and wears it constantly."

"Huh, he must be really sick. How old is he?" Oliver asked with sudden interest.

"Pff, not sure. Something between 70 and death, I guess."

"Alex! How can you say that?" Sophie scolded him.

"Well, I am just honest, Mom. The guy is in a wheelchair, he looks really sick and weak, I can't really tell how old he is," Alex explained his inconsiderate comment. "He is a video game developer. He was working for Atari, but before he was working on another game, the Polybius."

"No way!" Oliver was stunned. "I've heard so much about him. Everyone thought that he was dead. I thought they captured and tortured him."

"Yes, that's what he said," Alex continued. "But he escaped, moved to California, changed his name, and eventually started working for Atari. But he never fully recovered from the torture they subjected him to."

"Where is he now? Is he joining us?" Oliver's eyes lit up, he looked really enthusiastic.

"Yes, I should actually call him. I also found Maya, I told you," Alex explained and started blushing.

"Ah, the girl who you fell in love with," Oliver added.

The ladle suddenly banged and clattered loudly on the floor as Sophie dropped it accidentally from her unexpected surprise, "Oh my God, Alex! Why didn't you tell me!" She started screaming and running towards Alex for a hug, "So, you like Maya. Did you tell her already?"

"Mom, no. It's not like that!" Alex snapped, "Why did you say it? I told you it's not something I want to share!" He turned to Oliver with anger.

Oliver just patted his shoulder. "Sorry, man, I didn't know it was such a big secret. Hahaha," he laughed out loud.

Alex tried to peel off his mother's python-like embrace from around his body. "Mom, calm down, it's not happening. I didn't tell her anything. She has a boyfriend."

"Well, you better be careful before he hurts her. That guy is a criminal!"

Sophie grumbled with deep anger.

"Hurt her? What are you talking about? Is that what you were talking about earlier?" Alex was shocked. "Why didn't you tell me anything?"

"She made me promise not to tell anyone. But she's always covered in bruises and cuts. I don't understand how she can endure that beast," Sophie said emotionally. "He's been in prison twice already and just got released a couple of weeks ago when the pandemic started again."

"We could pay him a visit. Alex, what do you think?" Oliver suggested with a casual face. "Just to check on him, and he could accidentally bump into a wall a few times. What do you say?"

"No, that's not right," Alex shook his head. "We can't just barge in there," he added, though it seemed like he did consider it, judging by the emphasis in his reply.

"You know, Alex, I'm here. Just saying…" Oliver smiled.

Sophie pushed the cube further along the table to make some space for dinner. "Now, everybody, calm down. Let's eat first. Here are the plates, and we can discuss this later when we're less hangry, okay?" She diligently started to bring pots, bowls, trays, and some more pans to place in front of Oliver.

"Mom, you said kidney pie. What are these?" Alex grumbled.

"Come on, Alex, look at him. Do you really think the wind blew this together?" Sophie giggled, pointing to Oliver's giant body towering over the table while he was seated.

"Yeah, right," Alex rolled his eyes again and gave in to the mashed potatoes with a big spoon.

"I saw that, Alex," Sophie nagged. "You know, we don't make grimaces. It's not polite."

"Okay, sorry," Alex replied with an annoyed voice. "Let's just eat finally."

Bang-bang-bang. Loud banging came from the door. "Sophie, please, help me!" Maya's voice came through from the porch, and they all rushed to the door to quickly let her in.

"My God, Sweety, what on earth happened?" Sophie asked the crying Maya, standing in the darkness outside, her arm and face full of scratches and cut wounds.

"I tried everything; I can't stop him. He's totally turned insane. He was not like this before," she sobbed, burying her face in her palms.

"So, can we go now?" Oliver gave Alex a determined look.

"Hell yeah, I'll get this bastard myself," Alex replied with wrath and determination.

The two Gatekeepers left the headquarters and stepped out onto the dark street, ready to throw themselves into their first mission together. No bats or knives, just two angry men with bare hands and a wrath that could rival the mighty gods. Erm, okay, I exaggerated a bit, but they were pretty pissed off...

They spotted the guy very easily. He was running around under the neon streetlights with a butcher's knife in his hand.

"Boris! Is that you?" Alex shouted.

"What the actual hell are you doing?" Oliver turned to Alex with outrage.

"I want to make sure that we get the right guy," he explained.

"Do you see anyone else running around with a weapon?" Oliver snapped.

"Ha, you would be surprised. I already had a crazy neighbour. They are growing nowadays everywhere like wild mushrooms," Alex added.

Oliver just stopped and glanced at Alex with a disdainful smile. "I'd rather just take my chances when I see a guy with a knife the size of my left arm."

"Yeah, yeah. I mean that we should find Maya's boyfriend first," Alex nodded and raised his arms like a boxer in front of him.

The guy still just hovered and slalomed in a random zigzag throughout the street, but didn't reply to the name, so Alex went closer and shouted at him repeatedly again. "Boris! Boris!"

He seemed to slow down, looking at Alex, tilted his head, and suddenly geared up to full speed, running toward him while waving the knife menacingly.

Alex just stood there, waiting for the impact, but a sudden swinging hand stopped the guy just a step ahead of him like a brick wall. A loud knock followed the blunt thud as the guy bounced back from Oliver's sturdy arm, and his head banged on the bitumen. Alex looked down at him and then quickly glanced back at Oliver. "I was going to handle it!" He shouted.

"Sorry, he's all yours now." Oliver grinned, but they just realized that the guy had already stood up and swung his knife towards Alex, cutting his chest.

Blood started to run through his T-shirt, and Alex looked down at himself with utter desperation. He tried to look for Oliver, but he was already pulling the guy from his throat like a bag of potatoes and pinning him to the nearest tree with his bare hands, the guy's legs dangling a meter from the ground.

"No, wait!" Maya screamed from the distance as she ran toward Oliver. "Please wait! I know him; he's not himself. Please, let him go!" She begged Oliver with teary, bloodshot eyes.

Oliver turned his head, looked down at Maya, her distress truly moving him, and lowered the guy so he could stand on his feet. "If I let him go, he will kill you, I know. I can see it."

"What? You can't say that! You don't know him!" Maya cried uncontrollably.

But they couldn't make the final verdict because the guy suddenly stabbed Oliver in the side, deep between his ribs.

"Oh my God! No! No! No!" Maya screamed in horror, seeing the blood just beginning to flow down like a river on Oliver's shirt, right next to the knife wound.

Oliver didn't even look at his wound; he just slowly turned his head back and locked eyes with Boris, his gaze intense. The only sound was the faint cracking of Boris's larynx cartilage as it began to give way under the relentless pressure. Silent hissing and deep, slow breaths were exchanged between them until Boris gradually released his grip on the knife, and his lifeless hand fell to his side. Oliver released his hold, and Boris's body dropped to the ground.

"He's alive, don't worry. But we need to take him to the hospital," Oliver said firmly as he turned toward Maya and looked into those beautiful and hopeless eyes.

"But you're bleeding! You need to go to the hospital as well!" Maya said, trembling, torn between whom to assist. "You've lost a lot of blood; we need to take you." She stepped closer to Oliver, who had just now started to examine the massive knife protruding from his torso.

Alex and Sophie exchanged glances, and Sophie rushed to help Alex, who, although bleeding, was fit as a fiddle compared to Oliver. They gathered Boris, who was still rattled and shaken but breathing steadily, and they all headed to the car, driving straight to the hospital.

16

After waiting for long hours, finally, someone in a slightly stained green scrub entered the waiting room. The surgeon's face was exhausted, with his expression grave as he approached them. He cleared his throat while looking at the anxious group of faces. "I'm sorry, but we couldn't stabilize his condition. I know this isn't the news you want to hear, but it seems that any medication we've tried to give him just isn't working on him."

Maya burst into even louder sobs, turning to Alex, whose face had gone as white as a sheet. The prospect of losing Oliver felt like a declaration of defeat before they could even begin their journey to save the world. "I must see him, please, let me talk to him," Alex pleaded with a worried look on his face.

"I'm sorry, it won't be possible. We had to put him in an induced coma to prevent his condition from worsening," the doctor explained. "Until we understand exactly what's causing the pandemic, we can't wake him up."

"No way, we need him!" Alex shouted. "Please, we have to wake him up. You don't understand. Without Oliver, we're all lost."

The surgeon looked at his chart again, somewhat confused. "Oliver? I thought his name was Boris."

"Did you miss me?" Oliver's voice resonated from the far end of the corridor, drawing everyone's attention to the corner of the huge waiting room. He was slowly walking in with a broad smile on his face, his chest wrapped in a labyrinth of plaster and bandages. "I overheard my name, but I hope you didn't think you could write me off that easily."

The doctor, somewhat bemused, replied, "Ah, him? He's fine!" And he just waved with his hand, "It was really wise that you didn't try to pull out the knife. It seems that it saved his lungs from collapsing, but no other major organs were reached. The cut is still very deep, so we stitched him up and against our medical advice he already signed the papers that he wants to leave at his own risk, so he's good to go. Just make sure he has a few days to recover, preferably in bed rest, though it's entirely up to him. He made it very clear what was going to happen, and none of my colleagues could stop him. He is like a gladiator, so he's all yours now, and your problem," the doctor chuckled. "So, yeah. And what about the other gentleman?" He glanced at his chart again. "Boris his name, yes. You wanted to see him, correct?"

Maya, having finally dried her tears, appeared a bit unsure. "Well, you said that he's in a coma, and we should wait until we know more about what's happening with him. I'm sure he's in good hands here. Maybe we can just leave him for now," she suggested, looking around timidly for agreement, clearly eager to leave the hospital as soon as possible.

"Don't worry, Ma'am, we have patients every day with the same or even worse condition. I know that you just tried to protect yourself, it's obvious," the doctor looked at Maya with compassion. "We get most patients with really violent injuries; people try to protect themselves. Not everyone is affected in the same way. It looks like this condition brings out brutality from people who have records from before with this kind of behaviour. Most victims are just aggressive, but with a history of violence from their background it somehow tips over inside them something and they become extremely dangerous. So don't worry, you did the right thing. You are lucky that you had someone there to protect you." The surgeon touched Maya's arm, seemingly acknowledging her wounds and bruises.

The doctor's reassuring words seemed to comfort Maya, and she nodded kindly. "Thank you, Doctor," she said, feeling a bit less guilty about leaving Boris behind, knowing she had made the right decision.

With Alex's help, Oliver finally made his way back to the group, and everyone felt relieved with a renewed sense of purpose. After continuing their discussion with the doctor about the illness and any information he might have about the medals, it became even more clear to Alex that the healers' unique abilities in hospitals as Gatekeepers, while powerful, were only one part of the puzzle. However, it wasn't enough for the impending battle ahead of them. They needed to focus on finding the amulets, and even more crucially, the last missing element which could help them combat the imminent threat of the water infections.

Sophie, who had been overwhelmed with worry and speechless during their time at the hospital, now couldn't stop pampering Oliver on the way back home and it actually seemed to have a remarkably calming effect on him. She even managed to convince him to take some much-needed rest in the guest room after promising him a hearty chicken broth for lunch if he'd behave and follow her instructions to get a couple of hours of rest as a good patient. Who could resist such a tempting and persuasive woman?

And it finally allowed Alex a long-awaited moment alone with Maya in the kitchen, to express the whirlwind of emotions that had been brewing within him since their first unexpected meeting.

"Maya, I am so glad that you came here last night for help, but I'm a bit surprised you didn't mention anything to me before about how Boris has been treating you," he said, and stepped closer to her, giving in to the irresistible magnetism drawing him towards her, like a moth to a mesmerizing flame.

"You must promise me that you will tell us if you need help." Alex stopped and tried to repeat his words to come out as he actually meant them. To emphasize that she should turn to him, not anyone else. He felt deep responsibility for this beautiful creature, and just by looking at her, Alex felt ready to move mountains or travel through time and space just to save her.

But before he could muster the courage to continue, Maya gently interrupted him with her delicate voice. "Alex, I can't express how grateful I am for your help. I wish we had met under different circumstances, but everything feels so confusing right now, and I can't figure out how to find myself again," and she took a small step back from Alex, leaving him with the feeling of rejection. Slowly, she turned her gaze downward, her eyes fixed on the space in front of her. "The brooch gave me back my hope; I can sense my strength slowly returning, but I need time to recover, who I was before. Please, let me help Oliver first, he needs me. You see, I gain my power when I heal others. When I give, that's when I become stronger. Do you believe me?"

Although it seems like a paradox, Alex understood her completely. He would throw away everything just to make sure that Maya and Sophie were safe. And even just thinking about the impending battle to save the entire planet gave him unexpected strength over his doubts and vulnerabilities.

The idea of losing his hair, gaining wrinkles, or even perishing in the eternal cosmos seemed like a small price to pay for the indescribable pride he felt in possessing the power over the elements. To be invincible, irreplaceable, and above all: needed. Of course, the thought that there would be others to maintain order after him was reassuring, but he wanted to be the first, the one who is acknowledged and looked upon. Thus, with silent dignity he just smiled, nodded, and let her go to see Oliver, who needed her healing more urgently than he did.

Sophie approached them from upstairs, and as their paths crossed in the hallway, she gave Maya a big hug. But as soon as she sensed that they were alone, she leaned in closer to Alex, her voice barely a whisper tinged with excitement. "Did you tell her?"

Alex sighed deeply. "It's not the right time Mom," he replied, giving the hint to Sophie about the emotions swirling inside him.

"Alex, there's never a right time," Sophie responded, shaking her head gently. "Not for a talk, not for a kiss, not for a confession. If we keep waiting, we're just wasting our lives, always hoping to find the appropriate circumstances or right time. Don't forget, we are the ones who create those circumstances, we have to act before it's too late for a hug, a relationship or to start a family. Alex, I've never wanted to tell you how to live your life, but you are now 42 years old, and you're still waiting. For the weekend, for a holiday, for a new game, or a better job. Please, don't let the best things in your life just slip away, pass by you because you are waiting for the right time. It might never happen."

Sophie's words carried a gentle wisdom. Alex knew that she was right, and he made a firm decision that once they all had a bit of rest after the long night, he would gather the courage to speak with Maya and share his true feelings. But it was just so frightening, the thought of uttering those words out loud. Like suddenly his imagination could come alive and the thoughts of his harmless feelings would turn into irreversible reality, losing the money-back guarantee and leaving him vulnerable with a chain like a death sentence.

The truth is that he was still a coward, just as Daniel told him. He felt it was easier to shop in the excuses department, laying blame on life and circumstances, rather than going after what he really wanted. But the unspoken thoughts and feelings carry weight and energy of their own. Eventually, they could become an anchor, weighing him down and keeping him forever in the safe harbour. Never venturing out on the grand adventure, experiencing the depths of emotions and thrills, which could infuse his life with flavour and guide him through the storms of life. He understood finally that he needed to leave his comfort zone to become the person he wanted to be and find the destination he aspired to reach.

17

Merely a couple of hours had slipped by, yet the aroma of freshly brewed coffee and the mouthwatering scents of a hearty chicken soup awakened everyone from slumber early that morning. In the heart of the kitchen, Sophie was already bustling about; all the hobs were occupied with boiling pots, while the fragrant, steaming aromas escaped from under the lids, wafting through the entire house, filling the air with cozy warmth and happiness.

It's remarkable how such a seemingly small detail, one that would just soak up within the very walls of this brick-and-mortar structure, could transform a house into a true home. Just by adding a touch of warmth and enticing aroma, it becomes the power to cradle the essence of happiness and love within a family. No wonder why one of the real estate industry's best-kept secrets is the simple act of baking cinnamon cookies during property showings. It never fails to work its magic, evoking nostalgic and cherished memories of days gone by while also unconsciously signalling the promise of a precious family future.

"Good morning, Mom. You're up very early," Alex greeted Sophie with a warm hug, grateful for the heartwarming feeling she brought.

"I know you have a long day ahead of you all, and I want to make sure you have the energy for it, so you need to eat," she said, her caring gaze filled with tenderness. "Please go and check on Oliver, ask him how he likes his eggs, fried or scrambled, and we can have breakfast soon."

Alex made his way up to the guest room, and after knocking on the door, he entered. But he immediately regretted not waiting a moment longer. He would have preferred to gouge his eyes out rather than see Oliver lying on the bed in Maya's arms. They were just waking up, stretching, and yawning, greeting him casually, as if it were the most natural thing in the world.

"I'm sorry, I didn't know that Maya was with you," Alex mumbled, trying to look away, a sudden confusion clouding his face.

"I told you that I came to see Oliver; I needed to heal him," Maya explained with an innocent expression.

"Wow, look, Alex," Oliver exclaimed, standing up from the bed and beginning to open the bandages on his chest. "The wound has almost disappeared already. I can breathe, and I hardly feel any pain," He looked at Maya with admiration. "You're amazing; I could get used to this super-fast healing."

"Good, okay. I'm very happy for you," Alex nodded, using all his strength to hide the surge of anger towards Oliver.

Alex couldn't help but feel a sense of betrayal, but he fought to keep his composure, hiding the devastation he felt inside. He had already poured his heart out to Oliver about his feelings for Maya, and Oliver had even encouraged him to talk to her. And now, this half-naked guy was just casually getting dressed in front of him after leaving the bed he had shared with Maya.

"What a two-faced, lying hypocrite," he thought to himself but wanted to stay cool and just act like he had not fallen apart into thousands of tiny broken pieces. "My mother was asking how you want the eggs for breakfast, but we can just have a catch-up downstairs when you guys are ready," Alex said, his voice carefully neutral as he turned and walked away, feeling like everything had fallen apart, and nothing really mattered anymore.

He made his way back to the kitchen, sat down, and tried to erase the image from his mind - Oliver and Maya intertwined together.

"I can go and wake up Maya in a minute," Sophie mumbled while stirring the soup. "Just take the lid off if it starts boiling too much, will you?"

"No need," Alex replied quietly. "She's awake already. She stayed in Oliver's room."

"Oh, really? That's strange. I made a bed for her in the other room, next to mine. But I'm sure there's a totally reasonable explanation for why she had to stay there. Maybe she just checked on him in the morning before you entered," Sophie tried to comfort Alex, seeing the devastation on his face.

"No, they just woke up. She was there, but Oliver is almost fully recovered now, thanks to her," Alex said, his frustration no longer hidden in his voice. "Mom, she looked exhausted! Oliver could have healed on his own. He didn't need to take energy away from her."

"Good morning," Oliver greeted them as he entered the kitchen, Maya following behind slowly, her face a little pale but still graced with a gentle smile. "Hello."

"Oh, it's so nice to see you both, please have a seat. I am almost ready; I just quickly make the eggs and we can eat." Sophie replied politely. "I hear that you are feeling much better Oliver. I am so happy, that you recovered so fast. I know how important it is for all of you to have the strength and power to face these challenging days now."

"I was wondering, Alex, you mentioned yesterday that you should call that guy. Erm, Daniel if I remember his name correctly. Could we visit him?" Oliver seemed full of energy, eager to step into the next chapter.

"Yes, right. I just call him now, and perhaps we can visit him today. He lives roughly two hours away," Alex said, reaching for his phone.

"Alex, you said that you wanted to show me something," Maya stopped him with a sudden burst of curiosity. "Is it something about this guy?"

"Ah, yes. I didn't have a chance to explain yesterday why I wanted to speak with you and introduce you to us," Alex started to clarify. "I am quite sure that you already have a very good understanding of how unique your power is, and by now maybe you can tell that we are also a little different because of the power that we possess, derived from our medals."

"Uhm, I am not sure I can follow you," Maya replied. "I can see Oliver's incredible power, and I am so grateful for his help yesterday in stopping my boyfriend, I mean I should say ex, sorry, but I am not quite sure what you mean by 'unique power.' What power you are talking about?" Maya inquired with an innocent smile.

"Maya, we are the Gatekeepers," Oliver chimed in. "We need to protect the world from the epidemic by using our power. These medals are harnessing the energies that we embody from our family legacies. We represent the five elements, or Platonic solids. Maya, you possess power over the air, I control the earth, Daniel wields the water, and Alex combines the power of the Universe. We are only missing one more Gatekeeper, the final fire element. We need to find him, and we can stop the water pandemic if we are able to figure out how to work together."

"Yes, that's precisely what I told her earlier," Alex affirmed, a touch of annoyance in his voice as he realized Oliver had essentially repeated his words to Maya, who seemed more inclined to listen to Oliver.

"Alright," Maya began, her expression turned serious, "I've heard about this, I mean our family's power, but it all seemed like a fairy tale when my father talked about it." She looked at Alex, then Oliver, and continued. "Oliver, I can see your power, but sorry, I'm having trouble understanding how Alex fits into this. What exactly is this 'universe power'? It just doesn't make sense to me, I'm sorry."

"Alex is above all of us," Oliver replied, his voice filled with admiration as he gestured toward Alex like he was a messiah, explaining it to Maya. "We need him to create and unite our energies. He is the magician, you could say, who brings us all together."

Maya furrowed her brow, casting a long sceptical glance at Alex, but then nodded, still a bit unsure but willing to trust Oliver's judgment. "Alright, so we need to find some guy who has a medal with a fire element, correct? And how should we start?"

"Let me call Daniel, maybe he has some tips," Alex suggested, tapping the call button on his phone.

A few seconds later, Daniel's face appeared on the screen. "Hi Alex, how are you? I have some good news, maybe you could visit me and bring the Metatron's cube. I still can't believe that you were sitting on it for all these years. I would love to examine it up close." He explained in an excited tone.

"Hello, Daniel, I have news as well. I've already found two more Gatekeepers," Alex responded with a smile, turning the phone to Daniel, so he could have a view of Oliver and Maya. "Maya has an octahedron. Please, show it to Daniel," Alex asked Maya, moving the phone closer to her cardigan. "It looks like an open star, but it closes up when she's not wearing it as a brooch. And look, Oliver has a cube, and we've already travelled to some strange outer space dimension. He created a giant, round thunder. Like a ball lightning shield to protect us," Alex explained with immense excitement.

"Alex, that's amazing. In just two days, you've achieved what I couldn't in thirty years. I always knew you would succeed." Daniel sounded full of energy and determination. "So, you tapped into your power already. But how did you do that so quickly?"

"He was thinking about something beautiful," Oliver chimed in with a giggle.

"Shut your mouth." Alex snapped at Oliver.

"Something beautiful? What do you mean?" Daniel looked puzzled.

"Never mind, I'll explain to you later," Alex said, brushing off the comment. "Can we visit you today? We could be there around lunchtime."

"No problem. Just bring the cube. I'll send you the address. See you soon. Goodbye," Daniel replied, ending the call.

"What do you mean by outer space?" Maya asked, looking at them surprised. "What dimension are you talking about?"

"I told you, Maya, he's the magician; he can travel through space and time with his medal," Oliver added.

"Am I doing what?" Alex looked at him stunned and confused.

"Yes, we were out, in-between time and space, I told you." Oliver nodded.

"But you didn't tell me that I can do that! I thought that it happened because of what I was thinking." Alex said, with a seriously scared look on his face.

"No, you decide where you want to go and when. We can follow you, but without you, we can't travel." Oliver's words were just lingering in the air for seconds, leaving everyone just trying to process the information.

"But how do you know all this?" Alex asked with sudden curiosity.

"I inherited my father's power, but he passed away when I was young. His friend helped me, and my mother go through that tough time. He was a magician like you and taught me many things. Eventually, he stayed with us and became like a new father to me. We travelled together, and that's why I was able to come with you when you wandered off." Oliver smiled. "I just touched the ground to create the shield for us. Remember?"

"Oh, yeah, I didn't understand why you knelt down in front of me, but it makes sense now," Alex mumbled as he recalled the travel.

Sophie had to interrupt, bringing them back to the present. "Kids, let's eat. Maya, please help me with the plates. If you want to get to Daniel today in time, you need to hurry. I'll make some sandwiches for the trip for you. The soup will wait for you when you come back, okay? Quickly, you don't have all day. Eat up, eat up," she urged with a smile, bustling about like a diligent little fairy, placing all the dishes on the table.

18

The car journey started out a bit challenging. Oliver had the fixed idea that he was supposed to be the designated driver. Alex was concerned about his daring driving style but couldn't really find a way to address the situation without a heated argument. So, after a short dilemma, he came up with a clever excuse, citing Oliver's ongoing recovery from the terrible wound. He suggested that he just take it easy for a few more hours, hoping he might see reason eventually and embrace the idea of driving on the right side, I mean the left-hand side in the UK.

However, the tension in the car lingered during the whole trip as they navigated the eerily empty roads. In Alex's mind, the sting of betrayal over Maya's attention was still there, with the question of whether he could ever trust Oliver at all. But what he didn't know was that it was something way deeper that bothered Oliver. His face was full of concern and fear since they left. He kept cracking his finger joints, like a nervous teenager, and eventually, Maya leaned forward from the back with concern and asked, "Oliver, is everything alright? You can push the seat back further if you are not comfortable; I have enough space back here."

"No, I am fine, thanks, Maya. That's very kind of you. I was just thinking about my father," Oliver replied, his voice carrying palpable sadness.

"I lost my father as well; I know how you feel," Alex added, sensing Oliver's anguish. He suddenly felt a twinge of sympathy toward him. "But we were not that close. I wonder why he never mentioned a word about my grandfather. I should have learned all these things from him; I can't really understand why he chose to keep things hidden all these years."

"I am sorry to hear that, Alex, and you have to know that, whatever happens, you can count on me," Oliver said, his tone a bit odd, almost as if he were a gentle giant who'd just knocked over an entire porcelain store. "I can teach you, and if you want to practice, just ask me. I know it's not much, but we have to help each other. After all, we're cut from the same cloth. Remember?" Oliver smiled at him with kindness, like Alex never imagined that he was capable.

"Thanks, man, that really means a lot," Alex replied. "I need to learn a lot, that's for sure. And to get through whatever this mess turns out to be, we need to set aside our past differences."

Maya gently reached out from the back and put her hand on the guy's shoulder in the middle, like creating a bond between them, a unity. "I'm here for both of you. We're a team and come what may, we'll stand together. Agreed?"

"Agreed! Gatekeepers' team, at your service!" Alex exclaimed with a chuckle, and suddenly he felt a renewed sense of trust in his companions, even to place his life in their hands.

When they finally arrived, a very strange sight awaited them. Not unusual per se under any normal circumstances, but after passing through countless desolate towns and cities, this place was like stumbling upon the neon-lit paradise of Las Vegas during the Elvis impersonators' yearly convention on the Strip, just before the Celine Dion concert. It was crazy busy. I mean compared to the world around them, of course. Streets were teeming with people, shoppers bustled about, and cars and buses navigated the crowded lanes. It felt almost magical.

All three leaned out of the car windows, their faces illuminated by wonder and astonishment as they passed through the crowd, slowly pulling down the windows to experience this phenomenon. Passersby couldn't help but smile and kindly wave at them, clearly recognizing the newcomers' sense of awe.

"Where are we?" Maya asked, her voice filled with amazement.

"Bath. According to the map, Daniel's place is just behind the old Roman bath, on Abbey Green," Alex explained, still half leaning out the window as he soaked up the air that gently touched his face. "We can just leave the car and walk from here," he added and quickly parked the car.

It was like walking into Wonderland. A beautiful giant plane tree loomed over the quaint courtyard, where charming cafeterias and delightful little shops created an enchanting scene. Just around the corner, a sublime Georgian building stood tall, with its transom window above a pristine white panelled door.

Alex couldn't quite believe his eyes and checked his phone for the third time to confirm that they were indeed in the right place. With resolve, he pressed the intercom button. "Hi, it's Alex. I'm looking for Daniel," he said, and without hesitation, the buzzer unlocked the door. He turned back and waved timidly to Maya and Oliver to follow him.

As he gently pushed open the heavy Georgian front door, it swung open with graceful ease on well-oiled hinges. The foyer greeted them with its luminous charm and meticulous decor, like stepping back in time to an era of classic elegance and refined design. The walls were adorned with ornate wallpaper, the warm hues of gold, cream, and pale blue creating an inviting atmosphere. A mirror with an elaborately gilded frame hung on one wall, reflecting the soft glow of the crystal chandelier suspended from the ceiling.

Directly ahead, a grand wooden staircase with finely carved black balusters beckoned to explore the upper floors. Each step was covered with a plush burgundy carpet runner that muffled footsteps as you ascended. To the right, a set of double doors opened to the parlour, with large windows allowing ample daylight to filter in, highlighting the silk draperies and polished hardwood floors. Antique mahogany furniture was everywhere, elegant regal chairs upholstered in rich fabrics, with a marble fireplace standing in the heart of the room, its mantle adorned with delicate porcelain figurines.

To the left, another set of double doors revealed a sneak peek into the splendid dining room. A long wooden table, seemingly fit for a lavish gala of two dozen guests, complete with a fine porcelain set, glistening silverware, and delicate crystal glassware displayed in the glass cupboard behind. Above, a dazzling chandelier cast a warm glow over the room. The walls were filled with oil paintings, and a large tapestry added an air of sophistication.

Finally, a familiar sound approached from behind the staircase—the distinct squeak of Daniel's wheelchair on the polished hardwood as he maneuvered out from the elevator. "Ah, you are here. I am so glad; you have no idea," he greeted them enthusiastically. "Please follow me, have a seat while I find some refreshments for you. I hope you can forgive me; the housekeeper has a day off, so my partner went out shopping. We weren't expecting any visitors, but he'll be back any minute now. Please, please come in," he urged them as he guided them toward the library.

The room was a bibliophile's dream, its walls lined with floor-to-ceiling bookshelves, filled with leather-bound heavy volumes. A leather-topped desk with an inkwell sat near the window, inviting scholarly pursuits. Comfortable leather armchairs and couches were arranged atop a rich Persian rug, completing the ambiance of an intellectual retreat at the centre of the floor. "This is my favourite room; I hope you don't mind if we stay here. I try to avoid the direct glare of the afternoon sun in the sitting room, if I can."

Alex and Oliver looked at Maya, still rendered speechless, as if they had suddenly landed in the midst of a Jane Austen novel adaptation. Half-expecting Lady Catherine de Bourgh to enter the library with her haughty personality, expressing her belief on the urging matter of the intolerably situated dinner seating arrangement with domineering authority.

But after a few minutes of shared silence, Alex finally gathered his courage to ask the inevitable question that had been on all their minds. "I am sorry, just out of curiosity. Are you living here? I mean, it's amazing, but I had no idea you were so well-off. I imagined you made a fortune with Atari, but this... it's... like you're practically a modern-day Croesus."

"No, I live here, but it's my partner's home." Daniel chuckled, a warm smile gracing his face, and then he opened a concealed door, hidden behind a massive bookshelf, revealing a family-sized fridge stocked with drinks and snacks. "Guys, please help yourselves. Glasses are behind the left hidden shelf. Napkins, and coasters are in the bottom drawer," he explained, rolling back behind the gigantic desk, and started to search for something in the drawer. "We decided, Miles and I, that it would be best for both of us if I moved here permanently, at least until we can solve the enigma of the water pandemic."

"I think this place is awesome," Oliver exclaimed and bounced into a Mini Cooper-sized director's armchair, placing the huge box in front of him on the floor, which he had been carrying under his arm the whole time like a watermelon. "Finally, I feel at home; this chair fits me," he laughed and effortlessly flicked off the crown cap of his soda bottle with a nonchalant flick of his finger like a light switch.

"I am so glad we have the chance to meet you," Maya began to speak, her voice gently finding its place after a few sips of water. "Alex mentioned that you also have a medal, is that correct? May I see it?" she inquired, settling down next to Alex on the sofa.

"Yes, just give me a moment. I could've sworn I left it right here..." Daniel replied, continuing to open drawers with the air of someone searching for something of great importance.

"Daniel, what is happening in the city?" Alex turned to Daniel in a little while. "Everybody seems to be perfectly fine. I don't understand."

"It's all about the location," Daniel replied, glancing up and smiling at Alex. "Some places have always been considered sacred. Even in the Stone Age, people knew where the energy is coming from. They built Stonehenge, churches, and pyramids on these energetic points to harness the power."

"You mean the Gatekeepers built them?" Alex replied with growing curiosity.

"Exactly," Daniel affirmed. "Architects, scientists, alchemists, shamans—many were descended from the chosen ones. The knowledge has been passed down through generations, how to use the power of water, from father to son."

"Or daughter," Maya chimed in proudly.

"Indeed, in some cases," Daniel agreed, his face lighting up as he finally seemed to find what he was looking for. He placed the object on his lap and brought it closer to the team. "I wanted to show you this," he said, looking at Alex. "An old friend of mine called me when he spotted it on eBay. I thought it might be a joke, perhaps a prop from a theatre, or even just a fake caduceus. But it was worth a shot for £800. Take a look!" With that, he lifted the shiny metal stick, with two small snakes crossed at the top end forming a circle, with their heads resembling horns.

Oliver couldn't help but burst into laughter. "Wow, that must be one heck of an eggbeater for £800!"

"Ha, another funny guy," Daniel mumbled, visibly quite irritated. "Anyway, I can't determine if it's a genuine one or not, but look," and he pointed to the bottom end of the wand, "The Delphic Epsilon is engraved around the handle and on the eyes of the snakes at the top, just like the print on the cloth you found around the Metatron's cube. Maybe it's just a coincidence, but I've been trying to find out more about this staff, and it turns out magicians used to have these wands."

"Daniel, I don't mean to question your intellect or your level of education," Oliver began, trying to hold back his laughter, "I respect you, but seriously, even a five-year-old knows that magicians have wands." He chuckled, tears forming in his eyes.

"Yes, that's exactly what I mean!" Daniel replied with an annoyed expression on his face, then turning back to Alex, "It's likely part of your accessories or equipment. Just think about the tarot cards where the strongest major arcana, The Magician pointing his wand upwards with one hand and holds downward the other hand. It symbolizes 'As above, so below.' Do you know who said that?" Daniel waited a couple of seconds, but only the sound of crickets could be heard in the room. Daniel gave in, "Hermes Trismegistus."

"It was right on the tip of my tongue; I knew it!" Oliver interjected, wiping away tears of laughter.

"Seriously? I thought one clown was enough for a circus. Cut it out," Daniel snapped at him with unexpected intensity. "Alex, where did you dig up this caveman?" He turned back to Alex with a disappointed expression.

"Hey, I am not here to tolerate your scolding like a schoolboy." Oliver retorted.

"Then you'd better start growing up, fish out that crown cap you tossed under my desk, and buckle up because I'm not going to teach basic manners to an infantile ape in the midst of an impending apocalypse. Got it?" Daniel suddenly rose from his wheelchair, looking as though he were about to approach Oliver and rip his head off, like a praying mantis. Pretty scary, but what was even more intriguing was that he remained frozen in that position. He didn't move. He was actually standing.

Everyone stared at him in disbelief, as if witnessing a miracle on The Church Channel after a generous charity donation. Daniel stood on his legs, trembling but upright.

"What happened? Daniel, dear God!" A man rushed into the room and ran straight to Daniel just as he collapsed back into the wheelchair, crying with the force of a thunderstorm. It was a deep, uncontrollable cry that sent shockwaves through everyone in the room. "Tell me, are you okay?" He asked Daniel again, his voice filled with concern and care.

"Miles, I was standing. I can't believe it, after 40 years. I felt my legs again," Daniel sobbed like a child, tears streaming down his cheeks. With a shaky hand, he slowly turned the wheels of the wheelchair and rolled out of the room, "Miles, please take care of our guests; I'll be back in a couple of minutes."

"Are you sure? Daniel, I'll come with you," Miles replied, deeply worried.

"I just need a moment alone," Daniel whispered, and he quietly left the room, leaving everyone's eyes glued to the door.

This whole setup was like an extreme roller coaster ride without a safety belt, and from the front row at that. No one could utter a word, only the annoying sound of the crown cap scraping across the hardwood floor as Oliver crawled under the table on his hands and knees, trying to retrieve it. "I got it, sorry. I won't do it again," he said with an embarrassed expression on his face.

19

As the emotional storm slowly receded, Miles stepped in to thaw the atmosphere. He carefully placed coasters beneath everyone's drinks, a subtle gesture of hospitality that didn't go unnoticed.

"Please, take these," Miles insisted with a warm smile. "I must apologize for my lack of proper introductions. I'm Miles. I'm certain Daniel has mentioned me at some point," he began, striving to dissipate the lingering tension. "And it's safe to assume you're Alex and Maya."

With polite smiles and nods, Alex affirmed, "Yes, she's Maya, and I'm Alex Davis. I met Daniel just last week at the GameCon. And the other gentleman is Oliver," he introduced, indicating Oliver, who still appeared somewhat on edge after his recent dressing-down.

"I'm Maya Kogan. I must say, your home is absolutely beautiful," Maya joined in extending a warm handshake.

Oliver jumped up and rushed to shake hands with Miles. "I am Oliver Webster, thank you for the kind welcome, and sorry for the thing just before. I didn't mean to upset Daniel," he tried to excuse himself.

Miles, unfazed as a true gentleman, replied casually, "No worries. Daniel has always been a bit sensitive. But ever since he met you Alex, he totally changed. He is even more passionate than ever about this topic, and the whole water alien's story. Frankly, I can barely keep up with everything he is saying, but I know it's important for him, so I try to support him wholeheartedly."

Then, he turned his attention to Maya. "Kogan, is it? The name Kogan sounds so familiar. Perhaps you have some Russian heritage?"

Maya, intrigued by the query, nodded and replied, "Yes, my great-grandparents hailed from Russia, Leningrad. Although, how did you know?"

Miles, ever the conversationalist, continued, "I recall the name from an old article I read once. It was about Stalin, though I am sure that you've heard the whole conspiracy theories surrounding it."

"Yes, but not many people are aware of the real story. My family had to flee the country, seeking refuge in Poland, where we still had some distant relatives that time after the war." Maya explained and with a sense of vulnerability, she added. "I grew up in Warsaw, but when my parents decided to move to Israel twenty years ago, I eloped with my ex-boyfriend, Boris. I was seventeen, in love, and he wanted to come to England, so I followed him here. It seemed so perfect, he was promising everything, marriage, future... I was so naive and foolish... Years went by, and somehow that idyllic dream just turned into a nightmare." Her eyes glistened with unshed tears as she spoke. "I didn't speak with my father since, I don't even know how to reach them or if they are still alive after the attack. It's all my fault."

Alex offered reassurance to Maya; his voice laced with empathy. "Don't worry, I'm certain we can help you find your family."

Miles, with his refined English charm, chimed in as well, "Indeed, I might be able to offer some assistance. If you provide their names or any information you have, I'll explore a few options."

Maya, grateful for their understanding, nodded and apologized, "Thank you all. I appreciate your patience. These past few weeks have been incredibly overwhelming."

The screeching sound of a wheelchair grew louder and took everyone's attention in the room. Daniel was approaching slowly from the door. "It must be the cube. Let me check it," he was exuding a newfound sense of calm and excitement. He rolled over straight to Oliver.

"Here, please, let me put it on the table for you." Oliver offered, extending the cube. "I must apologize for my earlier behaviour. You were right; we're a team now. I just have to get used to the fact that I am not alone anymore, and we're working together."

"Yes, I was rather tense as well," Daniel mumbled. "We don't have much time, so we need to concentrate on one crucial goal: learning more about the Hydrons. That's the key to stopping the pandemic, and it must be our top priority," and he put his hand on the Metatron's cube with no hesitation. With his fingers gently tracing the cube's sides and each corner one by one Daniel began to smile, "I can feel it. It's like a thousand tiny ants tingling up my legs, it's amazing. This energy is coming from within the cube, bubbling like sparkling carbonated soda water. It's utterly fascinating."

"Does that mean you will be able to walk again?" Miles asked, his voice filled with hope.

Daniel's smile widened. "I'm not sure about that, but I haven't felt so alive since 1982," he quipped, turning to Alex. "Have you tried the staff? Do you think it's real?"

Alex appeared puzzled. "The... what?"

"The caduceus, the wand!"

"Oh, right! I forgot." Alex glanced around the room and picked up the staff from the couch. "Do you have any idea on how to use it? Any advice on what I should definitely avoid doing with it?" he asked with a playful smile.

Daniel chuckled and said, "Well, for starters, try not to turn me into a newt." Then he continued with his explanation. "As I was saying about the Egyptian magician Hermes Trismegistus, he was the first to use this kind of wand. They said he lived before the great flood and invented astrology, alchemy, music, writing, essentially the foundations of civilization. But above all, he created magic. Hermes influenced the Greek and Egyptian history and became a god in many religions, like Islam and Hinduism. During the Renaissance, his book, the Hermetica, was considered divine wisdom, even by the Catholic Church. For centuries, Hermeticism thrived in secret orders and among philosophers. Chess, card games, Freemasonry, witchcraft, and symbolism, they all grew from his teachings."

"Yes, I got it." Alex interrupted Daniel's never-ending story. "He's like a god, but how do I figure out how to use this wand?"

Daniel scratched his head. "Well, you're a magician, just like him. You need to find out," and he returned his attention to the cube. "Did you bring the wooden box and cloth also?"

Alex seemed a little puzzled by the question. "Uh, no. Do we need them?"

"Probably. If my theory is correct and this cube is what I think it is, then it is best to keep it in the box." Daniel added.

"And what is the liquid inside?" Oliver chimed in with curiosity. "I felt something sloshing in the cube."

Daniel took a deep breath and continued with an excited voice. "That's the elixir of life! In some cultures, it's called ambrosia, panacea, amrita, or the fountain of youth. Throughout history, countless emperors and brilliant minds have been searching for it. Alexander the Great, Genghis Khan, Caesar, Attila the Hun, Leonardo da Vinci, Newton, Napoleon, Hitler, Stalin—the list goes on. They all wanted to find this liquid to gain immortality, and it's right here in front of me. Unbelievable!" He exclaimed with a fascinated smile on his face.

"Stalin?" Maya asked with astonishment. "My great-grandfather was working for Stalin, until he suddenly died in 1953, and they deported everyone who was involved or knew about it to Siberia. They arrested him as well, and my family had to escape. That's why we had to leave Russia!"

Daniel's eyes widened with interest as he heard her story. "The doctor's plot in 1951?" He asked. "The newspapers wrote about the doctors and prominent medical specialists who were accused of a conspiracy to assassinate Stalin, but as far as I know Stalin gathered an army of doctors to find him the elixir for immortality. He wanted to live forever. Of course, after they created the cover story about the assassination attempt and cleared all evidence."

"Yes, that was the article I just mentioned earlier, about the whole antisemitic campaign after the doctor's plot." Miles nodded. "That's why the name Kogan was familiar, just like Maya's family name."

"I am so sorry Maya. That's horrible." Alex looked at Maya's gloomy face. "But it just all makes sense now. Our power separately is not strong enough. We all experience how much energy we have, but the more elements are gathered, the more powerful it gets. Maya, your great-grandfather was not enough by himself, or Oliver or Daniel alone. Or even me. We need to work as a team. But we still miss one more person. Just think about what we could achieve when we find the last Gatekeeper."

Daniel, his face lit with excitement, chimed in. "Alex, you have no idea how grateful I am for everything you've achieved so far, and with you, I am sure that we will find him," and he smiled. "But first, let's have a quick lunch. I'm sure you're all hungry, and we can continue after, shall we?"

Miles, brimming with enthusiasm, took the lead, ushering everyone toward the kitchen. "Alright, I quickly make a smoked salmon Fettuccine Alfredo. Does anyone have allergies or is vegetarian? It'll be ready in just 30 minutes."

As they walked away, Alex turned to Daniel, a sense of gratitude filling his voice. "Daniel, I never imagined any of this would happen to me. I owe so much to you, for believing in me. You guys changed my life."

Daniel nodded with a note of seriousness "Alex don't forget. This is just the beginning, we have a huge job ahead of us, and we all depend on you. No pressure, but the most difficult part is yet to come." Daniel touched Alex's arm in a reassuring gesture, offering his support.

The enticing aroma of fresh smoked salmon, infused with a blend of herbs and sizzling garlic, quickly filled the rustic kitchen, making it nearly impossible for anyone to think of anything else, even after Sophie's huge breakfast. In just a matter of minutes, they all eagerly gathered around the kitchen table, ready to taste Miles' homemade fettuccine.

"So how did you guys meet?" Miles asked while he started to prepare the plates on the table.

"Well, I met Daniel first." Alex started, "He told me about the Hydrons and the Gatekeepers."

Maya, her curiosity piqued, inquired, "Hydrons? Daniel also mentioned, but what are those?"

"Yes, I didn't tell you the whole story," Alex continued. "So, Daniel explained to me the theory about the alien civilization the Hydrons, who came to our planet from another galaxy. They tried to escape from an evil enemy who almost destroyed them with a plasma attack, but they managed to transform into water and carried all their ancient knowledge with them. When they arrived on Earth, they brought this knowledge within the water. They created life on our planet and billions of years later our human civilization. This water is the building block of our bodies and everything around us. It carries nature's DNA for life. But something happened with the Hydrons, and that's why people lost their feelings, their interest. People are turning into emotionless zombies without healthy water."

"Also, animals and plants," Oliver chimed in. "First, I noticed that wild animals just gave up eating, and birds behave very oddly. I am an environmental activist; I live in Bergen, Norway. My family owns land just on the coast, with a forest and a big estate. It was just devastating to see that one by one the moose, badgers, and foxes just disappeared. When I walked around in the forest, I found animals lying lifeless on the ground. No signs of wounds or poison, just emaciated and severely dehydrated. They weren't eating, making no attempt to escape or hide; they were simply waiting to die. That was the point when I knew that something happened. I called everyone, I reached out to every major environmental organization and research institute, but no answer. So, I decided to go to Paris and find out what the WHO and UNESCO know about the situation. That morning when I had my flight, Alex called me. I was already on my way to the airport."

"So that's why you had that huge bag with you," Alex remarked. "What were you carrying in that bag anyway?"

"It's probably better if you don't know about it." Oliver chuckled. "Let's say I had a plan. But after I met you at the station, I knew that with you, I have a better option to save the planet."

"Well, I am glad that I made a good impression on you," Alex said with a smile.

"Oliver is right. Everything is at risk." Daniel interjected as he drew a bit closer. "When we start eating the fruits and vegetables that have been watered with this tainted water, it will turn even worse. It's a chain reaction. We may have a few more weeks or days, but eventually, it will affect us too. While we have some protection through our powers, it won't shield us forever if we consume contaminated food. Not to mention the people in this city or the other groups who are sheltered now near the Earth's energy points."

"So how can we find the fifth Gatekeeper?" Maya asked with a worried expression.

"We are looking for someone who is probably a leader in the military, a politician, or someone really powerful and influential," Daniel added. "And most of all, he has a medal with the tetrahedron, which represents the element of fire."

"And how does that look like?" Maya looked around puzzled.

"Imagine a pyramid, but with only three sides and a triangular bottom," Daniel explained.

Miles interjected with hesitation in his voice. "A medal? It might be nothing, but I recall an interview from a couple of years ago," and he stepped to the table with a big bowl of pasta as he continued. "It was about a Republican politician who famously held several filibusters to block Democrat's bills. She was wearing a long necklace on a TV show that looked like a pyramid."

"Yes, Maya has a brooch, Alex has a medal. Apparently, it's only the shape that matters." Daniel replied. "And can you remember her name by any chance?"

"It was on The Late Talk show, on April 7th, 2018. You were at a conference that weekend in Taipei, and I was home alone watching TV, flipping through the channels when I saw this charismatic woman. I just stopped and listened to her story." Miles recalled, frowning as he dug into his memory. After a moment, he continued. "Abrams. Yes, her name is Debby Abrams."

"Wow, that's fascinating Miles. How do you remember all these details?" Alex asked, astonished, as he quickly searched his phone. Within seconds, a smile appeared on his lips. "Look, Daniel, I found her. She is wearing the medal in the pictures too," he said, turning his phone toward Daniel.

"Miles has an eidetic memory," Daniel explained then looked at Miles genuinely surprised. "If you remember all these things, why you never told me that you saw this medal when I was telling you about the Gatekeepers?

"You never told me that others are wearing it as a medal or a brooch," Miles replied, looking almost offended. "I thought it should be on a belt buckle like yours. How was I supposed to know?"

To be fair, Miles had a valid point. Our world is often based on the perception of the majority of the people. Everything seems straightforward, right, or wrong, left or right. But what if I were to tell you that what you see or hear is only your version of reality, your interpretation of the truth? And there are many other completely perfect truths that exist outside of our reality.

Just think about the infamous audio clip 'Yanny vs. Laurel,' that played a single word, and listeners couldn't agree on what word they heard. Some people claimed to hear 'Yanny,' while others insisted, they heard 'Laurel.' Actually, the recording contained acoustic information that overlapped in a way that some listeners, who primarily can hear higher frequencies only, interpreted as 'Yanny,' while others who mainly hear lower frequencies, heard 'Laurel.'

Our brain is a remarkable supercomputer that constantly learns from an early age how to process vast amounts of information from our senses and internal thoughts. Like a diligent spider, it creates a web to store and organize everything. But when something is missing from the picture, the brain tries to fill in the gaps with made-up, fictional information to connect the dots, to make it believable, and to find a recognizable pattern.

The shape of clouds, our cognitive biases, the Mandela effect – these are all tricks our brains play. Or is it? Replacing episodes from our past experiences allows us to construct possible futures and anticipate those scenarios of theoretical concepts. It helps us to adapt to new environments. The acceptable cultural norm that was taught by our parents to help us create a survival mechanism and fit within our own tribe.

Do you now see why it is so important to shape a child's mind before they turn seven years old? To create these patterns. To forget about previous lives, and imaginary friends we played with for years, and to break into the perception accepted by the majority of people. To have a blank sheet where you can build a green-grass, blue-sky matrix of collective memory with all the answers ready for you to digest in a bite-sized version of the world around us.

But when you feel déjà vu or have a vivid dream that you can almost touch, you just ignore it and sweep everything under the carpet with a wave of your hand, thinking, "That's impossible." It's such a shame to forget about all the knowledge we were born with from the water. All the shared consciousness, and the millions of years of history that we've experienced. Just to fit in and become average.

20

The atmosphere in the room shifted from uncertainty to a palpable sense of shared determination as the group delved into their next steps. Daniel suddenly realized that all those years he had tried to work alone and secretly recruit his team using the arcade game, while the solution was right there in his face. Miles with his unique perspective and exceptional memory made him realize what had always been the missing link: Teamwork. This was indeed their greatest strength, and everything started to fall into place once Daniel just let go of his own leadership.

Looking over at Miles, the man with an incredible eidetic memory who could recall every minute detail with photographic precision but couldn't simply connect two dots, just made him smile and admire him even more. "You're absolutely right, Miles. I should have considered it myself. I assumed that the shape alone would be enough context when I told you about the Gatekeepers. But it's clear we need to change the way we look at things and ask the right questions."

Miles offered a humble smile. "No offense taken, Daniel. So, what's our plan now? How do we approach this lady, Debby, and convince her to join us?"

Alex responded with a casual wave. "Simple, really. We just need to have a talk with her."

Daniel glanced around the room, his face a mix of caution and contemplation. "We have to be careful. Let's not forget, we're playing with fire here. Even if she is a Gatekeeper, we can't be certain she'll be eager to join our team. With power like hers, she might not want to play nice, even if she wears a shiny medal."

Miles suddenly piped up, a glimmer of hope in his eyes. "I might be able to help with that. My media connections can help us snoop around discreetly and get the lowdown on this Debby Abrams."

Maya chimed in, still puzzled. "Wait, why wouldn't she be on our side? I don't understand."

Daniel leaned forward, his expression deadly serious, "Imagine someone with that much power, ambition, and assertiveness. She is the fire, and you don't touch the baking sheet without an oven mitten. We need to be cautious, that's all." Daniel explained and turned to Miles. "It would be good to find out a bit more about her, just to be on the safe side. Could you help us, Miles?"

Miles nodded in agreement and got up, heading toward the door. "No problem. I'll get right on it. Be back soon."

As Miles left, Alex peered at his phone, his face shifting from puzzlement to concern. "So, I checked the internet, and it says she lives in Boston. Does anyone have any idea how we're going to get there? I doubt commercial flights are still up and running as usual."

Oliver, always ready for adventure, beamed with confidence. "What do you think Alex, how did I get here to London from Bergen? We can do this together easily."

Alex leaned in, mischief glinting in his eyes. "Well, I've got a couple of scenarios in my mind when you say casually, that 'we can do it,' but I am not sure which one is worst. You either want me to whip out my magical powers and whisk us away on a cosmic joyride like last time, but I must warn you, there's a teeny, tiny hitch. Instead of landing in Boston, we might just pop up in the Andromeda Galaxy, sipping ice lattes with aliens."

He paused dramatically before moving on. "Or you're suggesting we go all in James Bond style, waltz into an airport, and 'borrow' an airplane. You know, I hate to be a buzzkill, but last time I checked, airports are pretty keen on security. Cameras, guards, and radar that can spot a pigeon at 30,000 feet. Trust me, I don't think they'd miss when a jumbo jet trying to pull a Houdini, even now with the reduced military presence."

Oliver chuckled, his confidence unwavering. "Leave it to me, oh mighty Hermes. I know some people who can help us to slip into the airport under the radar, and don't worry, I can fly a plane. Trust me, we'll be jet-setting to Boston in no time," and he punctuated his assurance with a wink.

"Shouldn't we all go together? But what about Daniel? How could he come with us? And the others?" Maya's concern for their safety was palpable as she voiced her worries. "We need all of us if she's so powerful."

"I stay here with Miles; he needs me." Daniel chimed in. "The three of you can manage this, I'm sure. Just, remember, don't talk about the cube and caduceus until you're certain she's on our side."

Miles returned with his laptop and spun it around to show the team. "I've tracked her down. She's got an office right in the heart of downtown Boston, Court Square to be exact. She posted pictures from her office just a couple of days ago on social media. I'll write my friend in Washington, he's a great journalist and knows everyone in politics. By the time you get to Boston, we'll have her uncensored bio, I am sure."

Alex couldn't help but praise Miles. "Miles, you're the best. Thanks for your help. Alright, guys, it's back to London for us," he said looking at Maya and Oliver. "Oliver, you'll have to work your magic to secure a plane. Time's ticking, we need to be in Boston by Monday morning, so we have 2 days only to make this happen."

As they prepared to leave, a solemn mood filled the room. Daniel broke the silence first. "Alex, I hate to say this, but take the Metatron's cube with you," he said with a sense of selflessness. "It should be stored in the box. I am just worried to keep it here."

"But it made you feel better; it can heal you!" Miles objected. "Why would you want Alex to take it back?"

Daniel, however, had a different perspective. "I am not a magician; Alex should have it, and he has the wooden box. When this is all over, I am sure that we can borrow the cube and heal me, but for now, the mission is the priority, not me," he smiled.

Understanding the gravity of the situation, Miles accepted the decision. "Of course, Daniel, I am just trying to protect you. I hope you know that." he said gently, reaching out to touch Daniel's hand and encircling it with his own.

Alex, ready to depart, thanked their gracious hosts. "Thank you again for your hospitality and the amazing fettuccine. But we need to leave now. Please keep us updated about the politician lady, Debby, and you should join us as soon as we come back," and he cuddled Miles who was standing next to Daniel's wheelchair.

As he got closer and leaned down for a heartfelt farewell, Daniel whispered a cryptic message in his ear. "Look out for Oliver."

Alex was taken aback by the sudden warning and looked at Daniel confused and puzzled. Why would he say that? He had seemed to forgive Oliver for his childish behaviour earlier. Or was it something else he wanted to warn him about?

But Daniel just kindly smiled again, seemingly hiding in front of others his little advice to Alex and continued. "I am sure, you will be a great team and work out every problem you are facing. Don't forget, 'The whole universe is in your hand now,' Alex."

Miles waved goodbye to them from the doorway, and the little rescue team was on their way back to the car. All were quiet, each lost in their thoughts and questions about the trip. Alex, in particular, couldn't shake the nagging feeling and that annoying little voice again in his head about Oliver.

He can't trust him, not with Maya, not with the mission. But it's just so confusing. Like those wolves are fighting inside him, but which one to feed? Should he treat Oliver like a friend, who can help him unlock his potential as a magician, or like a rival, who might steal Maya away and even jeopardize the mission if he's not careful with him?

Alex decided to find out more about Oliver, feeling that understanding his past might shed some light on his intentions. "Oliver, you mentioned practicing a lot with your second father, the magician. What happened to him? Is he still in Norway?"

Oliver's face took on a somber expression. "No, I'm afraid not. One day he disappeared, never came back." Oliver explained as he opened the car door and tried to squeeze himself into the front seat. "He always warned me that one day he might not come back. Magicians' lives are really dangerous. Traveling through time or teleporting to other places isn't just overwhelming and exhausting; it's full of unknown dangers. You never know who might spot you, whether your arrival will be met with hostility or friendliness. And you must always assume that upon arrival, you might find yourself in trouble or get injured."

Alex's eyes widened with concern as he reached for the car's ignition key. "What do you mean by 'injured'? You never mentioned that I could get injured..."

Oliver rolled his eyes. "Come on, use your common sense. You manifest out of thin air, but how can you predict whether you'll land in the midst of a battlefield during a war, underwater in a river that dried out 5,000 years ago, or even in the vacuum of space, like last time with me? You need to practice and learn, but even after years of experience, there's one rule: energy cannot be created or destroyed; it can only be transferred or converted from one form to another. When you travel, you swap places with someone from that space and time."

Alex was in disbelief. "No, that can't be true. In space, I couldn't have swapped with anyone. There was absolutely nothing there; you saw it too." Alex shook his head.

Oliver sighed and continued, "No, that time, you took my energy. I gave you my shield, I told you." He explained. "When you travel, you must consider that someone will replace you here while you're away. I'm sure you've seen news articles about strange people appearing in photographs and places, looking lost, and explaining that they're from a different time. And shortly after, they vanish again."

Maya's concern was evident as she raised a crucial question. "But what happens with the magician if that person dies? Or gets arrested and thrown in prison?"

Oliver nodded, acknowledging the gravity of her concerns. "That's exactly why you need to be incredibly careful. When you leave, you need to make sure that you lock yourself in a place where only you can escape, not the person you swap with. If something happens to any one of you, you are stuck there. That's why you can't be away for a long time, maybe just minutes, but certainly not more than an hour. That's the rule."

Alex slowly started the car's engine and released the brake. "Well, I have a lot to learn," he mused, his eyes focused on the road ahead. "But bottom line, travel is only for the worst-case scenario, if I don't want to end up dead. Got it."

Funny how seemingly unrelated minor details started to make sense with time and fit into the bigger picture. Alex remembered these strange encounters he'd heard about in the media, which had always fascinated him. His father used to collect newspaper clippings about time travellers and discuss them during family dinners. At that time, it just seemed like a little quirk from his father, but maybe he was collecting information about people whom he had to swap with during his travels. Perhaps he wanted to prepare Alex and gather information about how to avoid problems and learn from his mistakes. "Let's hope the file with the clippings is still on his desk," Alex thought and glanced to his left at Oliver, who was buried in his phone.

21

Just as they left Eaton on the highway, Oliver emerged from his texting and turned to Alex. "At the next roundabout, take the right exit."

Alex glanced at him with curiosity. "Heading to Heathrow? Did you find somebody who can help us?"

Oliver grinned, looking rather pleased with himself, but quickly locked his phone's screen. "I have to meet a guy. I think he can help us. I'll go there, and you just wait for me in the car."

A few minutes later, they pulled up to a gate surrounded by tall fences and industrial buildings in the distance. Oliver swiftly stepped out of the car, walked to the gate, and effortlessly leaped over the nearly 6-foot-tall metal fence with an uncanny grace. His movements were a mesmerizing blend of fluidity and raw power, defying the laws of physics.

Inside the car, Alex and Maya exchanged incredulous glances, and then looked straight back to watch Oliver's distant figure disappearing between the massive warehouses. "I can't believe it. How did he jump over that fence?" Alex muttered; disbelief etched on his face. "Nobody can jump that high from a standstill. It's just not possible!"

Maya, still processing the spectacle, finally chimed in, "It was like a big cat leaping over a fiery hoop. Almost like those young kids doing parkour, jumping on buildings. Maybe that's how he does it."

Alex was still just grabbing the steering wheel, his knuckles turning white as he stared at the spot where Oliver had vanished. "No, that's not parkour. No human athlete would be able to do that. He must have some secret ability to do this, what we don't know about," he added, and now when he finally had a moment of privacy to talk to Maya, he quickly turned towards the backseat. "Please, promise me you'll be careful with Oliver. We don't know him that well. Can you promise me you'll tell me if you notice anything strange about him? Please."

Maya met his gaze with an understanding smile. "Of course, Alex, but you don't need to worry. I can see him. He's a good guy, I can assure you. When I was healing him, I saw his past, his thoughts, and he's with us. I'm sure."

Alex was taken aback by Maya's claim, his brows furrowing with surprise. "You can see people's thoughts and past? What do you mean? How?"

"Well, it's not like I can predict the future, but I can perceive their inner essence," she explained. "Not just the outer aura surrounding a person, but their energies, motivations, emotions, and intentions."

Alex felt a sudden chill, akin to a cold shower washing over him. He likely felt how the emperor did when the truth about his new clothes was revealed—naked and vulnerable. He realized he couldn't hide his feelings for Maya; she had known all along. "So, you mean you can read people and tell what they think?" he mumbled meekly.

Maya nodded. "Hm, yes, pretty much," Maya confirmed. "Like Daniel, he was talking with me the entire time we were there."

"What? Daniel was talking with you?" Alex interrupted. "You hardly exchanged a couple of sentences the whole time."

Maya clarified, "No, not in front of you. Not talking per se, we were just exchanging energies. He showed me his work—the Polybius, the Platonic solids, everything he knows and feels we'll need to convince Debby."

"But I didn't sense anything," Alex pointed out. "Why didn't I feel anything?"

Maya was thinking for a second before responding. "Maybe it has to do with the elements. About what we represent is how we connect, I don't know. It's not entirely clear."

"Hey, let's go," Oliver suddenly leaped into the car.

"CHRIST ON A BIKE!" Alex shouted, startled by Oliver's abrupt action. "I almost got a heart attack, don't do this again!"

"Alex, stop moaning and step on that pedal. We only have 4 hours. We're meeting the guy at midnight, Terminal One, Gate 26," Oliver urged, glancing at him. "The guy will bring us in and help to get enough fuel to fill up the plane. The rest is on us," he added with a grin.

"That's not much time. We need to hurry, okay," Alex agreed, and he swiftly put the car in reverse.

As soon as they returned home and picked up a few essentials for the trip, including the new lunch boxes from Sophie, they headed straight back to the airport. Alex carefully parked the car in a nearby area, and they started to walk through a bushy sidewalk path toward the old terminal building.

"I think there should be a road here that will take us to the gate," Oliver said, turning to Alex, as the three of them side by side ventured through the untamed terrain in the dark.

"How can you see anything? Do you have a torch, a lamp, or something?" Alex grumbled with each stumble, tripping over every little rock scattered across the ground.

"I can't see past my own nose in this darkness."

"I don't get why you're complaining, it's almost full moon." Oliver retorted. "We don't need light; use your senses."

"Sorry, buddy, but I must've missed the memo on how to develop night vision for my species. I don't know which planet you're from, but it's pitch black for my eyes."

"Guys, enough with the whining! We need to be stealthy," Maya whispered as they inched closer to the fence.

"So, what's the plan now?" Alex asked Oliver, his tone dripping with annoyance. "I'm not exactly a kangaroo to jump over, and I sure don't see a gate either."

"Just hang tight," Oliver replied with a mischievous grin, relishing Alex's struggle as he persisted in stumbling over objects and grappling with the unruly bushes along the way.

As a faint noise gradually approached from the other side, a utility van pulled up near the fence. Oliver raised a hand to his mouth and whistled, mimicking a bird's song with rapid notes. In response, an instant reply echoed from the other side, and a rugged, nearly two meters tall guy emerged from the van.

In the darkness, he almost resembled a grizzly bear. Still, Alex, applying some quick logical reasoning about the number of grizzly bear populations inhabiting the UK, confidently concluded that this must be a human. Also, he noted, bears couldn't drive. Nonetheless, Maya and Alex watched anxiously as Oliver effortlessly tore apart the wire fence with his bare hands, making it seem as easy as opening the poppers on a puffer coat.

"I thought you might never make it," the guy whispered, greeting Oliver with a firm handshake as he passed through the fence first.

"We had to go back to collect a few things, but we made it," Oliver replied, and he quickly turned back to help Maya slip under the gap. "Be careful with the wire," he cautioned.

The guy opened the sliding door on the side of the van. "Get in, we need to move. Quickly!" He promptly shut the door behind Alex.

Oliver assisted Maya in finding a seat on his duffle bag since there were no proper seats, just shelves inside. After a brief, bumpy ride with several turns, the van came to a halt, and the door slid open.

"Oliver, I've prepared this one for you," the guy pointed to a plane inside the hangar as Oliver disembarked from the van.

"Roger, you're the best," Oliver said, patting the guy on the shoulder. Maya and Alex clambered out of the van, still a bit wobbly from the journey. "These are my friends I told you about, Maya and Alex. And this hero is Roger, my old friend," he introduced, gesturing to the giant with a thick, messy beard and a bushy unibrow that practically covered his forehead.

"It's my pleasure to meet you," Roger rumbled in a deep, earth-shaking voice that sounded like Darth Vader on steroids. "I have to admit, I'm glad to see that there are people who haven't been affected by the pandemic. If you need anything, just let me know. You can count on me." He then turned back to Oliver and delivered a hearty slap on his back that could have crushed a smaller vacuum cleaner. "Keep me in the loop when you're coming back. Good luck."

Alex felt a tad uncomfortable, realizing that with Roger, who was twice the size of Oliver, suddenly he looked like a delicate little flower standing next to Maya. Not like it's a competition, but the presence of these two giants was pretty emasculating. Alex had to clear his throat twice to produce a deep, booming voice that somewhat matched theirs. "Uh, thanks, Roger. Um, we should be back in a couple of days. And definitely, keep in touch." He extended his hand for a handshake but instantly regretted it after hearing his joints crack in Roger's grip.

"Safe trip for you too, beautiful lady," Roger added, turning his gaze toward Maya. He then hopped into the van and reversed out of the hangar.

Oliver began to stride toward the plane and glanced back at them. "Are we going or what?"

Maya smiled at Alex, who was still trying to revive the feeling in his hand after the bone-crushing handshake. She took his arm and let him lead the way to the plane, while Alex was still trying to shake some life and blood into his beleaguered palm.

Oliver dashed up the stairs and dropped his bag on the first available seat, swiftly closing the stairs behind Alex as everyone got on board. He locked the door securely and then made his way to the cockpit.

"Alex, are you coming?" Oliver called out, his expression slightly annoyed, as he observed Alex comfortably settling into a leather-covered business chair next to Maya, almost ready to fasten the buckle.

"Coming where?" Alex's voice held a note of confusion.

"I need a co-pilot," Oliver replied, his tone impatient.

"But you said you can fly a plane. Why do you need me?" Alex's voice carried a hint of concern.

"This is a long-haul flight, over 7 hours. Do you think I should do it alone?" Oliver countered.

Alex didn't exactly exude confidence, but with palpable hesitation, he stood up and walked toward the tiny cockpit.

"Pick your side," Oliver smiled, pointing toward the seats in front of the myriad buttons and switches on the control panel.

"I don't know which one is the pilot's side," Alex admitted, looking puzzled.

"Doesn't matter, I can set up both sides. Just take your pick," Oliver said, gently urging Alex forward another step.

"Uh, okay. I pick the right side," Alex mumbled, carefully settling into the seat, his eyes darting around as if preparing for brain surgery.

Oliver glanced back at Maya, a mischievous grin on his face, and added with a playful tone, "It would be lovely if you could fasten your seatbelt, please. And, just in case, if you catch both of us snoring away, make sure to wake up Alex first."

Maya chuckled at Oliver's humor and settled back into her comfy seat.

"So, let's start with aviation 101," Oliver announced as he swaggered into the cockpit. "This is a Cessna Citation X jet with two Rolls Royce turbofan engines. The flight controls, these sticks and pedals can be operated from both sides. Over here, we've got the avionics navigation, radios, and our fuel system," he continued, pointing at various buttons and panels with an air of nonchalance. "Any questions? Feel free to ask, but, and I can't stress this enough, hands off anything unless I give you the official 'touch this' thumbs-up. Clear?"

Sheer panic was etched on Alex's face, and he suddenly felt like he wouldn't be able to repeat a word of what Oliver had just told him. Nevertheless, he played it cool and nodded confidently as if he understood everything.

"Okay, let's go," Oliver declared and started the engines.

The plane, moving as gracefully as an elegant Edwardian dowager navigating through a boring dinner party, slowly rolled towards the hangar's exit without a hint of hesitation. Oliver double-checked the panels, turned on the radio, and taxied out to the runway. He cast a final quick glance at Alex's terrified expression, and after quickly picking up speed, he effortlessly pulled the plane into the dark sky, disappearing into the inky abyss above.

22

"Alex! ALEX!" Oliver exclaimed, shaking his drowsy co-pilot awake. "Wake up!"

Alex blinked, disoriented. "What...? What happened?"

Oliver chuckled heartily, leaning back in his seat. "Haha, you either took a little nap or decided to pass out on me. Not sure which one." He grinned mischievously. "You've had a solid three hours of 'me time.' Now, it's my turn to recharge. Keep an eye on things, and if you hear anything odd or see flashing lights, don't be shy about waking me up, okay?"

Alex's expression was a mix of uncertainty and slight panic. "Wait, wait! I can't fly this thing! What should I even do?"

Oliver furrowed his brow, putting on a show of deep contemplation. Then, he pointed confidently at a display. "See this right here? Make sure the altimeter keeps the plane centred on the screen. And on this MFD, if you spot another aircraft, give me a little nudge, okay?"

"But I don't know how to..." Alex began, his voice trailing off in confusion.

"It's on autopilot," Oliver reassured him with a grin. "Bottom line, don't touch a darn thing. Just nudge me if things go haywire. Got it?" With that, he folded his arms across his chest, closed his eyes, and settled in for some well-deserved rest.

Those hours felt like an eternity for Alex, filled with anxiety and discomfort. As the minutes crawled by, Oliver occasionally glanced his way, chuckling at the sight of Alex sweating profusely, fixated on the display.

Finally, as the time neared its end, Oliver roused himself, glancing around. He found Alex slouched in his seat, drooling slightly as he slept.

"Wakey-wakey! Breakfast ready!" Oliver quipped with a hearty laugh.

Alex jolted awake, confused. "God! Where are we? Oh, sorry, I dozed off again. Are we there yet?"

"Almost. Just one more hour to go," Oliver replied. "Now, go check on Maya, grab some coffee for both of us, and then get back in that seat."

Alex, still feeling somewhat shaky and unsteady, stumbled his way over to Maya, who was sleeping peacefully like an angel. The ethereal aura of soft light enveloping her like a gentle mist, a sight that left Alex momentarily captivated.

"Where's my coffee?" Oliver's voice called urgently from the cockpit.

Maya opened her eyes, sparkled like luminescent emeralds, and smiled at Alex. "Hello, good morning."

"Hi, good morning. I'm making coffee. Can I get you one too?" Alex offered as if this was his sole reason for staring at her.

"Thanks, but let me come with you; we can make it together," she replied kindly and popped open the seatbelt.

"Guys, there's a little problem," Oliver announced from the cockpit. "Get that coffee brewing ASAP and strap in for landing."

Alex's voice tightened with worry. "Wait, what's going on?"

Oliver explained, "Nothing yet, but it seems that Roger slightly undercalculated the fuel. No rush, but we've got 15 more minutes to find a landing spot. So, get me my bloody coffee and prepare for landing."

That was a quick wake-up call for all of them, even without the caffeine. Maya and Alex exchanged a glance and rushed to the back of the plane to locate the instant coffee. In record time, they returned to their seats, watching as Oliver scrutinized the meters on the screen.

"It's not too bad; we just need to make it to Eastport in Maine. Shouldn't be too difficult," Oliver mused aloud.

"Eastport? Where's that?" Maya inquired from the rear of the plane.

Oliver turned his head to address her. "It's the first airport over the Canadian border, on Moose Island. Maybe it's even better than waltzing into Boston Logan Airport with a stolen plane. We can land quietly and then make our way to Boston by car. What do you think, Alex?" He glanced at Alex, whose face was etched with tension.

"I just want to be on the ground. I couldn't care less if it's Maine or Massachusetts, as long as I have my feet on the ground," Alex replied with a trace of exasperation.

"Seems like you're not a fan of flying," Oliver quipped with a playful grin.

Alex sighed. "Oliver, don't take it personally, but I'd rather be just about anywhere on this planet right now than on this plane."

Oliver abruptly shouted, "STOP, NO! Don't do it!"

"Do what?" Alex looked bewildered, but soon realized that the cockpit was starting to disappear around them, and he felt as if a massive, cozy white blanket had fallen on his shoulders.

For a few seconds, Alex sensed an unusual warmth coursing through his body, accompanied by strange noises echoing from all directions. He couldn't really make out what the noises were, but slowly they started to form words. Alex tried to open his eyes, but the light was too bright, and even just breathing seemed challenging and difficult, like operating heavy machinery.

When he finally managed to pry his eyes open, he found Maya's smiling face above him, mixed with a hint of concern. "Alex, are you okay?"

"Ouch, my head. Where am I?" Alex mumbled, his hand instinctively reaching for his throbbing temple.

"We're in a car, heading to Boston. Remember?" Maya explained.

"In a car? Wait, no, I was on a plane. What happened?" Alex felt confused and couldn't understand what happened.

"You wandered off again, so I had to stop you," Oliver cut in and turned his glance back on the highway as he continued driving, "I couldn't risk everyone's life."

"God! Did you hit me again? That's your only solution, that you just knock me out?" Alex hissed, clutching his head as if trying to contain the pain.

Maya carefully pulled him back onto her lap as they sat in the car's backseat. "Calm down. Let me finish your healing."

"Sorry, buddy, but I had no other choice," Oliver explained. "I had to give you a little tap; you banged your head, we safely landed, and all problems were solved."

Alex rubbed his temples and groaned, "And how long was I out?"

"Four hours," Oliver replied nonchalantly.

"Four hours? So where are we now?" Alex clambered out of Maya's lap and peered out the car window. But suddenly, his face turned white. "Oliver, stop. Right now!"

"What's wrong?" Oliver glanced back; concern etched on his face.

"Pull over immediately!" Alex shouted. As soon as the car came to a halt, he flung open the door and lunged out, finding the nearest spot to bend over and threw up like on a prom ball.

"Oh, poor thing," Maya sympathized, peering at him from the car. "Are you okay now? Feeling better?" She shouted after him.

"Never felt better, like I've just been reborn," Alex quipped, his voice tinged with sarcasm as he wiped his mouth and staggered back to the car.

"Alex, look out, behind you!" Maya suddenly screamed in sheer horror.

"Now what?..." but before Alex could finish the sentence, he was tackled to the ground, pain searing through his shoulder. He felt a terrible bite, and when he looked up, a massive bear loomed above him, its hot breath on his face as he lay pressed against the grass.

Out of the car, Oliver sprang into action, shouting loudly as he rushed to help Alex. "Argh. Argh! Come here, you beast. Pick on someone your own size!" he bellowed, attempting to draw the bear's attention away from Alex.

The bear stared up at Oliver, madness in its eyes, and foam dripping from its mouth. With a sudden lunge, it leaped toward Oliver, who braced himself for impact. With a twist and a turn, Oliver grabbed the bear's fur and threw it forcefully onto the ground.

It was a clash of titans, a fierce and ruthless battle, as they were rolling and twisting. Oliver and the bear fought with raw, furious passion, but suddenly the bear's colossal claws sliced deep into Oliver's thighs. Oliver's eyes darkened, turning into abyssal pools of primal intensity; his shoulders broadened, and his posture emerged, filling the space with an almost supernatural force.

An agonized roar erupted from deep within him, the sound resonating with an otherworldly power echoing through the forest, and his face contorted into something beyond human recognition. His veins pulsed visibly, his arms pumped up, his knee and elbow bent ready for attack. At that moment, he embodied the unstoppable force of nature, his gaze filled with raw and primal wrath as if he had tapped into a hidden source of power, unleashing it upon the world with the expression of overwhelming destruction.

Oliver's transformation and earth-shaking roar seemed to shock the bear, and with a sudden decision, it halted its attack and dropped down on its forelegs. Started moving backward, bowing its head in submission before Oliver's majestic power. Then slowly, it turned back and in seconds disappeared into the forest next to the road, vanishing as quickly as it had come.

Maya rushed to Oliver's side as he still stood there, like hesitating if he should go after the bear or let it escape from his anger. "Oliver. Are you okay? Did you get hurt? Please say something," she pleaded, her eyes filled with concern, seeing his still and tense muscular body, struggling to release the overwhelming urge that surged within him.

"I am okay! Nobody asked, but I'll be fine!" Alex exclaimed loudly, pushing himself up from the ground, while touching his injured shoulder, where the bear had bitten him.

"Oh, gosh. Sorry, Alex." Maya apologized, her attention shifting to him. "Please, let me help you!" She reached out to assist Alex, who was clearing his face and spitting grass from his mouth.

Oliver barely moved, standing like a statue. Slowly, he turned and without uttering a word, walked back to the car. He stopped and gently said, "I think it's better if someone else drives from here."

"No problem, I can drive," Maya offered. "Let me just get Alex in the car first, and we can go, okay?"

Oliver quietly squeezed himself into the back of the car in a fetal position and closed the door.

"Maya, I have to admit that until now I wasn't entirely sure, but at this point, I can tell you with absolute certainty that I need a fresh pair of underwear," Alex quipped as Maya helped him to her side, his arm leaning on her for support. "Wait, and I need to brush my teeth. So, let's keep a bit of distance, shall we?"

Maya chuckled softly at Alex's grumbling. "No worries, Alex. I'm just relieved you're okay and nothing worse happened." She reassured him with a kind smile as he limped beside her. In silence, they settled in the seats, and the car pulled back onto the road, their eyes fixed on the seemingly endless highway stretching out before them.

"Bloody grizzly bears," Alex mumbled after a little while as he examined the bite on his shoulder. "I think I need a tetanus shot."

A moment later, Oliver chimed in on a casual tone, "Actually, it was a black bear, not a grizzly."

"Poteto, potato. Same thing," Alex retorted, still nursing his wounded pride. "We'd better find a hospital before my whole left arm needs to be amputated."

23

They travelled for miles and miles with no signs of life in sight, while the empty road and the surrounding forests cast a somber mood inside the car. When finally, a small town emerged on the horizon, a glimmer of hope appeared on everyone's face, though for different reasons.

Alex was shaking, probably from the fever or exhaustion. He had long given up the search for a stray tic-tac in the glove compartment, but he still yearned and would gladly trade his soul for a warm shower in a heartbeat. Although Oliver's thigh was still bleeding severely from the bear's deep claw wound, his most significant inconvenience was the lack of space for his legs, making him feel like he was trapped in a sardine box at the back.

Maya glanced repeatedly at the guys, feeling helpless and anxious about her inability to assist them. So, she tried to stay focused on driving and finding a safe place as soon as possible with medical supplies to care for them.

Then, like a beacon of hope on the horizon, Alex spotted a road sign. "Look, there! A hospital! Exit 32…"

Oliver nodded, feeling his wounded leg throb with every bump in the road. "Yeah, it's just a slight detour, and we could find a place to lay low before heading to Boston. We'll stay there, gather our strength, and continue tomorrow. What do you think, Maya?"

"Perfect, I'm dying for a comfy bed and some food," Maya agreed, her stomach growling, and just a few turns later, they pulled up in the hospital parking lot next to the emergency exit.

When they walked through the reception area, it was eerily empty, nobody seemed to be around, just the heavy smell of antiseptic filled the air as their footsteps echoed through the long corridors. They ventured deeper into the deserted space, their eyes scanning for any sign of life, passing closed examination rooms with empty beds, and neatly organized medical equipment.

They finally reached the nurses' station, where medical charts and patient files were scattered all around, as if the hospital staff had vanished overnight, leaving everything behind. Alex began sifting through the rooms, searching for any clues as to where they would find the medical supplies they desperately needed, knowing their survival depended on what they could gather.

Maya kept a watchful eye on the entrance, her senses heightened by the silence that enveloped them. Suddenly, she heard the sound of soft footsteps and sensed danger lurking from every corner, fearing that they could not afford another injury. "Guys, I think I heard something," she whispered.

Oliver continued his search, rummaging through cabinets and drawers, hoping to stumble upon the tetanus, antibiotics, or bandages, what they needed most. "Maya, just be careful. Stay close," he replied cautiously, while he scoured the abandoned rooms.

A swing door slammed open, shattering the creepy silence, and someone's grip tightened around Maya's throat from behind, pressing a gun against her head. "Get out of here, now!" The suspicious voice shouted, filled with desperation.

"Hold on, hold on!" Alex exclaimed, trembling with fear. "We just need some help. We had a bear attack a couple of miles from here. My friend is bleeding, and I need a tetanus shot. We'll be out of your hair in no time, please, just help us."

Behind Maya, a woman tilted her head to look warily at Oliver's blood-soaked pants and torn Green Lantern T-shirt that Alex was wearing, but she kept her fingers tight around Maya's throat. Slowly, as if not entirely convinced, she lowered the gun, a glimmer of uncertainty in her eyes. "Where are you from? You don't sound like you're from around here."

"We're from England," Alex stammered, "Well, I am, and the lady here," he pointed at Maya, "And the gentleman over there is Oliver from Norway."

"Hmm, okay. My name is Olivia," and she released the grip from Maya's neck and stepped forward from behind her. "Take what you need and leave. You've got five minutes."

"Thank you, we're leaving," Oliver chimed in. "We just need some medication, and then we're gone."

Maya stared at Olivia for a moment, her hand still gently caressing her own throat to ease the residual pain. "And do you need help? Maybe we could assist you." Her words held genuine kindness.

"No, I need you to leave," she replied with an angry voice.

Maya glanced at Oliver and then back at Olivia. "If your father is in danger, maybe we could help."

"What do you want? How do you know about my father?" she shouted, raising the gun, pointing at Maya, and then turned to face Alex and Oliver.

"Please, just wait!" Maya pleaded, raising her hands defensively. "I can heal him, maybe. I felt him when you had your arm around me. We're like you."

A long silence hung in the air as Olivia contemplated Maya's words, and slowly she lowered her gun again. "How could you know about him? What do you mean by 'feel him'?"

"We all have our powers, like you," Maya explained. "Alex is a magician, I'm a healer, and Oliver protects us. When you touched me, I could sense your energy, and I saw that you want to protect your father. Is he here?"

Olivia sighed, her shoulders slumping. "Yes, I take care of him. He's in the final stage of cancer. He needs morphine to manage his pain and to be on a continuous IV drip 24/7. But everyone left a couple of weeks ago, and the last nurse disappeared after her family was attacked. She just stopped coming."

"Is there anyone else around who could assist you? Someone who is not affected by the pandemic." Alex asked with concern.

"I don't know about any survivors," Olivia's face became gloomy. "A few months ago, it all started with some strange accidents. People began disappearing, and others went mad. First, people didn't show up at work, and the whole city became quiet. The television channels constantly shared warnings about a new illness, telling us to stay at home, but eventually, the TV broadcasts stopped, the stores got empty, and people started looting, stealing, and breaking into each other's homes searching for food. Everyone is starving, and no one seems to care."

"Olivia, we are here to help, but we must find somebody in Boston," Oliver interjected. "If we can locate her, we may have a chance to stop this pandemic. We will try, but we need to get to Boston. Maya can have a look at your father, but we need to leave tomorrow. Could you help us?"

Olivia looked worried but eventually agreed and continued. "This way. He's in the sterile room on the other side of the building; follow me," and she turned back and led them through the endless halls of the hospital.

They stepped into the dimly lit room, the shades drawn, a plastic bubble canopy protecting the bed in the middle, a fragile defence against a dire illness. The man lay there, slowly breathing with painful moans that escaped his lips. He turned his head as they entered. "Olivia, who are these people?"

With a reassuring tone, Olivia replied, "Dad, everything is okay. They are just passing through. Don't worry, try to rest."

A wistful grin formed on the man's face as he looked at Maya, "An angel. Is it my time finally?" and he made a feeble attempt to lift his hand toward her. "You are so beautiful, just as I imagined."

Olivia looked devastated as she gently explained, "Dad, no. They are from England, and they are headed to Boston tomorrow."

"My name is Maya. It's nice to meet you, sir," and she stepped a little closer to the bed. "If you'd like, I can stay here with you for a little while."

"His name is Bernard. My father was the Chief of Police, but a couple of months ago, his condition quickly got worse with the pandemic, and now nobody is looking after the area," Olivia began to explain, her voice tinged with frustration. "I can't do everything on my own, and it seems that eventually, everybody here got affected. I can't find anyone who could help me, and I am just hopeless."

Oliver approached Olivia and placed a comforting arm around her. "Let us help. Maya can stay here with you and your father. We need to look for the medications. Do you know where we can find them?"

"Yes, let me show you," Olivia said and she stepped through the door pointing to the left. "The second room on the right. It's open. Nobody steals medication; there's no point in locking it." and as Oliver and Alex had left, she turned her attention to Maya. "Are you a doctor?"

"No, I have a little shop selling herbs and medicines, but everybody in my family is a doctor, actually," Maya explained. "Can I touch him? Your father."

Olivia nodded, and then pointed to the plastic shield covering Bernard's bed. "Only through the glove on the plastic cover."

Maya pulled a chair beside Bernard's bed and sat down, reaching for his hand. She closed her eyes, and within moments, a pale, blue mist began to flow from her veins and Bernard's hand started to tremble.

Olivia was shocked, couldn't believe her eyes. She gasped as her father opened his eyes, gazing directly at Maya's face with a profound sense of gratitude.

"My angel," Bernard mumbled. "Please take me. I don't want to feel this pain anymore. It's my time," he added, glancing briefly at Olivia.

"Don't say that Dad! You can't give up. You will recover; just stay strong." her eyes filled with tears; she couldn't contain her pain any longer.

Bernard seemed to gain a bit of strength and gently pulled his hand away from Maya. "Please stop, don't waste your time on me. I want to go."

Maya, her expression filled with confusion, tried to reassure him. "No, I can help you. Just give me some time."

"No. You don't understand. I want to go." Bernard whispered and his gaze turned grim. "This pain is unbearable. It has taken over my whole body. You can't reverse it; it's too late now," and he gently rested his head back on the pillow.

Olivia collapsed, crying with a bitter mixture of sorrow and anger. "No, don't say that. You can't leave me. Not now! I need you!"

Bernard seemed so peaceful. "Olivia, my dear. I will always be with you. You know that. But it's my time. Just let me go, please." His eyes were warm and kind as he looked at her.

Maya stood up and stepped close to Olivia. "Maybe he is right. He's waiting for you to let him go. He can't leave until you want him here, but it's too much for him." And she cuddled Olivia with a gentle understanding.

"I can't," Olivia whispered to Maya. "He is the only one I have in this whole world."

"I know, he told me," Maya replied softly and held her tighter in her arms.

Alex rushed in with Oliver. "We found the medications and bandages. We can leave now," he exclaimed as he walked closer to Maya and Olivia.

Maya glanced up, her look trying to explain to Alex Olivia's sad expression as she quietly wiped her face.

Olivia slowly looked at Alex. "Do you have a place to stay?" she asked, her voice trembling slightly. "We live not far from here on Bayview Beach. I don't have much food, but there's hot water and a bed if you need to stay for a while."

"I could kill for a shower," Alex replied. "And food is not an issue. My mom packed tons of sandwiches, enough food for an army. We can share, okay?" He smiled and looked around for agreement from the others.

"I'll take you there, but after I have to come back here, to look after my father. You can stay as long as you need," Olivia added and smiled kindly at Alex. "The food would be greatly appreciated. I haven't eaten anything in days. Sometimes I just use the IV drip from the medical supply when I really feel weak."

"Let's go. It's lunchtime, and we all could eat something," Maya suggested and glanced back at Bernard. "We'll be back soon. Have a little rest. It was lovely meeting you, Bernard." and she gently pulled Olivia away from his bed.

Maya quickly cleaned the wounds, applied the bandages, and administered the tetanus shots in no time to the guys. Her movements were like witnessing Tinkerbell flying left and right, with such grace and efficiency that it seemed almost magical.

"I'm actually glad to see someone else around," Olivia admitted as they were getting ready to leave. "For the past two weeks, you're the first people I've talked to."

"And your father?" Alex asked as he held the entrance door open for her.

Olivia was thinking for a moment before replying, "He hasn't spoken since last month. I need to give him very strong painkillers. Most of the time he's sleeping or just too weak to speak. It was a miracle that you could talk with him," and she glanced at Maya and continued. "I believe you now, that you are a healer. And maybe you are right, I just needed to hear my father say it so I could let him go."

24

Maya followed Olivia with the car, and after a short journey, they arrived at a picturesque beach. As they approached the shoreline, they navigated along narrow pathways that meandered amidst lush landscapes toward the tranquil waters. On one side, the pristine beach unfolded, while on the other side, a line of elegant residences stood gracefully at the edge of the forest. It was a place where the serene woods met the endless ocean, creating a sense of calm balance.

Olivia parked her Jeep in front of one of the charming coastal homes with classic beauty, exuding an air of timeless elegance. "My father built this house, but since my mom left, it's been just the two of us," Olivia explained as she opened the door. "Just follow me; I'll show you around."

As they walked in, they found themselves in a generously lit living room, with an open-plan kitchen at the far end. Olivia gestured towards the staircase, saying, "I'll change my clothes quickly; just make yourselves comfortable. I'll be back in a couple of minutes."

Oliver strolled over to the back porch, his gaze fixed on the towering glass wall that framed the breathtaking expanse of the boundless ocean, while Alex and Maya started to explore the kitchen. The cupboards were empty, and the fridge contained nothing but ice cubes. When Alex tried to turn on the faucet, strange noises and brown liquid came out, which made him cringe and quickly turn it off. "I think water is not an option," Alex declared, "But we can just use the ice; it will melt quickly."

Soon Olivia returned, and as they all grabbed their sandwiches, they couldn't help but watch in amazement as she devoured her food, practically inhaling it like a famished lion. "It tastes amazing; the meat is melting in my mouth," Olivia added with a full mouth, mumbling.

"Yes, my mom's roast is unbeatable," Alex grinned. "You must also try her beef sandwich with horseradish."

"This was an absolute lifesaver. Thank you," Olivia replied, still munching on the last bits of her toast. "I need to head back now; I can't leave my father alone for too long. There are four rooms upstairs; I suggest you all stay in one. Help yourselves to whatever you need, and feel free to stay as long as you like. Just pop by and say goodbye before you leave, alright?" she beamed, her grin radiating satisfaction as she delicately patted her mouth with a napkin.

Maya initially struggled to find the right words, but eventually, she simply turned to Olivia and asked. "Why don't you have your father here? You have plenty of space, and we could help you bring him here. It would be so much more convenient for you."

"I can't. Time after time, people break in, thinking there's still food. I can't protect myself alone. But in the hospital, no one seems to come searching," she explained. "You'll be safe if you stay close to each other at night, but I can leave a rifle here if you need."

"Thank you for your hospitality; we will not stay for too long," Alex added. "We have to meet a lady in Boston on Monday."

"Ah, that's less than two hours from here. You can leave early in the morning and stay here today and tomorrow night if you want," Olivia suggested.

Oliver's gaze wandered through the room, eventually settling on a nearby picture displayed on the coffee table. "Is that your father in the picture, Bernard?" he inquired.

Olivia nodded solemnly. "Yes, it's hard to recognize him now. He was tall, handsome, and strong, like a god, the protector of justice and the helper of the whole community. He devoted his life to these people, even her marriage. Probably that's why my mom left. But I don't want to bore you with my story."

Maya chimed in; her curiosity piqued. "No, not at all. By the way, where is your family originally from? I'm from Poland, but my parents are from Russia," she added friendly.

"I had a hunch about your accent. It's hard to miss." Olivia chuckled. "My family was among the early French settlers. But on my mother's side, she always said that our ancestry traced back to the Wabanaki tribe, the People of the Dawn."

Alex looked really intrigued. "By any chance, do you have a medal like this one?" he asked, pulling out the amulet from beneath his torn T-shirt. "Maybe your father or someone in your family had something similar?"

Olivia took a close look at the amulet, and her eyes widened in recognition. "Ah, yes! It does resemble the cube that my great-great-grandfather used to have on his sword. Come, I'll show you," and she walked to a painting hanging on the opposite wall. "Here he is, in his Civil War uniform. If you look at the end of his sword handle, you can see the cube. We always thought he must have been a big gambler and loved playing craps, that's why he had that dice," she laughed.

Oliver's eyes lit up with excitement. "And where is this sword now?"

Her expression turned somber. "We don't have it. They never brought him home; he was buried somewhere in Virginia with the sword," she said and then looked surprised. "But why do you ask?"

Alex and Oliver exchanged a knowing glance. They realized how fortunate they were to have these precious medals. During the chaos of battle, accidents, theft - hundreds, if not thousands, of ways the medals could have easily disappeared and been erased from history forever. And without the knowledge, the power of the legacy is obviously not strong enough to be a Gatekeeper.

"I can tell you more about it later, but I am sure you are eager to return to your father." Oliver replied. "If you don't mind, I could join you, and maybe we can look around in the town."

Olivia smiled and nodded, happy to accept the request from such a handsome guy. But the truth is that Oliver was really intrigued by her courage and strength. Despite her fragile appearance, her eyes held a fierce determination, and the way she held the gun at the hospital revealed a fearless Amazon. Oliver felt an undeniable attraction, and frankly, it was mutual.

"Of course," Olivia replied warmly, her eyes gleaming. "I could show you the gas station on the way; you'll probably need gas if you want to get to Boston. I can open it for you; I have the keys; it won't be a problem." and she reached for her car keys, ready to lead the way.

Maya and Alex finally had some time alone in the house to refresh themselves and relax after the long journey. As time passed, it became obvious that Oliver wouldn't be joining them, so they started getting ready for sleep.

Alex, ever the gentleman, offered the bed to Maya, making sure she had a comfortable place to rest, and he placed a few blankets in front of the door for himself, creating a makeshift barrier so nobody could enter the room. But most importantly, it allowed Maya to rest without losing her energy on healing him.

Morning arrived swiftly, and when Alex woke up and checked his phone, he appeared surprised. "Maya, look! Daniel sent the bio about Debby last night. I was sleeping so deep; I didn't even hear the notification. I just sent it to you and Oliver, read it."

"Gosh, Daniel was right, Alex. We need to speak with Oliver. Where is he?" Maya replied.

"I know just as much as you do, but he's a big boy. He can definitely take care of himself." Alex laughed, a bit hoping that Olivia could take Oliver's attention away from Maya.

But Maya seemed genuinely disappointed. "Ah, okay. I hope he's fine and will be back soon. Or we can text him to join us for breakfast."

That was not exactly the reaction Alex wanted, but he nodded and picked up the blankets from the floor, feeling that his gallant gesture might have gone unnoticed again. "Yes, I'll text him, no problem," and he just left the room so Maya wouldn't see his slightly crestfallen expression.

But as he walked down the stairs, he found Oliver already in the kitchen with Olivia. "Hello, sunshine. Long night? I thought you'd never wake up," Oliver teased.

"When did you come back? I didn't hear you," Alex said, looking surprised.

"I came back late, and I didn't want to disturb you, so I slept downstairs," Oliver explained and gave Alex a discreet wink. "I woke up early and invited Olivia to join us for breakfast." He moved closer to Olivia and took a coffee mug from her hand.

"Hello, good morning," Maya joined them in the kitchen, her keen senses picking up on the unusual atmosphere that seemed to hang in the air. As she looked at their faces, she couldn't help but feel that something was amiss. "Oh, Olivia, I am so glad to see you. I hope you can join us for breakfast."

"Hello. I'm just making a champion omelette for us. Actually, Oliver has been incredibly helpful. We managed to find quite a bit of food supply last night, so I'll be okay for a while, I think," Olivia replied, glancing at Oliver with admiration. "He's very handy in every way, I must say," she added with a giggle.

Oliver blushed slightly and quickly changed the subject, "I just read the paper that you sent me on my phone about Debby. It means that Daniel was right about her."

"What do you mean? Who is Debby?" Olivia asked, looking puzzled.

Alex sat down at the table, picked up a steaming coffee mug, and had a big sip as he began. "Yesterday, I mentioned that we need to get to Boston to find a woman named Debby. All we know about her is that she has a medal similar to what we have, and if we find her, we need to convince her to join us."

Olivia leaned forward, with curiosity in her eyes. "Join you in your quest to save the world? But why do you need her?"

Maya chimed in, her voice steady and determined. "We believe that Debby possesses a medal representing fire, an incredibly powerful element. Even stronger than ours combined together."

Alex reached for his phone and began scrolling through Daniel's message. "My friend Daniel has the water medal. He was telling me first about the Gatekeepers and soon I found Maya and Oliver. We already gathered four elements, with four amulets."

Olivia raised an eyebrow. "Wait, there are only four elements. You said that you already have four medals, I don't understand."

"Yes, traditionally there are four elements: earth, water, fire, and air. But ancient knowledge speaks of a fifth element, often referred to as aether or the universe. And she has the final, fifth amulet of fire." Alex explained and continued. "My friend, Daniel has some connections, and he found out that Debby seems to be working on a secret government project. Before she used to be a prominent figure in politics, but she retired suddenly in 2018. Out of the blue, she resigned from her senatorial position mid-term and started working pro bono as a child custody attorney. Quite an abrupt career shift, don't you think?"

Oliver stepped to the table, thinking deeply. "She must've got a better offer. Maybe that's when she started to work on that government project. To have a cover story, she's taking some cases, so she can work for the FBI or CIA on something highly classified."

Alex's eyes filled with terror. "Guys, this isn't good news," Alex said, his voice quivering with fear. "Remember Daniel? You both saw him. They did that to him—the FBI, CIA, or whatever they're called. They worked together on a project to torture him for months, extracting every bit of information from him. He managed to escape, but his soul... they destroyed him."

Maya's expression shifted from curiosity to horror as she realized the true nature of the vision she had encountered. "Oh my God, that was him. The creature I saw," she exclaimed. "It makes sense now why he kept saying 'me-me,' but all I saw was that tortured, wounded, zombie-like figure."

"You saw that creature too?" Alex looked concerned as he learned that Maya had also witnessed Daniel's carcass. "So, you understand that this is no game. They can destroy us and strip away our abilities if they want to."

Maya's face turned really gloomy. "When I first saw Daniel, I was really frightened by him. That's why I remained so quiet when we were there. I needed some time to gather the strength to heal him so we could finally speak."

Oliver suddenly couldn't contain his excitement as he pointed out a detail in Daniel's message. "Alex, mate, you've got to see this. Debby's family is from Laconia, Greece," he said, his voice filled with fascination.

Alex furrowed his brows, not immediately grasping Oliver's point. "I'm not entirely sure why this is important, Oliver. Care to enlighten me?"

"Laconic. It means to speak in a blunt, direct way, like Spartans. I'm surprised you've never heard of it." Oliver grinned like a Cheshire cat. "Now, Daniel's intel reveals that Debby's mother was abducted in 1948 during the Greek Civil War from Laconia. That's Sparta. More than 30,000 children between the ages of 3 and 15 were forcibly separated from their parents to be indoctrinated in refugee camps. When the war ended two years later, as soon as she turned fourteen, she got adopted and shipped to America."

Alex still seemed puzzled. "My grandfather was from Delphi, not Sparta. I'm not sure where you're going with this."

"Don't you think that this could explain your connections with the elements? You're a magician from the home of the future-teller Oracle Pythia, and Debby, well, she comes from the land of Leonidas, the legendary Spartan hero. Get it now?" Oliver replied with a content smile as he connected the dots.

"Oliver, I highly doubt that strolling into her office and sharing an anecdote about possible mutual great uncles or cousins would convince her to help us." Alex rolled his eyes. "As soon as I admit that I'm a magician from Delphi, she might just escort me to a torture chamber to dissect my brain. Why would I willingly do that?"

A sly grin appeared on Oliver's lips. "I think you haven't seen the movie '300.' Even Leonidas himself sought the Oracle's blessing at Delphi before going to war. You, my friend, are our very own Oracle."

"Oliver's got a point, Alex." Maya chimed in, clearly intrigued. "If you tell her that you've seen the future and have returned to help her, she'll believe you."

"So, you're suggesting that I pretend to have travelled through time, saw that she would help me, and even though she doesn't know me, she'll consider listening to me because she believes that it's already happened in the future." Alex contemplated the idea seriously and nodded with a smile. "I just have to come up with a convincing prophecy."

Maya continued timidly. "But if I could briefly touch her before you meet her, I could glean some insights into her plans."

"The problem is, we don't even know where she lives, just her office," Alex explained. "Daniel's sources have gone silent regarding Debby's private life. Plus, once she spots Maya with us, she'll realize that it was a setup. We might have to do first some old-fashioned detective work."

"What if we could gain access to her private files?" Olivia said with a sinister smile. "Hypothetically speaking, of course, if we had something like that in the police station. Suppose if such files existed, I might be able to discreetly check and offer a subtle hint about a couple of details, like where and how you could find her. I mean if we would have such files exist."

"Now that's what I am talking about. You're a gem, Olivia." Oliver exclaimed and started laughing. "Alex, we ought to find that bear and give it a big bear hug for leading us here. Don't you agree?"

Alex smiled appreciatively. "Indeed, Olivia, that would be a tremendous help. We'll need all the leads we can get," he then turned to Oliver. "Regarding our bear acquaintance, I must admit that my fondness for our furry friend doesn't exactly reciprocate yours, to say the least."

Ah, life—a series of coincidences, abrupt changes, painful decisions, and unexpected occurrences. It's almost as if that traffic controller orchestrating the rails of existence has a rather whimsical sense of direction. Yet, somehow, amidst all the chaos, it seems he knows exactly what he's doing.

25

Thanks to her dad, Olivia had unrestricted access to every corner of the town. Navigating the labyrinthine layout of the police station was a breeze for her, as she knew it like the back of her hand. In a rush, she checked a few rooms, gathering scattered papers, before heading toward a closed office. "This way, this is my father's office. We can use his computer; he has top-level security access to everything," she explained.

As she began typing the numbers and codes she had collected from the papers, her expression shifted to one of surprise. "Hmm, interesting. Normally, this code allows access to top-secret levels of government files. However, it appears that this woman's files are not managed by the government system, nor by any other county or organization. It's as if she works for an entirely different country or entity. That just doesn't make sense," she mumbled, continuing to type even faster.

Alex was watching her determination for a while but then felt it wasn't the time to be reserved. "I think I can help with that. Not my proudest moment to admit, but let's just say I know my way around hacking the internet. You need to create a pass to override it, probably. Can I give it a try?"

"Absolutely, it's all yours," Olivia replied, her curiosity piqued.

"The trick is that most systems nowadays have the same old defence protocols. But with the new AI supercomputers that those secret government services use, you first need to pass the security level, and then you can open and create a path to hack the server," Alex explained while they all tensely watched his moves on the keyboard. "It's not that hard... Ah, interesting," he paused and stared at the screen: "Access Denied."

A couple of seconds and numerous beeping sounds later, Alex's face lit up with a triumphant smile. "Look, there we are. She definitely has something to hide. The National Bank has a weaker defence system on their server than she does. So, what are you working on?... Let me see..." Alex mumbled while navigating through the pages. After a moment, he looked up at the team. "I think this is just a trap for hackers, not her real site. It's a decoy, a dead end."

"But what about her personal life?" Olivia inquired; her face filled with curiosity.

"Let's see. I can check her bank card or track her phone," Alex replied, his fingers flying across the keyboard. "Her account shows no transactions in the last four weeks, just one big withdrawal six weeks ago. She probably only uses cash, but that's because of the pandemic, it's normal."

"What about her phone? Can we track her location?" Oliver asked, his eyes filled with hope.

"Wait a moment, I think I've got it. Yes!" Alex exclaimed and clicked on the screen. "Look, her phone shows that she's at the address that Daniel sent us for her office. She hasn't moved since Friday."

"So, she's either dead or ordering Uber Eats," Oliver quipped.

"The location seems a bit random, but most of the time, it's in the same area as her office. She is moving, but it looks like only a couple of blocks away," Alex added.

"Uh, that's not much to work with," Maya said, her voice filled with disappointment.

"Whoever she works for, they've scrubbed everything about her. She's like a ghost in her private life and work, only the pro bono cases appear online when I search," Alex explained.

"And can you hack her phone for calls and texts?" Oliver inquired with a glimmer of hope.

"I can try, but we can't trace her for long; they'll find out if I hack it. Max for a couple of minutes, no more," Alex continued, noticing the grim expressions around him. "The only way is to go there and try to see what she's up to. We have no other option."

"Guys, I have to stay here with my father, but I wish I could help you more," Olivia said, her expression filled with hopelessness.

Alex smiled and gently touched Olivia's shoulder. "No, you've already helped a lot. We can go there now; we already know that she's in her office. We can observe her today, maybe find out a few more details, and meet her tomorrow when we're better prepared."

Oliver nodded. "Okay, it's better to get ready for the meeting there than sitting here discussing options. I say let's go now."

As they prepared to leave, Oliver turned to Olivia, cuddled her, and gazed deeply into her eyes. "Don't forget what I told you. Promise me you'll call. Okay?"

"I promise," Olivia replied with determination and desire in her voice as they slowly walked out of the office.

After the heartfelt hugs and goodbyes, they departed, each filled with doubts, questions, and fears. Only Oliver seemingly managed to maintain an air of calm and collectedness, sitting in the car like a statue of confidence, but his eyes couldn't hide that something was going on. Maya probably sensed it and tried to talk to him.

"Olivia was so lovely, don't you think, Oliver? I really hope we can see her again soon," she began, trying to cheer him up.

Oliver looked resolute for a moment, then paused as if he was carefully considering his response. "Yes, we have a lot in common. I hope she takes my advice..." but then he trailed off, a hint of uncertainty in his voice. "She'll be fine, and we'll probably see her after we sort this whole thing out."

Even Alex couldn't ignore the change in Oliver's demeanour. While driving, he stole a few glances at his friend, sensing something was amiss. "We're almost there," Alex said, breaking the silence. "We should find a place to stay tonight and come up with a plan before we meet Debby. Any ideas, Oliver?"

But there was no reaction, no response from Oliver. Alex checked the rearview mirror, looking for some kind of sign or explanation from Maya. She appeared puzzled too, unsure why the once assertive and fearless giant now seemed so humble and fragile.

Oliver's intense gaze remained fixed on the road ahead as they approached the city, and the effort it took to maintain this composure became increasingly evident. It was as though he needed every ounce of his energy to conceal the inner turmoil that seemed to be consuming him.

When they finally arrived in Boston, it felt like they had entered a deserted city from a dystopian movie. The streets were lined with closed shops, broken windows, abandoned cars, and piles of trash everywhere.

There was no sign of life or people, just a stomach-churning stench that clung to the air, emanating from suspicious mounds of clothing that concealed decaying bodies in every corner. As they slowly drove through the once-bustling town, the horrifying reality of the events that had transpired there slowly pieced itself together.

Oliver signalled to Alex when he noticed a little corner shop with flashing neon lights, not far from Debby's office. The door was open, and as they entered the curry-smelling shop floor, two figures emerged from behind the thick plastic shield, separating the entrance from the back of the store.

"Stop right there," the taller one barked, his voice filled with an air of menace, while the distinctive noise of the gun being cocked echoed in the tense silence. "Cash only."

Alex, trembling, began to explain, "Hi, we just need some information. We're from England, looking for somebody. Could you help maybe?"

The intimidating figure retorted and stepped closer to the counter, revealing his face while pointing the gun at Alex, "No purchase, no service."

"Y-yes, we can buy something," Alex stammered, turning to Oliver if he had any idea how to handle the situation. "Do you need something, Oliver, like chewing gum or water?"

Oliver slowly stepped in, casting a quick glance back at the car outside to check on Maya before closing the door behind him. "Depends. What do you have?" He looked at the guys with a non-contradictory expression on his face. "We need food, water, and ammo."

The man behind the counter replied with a listless tone, "We have a meal deal: a hundred bucks for two cans of sardines, two bottles of water, and ten rounds."

"Make it two." Oliver briskly ordered, placing three crisp hundred-dollar bills on the counter. "And maybe we can make a deal if you help us."

The cashier nodded to his companion to fetch the items and then turned back to Oliver, his demeanour growing hostile. "And what do you want?"

"Probably you know the politician, Debby Abrams. We need some information," Alex replied.

The cashier's eyes suddenly flashed with madness. "Get out! Now!"

"Hold on," Alex interjected, attempting to reason with him. "We just need to find her."

"I don't want any trouble," the cashier shouted. "I want you to leave. Now!"

Oliver nonchalantly retrieved his money from the counter and looked intently at the guy. "I think you've made a mistake. A big mistake..." In one swift motion, he shattered the plastic partition and ripped it off from the countertop like a Band-Aid. In a fraction of a second, he grabbed the guy's shirt and knocked him right between his eyes so hard that he just collapsed to the floor like a sack of potatoes, still clutching the gun upright like a national flag.

"Please, just take what you want!" The other guy screamed and rushed there, trying to rouse him. "Dad, dad! Are you okay?"

"He's fine," Oliver assured him. "In a few minutes, he'll be back among the living. Don't worry. We don't want trouble, but we need to find this woman, and you're going to help us," he continued and bounced over the counter with an elegant gazelle leap.

As Alex continued to stare in shock, Oliver swiftly scooped up the guy from the floor, wrested the rifle from his grip, and handed it to Alex. "Come, we have to check in the back." With a determined nod, Oliver signalled for Alex to follow him into the stockroom at the back.

The counter wasn't particularly high, barely hitting ninety centimetres, but it had the same width as a buffet table at a sumo wrestler's convention. Faced with this formidable obstacle, Alex decided to channel his inner PE class hero, resorting to climbing up and crawling over the counter on his hands and knees, like a determined inchworm, aiming to conquer this mighty Everest of furniture.

Oliver watched this somewhat undignified attempt with a stoic expression but couldn't resist and quietly whispered to Alex, "Seriously, bro, even a ten-year-old girl could leap over that thing with more grace than you just did. No offense, but we need to get you into training ASAP to make up for that PE waiver."

"Haha, very funny, it was actually pretty wide." Alex retorted, feeling offended and a little embarrassed at the same time, but deep down he actually knew that Oliver was right.

He was going to the gym… sometimes, and while he enjoyed playing football and envied guys with bulging biceps and six-packs, he couldn't muster much enthusiasm for the prospect of a sweaty PE class. As a child, he'd frequently skipped it, just to play a game or watch an episode of Star Trek. It was always more comfortable to find an excuse and choose the path of least resistance than enduring countless hours of inhaling the pungent fragrance of armpits in a crowded gym.

Of course, Alex did harbour moments of jealousy toward those chiselled physiques, but never quite reached the point where he felt bad enough to do something about it. It's like when you want to lose weight. You always say that you should cut down on junk food, live healthier, and then you buy that bloody expensive gym membership just to force yourself to show up, but after a couple of sessions, the urge just fades away. Because you say it, but you don't really mean it.

Until the moment you don't actually feel that your life depends on it, or you get sick and tired of your own bullshit, you will just keep shopping in the excuses department, moaning about how bad and difficult your life is, and then order the extra-large pizza for just two more pounds. After all, why not? You feel healthy, strong, and anyway, not everyone could look like a bodybuilder, right?

But the truth is that Alex finally started to understand the unique strengths of his fellow Gatekeepers. And it wasn't only Oliver's extraordinary power, Maya's unwavering spirit, or his own mind that conquered the challenges they faced. The balance of opposing forces, the equilibrium they forged, what made them invincible. As Daniel once told him, about the three layers that constitute human beings: the body, the ego, and the soul.

This trinity, akin to the Father, the Son, and the Holy Spirit, is much like a three-legged stool that symbolizes the stability each aspect brings to our lives. Neglecting one of these elements or obsessively focusing on just one could lead to a profound imbalance.

It was a concept echoed by philosophers and thinkers throughout history, from Plato to Aristotle to Confucius, emphasizing that education should encompass not only physical well-being and intellectual development but also the nurturing of spiritual growth.

So, Alex gathered his resolve, knowing that it was time for a change. Took a deep breath, and slapped Oliver's hand to seal their agreement to get his shit together and take responsibility for his own life, even if it was a bit uncomfortable. And hopefully, this time, it would be for good.

26

The stockroom in the back was like a crowded labyrinth of culinary treasures, packed with piles of tins and water bottles forming a maze through which one could wander. The air was filled with the heavy scents of exotic spices, mingling in a fragrant potpourri. Stepping inside felt like boarding a colonial merchant ship, fresh from its journey across the oceans, laden with the fabulous riches of mystical India. Every shelf and corner held the diversity of cultures and flavours that had found a home in this small shop, like the world coming together through food, creating a tapestry of taste that transcended borders.

Oliver placed the guy on a chair and gave his face a gentle tap. "Hey, wake up! We need to talk."

The guy gradually opened his eyes, looking quite scattered, probably not even remembering his own name. "Who are you? What happened?" he asked, blinking at Oliver with genuine innocence.

"We asked you about Debby Abrams. Do you remember? And you were going to tell us where we can find her." Oliver explained with a determined tone.

"Auch, my head. What's going on?"

"Dad, just tell them." The young guy begged him, his voice filled with worry.

"Ahh, you have to leave. Please, understand. I can't help you. It's too dangerous," the guy continued, his face showing true fear.

"We can't leave until you help us," Oliver replied, sensing that he knew something important but was too scared to share it with them.

"I'll be in trouble if I tell you. She is very powerful, please, just take what you want and leave."

Oliver glanced at Alex, but he seemed to agree with him and looked determined to stay.

"Okay, here's what's going to happen," Alex stepped forward and added. "We have to meet her, and if you tell us everything you know about her, I promise that she won't know that we were here."

"No, you don't understand. She knows everything, she's everywhere! I just wanted to make a living, and provide for my family, but she has so much power, she's controlling the whole city." the guy looked up and turned to Oliver. "She is like acid poured into your eyes, burning into your skin, and filling your lungs with a sour breath. You can't say no to her, she destroys you if you object."

Oliver and Alex just stared at the guy, who a few minutes ago had been so cocky and confident but suddenly went from Mr. Tough Guy to a shivering chihuahua in no time, at the mere mention of this woman's name.

So, Alex, being the diplomat here, decided to have a little chat. He grabbed a chair and sat down next to the guy. "Okay, my name is Alex, and this is Oliver. We're on a mission to save the world from the pandemic, but it seems this powerful lady is the missing link and we need to track her down. We get it; she's got some serious power vibes going on, but do you know what? That's exactly why we need to meet her. Do you understand?"

The guy was hesitant, like he was considering his life choices at this point. He glanced at his son's terrified face, then he slowly sighed and nodded. "My name is Zahir, and my son is Amir. This whole mess cost me everything and everyone, my wife, my family, the whole shebang. Only Amir survived the madness. We're just trying to stay alive. Since the pandemic started, everyone seemed to disappear one by one. Just a handful of people still come here for food and water, and one day, this lady - I recognized her from TV, and let me tell you, she's even scarier in person, like Shiva the destroyer - she strolls in. She wanted a few things, but then she asked me to deliver them to her place. When I refused, her smooth talk turned blunt, and her words felt like poison-tipped darts."

Alex raised an eyebrow and leaned in. "So, you've got the address where she lives?" Alex asked with a glimmer of hope in his eyes.

Zahir winced and lowered his voice. "Nah, she lives in her office now. That's the snag - I've got to deliver everything there. Amir needs to go there like a pizza delivery guy, nearly every other day." Zahir explained.

Oliver looked at Amir, the young guy, and noticed that his hand was shaking. "Amir, we're the good guys. You don't need to be scared. Just tell us what you know about her, okay?"

Amir glanced at his father to gather courage before he started speaking. "Well, I knock on her store window when I drop off her stuff. It's like our secret 'I'm here' signal, and she opens the door, grabs the bags, and pays up. But that's it. That's all I know."

Alex leaned back, raising an eyebrow again. "So, you've never been in her office? Have you ever seen anyone else there? Are any henchmen, or sidekicks with her? People in her office? Somebody working with her?" he inquired, trying to squeeze out more intel.

Amir shook his head, "Nope, not a soul. I've never seen anyone; she doesn't allow me to step in. But there must be, I take enough food for an army," he replied, his voice quivering with fear.

Alex appeared quite frustrated as he glanced over at Oliver. How in the world could they gather any useful information about this woman if she never leaves her office? But there was something else on his mind also. Who were these two guys, and why weren't they affected by whatever was causing this chaos?

"Zahir, can you tell me if you have a medal or amulet that looks like mine?" Alex asked, pulling out his dodecahedron to show it to both of them.

They examined it closely, but it didn't seem to be familiar, and Zahir just shook his head, "No, I've never seen one like it. But it does resemble the one that lady wears."

Alex got up and walked over to Zahir. "Please, give me your hand; I need to check something."

A bit bewildered, Zahir extended his hand to Alex and began to smile. "You're definitely here to help. I can sense it. Your hand feels like soap, bitter and calm."

"That's the strangest thing that anyone ever told me." Alex laughed. "What do you mean, 'bitter soap'?"

"You're the complete exact opposite of that lady. You give off an aura like bitter soap, although I can't explain it any better," Zahir replied, furrowing his brow.

Alex scratched his head and chuckled. "Well, Zahir, that's certainly a unique way to put it. I suppose being the opposite of this lady isn't such a bad thing."

Oliver chimed in, his usual sarcasm intact. "Yeah, I mean, who wants to smell like a ruthless and poisonous politician when you can have the fragrant aroma of bitter soap?"

Zahir's son, Amir, couldn't help but smile at their light-hearted banter amidst the tension, but his voice still carried a hint of fear. "Well, it's good to see you guys can laugh in a situation like this. But that woman... she's no joke."

Alex's smile faded as he turned back, "You're right, Amir. We need to find a way to get close to her. You must've been really brave, dealing with her. We'll make sure to protect you and your father as best we can."

As they continued discussing their next steps, an idea began to take shape in Alex's mind. He believed that if they couldn't go directly to Debby, they might be able to bait her into a meeting. But they needed a plan and a convincing reason for her to see them.

Maya, who had been waiting in the car, suddenly burst through the door of the stockroom, her face a mix of concern and excitement. "Guys, you won't believe what just happened!" she exclaimed, catching her breath.

Alex and Oliver turned their attention to her, their curiosity piqued by the surprise in her voice. "Maya, what's going on?" Alex asked.

"I was sitting in the car, keeping an eye on things, when I saw someone heading toward the shop," Maya explained. "I thought it might be her, Debby Abrams."

Oliver raised an eyebrow. "And was it her?"

Maya nodded. "Yes, it was. She was dressed in all black and had a couple of bodyguards with her. As I watched Debby come closer, I couldn't help but wonder how she found out so quickly that we are here."

"I told you!" Zahir interjected with anger and fear in his voice. "She knows everything!"

Maya looked at the two strangers a bit surprised, but then continued, "She just stopped beside the car and peered inside as if she was trying to find out if I was alone. I had to make a quick decision, so I rolled down the window and asked if she could help me find the way. She seemed a bit suspicious, but it appeared she already knew that we were here and was waiting for us."

Alex pondered for a moment. "Waiting for us?"

"Yes, she came with those guys to check where we were. So, I got out of the car to talk to her, and that's when I noticed a bandage on her arm. I asked if I could have a look and heal her, and she agreed without hesitation."

Oliver's eyes lit up. "She sounds like a friendly kitten. Something is off."

Maya continued, "No, she's anything but friendly, more like a wildcat.

But I touched her, and I could sense that she needs us. She told me to call you."

"This must be a trap," Alex chimed in. "I can't imagine that we just walk into her office, and she'll be waiting for us with open arms."

"No," Maya added, "I saw what she wants—the Metatron's cube. She'd do anything for that cube; she's obsessed with it, but she's terrified of opening it."

"Open it? She knows about my cube?" Alex looked shocked. "How is that even possible?"

"I told you, but no one listens to me!" Zahir interrupted again in an annoying high-pitched tone, sounding like a child.

"Is she still outside?" Alex asked.

"No, they left. She wants us to go to her office." Maya replied.

Alex and Oliver exchanged an annoyed glance, but both of them stood up, understanding that it was time to go. Maya led the way out, nimbly slipping through the hidden gate of the counter. Alex couldn't help but mutter, "Oh, come on... Don't tell me we've gone all 'Mission Impossible' again when I could've just lifted the counter flap. Brilliant..."

He then turned to Oliver and continued, "By the way, it was a tad reckless to fight against two men with loaded guns, don't you think?"

Oliver gave him a sly smile and replied, "I knew only the older guy had a gun; there was just one gun click!"

27

Debby's office, hidden away in the heart of Boston, concealed its intriguing secrets behind a facade of normalcy. From the outside, it might have seemed like another retro-style lawyer's establishment nestled on the ground floor of a towering building, just behind the Victorian grandeur of Old City Hall. The quaint establishment was ensconced in a narrow alley, sandwiched between its neighbouring properties—an abandoned laundromat and a shuttered coffee shop.

As you approached, the weathered glass window shop bore the faint traces of past business signs, silent witnesses to the passage of time. Peering inside, curious eyes would catch glimpses of a few chairs, arranged around a spacious table, and a pair of cluttered cupboards, their shelves groaning under the weight of countless paper stacks and an enormous printer.

When Alex knocked on the door, a figure emerged from the shadows in the back to open the door. "Well, hello. I see that you've finally made up your mind. Come on in," Debby greeted them as she popped her head out to inspect the group.

Her beautifully styled grey hair framed her mature face perfectly. She was one of those who won the genetic lottery, and the iron teeth of time couldn't seem to find a grip on her to do much harm. As the saying goes, beauty is like a well-maintained ship. It can take you to far places and serve you well for a long time.

As they entered, Alex began politely, "It's really kind of you to invite us he..." However, as the door shut behind them, the atmosphere quickly shifted. Debby's intense gaze and a suffocating pressure gripped his throat from the inside, making it impossible to speak.

"I know who you are and what you want," Debby declared in a commanding voice, her expression growing more severe. "I would appreciate it if you don't try to waste my time, and we get straight to the point. Am I clear?"

The team attempted to respond, but they couldn't muster more than nods. Debby's presence had rendered them breathless, their lungs strained by a painful oppressive force.

"What I am about to show you is my gesture of goodwill, but let's not misunderstand me. I can crush you like tiny bugs if you don't follow my instructions," Debby continued, then began walking toward the left wall, just beside a filing cabinet, behind a table. "Follow me and concentrate only on what I tell you."

She suddenly walked right through the wall, leaving the team astonished. Although the intense pressure on their chests dissipated as Debby disappeared, the shock of witnessing someone walk through a solid wall left them breathless and bewildered.

"Come on, we don't have all day!" Debby's voice echoed from the next room, which was supposed to belong to the laundromat they had seen from outside, right next to her office.

They exchanged awe-filled and puzzled glances, then decided to follow Debby through the cabinet. The seemingly solid material turned out to be illusive, almost like mist or fluffy air.

"This is really cool," Alex exclaimed. "I bet it's a hologram, right?" he asked with an admiring smile as they joined Debby on the other side.

Debby gave a slight grimace. "I expected a bit more from a time-traveling magician. It's a far more complex technology from the future, using a type of aerogel, but okay, for your sake, you can think of it as a hologram."

The interior of this place was akin to stepping into a spaceship. It was entirely composed of plain stainless steel and white marble. Nothing about it bore any resemblance to a laundromat, as it appeared from the street. As Debby briskly advanced, a sliding door in the centre of the room slid open to reveal a vast hall filled with glass-walled rooms. Inside, the spaces were packed with high-tech machines and equipment. The group exchanged curious glances with the people working there, some clad in white medical coats and others in black security uniforms.

"It's intriguing," Alex mumbled, his eyes scanning the room filled with people seemingly unaffected by the pandemic. "I don't understand. Are all these people Gatekeepers?"

Debby replied in a casual tone, "We've been working on this project for decades, gathering nearly everyone with connections to the ancient tribes of Hydrons. The projection you saw from the outside is somewhat useless now, but it served its purpose by allowing us to blend in, maintain a low profile, and safeguard the anonymity of the people working here."

"And you project this hologram onto the window? What if someone just walks in?" Alex asked with curiosity.

"When you entered, the system scanned your DNA, adding your biochemical details to the security system, allowing you to see what lies beyond the projection," Debby explained. "Reality is what your brain can comprehend."

"So, someone comes in to do their laundry, and if they're Gatekeepers, they see another room. But if not, they just see the washing machines... Very clever," Oliver chimed in.

"Again, it's a bit more complicated, but you get the idea," Debby continued, her voice tinged with annoyance as she walked toward the glass rooms at the end of the corridor. "Not everyone here is a Gatekeeper. We've developed a treatment that slows down the effects of the pandemic, but it only works about 20% of the time."

"20%? I wouldn't call it a cure," Maya began, joining the conversation after her initial surprise.

"That's precisely why you're here, isn't it?" Debby replied. "You want to stop the pandemic. So, show me what you've got," and as she reached the elevator, she firmly pressed the button before stepping inside.

As the elevator stopped, the door opened into a vast room, reminiscent of the Oval Office in the White House but five times larger. "Please, make yourselves comfortable," Debby said. "If you're hungry, I can have something brought from Zahir. You've already met him and his son, I assume."

"It was just a coincidence that we went into his shop; he doesn't know anything!" Alex explained.

"I know. Only the spices keep them alive," she added in a cold tone.

"Spices?" Maya looked surprised. "What do you mean?"

"Well, he's not a Gatekeeper, as you probably know by now, but there are countless different spices from around the world in his shop, and something keeps him energized. It's kind of an enigma, and our team is working on it, but at this point, we're still just trying to analyse what it could be exactly. With other people, mostly, we use lactated Ringer's IV drips with dextrose to slow down dehydration."

The team exchanged glances, realizing that this was exactly what Olivia was giving to her father. It all made sense now.

"Debby, sorry to interrupt, but if you have all these people working for you and you have the solution, why do you need us?" Alex leaned forward, a hint of concern in his expression.

"Good question. Let me show you something," Debby replied, walking up to a huge cabinet and opening it. "Come and have a look."

The shelves were crammed with carefully crafted Polybius amulets and medals in various metals and finishes, representing every Platonic solid possible.

"My God, it's my father's original four-pointed star medal. Where did you get that?" Maya cried out, nearly on the brink of tears, as she picked up the octahedron from among piles of other solids, all arranged by elements.

"I'm sorry, darling. He passed away almost ten years ago in a car accident with your mother. Please accept my deepest sympathy. So, what I was saying..."

"Wait, what?" Maya shouted. "You're telling me this now, casually? You knew, and you didn't even think you should have told me earlier?"

"Darling, let me be bluntly honest with you. I don't have the luxury of time nor the crayons to simplify this for you, so listen carefully," Debby began, her voice a blend of anger and frustration. "I'm not here to coddle your emotions. You abandoned your parents and neglected them for decades, to live your pathetic fantasy that you could somehow change that lowlife boyfriend of yours, who, by the way, cheated on you with every single person in town. Your escapade is a remarkable exercise in questionable judgment, and I don't think I'm the one who should apologize for making the wrong decisions in life."

Maya's expression twisted with rage and anger. "How dare you talk to me like..." But she couldn't finish the sentence; her voice faded, her lungs devoid of air, and her lips slowly turned purple.

"I will not tell you again. I am not here to care for your problems. You'd better pull yourself together, or I don't need you here," Debby exclaimed, seeming to have Maya in her grip, somehow using her power.

"Wait, wait. Everybody, just calm down," Alex interjected, jumping between them. "We're not here to fight. We have a mission, and we need to put our differences behind us. Both of you, please!"

Debby's gaze softened, and immediately, Maya started to breathe again, gasping for air.

Alex managed to quell the fight, but when he looked at Oliver, he noticed his body was contorting, his face nearly unrecognizable. "Oliver, what's going on? Are you okay?" Alex asked with genuine worry in his voice.

"He's transforming soon," Debby chimed in. "We'd better lock him down for tonight."

"What on earth are you talking about?" Alex retorted, casting a puzzled glance at Debby.

"I see. He didn't tell you," Debby said, arching her eyebrow. She walked over to Oliver and slowly raised his face with her hand, squeezing his chin in disdain. "He's a Conriocht, a shapeshifter."

"I don't understand a word you're saying," Alex replied, clearly confused by Debby's statement.

"He's a werewolf!" Debby exclaimed. "Like all his kind. What's so hard to understand about it? Tonight, we should keep him safe before he loses his mind completely. It will be a penumbral lunar eclipse, probably why he looks so out of shape."

This was the last drop in Alex's glass of patience. He collapsed on the couch, shoulders slumped, leaning back. In his mind, everything felt like it was falling apart. The solid ground he had wanted to build for this whole mission was the strengths of the team, the other Gatekeepers. But as he looked around, Maya was crying uncontrollably, tears welling up like a little girl, and Oliver was shaking with an expression like he'd just thrown up after drinking six Jager Subs in a row at the local pub.

How could he possibly gather the team and convince Debby when their powers were so fragile, like a house of cards? Countless thoughts swirled in his mind, each painting a bleaker and bleaker picture of what might happen. How had his grandfather managed to do this on his own? It seemed impossible. As Alex looked down, he fished out his medal and tightly gripped it in his hand, trying to remember the kind old man, Arion, and his words: "The whole universe is in your hand now."

28

Suddenly, the air grew heavy with the mingling scents of salty sea breezes and exotic spices, carried on the winds toward Alex. The warmth of the sun on his skin was familiar, but as he opened his eyes, he was surrounded by a wild manifestation of an ancient, unknown world that he could not fathom. The Sun's rays played on turquoise waters in the distance, casting shimmering reflections on worn cobblestone paths. Bewildered and captivated, Alex stood there, feeling lost and confused in this strange place.

A mysterious figure slowly emerged from the mirage of the path. Draped in flowing white robes and donning leather sandals, his dark brown hair and thick beard danced with the ever-changing wind. He exuded an aura of otherworldly power, commanding attention with his very presence. Alex's curiosity couldn't resist the pull of this captivating figure, and he turned toward the man as he approached.

The stranger's gaze was intense and sharp as he scrutinized every detail of Alex with a hint of disbelief.

"Hi, my name is Alex," he tried to introduce himself, but the man instinctively stepped back in fear upon hearing the unfamiliar words. Alex smiled and pointed at himself, repeating, "Alex."

The man seemed to be trying to process these strange words and hesitantly echoed, "Alex. Alexandros?"

"Yes, Alexandros, that's me," Alex said, pointing to himself again with a big smile.

The man also pointed to himself and smiled kindly, "Simon. Simon o magus."

"Magus? Magic?" Alex attempted to repeat the words, wanting to ensure he understood correctly. To his surprise, the man nodded in agreement. "This is unbelievable; I'm a magician too! Magus, that's me." Alex declared, pointing to himself once more.

Simon raised his arm high into the sky and then pointed it down at the ground, his eyes fixed on Alex, brimming with curiosity. He uttered words in an unfamiliar dialect, "Pothen ei?" However, no answer came from Alex, only a puzzled expression on his face.

Seeing that Alex couldn't grasp his words, Simon went down on his knees and began to draw with great haste in the dusty soil at the side of the path. At first, he sketched lines and circles, speaking in a language that sounded like some Greek dialect, but nothing seemed to make any sense for Alex. Yet, as Simon continued to draw with his finger, he invited Alex to join him and began to outline a map that stretched from Italy through Greece, Egypt, and all the way up to England. Alex pointed to the middle "Rome," recognizing it on the map.

This familiarity seemed to encourage Simon, and he placed small pebbles on the sketch in the dust, naming cities like "Athenai," "Babylon," and "Alexandreia." Then, he pointed to a dot in the middle of it all, saying, "Tyros." He lifted his hand and gestured toward a city not too far in the distance.

"Tyros? Wow, okay. I wish I had paid more attention in geography class. I still have no idea where we are," Alex scratched his head embarrassed, then continued drawing on Simon's map, pointing to England and himself. "Me. Here. England, London. Ahh, wait, what am I doing? Maybe London doesn't even exist yet."

Simon regarded Alex with a curious and kind smile. He then stood up and waved for Alex to follow him. With big sweeping hand movements and loud, repetitive mumblings in his strange dialect, slowly Simon's white robe began to sway as if caught in a gust of wind. But as Alex looked closer, he realized that Simon's leg was in the air, and he was levitating like a majestic kite, poised for flight in the sky.

At first, Alex thought that he had probably fallen asleep on the couch or that Oliver had slapped him again for some morbid amusement and that he would wake up any minute now, but everything around him seemed all too vividly real. The fresh air, the warmth of the sun on his skin, the unusual scent of the citrus mixing with the earthy musky smell of sweat —it all felt oddly familiar.

Simon extended his hand, silently inviting Alex to join him. Somehow it was natural but as they touched, something extraordinary happened. They were encompassed in an invisible bubble, almost hidden from outside view, but as Alex stepped closer to Simon, a magical view slowly opened up around them. It was as if his eyes had become magnifying lenses, revealing a hidden reality.

The sky, the ground, the trees, and the water all became nearly transparent, and millions of tiny particles seemed to connect with one another, dancing in front of him in a mysterious and mesmerizing rhythm. It was as though the materials comprising everything around them unravelled, revealing the intricate, microscopic components hidden within. Alex could see the captivating colours of atoms and feel the resonating, humming energy that permeated the physical world, as if it were a web of flowing vibrations.

"This must be it," Alex exclaimed. "The matrix of energy."

However, when he tried to look at Simon's smiling face beside him, suddenly he was struck with fear. It wasn't just Simon who met his gaze, but there were all of them. All of his existence spans through past, present, and future generations, and across countless dimensions. The thousands of years of long-gone ancestors' faces mixed with every single potential future form he will be. At one point and time, yet in a chaotic and infinite shape-shifting convergence.

Alex's mind struggled to comprehend the overwhelming sight, which seemed to defy all logic. The sheer intensity of the energy just wanted to burst his head wide open. Sensing his distress, Simon gently slowed his movements, allowing them to descend to the ground. As the transparent bubble dissolved around them, Alex started to feel better, and looked around hesitantly, wondering where the surreal vision disappeared. However, everything was the same as before—the same landscape, the same sun, and even the same musky armpit smell.

Simon kindly embraced him, but gosh, that was not a good move. It was an even stronger reminder that this was indeed reality, and Alex found himself in the python grip of a brilliant, genius magician with very loose hygienic standards.

"Yes, thank you, thank you," Alex managed to extricate himself and took a step back, desperate for a breath of fresh air. "It was amazing, and I can't thank you enough for this journey, but I must go now. I'm sure my friends are sick with worry," and quickly he retrieved his medal from under his t-shirt.

"Dodekaedro tou Platona!" Simon exclaimed, nodding in front of Alex as a sign of admiration.

"Yes, Plato's dodecahedron. My grandfather gave… Wait, why do I even bother to say this?" Alex started to explain, but quickly realized the futility of it. "You don't understand a word I'm saying, do you? Anyway, I need to get out of here… It was lovely to meet you. Goodbye, my friend," he muttered, closing his eyes, and gripping the medal tightly.

After a few seconds, Alex felt a gentle tap on his shoulder and opened his eyes shyly. To his surprise he was greeted by a confused expression on Simon's face as he was still there looking at him.

"Ha, something's wrong. Maybe I didn't concentrate hard enough. Sorry, let me try again," Alex muttered. He pressed the medal even harder against his chest and took a deep breath, attempting to repeat his grandfather's words.

A gentle breeze touched his face, carrying a fresh scent of a slightly sweet, woody aroma, resembling Chanel No5. Definitely a luxurious upgrade from the stinky armpit. Yet the firm clutch still held him, cradling him tightly in a friendly grip. Alex tried to pry the hands away as he opened his eyes. "That was enough. Please, I must leave now. Let me go," he said, slightly frustrated. But when he looked, it wasn't Simon, but Debby who held him, her expression shocked, as if she'd just seen a ghost.

"Ah, you're back. Sorry, I was just hugging Helen." Debby explained, pushing Alex away with a hint of embarrassment. "Well, I must admit, you exceeded my wildest expectations, Alex. And I should thank you for the gift."

"G...gift? What gift?" Alex asked, looking around the room with a puzzled look, and exchanging worried glances with Oliver, who seemed to be slowly recovering on the couch, and Maya, who was less upset but now appeared genuinely concerned, probably because of the whole Houdini trick.

"Helen! You switched with Helen, the consort of Simon Magus." Debby explained, her eyes ablaze with excitement. "The reincarnation of the first female deity. She was here, speaking with me," she smiled with a victorious expression.

Alex stood still for a moment, as he tried to wrap his head around the situation. He kind of started to slowly pin things together in his mind like constructing a puzzle, brick by brick, from the moment he remembered his grandfather and touched the medal. It was clear that he must have accidentally travelled again and swapped places with this Helen.

While he was with Simon, Helen came here and spent time with Debby and the rest of the team. But wait, why Simon and Helen? Where did this come from? Why not his grandfather, Arion? There had to be a logical reason, a rational explanation, even though at this point, it all seemed to make no sense whatsoever.

29

Debby's face radiated happiness as she looked at Alex. "I bet it was challenging for you as well to converse with Simon. Nonetheless, I managed to gather most of what Helen was saying. She used this incredibly old and obscure Greek dialect; one I've never heard before. It must've sounded like Shakespeare in Greek after two thousand years," she mused, her gaze drifting off into the distance. "This woman! She's the most powerful being I've ever witnessed. I must thank you, Alex! It was truly inspiring and enlightening to meet her. She explained so much about us, helping us understand the true purpose of the Gatekeepers."

"Really?!?" Alex added, feeling pretty disappointed and rather useless after comparing his encounter with some hobo shaman, with whom he couldn't even exchange a full sentence, just drawing in the dust like two infants in the daycare. "Well, it seems like everything went just as I planned," he continued with a straight face, trying to hide his failed attempt with his best weapon in hand - the desperate display of confidence.

"Helen said that she was just going to meet Simon to convince him to be baptized by Philip in Samaria, so they could begin spreading the word of the new order and share the knowledge of the Gatekeepers…"

"Debby, hold on," Maya interjected, with astonishment. "Are you talking about Philip the Evangelist from the New Testament?"

"Yes, right. Apologies, I was not translating for you guys." Debby replied. She turned to Oliver and Maya and continued to explain with fervent excitement, "Helen is—or was in every creation epic—the first manifestation of the supreme light, or what scientists today call the Big Bang. The founder of the material universe, the elements, and all the other deities and angels. They called her by different names in various religions, like Ennoia, Sophia, or Gaia, the one who came to Earth to bring salvation to humans through knowledge. Her and Simon's work in Gnosticism is even mentioned in the New Testament by the Apostles, but, of course, they're portrayed as treacherous charlatans. History has been written by the victors only, and the Catholic church prevailed over the Gnostics, so they painted them as villains in their story."

"Wait, so she is a Gatekeeper? But from which tribe?" Alex asked with a fascinated expression.

"No, she is not just a Gatekeeper; she's the mighty source itself. The mother of the Hydrons, who is trying to protect them and us humans, because we carry them in their water form. She has the wisdom and profound knowledge above all, but throughout our male-dominated documented history, her importance has always been deliberately repressed. She was doomed ever since the male gods and rulers overturned the ancient primeval matriarchal religions, forcing people into a phallocentric, patriarchal worship of gods. Think about the eternal question, and you have the answer: which one comes first, the chicken or the egg?"

Alex was pretty confused as he glanced around. "But she is the mother of all the other gods, you just said. Do you mean that her own creatures turned against her?"

Debby casually waved her hand. "We are made in the image of the gods, and they fight, are jealous, and vengeful just like us. Don't forget, power corrupts, and absolute power corrupts absolutely. Gods, humans, we are all the same. Once we taste power, we want more and more."

"So, why does she want to protect us? Or does she just want her power back?" Alex asked with suspicion in his voice.

"Alex, I can only explain it to you. I can't understand it for you, okay?" Debby retorted with an annoyed voice. "Yes, she probably wants her power back, but nobody is perfect. As far as we care, she wants to save life on earth, unlike the Ouron, so that is the most important thing. And frankly, right now, it's our only chance."

"Ouron?" Maya snapped, looking shocked. "What Ouron? Who are they?"

"Darling, I might look old, but I wasn't there 13 billion years ago at the creation of the universe to give you an exact description. So, I can only tell you about the suspiciously similar myths, repeated in every ancient civilization. They all describe the beginning of time exactly the same way: Ouron was created as the counterpart of Helen, like Uranus was to Gaia in Hellenic religion, or Osiris to Isis in Egypt. And if we believe the myth about the severed genitals of Uranus and Osiris, we can understand why Ouron is so furious and would do anything to slaughter the Hydrons, whom Helen created to help her. Bottom line, Ouron wants revenge since they escaped and aims to bring back the primeval chaos by overtaking life on earth."

Oliver slowly pushed himself up on the couch, still looking rubbish, as he began to summarize Debby's monologue in a weary voice. "Okay, so we can expect anytime soon the full-time wrath of this bloke with a missing dick. It's like restarting the War of the Titans, Ragnarök with Thor, and Odin, and not to forget the infinite inferno of the apocalypse from the Book of Revelation, all at once. That's what coming our way if we don't stop the Ouron, correct? Did I miss something?"

"Ah, our wolf man is back. Glad that you managed to finally join our humble company," Debby remarked with a hint of condescension as she looked at Oliver, then continued, "In fact, we've been working for months on collecting and analysing samples from around the world. But sadly, we still don't know with full certainty what caused the pandemic in the first place. What we do know is that the water is changing at an alarming rate and losing its power because the Hydrons are dying. The truth is, we have maybe two or three more days before we all turn into vegetables."

Debby slowly closed the cabinet with the Polybius' amulets and sat down at her desk with a gloomy expression. "I have to admit that there's a possibility they are ill because they sense the arrival or the closeness of the Ouron. Even worse, if he's already here, his actual plan might be to watch our slow and painful extinction from the front row, rather than a quick vendetta. We can't be sure."

An eerie silence descended upon the room. It felt like a cold crypt, a catacomb where each person's name was meticulously etched into the walls, in beautiful distinctive gold capital letters, waiting for the inevitable moment. Not a matter of 'if,' but 'when.'

After a moment of processing this grim omen, Alex finally gathered his courage. "Debby, if you've been working on this for months with everything at your disposal – the medals, the people, the funds – and you couldn't find answers, what could we do? What do you want from us?" He looked directly into her eyes. "You can't expect me to just hand over the cube."

Debby laughed heartily. "Don't underestimate me, Alex. We've already collected more than enough artifacts. I don't need the cube," she retorted and slowly advanced towards Oliver. "Instead, you should rather ask this friend of yours why he joined your quest. Am I right, Conriocht? Did you tell them?" She leaned closer to Oliver, who was still shivering on the couch.

"Oliver, what is she talking about?" Alex looked at Oliver with a surprised expression, as if he had been caught stealing a chicken.

"She wants us to fight, don't you see? That's her plan!" Oliver exclaimed with a defensive tone, pointing at Debby.

"Ah, my plan?" Debby turned her gaze to Oliver. "Okay, so show me your cube then. Show me, damn it!" she shouted at the top of her lungs.

Debby's voice echoed through the room like a sudden thunderclap. Everyone flinched, and Maya, in her startlement, let out a small scream, clapping her hands to her mouth. "Oliver, just show her. We are here for you," Maya implored him, concern evident in her eyes.

"It must be a mistake," Alex interjected, quickly rising to his feet. "I know he has his medal."

"Really? Did you see it with your own eyes?" Debby inquired, her tone dark and suspicious.

"Of course, I've seen it. I was with this girl, Luna. She gave me Oliver's number, and then I met Oliver at the station, and we travelled… erm…" Alex unexpectedly stopped and slowly his face started changing as he continued. "At Olivia's place, only I showed my medal. You didn't take out yours. You just asked her for the sword. It was a little awkward."

"Hm… Well, you better ask, who is the real traitor here?" Debby replied, then turned around triumphantly, and walked back to her table as she continued. "Oliver lost his cube months ago. He wanted to come with you, Alex, so he could use you and travel with you."

"No, that's not possible. He came to help us, to stop the pandemic. Please, Oliver, tell her," Alex implored, turning to his friend.

"Sorry, Alex. She's right. I lost it the last time I changed. Somehow I must've dropped it."

"Even after thousands of years, and still no one put a pocket on that wolf-skin costume of yours? Ha, no wonder that you lost it," Debby scoffed.

"But I saw you take me to the dimension with your shield. You have your power! You leap like a tiger, or correction, apparently like a wolf. I don't understand!" Alex said with desperation in his eyes.

Debby replied instead of the silent, devastated Oliver and began to explain. "Alex, all Gatekeepers have the ability. Polybius only created the medals to enhance the power that was fading away after hundreds of thousands of years, and to store extra energy, like a battery or something. What do you think Gatekeepers were using before the medals? Hm? From the beginning of time, we had our tools. The staff of Moses, Thor's hammer, the rod of Asclepius, the sovereign's orb, swords, crowns, belts, you name it, not just medals. Once you inherit the knowledge and master the element of your tribe, you don't need the medal or tool, unless you're sick and need to heal yourself and recover."

"But why did you want to come with me, Oliver? Tell me!" Alex demanded anger in his voice.

Oliver lowered his gaze with shame. "I have to go back to find my father. I can't travel alone in time; I need your help."

"But why didn't you ask, Oliver? You should've just asked!" Alex retorted with a bitter, angry voice, feeling betrayed. "How can I trust you if you don't tell me anything? How can this work if we have secrets?"

"Leave him," Debby continued. "Alex, you need to understand something. This is not a game or some sort of gallant knighthood challenge. This is a war, and we are here to fight together, but we are not cut from the same cloth. Think of it more as Hermetism describes the universe. Do you know what Hermes Trismegistus meant with his quote, 'As above, so below'?"

Alex felt too exhausted to even bother thinking and just slumped into an armchair before responding to Debby. "Danel, my friend, you probably know him already, he mentioned this guy before, but I don't know exactly what you mean," he added, carefully avoiding mentioning the caduceus that Daniel bought online. Hm, honesty above all, right?

30

Debby pressed a button on the table, and a vibrant hologram emerged in the middle of the room. "Now, this is what a hologram looks like, for your information," she remarked casually and began to point out details in the images displayed before them. There were pictures of ancient writings on various tablets from Egypt and Mesopotamia, along with detailed illustrations from numerous medieval encyclopaedias. "Hermetism was based on drawing parallels between the microcosm and macrocosm. In other words, humans, and the Universe. Just as the Sun and the Moon affect the Earth, our souls and spirits affect our bodies. From the smallest particle in our world to the entire universe, including humans and gods, we are built the same likeness to each other."

Maya looked at Debby with an intrigued expression. "Just like the Bible says: 'God created mankind in His own image'."

Debby nodded in agreement. "Precisely. The blueprint is just a copy-paste but scaled infinitely. People in ancient times might not have known about quantum physics or subatomic particles, but they believed that physical materials were composed of tiny atoms, just as our bodies are made up of organs, stars and planets build galaxies, and galaxies build the universe. 'As above, so below,' as Hermes Trismegistus put it."

Alex watched the hologram images intently, his brows furrowing in concentration. "Yes, I get it. The Fibonacci spiral in a sunflower and the shape of a galaxy, the fractal patterns in a tree's branches, or the connections between the brain's neurons and the expanding universe. But what does this have to do with us and the Hydrons?"

"Thousands of years have passed till we were able to prove their theories," Debby continued. "But those ancient philosophers were actually right! And soon, we discovered that these atoms are composed of even smaller subatomic particles: protons, electrons, and neutrons. Strangely, they assemble in the same way as our society's smallest units, families—a female positive proton, a male negative electron, and children, neutrons, connected around the proton. The more protons an element has, the more neutrons can bond to it, surrounding the protons in the nucleus as isotopes. Meanwhile, the electrons are constantly in motion, forming bonds with other atoms, creating larger, more complex elements or chemical compounds."

"So, you mean humans behave like the elements on the periodic table? That's a bit farfetched." Alex said, looking at Debby with a surprised expression.

"The concept of hermeticism refers to alchemy and astronomy, as Gods' magical power: ancient theology or universal knowledge," Debby explained, moving forward with the projection, displaying images as evidence for her statement. "Human families and atoms operate much like the tribes of the Hydrons. We, the Gatekeepers, are not equals, nor opposites, but rather the building blocks that create a delicate equilibrium. I understand it may sound absurd, but my point is that once you comprehend how the system works on a small scale, you can predict and establish balance on a larger scale as well."

"This is nonsense, just a theory." Alex remained sceptical, shaking his head in disbelief. "You're comparing creation myths to quantum physics and cosmology. It's like building a foundation based solely on the law of large numbers, cherry-picking statistics to fit your agenda. Of course, there will be similarities between forms and events if you analyse them within the frame of infinite time and space, but that doesn't mean they fundamentally operate in the same way." He replied pacing back and forth in the room, like a caged lion, his hand gestures reflecting his confusion.

"Alex, Debby has a valid point. Think about it," Oliver chimed in weakly, but seemed excited by the idea. "Magicians are the only Gatekeepers who can travel in time and space. Like electrons, they move around to create connections with other Gatekeepers."

Debby closed the hologram with a swift hand motion and walked closer to her desk. She paused and glanced back at Alex. "This isn't just a theory. If you're familiar with Occam's razor, you know that there is nothing random in nature. Everything happens for a reason, and the most simple and logical explanation is probably the correct one."

It's hard to argue with thousands of years of philosophers and spiritual leaders when they all seemed to point to a similar conclusion, while understanding the original meaning can be difficult sometimes, because they conveyed profound physical realities either symbolically, metaphorically, or even literally.

Imagine trying to explain life and existence using simple, kitchen language to people in the Stone Age 3.5 million years ago, who had no prior education, concept of writing, or complex language beyond words for food and body parts. Hmm, a bit like playing charades in a nursing home for people with dementia—not impossible but pretty challenging. So, you try to keep it simple, easy to understand, using common expressions like man and woman instead of attempting to explain the concepts of gender neutrality, non-binary, or transgender. Life itself is remarkably simple, but the human mind is not always able to grasp complex connections.

A common analogy often used to explain our limitations in understanding higher dimensions is that of Joe, a two-dimensional being peacefully living on a flat sheet of paper, when he suddenly hears a voice from the third dimension. Joe can perceive his world in two dimensions— left-right and forth-back—but no matter how hard he tries he can't fathom the third dimension above him, so he's thinking 'It must be God who's speaking to me.' Like us, we, as three-dimensional beings, are incapable of fully comprehending the fourth dimension, we can't see it, because from our world it's not visible.

You could say: 'But wait, we have our fourth dimension, it's time.' Well, where I am coming from, Einstein's theory of relativity is just one of dozens of others, and frankly, it's only applicable to this world's physics. Even quantum mechanics proves that using time as a fourth dimension is incorrect. Time doesn't quite fit the definition of a spatial dimension and can't be treated as a dimension, because it doesn't specify a point in space. The concept of time is life itself, the continuity of our existence. The infinite cycles of the seasons in the symbol of the curled-up snake that bites its own tail, the Ouroboros. If life were to vanish from Earth, time would cease to exist, but space would remain.

Can you now see why we're so utterly fragile and doomed? And how our huge problems about rising electricity bills, unending wars fuelled by politics and religions, and cheating husbands' shenanigans are so inconsequential. They are just insignificant, mere grains of sand on the boundless ocean shores of our existence. We are constantly fighting about life, for every aspect of our existence, money, love, and work, never truly appreciating the fact that we are here to create something precious. To leave a mark behind in time—a legacy in the form of a child, a sonnet, or a magnificent structure—for the next generation to build upon.

From simple words, we created the Tower of Babel. Out of envy, fear, and anger to confuse people's languages and make it easy to rule over them: divide and conquer. From simple life in Eden, we have needlessly complicated everything, pretending to explain the simplest truths until even scientists with four PhDs find them challenging to grasp, just to showcase our intellectual superiority over other human beings. With great innovations, things have become so complicated that we no longer know how to fix things anymore.

From the beginning of our civilization, we were capable of constructing beautiful palaces and embarked on expeditions to discover new continents. We haven't grown any smarter since or developed larger brains in the past few millennia; instead, we've just fragmented and divided our collective knowledge, making it more challenging to understand it as a whole. Fifty years ago, a man could build a house by himself, but now it requires two technicians to change a lightbulb—one to loosen it to the left and another to tighten it to the right—I'm not kidding. To change a spark plug you need a certified mechanic to open a car's bonnet, lest you void the warranty.

To be honest, we've reached a point where we expect everything to be so complicated that we don't even make an effort to address issues or attempt to fix things ourselves because we assume that they're beyond our capabilities. Whether it's our relationship, the intricacies of the legal system, or the complexities of tax regulations, we frequently opt for the path of least resistance, hoping to avoid becoming entangled in bureaucratic red tape or facing online shaming from complete strangers who have zero insight into our lives, just opinions on virtually every topic.

No wonder Alex had a hard time accepting the notion that just because you can't see or understand something clearly doesn't mean it's not there or can't be done. Sometimes you just need to believe that faith or destiny will show you a way how and what to do, and even if it's not to your immediate advantage, in a broader sense, it will support life.

Alex eventually slowed down and came to a halt, ending his nervous pacing in the room next to Oliver and Maya. His face became relaxed and he burst into a hearty and genuine laugh, leaving everyone in the room with baffled expressions.

"Did I say something funny?" Debby asked, her face showing a hint of annoyance.

Alex paused, wiping away the tears of laughter before responding, "Ha, sorry, no. I was just thinking that when I imagined this meeting with you, I had plenty of different scenarios in my mind. Scary, violent things. But I would've never expected that we'd be talking about couples therapy with you to save the world."

Debby replied with a tiny smirk in the corner of her lips, "I'm glad that you can see the funny side of the situation. The truth is that's exactly what we're going to do. But first, we need to prepare for tonight. Oliver has maybe a couple more hours before he turns into a full-blown aggressive furball," she added, glancing at Oliver's unrecognizable face, already showing big patches of uncanny hair on his forehead.

"Could I borrow one of the cubes from your collection, Debby?" Oliver asked in a weak, humble voice, gazing toward the cabinet.

"Oliver, you know it won't help. With or without the medal, you will change." Debby responded with surprising care in her voice. "I can only offer you a nice and cozy padded room for tonight, but I can't move the Moon out of Earth's shadow."

Maya moved closer to Oliver on the couch, gently leaned into him, and put a comforting arm around him. "We will be with you, don't worry."

"Darling, I seriously doubt that. Nobody wants to be there; I can guarantee you." Debby chimed in glancing at Oliver's unsettling expression as she picked up her bag, ready to leave. "We should go now. We take care of Oliver first and you two can stay at my place today, shall we?"

Alex and Maya helped up the precarious Oliver, carefully guiding him out of the room and back to the elevator. As they moved, Maya tried to catch a glimpse of Alex, her eyes seemingly wanting to convey something, but he was too busy checking out Debby's every move while she operated the elevator, pressing buttons on the panel.

As the door opened again the light turned on revealing a long, white corridor with dozens of unmarked doors, each without handles. Debby suddenly stopped in front of one of the seemingly random rooms. A beam of light scanned her face, and the door silently slid open, giving a glimpse of an empty chamber, which resembled a cell in an asylum for the mentally ill, with padded walls, and floor.

Debby turned to Oliver, her voice carrying a mix of concern and firmness. "Oliver, you know that we're doing this to protect you. We can't let you do something reckless tonight, but we'll be back for you tomorrow morning."

Seeing Oliver's struggle, Maya unwittingly started weeping, sensing the overwhelming multitude of thoughts racing through his mind. She felt the excruciating pain he was experiencing, as the agonizing fear coursed through her. It almost paralyzed her thoughts, leaving her unable to offer real comfort. Being an empath was a heavy burden, as it often meant physically feeling the pain and suffering of others, making it nearly impossible to separate the emotions of others from her own. Maya had lived through the world's misery, carrying everyone's cross on her heart.

She often felt this unbearable pain, as the hopeless fear surged through her mind after each interaction with people in need, while the unsettling images stuck inside her and became her own memories. As a little girl, she

172

often spent time alone, hiding in the school's bathroom just to avoid other kids. Every hug and friendly touch sent a wave of shock down her spine with terrifying pictures of abusive fathers' drunken, violent hands or unapologetic mothers' aggressive screaming outbursts over inexplicable issues.

After a while, she just unconsciously tried to stop herself from allowing people to get close to her. Kids often don't fully understand the world around them; they just live through the pain until they learn the reasons behind it. Not knowing the causes and why it happened they slowly build emotional walls and behaviours just to block the trigger.

Everyone needs to burn themselves to understand the fire; you can't explain the burning pain just by looking at the flame. But most of these scars of burnt and damaged wounds get buried deep in their unconscious little minds and stuck there as silent templates for future behaviours, influencing how they navigate the world and deal with pain.

Of course, Maya knew how blessed she was that her unique power brought comfort to others, but it couldn't diminish the effect it had on her. Over time, she had learned to treat people with gentle sympathy, but the deep scars never truly disappeared and remained in her mind as open wounds, constantly sprinkled with the salt of others' suffering.

They say, 'What doesn't kill you makes you stronger,' right? Apparently, she should have been a block of steel by now, but somehow every touch seemed to melt her heart over and over again. Just like when Prometheus, punished by Zeus for giving fire and knowledge to humanity, was chained to a rock, and an eagle was eating his regenerating liver, tormenting him endlessly every day for eternity, causing him never-ending suffering. It's a pretty nasty form of torture, and Maya willingly endured a similar agony to ease the pain of others like a saint.

As the door shut on Oliver's chamber, Alex extended his arms, offering solace to the crying Maya, who had suddenly collapsed in his embrace. Her body felt incredibly fragile, almost weightless, weakened from dehydration and exhaustion after the long days of travel, which had obviously taken a toll on her. Holding this delicate and beautiful creature so close to him, Alex couldn't help but feel an overwhelming urge to protect her. Gently, he scooped up Maya and cast a silent glance at Debby, gesturing for her to lead the way out of the building.

31

The morning seemed blissfully unaware of the harrowing night Oliver had endured, and it cheerfully ushered in a new week. The soft sunlight gradually filled the room, dispelling the dark shadows that lingered in the corners. Maya raised her head and rubbed her eyes in an attempt to wipe away the remnant haze of her dreams, and to her surprise, she found herself in a beautifully decorated, elegant bedroom.

She slowly scanned her surroundings, her gaze gradually focusing on a familiar figure, curled up on the floor, wrapped in blankets, laying in front of the door. She whispered in a hesitant voice, "Alex?"

The body on the floor stirred, and Alex's smiling face emerged from the blankets. "Hey, good morning. How are you feeling?" he replied as he stretched and tried to coax life back into his stiff limbs.

"Good morning. What happened, and where are we?" she asked, her voice still tinged with drowsiness.

"We had to get you an IV drip, and after Debby took us here, to her home," Alex explained, stifling a yawn as he pushed himself up from the floor. "You need to see this place; it's amazing! A Colombian drug lord's palace would look like a dirty ditch compared to this 'humble abode.' I'm telling you; she's loaded! I swear I saw at least three Van Goghs and a Picasso on the way in. Maybe two, couldn't tell for sure."

"IV drip? I can't remember," Maya mumbled with a confused look, her gaze drifting into the air as if she were sifting through the fragments of her memories.

Alex realized that Maya didn't really catch his monologue, so he added an explanation, "You fainted when we left Oliver."

"Oh my God, yes, I remember now. How is he?" she exclaimed, instantly jumping out of bed.

"I don't know. Not sure, but our first stop will be to the office to check on him. Don't worry; he'll be fine," Alex reassured her, though his face bore a familiar look of disappointment, yet again.

"And why did you sleep on the floor?" Maya paused and stared at the makeshift rabbit nest on the floor, where Alex had slept. "The bed is huge; you should've just slept there next to me."

Alex's heart skipped a beat, and a dry lump formed in his throat and stuck there like a stale chicken breast. He stammered, "Erm... I... was just thinking that you need to rest. And... it's better if I don't take up your energy so you can heal."

"Ahh, you know what, Alex? I don't even care. Next time, just use the bed. I promise that I won't bite you or climb on you. You shouldn't worry so much," Maya responded sharply, and her tone got a mix of anger and frustration as she continued. "Anyway, you're always so conceited with me. And frankly, I don't understand what I've ever done to you to deserve it. Like I'm so beneath you."

"Whaaat?" Alex retorted, feeling like he'd been hit by a freight train. He was having trouble even processing her words. His mouth moved like a talking fish in the tank before he finally managed to blurt out, "Conceited? Why?"

Maya was clearly upset as she added, "Yes, you always seem to disdain me. But I'm not sure why you're avoiding me like I have leprosy or aiming to steal something from you."

"Gosh, no. You're mistaken. Actually, it's quite the opposite. But I didn't want to bother you with my things."

"Your things? What are you talking about?" Maya's expression was a mix of annoyance and hesitation.

Alex was a little confused, "Wait, you must've known how I feel. You can read people's minds, right?"

"Well, yeah, intentions and emotions. But with you, I just feel a block, like you're pushing me away, but I can't figure out why." Maya replied, then quietly sat down on the corner of the bed and looked at Alex really befuddled.

"Wow, that's definitely not what I expected. I just wanted to give you a bit of space after you broke up with Boris. And every time I tried to come closer to you, something happened. But I thought you could see how I feel."

"You tried to come close to me?" Maya frowned, slightly in annoyance as she said, "When? You can't even stay in the same room with me, and always talking with somebody else. I remember in the hospital when we visited Maggi, for hours you didn't even look at me. Or in the car when you took me home, your hand was tapping on the steering wheel, just waiting impatiently for me to get out of the car. At that time, I was still thinking maybe I just came across as too pushy, you need time to get to know me. I even waited in front of the door for minutes, pretending to look for my keys, but you just nodded and drove away in haste. I mean, every time you just pushed me away and behaved like I was worth nothing!"

Alex arched his eyebrows as he contemplated the right answer, considering how he could explain the multitude of emotions he felt for her without looking like a total idiot. Yet, at the same time, he actually got surprisingly defensive by all the accusations thrown at his doorstep. "I didn't push you away. You were the one always saying it's not the right time and paying so much attention to everyone, especially Oliver. Of course, I just kept my distance to give you guys space."

Maya winced and responded with a resigned tone, "Fine, I appreciate it. At least now I know how you feel. Good!"

"Fine. Good," Alex retorted, feeling pretty silly, like he'd just won a battle but lost the war.

A sharp knock on the door interrupted their conversation, and Debby stepped in with a curious expression. "Hey, is everything all right? I heard noises. Are you guys ready? We should get going soon."

Maya replied with a polite but forced smile, "Yes, sorry Debby, could you please show me the bathroom? I just need to freshen up a bit."

"Of course, this way," Debby nodded and gestured to the other room across the hall.

Maya picked up her cardigan with a pouting expression, like an upset little girl, and stormed out. Debby just glanced back at Alex, wondering what the hell he could've said to her to make her so upset, then quickly followed Maya to show her the way to the bathroom.

As they walked down the hall, Maya's eyes marvelled at the luxurious satin wallpaper, the sophistication emanating from the apartment's classic design, and the carmine red carpet throughout the crisscrossing hallways, creating a unified and elegant ambiance. Debby's place looked more like the Metropolitan Museum during a gala dinner, complete with all the antique sculptures and paintings, rather than a typical living space. The bathroom, in particular, resembled a lavish jewellery box with golden embellishments, radiating and reflecting in the numerous mirrors throughout.

Debby sensed that something was up and tried her best to initiate a 'heart-to-heart' chat with Maya, "If you need a change of clothes or to remove that plaster-thick makeup from your face, just let me know."

Maya's eyes widened in shock at this blunt comment, and she replied with a somewhat huffish tone, "Hm, thanks, I'm fine." But she was clearly feeling a bit defensive.

"Darling, obviously not, so let me help you," Debby responded and opened the vanity drawers to take out some cosmetic jars. "So, anyway, what is going on with the tons of makeup, and this gruesome, sluttish dress? What are you trying to achieve with it? I don't get it."

"Excuse me? What are you talking about?" Maya retorted; her voice laced with indignation. However, as she caught a glimpse of herself in the mirror, a disconcerting image stared back at her after unconsciously sleeping with full makeup on. She panicked and hastily reached for the tap, desperate to wash off the remaining heavy eyeliner and mascara smudges, but it only seemed to worsen the situation as she frantically scrubbed her face. Slowly, her tears began to mingle with the water, a silent testimony to the emotional turmoil swirling within her. And despite her best efforts, the telltale redness in her eyes betrayed the turmoil she sought to conceal.

Debby took a step closer and handed Maya a towel to dry her face. "You don't need to hide behind layers of makeup," she gently added. "I'm sure you know that as a strong, independent woman it's always harder to survive in a man's world, but with your strength and beauty, you don't need to hide. You should embrace yourself instead! Be proud of it!"

Maya slowly stopped, and as she listened thoughtfully to Debby's words, she slumped into a chair, wiping away her tears with a stoic expression. "I'm just so tired of trying to fit in and please everyone, Debby. I feel like I am constantly walking on eggshells to be accepted by everyone, but no one seems to care who I am or what I really need."

"Of course, we care, darling. We all care about you. And that's why I am telling you now, that this has to stop. THIS WHOLE THING!" Debby theatrically circled her index finger in the air around Maya's sitting figure, with a strange grimace, "You're only setting yourself up for failure with this attitude."

Maya was still sniffling a little from crying as she glanced at Debby, "I don't understand what you mean."

"Look, darling, most people are not aware of this, but our role is crucial. We are the ones who make the decisions, and it is our job to run the world and keep it moving. NOT MEN! They may seek adventure, and fight wars, driven by their inflated egos, but they are only good for creating conflicts and leaving destruction in their wake! BUT WE, we're the ones who must pick up the fallen pieces, mend the wounds, and carry life forward. I understand that you long for appreciation, love, and recognition. BUT MY DEAR, you're barking up the wrong tree! You don't need to prove yourself to anyone," Debby said, her voice suddenly becoming gentle after her heated speech, as she reached out and touched Maya's cheek, "By lowering yourself, you won't become more lovable, just more accessible. Like the end piece of a loaf of bread. Everybody touches you, but no one wants you."

Debby's words struck a deep chord with Maya, and it was as if one swift movement opened a wound, revealing past traumas, buried beneath her seemingly peaceful demeanour. A pained sigh burst out from Maya, desperately seeking the right tone to explain all the hurt and struggle she was carrying within. But gradually her anger started to mix with a profound appreciation for Debby's honesty, somehow calming her response to a mere question, "But how can I ever be enough?"

"Maya, you are enough. You have the power to create everything you desire, and you don't need anyone's validation. PERIOD! And if someone cannot recognize your worth, it's not your responsibility to convince them." Debby responded with conviction and then jokingly added, "Don't forget, if you want to play chess with a pigeon, you have to be prepared for it to knock down all the pieces, shit all over the board, and then stroll around like it won the game."

Maya's tension seemed to fade, replaced by a heartfelt giggle as she remarked, "That's so true."

"Trust me, it's easier to win them over with food than common sense! You need to understand that we may not speak the same language as men, but we can accept our roles and learn to work together."

Maya sighed again deeply as she leaned back in her chair, her gaze empty and distant, "Ahh, Debby, I'm just so tired."

"I feel your pain, honey, don't worry. But first things first: You need to get rid of that awful makeup and dress. They're screaming desperate for attention, and you deserve better. Trust me on this one!"

Maya winced but managed a bitter smile, reluctantly acknowledging Debby's criticism. "Fine, I get it. Just give me a moment. I need some time alone."

Debby nodded in understanding and left Maya to absorb her candid words. Frankly, we've all found ourselves in this place at some point. There are times when you know exactly what you should do, what reality demands of you, but you opt to mask it with some lame excuse, hoping to deal with it later. Maybe it's just another layer of makeup to conceal dark circles, a well-hidden shapewear to tighten some loose bits, or a completely unreasonable splurge to max out the credit card when you're feeling down. But it's just a quick fix, until the problem inevitably resurfaces again, often hitting you in the face like a brick at the worst possible moment. We've all seen Bridget Jones's diary.

Life always gives you choices, and if you don't seize those opportunities, it will attempt to guide you back, with more and more 'subtle' hints. Perhaps it's about the job you should have taken, the city you ought to move to, or a simple apology call you should have made. But you resist, clinging to your comfort zone, and you stumble again. It's at this juncture that you might start wondering, "Why am I so unlucky with everything? Why can't I get anything right, with even the simplest things turning into a disaster?" It feels as though the entire world is conspiring against you.

This is the point where you need to pause, sit down, and question yourself. Why does it seem like life is hell-bent on beating the crap out of you? The answer is that you hushed that inner voice within you—the gut feeling, your sixth sense. It's never about the small, everyday mishaps that make you feel miserable and unlucky. The truth is that you should find the root cause of your problems because somewhere along the way you took a wrong turn, and you got on the wrong train in the wrong direction.

Humans can't go back and change their past choices. In this three-dimensional world, time follows a linear, one-way course. However, if you can't swim, it's not because the water is stupid. Simply, you just don't know any better in this particular space and time. The only way forward is to get off that train and embark on a journey to discover where you genuinely want to go: the right place, at the right time. Plain and simple.

32

The muffled static from the walkie-talkie echoed in the hallway when Maya stepped out of the bathroom. As she walked further towards the noise, towering security guards stepped in front of her to lead the way with an air of silent assurance, guiding Maya through the maze of the opulent mansion.

As they approached a heavy door, the taller security guard opened it with a courteous gesture, revealing a baronial sitting room where the other members of the team awaited. Maya's eyes swept across the room, taking in the luxurious surroundings, before settling on Debby, who began to explain the presence of the security guards.

"Sorry, Darling, I didn't mention before. I asked these gentlemen to look after us last night since we had to come to my place," Debby started, her gaze meeting Maya's questioning expression. "But we should really go now to the office to have breakfast. I'm seriously starving. You know, I can't keep any food here for obvious reasons."

Maya nodded understandingly; her gaze swept admiringly across the vast living room. In the midst of the luxurious surroundings, her eyes met with Alex's, who appeared to be sitting on pins and needles. The anticipation in his gaze suggested an eagerness to say something to her.

Without hesitation, Alex jumped up from the armchair, his hurried steps closing the distance between them. An uncertain smile played on his lips as he approached, a subtle mix of apology and hope etched on his face. It was as if he was wondering whether Maya might react with the ferocity of a praying mantis after the recent incident or respond with a more welcoming twinkle in her eyes.

"Perhaps first we can pick up Oliver from the office," Alex suggested cautiously. "Hopefully, he is in better shape by now."

"Oh yes, it doesn't last too long normally. He should be okay, just the transformation part is a bit scary," Debby continued, while she ushered them towards the exit. "But I'll tell you more on the way."

The three guards formed a protective barrier around the small group as they ventured into the quiet street. The leader, positioned at the forefront, skilfully navigated ahead, his communication flowing seamlessly through a discreet headpiece. His gestures signalled the group to follow, indicating a clear path through the urban landscape.

In the shadows behind, the other two guards maintained a watchful stance. Their discerning eyes scanned the surroundings for lurking threats, scrutinizing the dark alleys and the creaking doors of abandoned shops. Swift and agile, they responded to every rustle of plastic bags as they danced peacefully in the wind, while suspiciously keeping their right hands, strategically above their pockets.

As the group moved, Alex stepped closer to Debby, unable to contain his curiosity, "Debby, just a quick question. Are these guys also Gatekeepers?"

"Actually, yes. Otherwise, they would be useless, just like the rest of the population by now," Debby responded with a gloomy expression. "The only difference is that they didn't have the initiation, as we did. So, they don't have the power to use the medals, but they're more resistant to cosmic changes. Similar to Olivia."

"What?" Alex snapped in shock, "How do you know about her?"

Debby, wearing a sly grin, admitted, "Well, let's say we all have our tools. I may lack the ability to foresee the future or delve into minds like you guys, but I know how to wield the power of law and order. And no, I don't have eyes on the back of my head. So, when I need to know what's going on, the SFRS comes into play — the Worldwide Satellite Facial Recognition System."

"Excuse me, what? You can't see faces from a satellite," Alex interjected. "That's impossible!"

Debby, maintaining an air of nonchalance, explained, "Actually, yes. You can discern even a penny, whether it's heads or tails, in your hand from a satellite image. It's just encrypted for public use. Anyone around the world can be tracked down in 30 seconds, the moment they step out of their apartment. Correction: even when you're at home, but we don't need to delve into unnecessary details for now."

Maya and Alex looked at each other with horrified expressions.

"Oh, come on!" Debby, scoffing at their apparent disbelief, continued, "Don't tell me you thought I just get visions and figure out magically where to find people and what they're doing? Of course, we use technology! We're aware of Daniel and his partner, Olivia and her father, and every fiasco Oliver has been embroiled in for the past two decades. We keep an eye on people, checking what they're up to. No harm in looking at the menu if you don't order, right?"

Alex, raising a sceptical brow, retorted, "It's actually pretty alarming that you can just dig into people's personal lives without their knowledge and consent. I'm sure it violates personal privacy and goes against basic human rights, though I can't recite the specific paragraph."

Debby, undeterred, defended her stance. "You know, Alex, without our technology, we'd have no chance now to defeat this pandemic. People are always afraid to let the wolf in, but they're happy to pay a complete stranger a fortune in advance, to slay the dragon. It's nice to live in a fairytale and believe that a knight in shining armour gallops in, and saves the world with his trusty steed and servants—aka your little team. But in reality, you need resources. And this is what I bring to the table: unlimited data, insights, and connections. So, whether you like it or not, I'll do whatever it takes to secure these resources and make this happen. Even if you question the ethics of my methods."

As they reached the window of the laundromat, Debby halted abruptly. Turning to face Alex with unwavering determination, she added bluntly, "Don't forget, you might be a magician, but I own this circus," before stepping through the door. The weight of her words lingered in the air, leaving Alex and Maya to grapple with the unsettling truth of Debby's arsenal and the enigmatic circus that had become their reality.

On the way in, through the scanner and within the confines of the elevator, a thick silence enveloped the group. The air carried an unspoken weight, akin to the anticipation of having one's heart weighed at the final trial of moral justice in the presence of God's judgment.

Doing what is right and adhering to the law is not necessarily the same path, and this dichotomy hung in the air like a double-edged sword, dangerous to wield. It's a heroic job, definitely not fit for everyone, and it took a huge toll on Alex, far surpassing the complexity of merely stealing a car, bore down heavily.

Maya was seemingly more laid-back, as if balancing the considerations from both sides. Yet, beneath this calm exterior, her silence served as a shield, a means to bide her time until the charged atmosphere settled. Her true concern lay with Oliver, and her tension only grew as the elevator carried them closer to the chamber rooms.

As the light beam scanned Debby's face and the door slid open, an unimaginable scene awaited them. The room lay in ruins, wall paddings ripped apart, blood and torn cloth remnants scattered across the floor. Oliver sat quietly in a curled-up position at the far corner, wearing a timid expression, reminiscent of a little puppy on the first day in a shelter.

Maya, shocked, screamed, rushing to Oliver's side. She fell to her knees, embracing his bleeding shoulders without hesitation. "Oh my God, Oliver! What happened?"

Debby, with a frown, assessed the situation. "Wow, that's worse than I expected. I guess it's time to find you a medal from the cupboard. Let's go."

Alex picked up Oliver and helped him find his balance, but immediately noticed something peculiar. Somehow, Oliver seemed different—shrunk and lost all his muscles, looking more like your average Joe from Home Depot in the clearance section. "MAN, this transformation is still not complete. You look pretty shitty," he exclaimed.

"No, he's already back since 4 am. I saw him on the cameras. This is his normal form," Debby interrupted casually.

"What? Nooo! He's nothing like Oliver, at least a foot shorter and half his size. This can't be…!" Alex retorted.

"Well, actually yes. This is him, the real form. You are probably talking about his aura, what you saw when you met him," Debby continued.

Alex looked rather confused, glancing at Maya, seeking to get confirmation that something was wrong with Oliver, but even she stared back at him, looking puzzled about his hesitation.

"I remember Oliver. I saw him, we spent the last three days together nonstop, and this guy is not him! I'm telling you," Alex mumbled, still checking Oliver's calm and exhausted expression as he laid on his shoulder.

Debby swung open the door to her gigantic oval room, gesturing towards the couch for Oliver's repose. "Just let him rest for a couple more minutes, while I find that cube," she instructed, heading straight for the cupboard. As she searched, she continued her explanation, "What you saw reflects how you feel about him—admiration, intimidation, or maybe fear. Our immense strengths allow us to alter people's perceptions. In ancient times, they described us as giants, lions, flaming phoenix birds, or angels with wings and halos. It's all in your head. The energy we emit creates our aura, like a vibration map."

Maya's face lit up suddenly. "Exactly! This is what I see! When I touch somebody, I can see deeper: intentions and past events. But it's this aura around everybody that I can sense instantly, like a vision of a colourful bubble. It shows how they feel: when they are upset, scared, or exhausted, like a map, just as you said!"

Alex slumped into a large armchair, wearing a contemplative expression. "So, everything I saw was just my imagination? But then how did he jump over the counter, gates, and lift me up on his shield?"

"Hm, not exactly. Probably it all happened, but what you see and how it makes you feel depends on how you process it," Debby explained. "Your brain decides to see or ignore particular details to create a vision and form a memory. That's why animals puff up their fur, making them appear larger and more intimidating, like when you get goosebumps. Or changing colours during mating times to attract a suitable partner and show health and fertility, like chameleons, octopuses, or peacocks. It's all about showing self-confidence and vitality."

While still scanning the shelves, Debby suddenly halted and picked up a silver crucifix, made up of six identical square plates, that together formed a cross. "Hm, this is what I was looking for!" she exclaimed, folding the intricately decorated cross into a hollow cube, and placing it in Oliver's hand.

She signalled for Maya to assist her. "You make sure that he holds this tight in his hands until he gains back his strength. It's best if you sit close to him and allow the energy to flow between you."

"Hey, wait," Alex interjected. "Oliver will take Maya's power, but it makes her lose strength, you know what it means! He's going to take…"

"Thank you, Alex. I don't need you to mansplain how it works," Debby scoffed. "I know exactly that she will age, get wrinkles and grey hair in the process. I understand what it takes to heal someone, but if we get the energy from each other, the impact is way less intensive, literally insignificant. We can recharge each other with minimal energy loss in the process."

"Damn, why didn't anybody tell me that before?" Alex lamented, realizing how many opportunities he had already missed with Maya, due to his cautious politeness.

33

As Debby gracefully retreated, a faint mist began to emanate from Maya's hand, gently sinking into Oliver's arm. It hummed quietly, flowing between them, and creating a translucent bubble that seemed to envelop them in a delicate dance.

"Let them work, and in the meantime, we can discuss how to get Daniel here," Debby suggested, her gaze returning to Alex's disappointed expression.

"I don't think that's an option. Even if he could come here, he would never willingly walk in after what you did to him," Alex replied, his brow arched, conveying a sense of blame.

"Yeah, you're right. But that was like 40 years ago! Way before me," Debby said, acknowledging the weight of the situation. "Look, I had nothing to do with it. Things were different back then, still in the midst of the Cold War."

"Debby, you shouldn't try to convince me. Instead, tell him why the CIA or whatever organization you work for destroyed and tortured him, until he was bound to a wheelchair for a lifetime. I mean, if he even wants to listen to your side of the story," Alex remarked, shaking his head in disbelief. "I wouldn't, but you can try."

"Hm, you have a point. I should go there and talk to him myself and apologize. Back then, it really got out of hand, and things escalated quickly with certain unnecessary measures. But we definitely need him; he is the only one we know with an awakened sacral chakra."

"Sacral chakra? What does that have to do with tantric yoga and esoteric tradition? The five Platonic elements are different, nothing like the Buddhist seven chakras," Alex said, looking puzzled and struggling to grasp Debby's explanation.

"I know, it's a bit confusing. Not everything seems to align with our current view of the universe and the understanding of nature. But, as I told you, we should start from the small system and apply the template on a larger scale to find the pattern—from atoms to the universe," Debby explained with a simple smile. "For example, the five Chinese elements are based on the same principles as the Platonic solids, yet they focused on the generating interactions between the elements instead of the key attributes. Water is nothing like the ether in our minds, yet they are both represented by the planet Mercury, and both are said to create a soapy taste in your mouth, just as the negatively charged electrons of the pH base is creating the baking soda's bitter taste."

"Soapy taste? Funny you say that. In the shop, Zahir told me that my hand feels like bitter soap," Alex smirked.

"Of course, because you are a magician. Flowing like water in the ether, creating invisible connections between atoms to bind energy with gravity. That's why you are the only one who can travel in time and space," Debby explained. She then turned to Alex, locking eyes with him. "Do you know what your representation is in the Chinese elements? The black tortoise entwined with the snake. The heavy world turtle, fighting gravity, pictured together with the never-ending ouroboros snake, biting its own tail in time forever. A very apt analogy, don't you think?"

Alex sank deep into his thoughts as he listened to Debby, attempting to discern the parallels between various symbols and cultural beliefs, trying to carefully place each piece in its respective context. However, the complexity of the task overwhelmed him, and his mind gave up, pulling down the shatters: closed for business. It wasn't a blackout, just a hiatus from thinking, akin to opening the box in your head labelled 'Nothing.'

It doesn't mean you are doing nothing; your processor is simply overheated and needs time to calm down. Reading a book, washing dishes, watching the stars, or going fishing—everyone has this mental box, as a built-in feature to prevent brain overheating. It felt similar to when Alex travelled in that bubble with Simon Magus. His brain couldn't process any more information; the drive was overloaded.

Imagine life as a 3D Mario game, where we navigate through levels of challenges and growth. Picture it like playing on a cutting-edge video game console with a super realistic video card, where each level introduces new, ever-changing obstacles. You, the player, evolve with each experience, much like advancing through the game's increasingly complex stages.

Think about it – you've tackled the earlier levels countless times, and what once felt overwhelmingly difficult just a couple of days ago, now seems surprisingly manageable through your relentless practice.

In real life, there's no Super Mushroom, to grant us an extra life or shield us from additional hits. We're uncertain about our time limit for each level, and we never know when we might encounter a Boss Battle. That's when hitting the pause button becomes essential – a moment to reflect, recharge, and ground ourselves before bravely facing the challenges ahead, much like preparing to confront Bowser's castle in the game. Life, like Mario's adventure, is an epic journey of growth and resilience.

From the outside, Alex appeared quite ridiculous—a thousand-yard gaze with a blank resting bitch face. Eyes and mouth wide open, staring into the abyss, barely breathing, and no blinking. Kind of creepy.

"Alex, do you hear me?" Debby stepped closer, worried about his sudden zoned-out zombie gaze.

"Oh, yes, sorry, I was just thinking. Yes, you should apologize to Daniel. That's the only way."

"Hmm, okay. We already agreed on that. What's going on, Alex? Are you okay?" Debby inquired with genuine concern.

"Um, nothing, really. Probably just my brain trying to reboot from the last accessible point," he laughed wholeheartedly. "So, you said something about Daniel's chakra."

Debby continued, but her gaze remained on Alex, a slight worry lingering in her eyes. "Yes, so it's not about the per se tantric chakra opening, in the traditional meaning. It's more about the ability to channel higher energy with the knowledge inherited from his parents. That's not something you can just learn from a yoga class."

"Okay, so how do you plan to get back to England and meet him? Do you have a spare airplane? Because due to some unfortunate circumstances, I can't remember where we left ours the last time we got here," Alex quipped, tilting his head to catch a glance at Oliver, who was still peacefully resting in Maya's healing-session bubble.

"We can't waste more time going back and forth. We have to go there together, pick up Daniel, and figure out what to do next," Debby responded, lifting her shoulders in doubt, looking somewhat at one's wits' end.

"Ah, okay, so you have no plan either. Great! Marvelous," Alex exclaimed, slapping his hands on his lap.

"I don't appreciate your sarcasm!" Debby retorted. "It's not like we've ever met before. How should I instantly figure out what you are able to contribute, or, as a matter of fact, the others? We all need to dig deep into our pockets, put all our cards on the table, to see the pieces, what abilities we possess, before we can complete this puzzle."

"Yes, yes, sorry. It's true, you're right! I am just frustrated. I feel like I'm a fly on the wall, just waiting for the big hand from the air to splash me, not even knowing where I should expect the hit will come from."

"That's why we need to stick together," Debby reassured Alex with a pleasant touch on his shoulder, but suddenly a very sharp electric charge sparked between them.

"Ouch, you shocked me!" Debby exclaimed, looking stunned at Alex.

"Oh, sorry. Maybe my clothes got static?"

"Hm, I think it's more about the energy between us," Debby replied with a wondering expression.

"Ha-ha, you two looked like sparklers on the Christmas tree," Oliver chimed in on a weak voice, seemingly entertained by the visual effect.

"Welcome back! I'm glad you're feeling better, and see that apparently your humor is still intact," Debby snapped back at him.

"Hey pal, you're looking so much better!" Alex smiled, quickly going closer to give Oliver a big hug.

"Debby, I understand that you said it's just my imagination, but frankly, this guy looks way bigger than ten minutes ago, I swear," Alex giggled, poking Oliver's tree trunk-sized arms with his finger. "It can't be a hallucination."

"Okay, kids, enough playtime!" Debby exclaimed. "Quick food and then off we go. Our next stop is Daniel's place."

"Wait, Debby, just one quick question. Is this the cube the one I lost last year?" Oliver glanced at Debby with a somber expression.

"What if I just say that we found it? Would that satisfy your curiosity?" Debby responded, turning away quickly to call the elevator.

"Hm, okay. Fair enough," Oliver mumbled as he slowly emerged from the couch. "But I am going to have a couple more questions later, when I finally lose my night vision. I still can't see clearly; everything is so bright."

Maya gently offered him a hand to lean on, asking, "Oliver, what was this transformation all about? And why didn't you mention anything to us?" Her voice was gentle, while she seemed a bit dizzy herself from the healing.

Oliver lowered his head and began to explain in a shy voice, "I never had this strong urge before. Normally, I have my medal to control me, and it somewhat helps to keep my balance. But if I don't have the medal, once the transformation starts, I can't turn it back."

"Last night was a penumbral lunar eclipse," Debby began to explain, waving for the rest of the team to join her in the elevator. She continued as the door closed, "It was a really rare eclipse, and this is the most dangerous kind for him. Sometimes, three years go by without this phenomenon, but last year in May and yesterday, it happened just ten months apart. This type of eclipse means that the Earth only partially cast a shadow on the full moon, and this distorts the gravitational energy between the Moon and the Sun. The effect is unpredictable, especially if you can't shield yourself with your power."

"Debby, did you say last May? Oliver lost his medal last year in May, correct?" Alex looked around with a surprised expression. "I mean, it could be nothing, but wasn't that the time when the whole pandemic started?"

"Hmm, not likely. A penumbral eclipse is not a super-rare cosmic event, like a once-in-a-lifetime planetary alignment. Also, very unlikely that it was caused by Oliver's negligence of losing his medal, so not sure if it has any connection," Debby added with a hesitant expression.

Alex's face turned gloomy as he exclaimed, "It was just the following week after the Coronation weekend. I was at home one of the evenings, and I felt this... horrible pain. All the screaming and the visions. That's when it started! It was mid-May, last year."

The elevator door rolled open, paused, and then slowly closed again with a harsh clicking sound. But nobody moved, just stared at each other. It was literally possible to hear the little cog wheels in their heads turning backward, attempting to calculate the months and the days back in time. Then sudden realization cast a murderous rage on everyone's expression. Except Oliver.

"WHAAAT?!? Why are you looking at me? I didn't do anything. I mean..." Oliver got quiet and started to gaze up, rolling his eyes, as if he were seriously concentrating to recall what he was doing on that night when he lost his medal. He added, "No, I am pretty sure." Then, with an air of nonchalant ease, he pressed the opening button and walked out of the elevator, as if he just arrived at his coronation ceremony to greet his subjects.

A few seconds later, Maya and Debby followed him, shaking their heads and still contemplating in silence. But Alex's face remained frozen in despair, standing there like a salt statue. Only the repeated nudging of the closing doors on his arm forced him out eventually.

"I can make a call, to check again the video footage from that night,"

190

Debby turned back, with a wince on her face.

"I am going to kill you with my bare hands if this was you. I am bloody serious!" Alex rumbled furiously.

"Come on, guys! First of all, I was pretty much A-OK the next day... sort of. So, I doubt that I did any major damage," Oliver replied with a defensive tone. "Second, I was out, not myself. And third, until you have no proof, I expect you to treat me as innocent, so no blamestorming!"

"You piece of stupid meat-tower, I'm..." Alex yelled and started to run towards Oliver like a freight train when a sudden rush of flaming air pressed against him. Hot, dancing flames licked his face, and a hungrily crackling fiery circle reached out to push him away. He tried to stand still, but the force was so strong that he couldn't withstand the power, and he bounced back, like a wrecking ball against the metal wall.

In the middle of the roaring fire, a silhouette emerged, and Debby's voice shouted at him, "STOP RIGHT NOW!"

Alex got paralyzed from the shock, and his hand stopped in the air protectively. The burning circle suddenly seemed to shrink, and the heat of the inferno quickly calmed to a fading, sparkly flame in Debby's hand.

She had a surprised, swift glance at the group and firmly exclaimed, "We have five seconds to leave before the CO_2 suppression system shuts down the doors, and we're stuck here for 3 hours with no air. RUN!"

Panic burst out, and more and more people gathered, glancing around bewildered. Then the loudspeaker announced, "THIS IS NOT A DRILL. ALL LEAVE THE BUILDING IMMEDIATELY. I REPEAT, THIS IS NOT A DRILL." At that moment, everybody started to sprint towards the exits, and exactly at the same second, the safety alarm's sound blasted out, and massive fire doors descended steadily from the ceiling.

On the street, a small group of people gathered with unsettled expressions, all from the office, staring at the building. As she checked around, Debby received confirming nods from all the guards that everyone was out and well. Just then, she turned around to face the team and stated with slight embarrassment on her face, "This...! This never happened before with me. I am so genuinely sorry. Your magician presence seems to exponentially magnify my power."

"We were just leaving anyway," Oliver grinned like the Cheshire cat. Debby's eyes turned red, "YOU! You better shut your pie hole and listen carefully," she retorted to Oliver, then took a deep breath, and continued in a slightly more diplomatic tone, "Gentlemen, I won't tell you this again, so please pay close attention! I will allow you to work this out between you because, A, you're both amazing Gatekeepers with superpowers, and B, as for who gets killed first in your pathetic testosterone tantrum, I couldn't give the hairy ass of a rat's behind, but only after we're done. Got it? GOOD! Now, we can go."

34

It was difficult to recall memories of the old world, just a few months ago, still bustling and fighting for life. Now, it had surrendered its last hope and was barely existing. The water, once life-giving, had turned barren, offering no nourishment to nurture the earth or quench anyone's thirst. The worst part wasn't the dryness but the absence of life that once flourished, making it unbearable.

As the small group gathered on the street in front of the office, they resembled the last tiny drop of life in an ocean standing still. Looking at their faces, the desperation was impossible to miss. Each person had lost someone—family or friend—and they all knew their only hope lay with the few Gatekeepers standing there, fighting amongst themselves like crazed dogs.

Surrounded by these faces of despair, Alex and the team suddenly felt the rising urgency and the weight of their sole responsibility. Until now, it was all about their own fears, struggles, and self-doubts. But looking around and sensing the unspoken pain of these people, it cut deeper than any torture device could to the flesh. As they walked away in silence, the guilty shame weighed heavily on their shoulders.

Debby, the only one able to maintain her dignity somewhat intact, wasted no time arranging a pick-up with a direct flight to Bristol. In an hour, they were sitting on the plane, still speechless in silence, contemplating how childish and selfish their actions had been. As they ascended into the air, Debby finally joined them, sat down, and after taking a deep breath, began to explain, "We have a good chance that by 4 pm, we can land and get to Daniel in Bath around 5."

Nobody responded, they just cast their eyes downward. Debby got frustrated and continued, "Okay, I say it because nobody has the guts. We can't screw this up. So, no more fighting, arguing, or ego-trips. If we fail, it's over for life on this planet." She glanced around, leaned back in her seat, and then casually added, trying to change the subject, "We should've eaten. In a couple of hours, we could fall into a coma from dehydration. The only option left now is IV drips. So, everyone needs to get one at least every six hours, and Oliver, you need to help in the cockpit and pitch in with the pilots, to give them a break until they receive their ration. They are much weaker than us; not even sure if they would last three hours at a time."

Oliver nodded and stood up right away, "I better check now, see how they're feeling, and swap with one of them to start."

"Thank you, Oliver. That's generous of you. But before you go, I need to tell you something. Please sit down," Debby said, her expression suggesting that the news she wanted to share was of great importance. "We checked the video footage from the night in May when you disappeared. It was not you who caused the change; that is definite. You were spending the night in the forest near Trondheim, unconscious after hunting down a moose and passing out on the carcass, dead drunk. So, the mystery is solved."

Alex and Maya glanced with horror at Oliver, "Hunting a moose? Did you eat it?" Alex grimaced.

"Well, he's a werewolf, so most probably. But the main point is that he has nothing to do with the pandemic," Debby continued. "On the other hand, I think we have some possible explanations for what could have happened. The penumbral lunar eclipse on the fifth of May was followed by a solar conjunction with the planet Uranus on the ninth of May. At first, it seemed irrelevant, but we noticed that the gravitational forces were abrupt. At that time, we thought it was just an error, a malfunction in one of the observatory's superconducting gravimeters because none of the spring or laser-based devices detected any disturbance. But now, we ran the data again, and it is clear that only a rapid movement of a cosmic object with an enormous mass could have caused this temporary imbalance."

"Debby, but nothing happened since. Where is this object?" Alex asked with a puzzled expression, "We would already know if a comet or asteroid would enter our galaxy. We could see it."

"Yes, that is the point. If we could see it," Debby added with hesitation, "In the last hour, we contacted every scientist who is still able to work and collected any information that is available, but we still need to run some calculations. If the theory is correct, then sometime during the conjunction, just around the time of the eclipse, when the Sun reached the position between Uranus and the Earth, an unidentified object without visible mass entered our galaxy."

"Sorry, what do you mean by without visible mass?" Oliver was bewildered.

"Okay, I don't mean to paint the devil on the wall, and we still need to..."

"Yes, we got it, just spit it out!" Oliver snapped.

Debby shivered from Oliver's rumble, then glanced back at Alex, "Well, it's possible that there is a gravitational sink, a type of dark star that appeared out of nowhere."

"NO! Impossible. Do you mean a black hole?" Alex interjected, "It would already eat up the whole solar system. We wouldn't be alive!"

"I know, it's controversial, that is why I don't want to use the term: black hole." Debby answered in a calm tone, "The theory, as I mentioned, is that this is a black star, about the size of our Moon, a gravitational object composed of dark matter. And apparently, it's in a static phase, almost as if hiding behind Uranus, because in the past 10 months, not a single detector or device has shown any changes, besides that one night when Alex had those visions."

"It happened on Tuesday, the ninth of May, correct?" Alex looked at Debby with a wince on his face.

"Yes, you were right. What you were feeling that night was the gravitational wave caused by the dark matter." Debby replied, then added, "It's important to understand that our fundamental forces, what we know to exist and run our universe, have two types. One, whose effects can be seen in our everyday life, like gravity and electromagnetism. The other type is only applicable on subatomic distances, such as the weak force of radioactive decay, and the strong force which bonds together the atomic nuclei. But the science of physics has been long debating on the reason why the gravitational force has only one charge as direction, unlike all other three interactions, and why it's significantly weaker than all other forces. Yet, on a larger scale, it's able to hold the entire mass of the universe and determine the motions of planets and galaxies with seemingly limitless power, unlike anything that we could even imagine. The accepted explanation is that there must be another source of the gravitational energy with a huge attractive mass, which consists of invisible particles."

"Yes, I read about this before." Alex continued, seemingly intrigued by the topic, "They said that that's why Einstein's field equations can't be solved about the spacetime problem around two interacting massive objects. Like between the Earth and the Sun, or in a binary star system. Gravitation and light don't act like any other energy form. That is why they assume that visible mass constitutes only 5% of the universe, and the rest is made up of dark energy and other invisible particles."

"Precisely. I see, you know a lot about physics." Debby added with admiration, then she continued, "The ancient Greek Aristotle believed that the universe is made up of five elements. Four the classic terrestrial, and the fifth celestial type, called aether, a special weightless and incorruptible element, which fills up the whole universe and is responsible for the propagation of light and gravity. This unchangeable element was thought to be a pure quintessence that the gods breathed, and filling the space where they lived, unlike the air breathed by mortal humans."

Debby paused, and I could swear that I saw a tiny teardrop forming in her eye, but she shook it off and continued again on an acrimonious tone, "The worst part is, that since the beginning of time, all the teachings and knowledge have been here and accessible just at our fingertips, but even today, we are still struggling to grasp what they said and how to interpret it. People argue pathetically about the minute details, what is missing, and contradict these teachings and myths, trying to prove that our current civilization is so much superior. It's just so painfully frustrating."

After a couple of seconds of silence, Maya leaned closer to Debby with a comforting expression, "I can sense your anger, and I know how you feel. You know, when I was a child, I often complained about my strengths. I was upset and crying about why people can't understand what I am going through and how I felt. My father was a very smart man, and he told me a story to calm me down. It was about a world where all humans were kept as prisoners, chained inside a dark cave, facing a big wall. They have been there since birth and were unable to see anything other than the grey shadows projected on the wall. These shadows were their only reality, which were coming from behind the wall to cast light from the objects outside of the cave. One day, a brave soul escaped, and although at first, he was painfully blinded by the dazzling sun, his eyes eventually got used to the bright sunlight, and he discovered the true world that was surrounding him. He felt so happy; he wanted to share all these beautiful, colourful visions, so he returned to the cave to enlighten the others and rescue his friends. But instead of embracing him, they resisted, preferring the familiar, old grey shadows, and refused to go out to the blinding sunlight. They clung fervently to the shadows that had been their only reality, and they threatened to kill him and anyone who would ever try to drag them outside again."

"Wow, that's definitely not a child-friendly, cute fairy tale. Your father had a strange, dark way to show his love." Alex sighed with wide-open eyes, looking surprised at Maya.

"Well, different cultures, and habits," Debby interjected, with a subtle smile, "But you are right, Maya. Your father was a very smart man. Plato wrote down this allegory of the cave, and it is about his teacher, Socrates' struggle in ancient Athens, just before the jury sentenced him to death. His only guilt was his method of questioning and challenging the traditional beliefs of the time, which made him unpopular among some influential figures in the city. So, instead of embracing him for his teaching, they killed him. Can you see it? Just like us, venturing into the unknown, seeking truth, but realizing not everyone may be ready to see the light we've found. This is the reason why everything is coded and shrouded in mystery. We were constantly hunted and condemned because of our power, treated like evil witches and common criminals. The Gatekeepers couldn't just write down on a cave wall how to build a power plant or make electricity. We would find ourselves easily killed by some ruthless tribe leader or dictator."

"This is quite hypocritical for you to say that. Don't you think? Especially after what happened with Daniel," Alex exclaimed, "You work for the same people who almost destroyed him."

"I already told you; it was before I took over the organization. I had nothing to do with it," Debby replied defensively, "On the contrary, I helped him as much as I could to protect him, and secretly I helped his work in the past five years."

Oliver slowly stood up and glanced at Alex, "I think I've heard enough. We have an important job ahead of us, so we should focus on the future, instead of what was in the past. Am I right, Debby?" and he turned to her with a questioning face.

Debby nodded, but when she lifted her head and met Oliver's gaze, a sudden cold shiver ran down her spine. There was something in his look that made her uncomfortable, but she couldn't really tell why.

As the time passed and everyone, one by one, visited the separated little area in the back to get their IV drips, Debby was left alone with Alex, while Oliver showed his best moves to his new pals in the cockpit.

"Can I ask a personal question, Alex?" Debby started, turning towards Alex, "What is going on between you and Maya?"

Alex felt a bit compelled to answer by her piercing gaze, so after a deep sigh, he started, "I don't know. It's just every time I say something, it's the wrong timing. If I want to help, she gets offended. I just don't get it."

"To get what?" Debby grinned.

"Ah, you know. How she feels about me."

"Look, Alex, can I be bluntly honest with you?"

Alex hesitated a little but nodded, curious about anything that could make or break this constant seesaw feeling inside him, like sitting on a roller coaster every time Maya was in his two-meter vicinity.

"Leave her alone."

"What? Why? Why would you say that?" Alex asked in an offended tone.

"Darling, I can see how you look at her. It's obvious, and deep inside, I want to cheer for you, and see this 'beautiful thing' or whatever you nurture in your head to bloom into a flower, but the truth is, it will never happen. And FYI, you need to grow a pair."

"That is really rude!" Alex snapped back at Debby, "I know that I can give her what she needs. I really believe that she is beautiful and I really like her. And…"

"Stop there, Alex. You only see things from your own perspective: what you feel, what you want, what you can give. But have you ever asked her what she wants? Even just once?"

"Erm, I don't understand. What do you mean?" Alex looked puzzled.

"Okay, I'll try a different way to explain this to you. How do you feel about Oliver? Do you trust him? Would you let Maya sleep in the same bed with him?"

"Ha, I guess you have to rephrase your question; it's already happened." Alex rolled his eyes with an annoyed grimace.

"Right, I didn't want to ruffle any feathers. But my point is, that you see him on a pedestal, you look at him, and you see your own fears. Not the real guy, but your competitor. Someone stronger, bigger. It's obvious that you won't trust him. While the reality is, that you guys are almost the same height, plus you are a magician and he is just a werewolf. Do you see my point?"

"Sorry, Debby, but you're not helping. You are not explaining it to me. I think, I need a little more detail."

"Alex, your assumptions are blinding you. Maya is from a different country; her love language is totally different. Just as an example, remember when you snapped, that her father's story was harsh. You offended her, but you didn't even realize it. Plus, the way she sees you is just as distorted as you see Oliver. She finds you intimidating. Your power, presence, and behaviour. She can only see your aura, what you created."

"But I like her! I want her to be safe, and I want to take care of her! Why is she not getting it?" Alex burst out, but suddenly realized that it was maybe too loud, and took down his voice, "I think she is perfect!"

"Again, you are thinking selfishly. You like something, and you want to take it. You see a beautiful flower, and you want to pluck it. You like fish, and you fry it and eat it. This is exactly the problem with men. If you love her, let her choose. And if you are not sure what she wants, just ask her.

Quite simple. Expectation is the root of all heartache, and assumption is the mother of all screw-ups."

"Debby, I appreciate you trying to help, but you don't."

"Okay, suit yourself. I warned you! But if you don't change your approach, you will find her in Oliver's arms in no time."

Maya's figure approached between the aisles, so they stopped the heart-to-heart conversation, but Alex couldn't stop thinking about the vivid image in his head, as Oliver is hugging Maya and she melts in his arms.

Humans have overly complex and confusing mating rituals. Dancing, singing, writing poems; a million ways to express their feelings, besides the unique ability: God's gift of speaking, to talk about their feelings elaborately and clearly. Yet, they made the entire process so overwhelmingly exhausting, that it got to a point where they needed a phone application to swipe left or right to avoid all of this, just to get laid. Kinda a bummer.

35

The rain descended eerily upon Bristol, defying the laws of gravity when they arrived. The fine mist, almost motionless in the air, seemed to challenge the very principles of physics. As the team disembarked from the plane, the wind tirelessly attempted to blow tiny droplets on their faces, but an uncanny absence of weight or moisture left them in a surreal void. A strange, otherworldly odour wafted around them, a malodorous prelude that unsettled their senses.

As they gazed upward, the sky bore an ominous visage, heavy with dark, thick clouds obscuring any glimpse of the celestial realm. Shades of grey mingled, creating an ominous forewarning on a swirling atmospheric canvas. The air hummed with a supernatural tension, as if the elements themselves conspired to issue a warning.

Awaiting them was a disciplined line of army men, the leader, an older man with the deepest wrinkle frown between his brows, walked straight to

Debby. They exchanged words in hushed tones, and a quick nod of agreement followed. Yet, when the leader's gaze met Oliver and Alex, a palpable disbelief etched his face. As they walked toward the cars, a young soldier attempted to assist Oliver with his giant duffle bag, only to receive a threatening fist and a stern indication to step back. It was a clear signal for personal belongings, and the soldier quickly retreated, wisely choosing not to escalate the situation.

The Gatekeepers found themselves sandwiched between two military vehicles as they settled into the minivan. With military precision, the convoy was soon on its way without any delays. As soon as they were seated, Alex whipped out his phone, desperately attempting to get a signal. After futile attempts, Debby pulled out her cell, offering it to Alex. "Here, just use mine. I don't think you can get a signal on your cell phone any longer."

Alex looked puzzled as he took Debby's phone, "Thanks, Debby. Not sure what's wrong with mine. A couple of days ago, there was still service."

"That was a couple of days ago. We are now in a State of Emergency. Most power stations are already shut down, with nobody to operate them. The emergency reserves, essential for minimal system functioning, are controlled by the handful of remaining army personnel. Most services have already been discontinued: phone, gas, electricity, and even the water pumping systems," Debby explained in a concerned voice. "Cities will be flooded in days, but the biggest concern is sewage water, spreading waterborne diseases in the cities soon—cholera, hepatitis—and possibly contaminating any remaining food sources for survivors. The pandemic was only the first step. The lack of human interaction to control the cities and the environment will cause even more devastating problems and lead to the final Armageddon."

"Gosh, this is terrible. In just one week! But the pandemic has been here for months, and nobody has done anything?" Alex's face displayed horror.

"This is not a virus or bacteria that can be contained by quarantine or by inventing a new vaccine. In the beginning, no one believed us in what we were fighting against, and the impact was so rapid and unprecedented that nobody even tried to come up with any actual, useful plan until it was too late. The main problem is that people lost their will to live, gave up the fight even before it started, and the pressure fell on random people who were not trained to act in such events."

"I had a plan," Oliver chimed in, "But obviously, with Alex, we have a much better chance now."

Alex raised his brow with confusion, "A better chance? I appreciate your enthusiasm, but we still have no clue what is happening and how to stop it. Nobody can tell us what is going on, why the water got sick, or how we can work together. We have nothing—no answers, just questions."

"Alex, stop whining and call Daniel. Tell him that we are on the way and to pack, get ready as soon as possible," Debby ordered him, then added a bit hesitantly, "And maybe mention that I am coming, so he won't be...erm, defensive when we meet."

"Hmm, okay. But we need to make another stop. I need to go to London after we've taken Daniel."

"Sorry, Alex, but we have no time to bring your mother. I understand that you are concerned, but we all need to make sacrifices."

"What? No. You don't understand. I need to go home; I can't leave her," Alex exclaimed with a firm voice.

Debby hesitated for a second but replied bluntly, "Alex, every hour counts. I can't allow you. Hundreds of people get killed in the search for food or die of starvation and dehydration every minute around the world. You must understand that."

Alex was devastated, his face drained of colour as the shocking realization hit him. The world around him was crumbling, but he hadn't expected it to tear him apart from the inside first. In an attempt to comfort him, Maya gently reached for his arm, but he pulled away, focusing on a painful task at hand – calling his mother.

"I need to call her. That is the least," he declared, with determination in his voice.

"After you've called Daniel, you'll still have time. Set your priorities. I won't ask you again," Debby's response was cold, like a sharp icicle straight to his chest.

Alex cleared his throat, deleted the numbers from the display, and with a heavy heart, began pushing the buttons at a snail's pace. The phone rang for what felt like an eternity before a faint voice answered.

"Hi, it's me, Alex," he replied immediately.

"Alex? Hi, I can't tell you how happy I am that you called. Please tell me, what happened?" Daniel's voice carried kindness but an immense sadness.

"Daniel, it's so nice to hear your voice. I'm on my way to you. We're coming to pick you up. And I bring someone, but you need to let her speak first. It's important. Can you promise me?" Alex asked, almost begging Daniel.

The line fell silent for a couple of seconds, and then Daniel responded, "I guess I don't have any other option. To be fair, I was kind of expecting it, just not now, but years ago. Well, please tell her I'll be ready. Let me know when you arrive."

"Maybe 50 minutes more, max an hour, we can be there," Alex assured, glancing at Debby for confirmation. "And don't worry. You can trust her. If you know what I mean. See you soon!"

Alex hung up the phone, turning to Debby, "I'll make that call now. Just give me 5 minutes."

Debby nodded and leaned back in her seat, seemingly giving him some privacy, as Alex pulled closer to the window and pushed the buttons. A strange feeling tightened his chest, a familiar image of rushing home from the GameCon flashing in his mind. As the phone rang, his heart raced, and he began banging his head against the window, feeling utterly useless. The painful memory of finding his mother alone and abandoned resurfaced. He realized that he had completely forgotten to call her again, and in the last few minutes, when it was probably too late, he started to worry and foolishly cry over spilled milk.

"Please pick up! I promise I will never forget to call you again. I swear, I will come home every week, just please, please pick up," he mumbled quietly, begging for one last stroke of luck.

"Hallo!..." Sophie's voice seemed distant at first as she picked up the phone.

"Mom, hi, it's Alex. How are you? How is everything?" Alex fought back the tears; his tone unsettled. "Do you have enough food? Do you need something?"

"I'm fine. A little weak and tired, but all okay. I'm just worried about you! What's happening? How is Maya? Where are you now?"

Alex was overjoyed to hear his mother's nagging voice, a comforting sound. He quickly wiped his tears, hiding the wet streaks, and continued, "We're fine. Still on the way, and it might be a couple more days until we can come home. But I wanted to hear your voice. Oh, and one more thing, Mom. You know, in my room, next to the bookshelf, where you keep my old toys. There is something for you. You know what... Please, use it! Just be careful, it's like Pandora's box, remember? But it helps, I promise!"

"Oh, that Godforsaken thing! I would not touch it for the world!" she snapped.

"Mom, just promise me. Keep it safe and stay close to it; it will help. Do you understand?"

"Yes, yes! I'll take care of it. But you make sure that you look after Maya. Okay? Please, be careful! I don't want to lose you like your father," Sophie replied, but suddenly the line started fading, and after a couple of beeps, it disconnected.

"Mom? What do you mean like my father? MOM!!!" But there was no answer. Alex glanced around with a bewildered look, finding the others' affectionate expressions staring back at him.

All of a sudden, he felt as if his soul had just left him, observing himself from an ethereal distance. His hands and legs felt numb, his mind shut off and senseless, as all surrounding noises faded into a distant hum. "This can't be happening. I'm just dreaming this whole thing," echoed a small voice, watching him from above like an audience observing the actor on the big screen.

Sitting in silence, a strange feeling began to surge within him. It was the realization that comes when you recognize yourself and try to figure out what just happened. He became an outsider, detached, and liberated from his own body. Simultaneously scared, lost, and confused in a way he had never experienced before.

If you've ever had this feeling, you understand what I am saying, and you're probably one of the few who had a chance to take a good look at what is out there. Maybe it happened while you were dreaming or in a life-changing moment when choices needed assessment, to find the right answer. To make that wise decision, get off the train, and change the destination. Or sometimes, you've just had enough, you look up into the bright light and shout, "No, that's it! I don't want to play this game anymore. I'm done! Get me out of here!"

And those who return from such experiences often describe them in the same way. Some may have become religious or turned to spirituality, but all attest that there is something more out there. People always have a choice; they decide which game they pick. In a vast store, according to their interests and experience level, they chose a game to spend their precious time on — to entertain, gain experience, or have fun. But above all, to learn with each life.

Alex couldn't discern how much time had passed, but when he heard Maya's voice, it felt like an awakening, orchestrated by an angel's charms. "Alex, please, let me help you. Give me your hand," she said kindly, pulling him closer.

Her soft hand gently enveloped his arm, and it felt like heaven. The pure, innocent sensation of love coursed through his veins — the kind you feel as a child. Honest, naïve, and boundless, like the ocean. Unconcerned about what others might think, he couldn't help but lean his head on Maya's shoulder, utterly exhausted.

The highway stretched endlessly before them, disappearing into the hazy distance as the rain continued its enigmatic dance. The radio crackled to life, and after a brief exchange, the man in the front gave some instructions to the driver. As they approached the city's outskirts, the convoy slowed, revealing a scene painfully familiar: abandoned cars with open doors lining the streets, empty shops, and piles of garbage, without any sign of human life. Even this little oasis had met its fate eventually, succumbing to the same destiny as the rest of the world.

When the cars stopped in front of the house, Daniel awaited them at the entrance. He turned and rolled toward the hall, heading straight for the library to lead the way.

"Come on in, I need just 10 more minutes," Daniel said, pushing the wheels to reach his giant desk.

The team stopped in the middle of the room as Debby walked in, wearing an ominous expression. "Hi, Daniel. My name is Debby Abrams. I've heard so much about you."

"Hi, the pleasure is mine. But before you say anything, please allow me to tell you," Daniel replied, turning his chair towards her. "I'm not expecting you to apologize for what happened. But I want to understand, why?"

"Daniel, I know it is not the right time or place, and most of all, I am not the right person, but I need to say that whatever was done to you 40 years ago was absolutely unacceptable. It was wrong and very evil, and I have to take full responsibility for what happened. As soon as I learned about the incident, I took the necessary measures, but what is done, I can't take it back. I can only apologize and promise that it won't be ever repeated to anyone, ever," Debby declared with determination, followed by a deep sigh.

"Thank you; it's nice that you made the effort to prepare this little speech," Daniel commented, looking deep into Debby's eyes. "But I need to know, why?"

"You have to understand, it was a different time during the Cold War, and people were seeing enemies everywhere."

"WHY??? Just tell me why? That's all I want to know!" Daniel screamed.

"The fear! Daniel, you know very well! The fear of the unknown makes people mad," Debby exclaimed with a shaking voice.

"Hm… This is not the right answer. We all have to face the unknown, but not everyone chooses to give in. Fear is what you create to avoid facing reality. It's just an excuse but never the solution. I have done nothing to deserve the pain I had to live with, but I need to believe that by going through all the suffering, I have made a change, and it was worth it."

For long seconds, there was silence. Then, gathering her courage, Debby stepped closer to him. "I was playing your game, The Polybius. In 1981, a friend invited me to spend spring break with her family in Portland. There, not far from her place, was an arcade game club. One night, we stopped by just to have some fun and try this new, strange game everyone was talking about."

Her eyes reflected memories, both distant and vivid. "Your game was wild, exciting, mind-blowing, and the next day I went there again, but then it disappeared. They said some guys from the government came and took every machine." A pause lingered, and the room seemed to hold its breath.

"The following weeks, I had crazy, vivid dreams. When I got worse, I told my mother about it. That was the first time she opened up about our past, explaining everything about our lineage and ancestors. Although she made sure to pass on the knowledge and initiated me when I was six, I never had the medal. She lost it during the war."

Debby's gaze met Daniel's, and her expression conveyed gratitude and vulnerability. "I would never have realized my power and background if I hadn't played your game. From that point, I spent my entire life searching for the medals and becoming the best Gatekeeper I could ever be. I know it's not much consolation for all the horror you had to live through, but I am who I am because you created that game, the Polybius."

Daniel's face displayed a myriad of emotions—sadness, pain, and a mix of sentiments all rolled into one look. Slowly, he turned back with his wheelchair and rolled behind his desk. From a drawer, he extracted a long pouch and gently placed it on the table. "Thank you for sharing this with me. I think, I got my answer, and although not what I imagined, it's more than I can hope for. Please promise me that whatever happens, the knowledge will never be lost. That's all I want."

She placed her hand on her chest. "I promise you. The whole universe is in our hands now."

36

Time was running out, and now, with all five Gatekeepers finally united, the team was complete, ready to form a plan for their urgent mission. To show his support, Alex walked up to Daniel and leaned in for a hug. He then pointed to the pouch on the table. "The caduceus? Did you manage to figure out how it's working?"

"Yes and no. We were researching with Miles, but since he got ill, I was looking after him and couldn't spend much time on it," Daniel replied with a gloomy tone.

"Oh, no!" Maya interjected. "What happened to him? Maybe I can help."

"He's upstairs. Last two days, he can't lift his head, really weak," Daniel explained. "I tried everything, but it's beyond my strengths. My medal barely keeps me alive, and I can't find a way to help him."

"Let me see him," Debby chimed in, glancing at Maya. "Come with me. I'll bring medication, but first, you need to start to heal him. His circulatory system is probably collapsing. Just give him enough strength until we can administer the IV drips."

Maya and Debby swiftly turned and left, leaving the boys in the library.

"I hope they can help him," Daniel added with a heart-wrenching voice. Slowly, he continued, "Well, about the caduceus; the only thing we could figure out from ancient sources is that it somehow helps to generate energy or combine forces, like a resurrector or defibrillator of sorts. But Miles suggested that it was probably more like the representation of the DNA spiral originally. The nucleic double helix in the form of two snakes intertwined on a rod. As he said, all the knowledge needed for life is stored in the code of DNA, created by the magician with his wand, bonding the nucleic bases with the hydrogen. These bonds, the combinations of the four elements, determine what type of life form he is going to build. So, probably, this is how it looks for an observer, with the nucleotides or elements twisting up around the rod with a wings-like energy sparkle."

Alex picked up the pouch and pulled out the caduceus with utmost care, being really cautious. He held it up in the air and made a faint-hearted swing, as if waving a lightsaber.

"Hm, I'm not sure that in Star Wars, I saw this kind of thing," Oliver grinned. "It's too fancy looking."

Daniel mumbled on a sarcastic tone, "Too fancy... too fancy. Of course, it's fancy; it's from the 17th century. It probably belonged to

Newton, Kepler, or Galilei. It should be fancy!"

"So, this is just a representation of my power, correct?" Alex inquired with a fascinated expression. "And this is how it should look like when I use my power. Hm... Interesting."

"Well, not much help, I know, but we couldn't figure out more," Daniel tried to excuse himself. Then he added, "But tell me, what about Debby? How is she? Do you trust her?"

"She wants to help us, that's for sure, but she does have a pretty blunt way of getting her way when she puts her mind to it," Alex responded with a pondering expression. "Just one thing I can't get out of my head. I really don't understand. When Maya first said that she touched her, she felt that she was crazy about the Metatron's cube. But when I mentioned it, she just quickly waved it off, like she has all types of relics and doesn't need more. It's kind of odd, or could Maya be wrong about her vision?"

"Hm... Maybe Maya saw her intention in the past, or her fear of the cube. Perhaps Debby wants you to help her open it. We can't be sure, but again... Just be careful with her."

Debby's distinct, strong footsteps approached, and the guys' glances turned toward the door, looking like they were just caught red-handed.

"Gentlemen, no need for this dramatic look," Debby exclaimed with a subtle smile, "We already stabilized Miles' condition. Maya is still with him for a couple more minutes, but an army nurse will set up a little station for him while we are away." Debby explained with a reassuring expression. "Now, where were we? Any idea what the next step is?"

Oliver started with his unwavering wit, "Erm, we were just talking about this caduceus, but besides that, Alex tried to use the Force with his new lightsaber against the Dark Lord... not much."

"Grow up, Oliver, seriously." Alex snapped at him in an annoyed tone.

"No, actually, he has a point," Daniel chimed in, "With the Gatekeepers, you are always the key figure with the creative power: the 'Force.' And you are the one who fights against the 'Dark Lord,' let's call it the dark, invisible energy, in every creation myth and religion. But can you think, what you have what the dark side wants so much? What could be the reason for the battle to be fought over billions of years?"

Debby interjected while she nonchalantly hopped into an armchair, "Power. It must be power."

Daniel shook his head, "No. The universe contains four times more dark energy than we have. They don't need power. It has more mass, more space, and more energy than we could ever imagine. I believe it's something way deeper: They don't have time!"

Everyone furrowed their foreheads, looking puzzled by Daniel's statement. Alex glanced at Debby and added, "Actually, we don't know if time is the fourth dimension or a fundamental force, like gravity or electromagnetism. It kind of fits into the spacetime equation, but just because three times two equals six, it doesn't mean that three plus three equals six is the same process. There might be a reason why we can't work out higher dimensions or why we perceive time and gravity only in a one-way direction and can't travel back in time."

A soft scuffing noise emanated from the hall, and slowly, Miles walked into the room, leaning awkwardly on Maya's shoulder while pushing the IV pole with the tubes in front of him, like a huge walking stick.

"Sorry, I couldn't keep him in bed; he wanted to come and speak with you," Maya explained with an anxious expression.

"No, don't worry guys. I'll be fine! Darling, your hand is like a power station; it charged me up." Miles beamed at Maya, "But I can't stay in bed and just wait for the end, thinking that I could be here and help you."

"Oh, Miles, you are a true friend," Daniel exclaimed, "Please, come and sit down, but spare your energy. For sure, we need all the help, and especially with your eidetic memory, it comes in handy if we could pick your brain."

Debby nodded as she glanced at Miles and added, "I always admired people with such genius. It is my pleasure to meet you, Miles. We were just talking about time and what could be the connection between dark matter and this pandemic."

"Ahh, I don't know about that, but I have a theory. Have you noticed the way how the rain falls?" Miles asked, looking around the room with an excited glance on his face, "In the last two days, I had plenty of time watching the raindrops, hitting the window. But they seem to defy gravity and just hang almost weightless, hardly flowing down on the glass. It's really peculiar, don't you think?"

Everyone's face turned perplexed as they recalled the same strange phenomenon, but it didn't ring a bell with anybody before.

Debby started first, trying to make some sense, "Yes, you're right. It is really unusual, but we are constantly measuring the gravitational energy, and dozens of scientists are analysing the chemical composition of the water, but nothing has changed. So, what is your theory?"

Miles smiled and gently tried to push himself up on the couch, then he continued, "Well, if the mass weight and composition of the water are the same, then what could've changed to defy gravity? Hm?"

"Life… It gave up life." Alex exclaimed.

"Yes, correct! We can all agree that life is a form of energy, or you can call it vibration, resonance, quintessence, whatever. And if it's gone without any physical or chemical change, then it must've been replaced by another energy with the same mass."

Debby opposed with palpable hesitation, "Hold on, it still doesn't explain why the water is floating in the air. Gravity causes mutual attraction between objects, but if the mass is the same, then gravity should've changed, and there is no indication that the gravitational field was affected since that wave."

"What wave?" Daniel flinched, "What are you talking about?"

"Yes, we didn't mention you yet." Alex interjected to explain it further, "We had a little episode with Oliver yesterday due to the penumbral lunar eclipse. But that's not the point… So, anyway, as it turned out, last year in May, there was another eclipse, followed by a conjunction where the Sun covered the pathway between Uranus and the Earth. During that time, a colossal dark star flew into the solar system, and it's currently hiding behind Uranus. On the night, last year when I had those visions I told you about, it was caused by a gravitational wave. The sudden stopping movement of the star created a wave, what hit the Earth."

"A dark star?" Miles' eyes widened; he was almost leaping up, "That's it! That's why we are witnessing these changes. The gravitational wave sent radiation energy, impacting Earth! That's what happened. The radiation initiated a chain reaction, slowly replacing life with this dark energy from the star. Same mass but opposite force."

That was a bit deep, and they needed a couple of long seconds to digest what Miles had said. They were all just blinking like frogs in a pond, rolling their eyes, grappling to piece together what this actually meant.

"Okay, so you're suggesting that this radiation contaminated life, much like the radioactive exposure from an atomic bomb, just with gravitation?" Alex responded with astonishment.

"Hm, yes. That's about right. Dark energy was transmitted from the star through gravitational radiation, likely mediated by graviton particles, and now it's gradually draining the life force from the water." Miles nodded with an explicit expression etched across his face.

"Wait, what?" Oliver was still trying to process the information, "I hardly get what you just said, but what it have to do with time? You said that the dark side has way more energy than us. Why would they need more?"

"Guys, can you see?" Daniel exclaimed with a Eureka spark in his eyes. "It's not about energy; it never was. We treat time as a dimension, but in reality, in terms of the universe, it equates to life! Just think! Remember when I told you about the Egyptian Osiris or the Greek Uranus? Damn, why didn't I think of this earlier: Ouron is Uranus, like the god and the planet! It's the same thing; just the spelling or pronunciation changed slightly!" he slapped his forehead.

"Daniel, slow down. What do you mean?" Debby exclaimed, "Time is life? How?"

"Yes! If you played the Polybius game, you know the story," Daniel nodded and continued with immense enthusiasm, "It all started when Ouron lost his manhood in a fight with the Hydrons. And they escaped, apparently taking his 'thing' with them. Think about it, what does manhood represent? It's reproduction, the creation of life! In every creation myth, it says that after the battle he lost his... you know what..., and then life goes on, but without him. Osiris got the underworld and became the first mummy, and Uranus… well, we never heard of him again… Case in point: he wants back his manhood!"

"Great, but how? We can't do that; we can't let him. We're going to die. That's not an option!" Oliver started to lose his cool, yelling and waving up and down, obviously frustrated by this disturbing dick scenario.

"I know, I never said we can, or will. Just hold your horses," Daniel added in a reassuring tone, "What I am trying to say is that we finally know what he wants and how he did it. That's more than we've gathered in the past 10 months, and all in just 10 minutes since we've been together."

"Daniel, I'm not trying to be a nag, but you still haven't told us why you think Ouron wants time. I just don't get it." Debby seemed a bit annoyed.

Miles leaned forward, holding on to the IV pole, and added in an ominous voice, "I think, I know the answer; I tell you: Without life, there is no time. And without time, eternity takes on another meaning. Heaven and hell could be governed by pretty much the same rules according to string theory's supersymmetry. Except from hell, there's no escape without reincarnation. Once you are there, the game is over, and I guess, that place is really not a joyful holiday destination."

Oliver scratched his head, "Bummer, I kind of start to feel sorry for that bloke."

37

A palpable tension filled the room after Miles' chilling revelation of the grave prophecy. The weight of their heroic mission was etched across Daniel's face as he leaned forward. His eyes surveyed the team with a determination that echoed the enormity of the responsibility before them. "We must find a way to reverse the effects and bring life back to where it belongs. But to do that, we first have to understand how Ouron manipulated gravity."

Alex, holding the caduceus in his hand, pondered aloud, "Okay, this symbol represents creation, right? The entwined snakes and wings. The cosmic power to bring life into existence. Hm... Maybe this is a key, and I have to open some portal to restore life, the same way as it happened before."

Maya, who had been silently observing the cityscape through the window, turned to the group with a thoughtful gaze. "Alex is onto something. If time is life, and life is energy, maybe our collective abilities hold the key to create a force strong enough to fight back this dark energy."

Despite his weakened state, Miles straightened up with newfound vigour. "There was a study that proved from the perspective of a photon, there is no such thing as time or distance. Trillions of years could pass from its creation until it's absorbed, but since it's moving at the speed of light, a photon experiences everything simultaneously, without the constraints of time or distance. Time is only our illusion, relative to the observer. Just like they say, if a tree falls in a forest and no one is around to hear it, it makes no sound. Like if it never happened."

Puzzled by Miles' seemingly cryptic remark, Alex asked, "Sorry Miles, I am not sure how this works in our favour? What do you mean?"

Miles gestured animatedly, "I have this picture in my head from a science magazine, about a light cone, where a flash of light travels in the form of an hourglass in opposite directions simultaneously to the past and future. While this theory only applies to measurable particles and not dark matter, I found it fascinating and gave me an idea. Currently, we imagine the arrow of time like this pole, pointing down in the direction of Earth's gravity."

Using his IV pole as an impromptu visual aid, Miles pulled it closer and explained further, "In the arrow of the pole, the cones, like an hourglass, contain grains of sand that represent time. In the top part, there is our unpredictable future, with all the possible outcomes. Whereas at the bottom, there are the past fallen time capsules, which we can't visit but faithfully remember and keep track of, in a recorded order as our history."

Miles continued with starry vehemence while pointing in the middle, "We are waiting for the particles to squeeze through at the only one point where our world is visible, observing the present moment in the middle, at the neck of the hourglass. It's like waiting to reveal Schrödinger's cat; until we don't open the box and see the outcome, we won't know if the poor cat is dead or alive."

Debby, absorbing the conversation, interjected, "It's also worth mentioning, that in ancient teachings, there's a recurring theme about cosmic balance, and time is often depicted as an hourglass. Just as you said, similar to a double cone, but with a mirror in the middle."

Miles nodded and furrowed his brow, "That's it, but for the photon, time doesn't exist. Traditionally, we use the arrow in the middle of the axis to show how our linear perception of time flows and moves downward to entropy with gravitation. But in reality, the photon exists at the same time everywhere. Time is not just one point in the middle when we observe it; it's a circular rhythm, like a big serpent biting its own tail as it cyclically moves around."

With a confused expression on his face, Daniel voiced his trouble following Miles' lengthy explanation, "I hate to say it, but I just can't figure out how gravity connects with light and time. Every piece makes sense separately, but I can't see how it could work together."

"Sorry, I can be a little confusing, jumping back and forth in my explanation. Just stick with me," Miles responded with an apologetic smile, "Now, try to imagine a similar shape, but as a yo-yo with a wormhole on the axis, where life is a circling ring in the middle. The rotation is created by the kinetic energy of the spinning motion as it looped around the neck of the hourglass, and always rolling in one direction: that's time. All this is nicely packed within a next-dimensional Euclidean two-surface nested torus, or you could just say: a twisting doughnut turning inside out, with a fractal ripple of the toroidal torque. But in the middle, the two-cone shape wormhole of the yo-yo is not our past and future pointing up and down; it represents the two opposite sides of matter and antimatter. And gravity, as a string, wrapped around in the middle, keeps time in constant motion, by pulling it toward entropy."

Miles took a deep breath to suspend the tension, then continued his intricate explanation, "I believe I know what happened. When the radiation wave hit our planet, it changed gravity's linear energy. The point has shifted, where life is created by the balance of angular and linear momentum. The Ouroboros ring lowered from the habitable equilibrium, closer to the other side, in the direction of antimatter. And if we can't stop in time the falling ring, the point of creation will flip into the other side, into the antimatter."

Alex, suddenly frozen, stared at Miles with astonishment. "I have absolutely no idea what you just said. You lost me in the yo-yo part. But that ring you mentioned, the circling energy pulled by gravitation, sounds familiar. Seriously, it's exactly what I feel when I travel! The air seems to tighten and wrap around me, like standing on an invisible spinning top that pulls me up, towards a centre point. But it's just a fraction of a moment, not like I'm flying in space on a trip, or journey through an endless wormhole. I just blink my eye, and the next moment I already smell and feel instantly the new surroundings, like it happens in a second."

"Exactly! That's the moment when you touch creation or the 'zero point,'" Daniel chimed in, explaining with a big smile. "Remember, you are the Gatekeeper of the fifth element: the aether. You have the same knowledge as Ouron, that's why you can control light and gravity."

"Wait, but if he has the same ability, that would mean he can also create life. I don't get it." Alex responded with a surprised expression, "Why would he need the time from us?"

"It's true, but he needs all the other elements together for the process," Daniel interjected, "You have us! And he's alone!"

Oliver shot up his hand abruptly, as if he were in a classroom, obviously eager to share something very important. "Guys, I think I know what he's doing. Many years ago, I was traveling to Egypt with my stepfather, and he took me to the Hathor temple in Dendera. He showed me a painting, an astrological ceiling, with some primordial gods, all lining up in front of a huge, round mirror. I was maybe 15-16 years old, but I remember that he told me that the eye of Horus is there in the middle to protect our universe, and it's guarded by Thoth the magician, who is standing on the right. That mirror, he said, is the gate to the other side, and if it's ever been moved, life will end."

Debby suddenly jumped up, grabbed her cell phone, and swiftly pressed the buttons like a Gen Alpha teenage girl. She exclaimed into the phone, "Hallo, general! We got the location. Prepare the plane, Operation Adelie is in place, now!" Hanging up, she glanced around at the curious faces with a sigh and a hint of a smile. "We are going to Antarctica. I hope you packed warm clothes too."

Oliver, still grappling with processing the news, finally broke the silence. "Erm, Antarctica. Care to explain?"

Debby laughed, "Of course, yes. We already had several possible scenarios for the final stage, but we couldn't narrow down exactly what would be the location. So, we prepared a few plans, and Adelie is the closest station in Antarctica to the Earth's magnetic south pole." Debby continued, her eyes sparkling with the sudden satisfaction of her revelation. She turned to Miles and added, "I hope we can count on you. We desperately need your help, and although I understand if you feel that it would be too dangerous, I can guarantee that…"

"I'm in," Miles snapped, impatiently interrupting Debby. "You couldn't hold me back, not even with an oxcart. So, I'm in!" He beamed with unwavering determination.

"Hey Debby, again, sorry," Oliver nagged her, "Why? Why Antarctica? And what does it have to do with the magnetic south pole?"

"Time to go. I'll explain it in the car," she said and walked out with hurried steps. "I guess we can get you some suitable, warm clothes too, and diving equipment."

Alex and Oliver's eyes brightened up, like little kids in a toy store. Only Maya looked shocked as she glanced at Daniel's hopeless expression, questioning what on earth she meant by diving with his condition, but Daniel took the news surprisingly well.

Without further delay, the determined group was on their way, ready to confront cosmic forces threatening not only their lives but the very fabric of time itself. In the car, they sat in a contemplative silence, gazing into the unknown, each face marked by a solemn dedication to the mighty gravity of their mission. As the rain continued its mysterious dance outside, providing a haunting backdrop to their shared purpose, they began to lay out their plan.

Debby broke the silence, addressing the urgency of their situation. "I hate to say this, but we are in the last minute. The full moon was last night, meaning we have maybe 10 or 12 hours left before the gate closes again. We can't wait another 28 days; we need to find this place tonight."

"Ten hours? We have ten hours to go to the South Pole?" Oliver's desperation echoed through the car. "That's impossible! We might have an hour left after we get there. We need to find another way; we don't have enough time!"

"Calm down, Oliver. I understand, and we have three military aircraft already waiting for us. We take a direct flight, and from the base, we use speed boats to approach the magnetic pole," Debby replied confidently. "I take care of the details, but if we miss this window, we might have nothing to fight for."

Daniel glanced at Debby, curiously watching her tense expression, "So, how did you figure it out? The location?"

She hesitated for a second, placing her hands on her lap, seemingly trying to collect her thoughts before answering, "The Hathor temple in Dendera, what Oliver mentioned... With the picture on the ceiling depicting the gods and the huge mirror... Well, we know where the mirror is."

"Excuse me?" Alex exclaimed, his anger evident. "You knew it? You knew all this time where the gate is? Why didn't you tell us?"

"I was not sure, I had to wait!" Debby snapped back, still fiddling with some invisible crease in her skirt before nodding uncertainly. "As I told you, we had some options; we were just not sure which one is correct."

"SOME OPTIONS? You had some options, and you didn't say anything about it to us?" Maya yelled at Debby in fury. "What were you waiting for? Till we all are going to die?"

"Okay, everyone! Calm down! NOW!" Daniel intervened, demanding calm. "We can't jump to each other's throat. I am sure that she has some reasonable explanation, correct?" And he looked back at Debby's shamed expression.

"We didn't know if it was the energy field or an actual physical change that caused the pandemic," Debby explained. "And you know as well! It was unexpected, unprecedented! And yes, we had some options to deal with the situation. But until the moment when Oliver mentioned the mirror, it didn't click in my mind, why the magnetic pole moved so rapidly in the last couple of months."

Alex shook his head, his voice filled with anger. "'Everybody, dig deep into your pockets, pull out all your cards, and put them on the table, to see...' 'We need to work together...' It was all bullshit! You just use us, if and when you need!" His voice seethed with frustration. "What else did you forget to mention? Hm? What else should we know before we go there, barging towards our demise like mindless animals to the slaughterhouse? NOW, TELL ME!"

"Ma'am, is everything all right back there?" A soldier turned back from the front seat, concerned about the commotion.

"Yes, thank you! Everything is alright," Debby responded quickly, attempting to defuse the situation.

"Okay, just let me know if you need something," the soldier replied, nodding politely. "We have ten more minutes till arrival at the airport. All supplies are packed and ready for departure at twenty hundred."

Life has sometimes pretty twisted ways of throwing unexpected challenges our way. But ultimately, it's how we respond to them, that defines us. In times like these, it's interesting to observe people, how they navigate problems. It's during these moments that one's true character is revealed.

Perhaps as a societal initiation, it should be made compulsory to give every engaged couple a ten-year-old laptop with dodgy Wi-Fi connection and spend 24 hours on a desert island, before they get married. Just to get a real quick reality check about the unfiltered truth, before diving into the illusions of an Insta-perfect life. It could be truly eye-opening.

The human body, a marvel of complexity, is constructed from the same tiny particles and assembled with the same old fundamental pattern as a banana or a creaky garden gate. Vibrating atomic molecules connecting with electrons—nothing more, nothing less. Yet it's capable of healing, feeling, and expressing emotions in a million different ways. Remarkably resilient and easy to repair, compared to other life forms, with a multitude of enzymes and hormones working tirelessly to maintain a healthy balance.

Given proper fuel and minimal maintenance, it can endure for 120-150 years or even more easily. This beautiful machinery has the opportunity to experience all the love and light the world has to offer. Yet, it inexplicably chooses conflict, violence, hatred, and destruction time after time, seemingly never learning from the cycle.

The most bizarre part is the human ego, which as an essential, built-in survival tool, serves a crucial role in infancy. Gaining attention and sustenance from your parents through crying and tantrums is what keeps you alive. Otherwise, your mother may simply forget to feed you, or your father leaves you at the grocery store...

But just like breastfeeding, it can and should be outgrown. Learning to ride a bicycle requires relinquishing the tricycle. Burning oneself prompts an avoidance of fire. Yet, for the majority of people, the ego somehow remains, leading them to blame circumstances for their poor life choices.

Rather than taking responsibility, people across millennia await a messiah in various religions, hoping for someone else to solve their problems, rather than taking action, to become the change they wish to see in the world. This cyclic blame game unfolds with excuses like "My ex was crazy," "The boss mistreats me," or "The neighbour's grass is greener." And what is the proposed solution?: "Let's stone him! Burn her on the stakes!"—the madness rooted in vengeance.

The ego stubbornly clings on, hindering personal growth. This perpetuation for penchant victimhood, this eye-for-an-eye mentality for scapegoating and blaming game is not only destructive but already become profitable and entertaining. As the Romans said, "Two things only the people anxiously desire — bread and circuses," echoes through time, while switching through the TV channels with soap operas and reality shows.

Love is divine, and light is limitless, this is what every ancient teaching says, but the vicious cycle, stemming from constant stress and fear, claims too many human lives prematurely. And as the inevitable conclusion approaches, one doesn't yearn for more wealth; only time becomes the most precious commodity. Regrets don't centre around past mistakes, but rather the time spent in misguided pursuits.

38

The profound nature of the universe lies in the intricate interplay of atomic particles, each with distinct flavours and charges, driven by the fundamental principles of life. At the heart of every atom lies a nucleus, a cosmic composition of protons and neutrons, each built of distinct quarks. The union of these quarks is governed by the strong force, with the mediation of bosons, known as gluons.

The proton, for example, the bearer of a positive charge, is an amalgamation of three quarks—two 'up' and one 'down'—each possessing unique properties. These properties contribute to the formation of our physical reality, adding both complexity and stability.

The scientific narrative may seem complex, yet it offers insight into the age-old adage that within every good thing, there is something evil. And explains why the road to hell is said to be paved with good intentions. Debby, too, navigates the complexities of her role, doing what she must to keep the machinery in motion. Juggling balls and spinning plates, she harnesses the power to attract both the forces of good and evil, forging a spectrum of energies to create white light.

You can't blame a tiger for slaying an antelope to feed its cubs—it's nature's order. And there's no reason to sit around in silent rage, hating someone for earnestly doing the best they can in a complex situation. Yet here we are again, everyone was huffing and puffing, caught in the ebb and flow of emotions. As the team boarded the jet, they gazed back at the dark spot of the city. Left behind in solitary beneath the expansive, empty sky, a poignant backdrop to the silent turbulence within each of them—a reminder of the complex interplay between nature, necessity, and the human spirit.

Only Maya had the notion to put an end to the nonsense and extend an olive branch, "I can't do this. I can't hold it together if everyone is so negative! Please, we need each other. To work together. That's our only chance!"

Like grumpy kids after a tantrum, feeling exhausted and defeated, they glanced around, measuring the tangible damage caused by their ego-trip. "Please, let's try to hold each other's hand, one time, and try to heal," Maya suggested, opening her hands toward everyone around her.

Subtle smiles and agreeing nods approved her suggestion, and they all gathered in a small circle, holding hands from their seats. Slowly, as they closed their eyes, a tiny dot emerged in the middle, like a random, timid light source in the middle of the ocean, lit up from a distant ship. So small, yet so powerful, it was hardly possible to look straight at or see its close details.

The little spot seemed to wander and slowly began to circle around in the air, one by one approaching the Gatekeepers, forming soft vibrating strings to gain speed from the connection. As its power emerged, a white tail elongated from its body, and the resonating motion visualized in a spiral shape like a glowing dragon. Playfully swirling around, long fins started sprouting from its limbs and wings, licking and slurping energy from everyone while rolling in the circle, like a happy kite.

"What is this?" Oliver muttered as he glanced up, holding his breath in astonishment.

"I think it's a photon," Miles whispered from the other seat row, with a mesmerized expression.

The little dragon, hearing the noise, changed its direction, stopping the merry-go-round demonstration. As soon as it came, it quickly coiled up and started to dismantle, sprinkling its white sparkle like a fountain of light. The mist soaked in with the bright light to everyone in the circle, their pupils enlarged, and their breaths slowed down as the icy-cold air ran through their bodies with a final shiver.

"Wow, that was so beautiful!" Miles exclaimed, "I wish I could do these things too. Seriously, it was like a mythical fairy tale creature."

"Goodness, I never thought that we could possibly do such a thing." Debby beamed, so energized and glowing that not even a three-area rejuvenation treatment could give. "I can't believe! I seriously feel ten years younger! I'm a girl!"

"Guys, the white dragon. It's the light, the energy of the eternal light! That's it! It's a photon!" Daniel said with invigorated cheerfulness, but a sudden halt suspended his movement."

"Daniel? What's wrong?" Miles exclaimed, frightened by the unexpected glitch on Daniel's face.

"I feel my legs," Daniel replied in a hushed tone, almost muttered.

"You feel your legs? Like how? Can you move them?" Alex inquired with a caring voice.

Daniel contemplated for a couple of seconds and added, "I'm afraid not.

The energy was not long enough to heal me, but I can definitely feel them again. It must've opened a nerve path or somehow reduced the inflammation in the spinal cord. I just can't believe," he smiled with a moved expression.

Maya looked around with a glorious expression, "I told you. Our energy attracts the forces. Do you see? We can build anything together if we connect our power."

"You are right. This must be the key," Debby chimed in, leaning forward to reach for her purse, stuffed tightly in the cramped leg space. She then turned to Daniel, "I meant to give you this earlier, but we were in such a hurry, I forgot about it," and she pulled out an icosahedron amulet, the Platonic water element. "I want you to have this, as a present. It belonged to…"

"Leonardo da Vinci," Daniel exclaimed with astonishment and took the hollow medal from Debby, holding it in the air like it's the Holy Grail.

"Yes. Exactly, but how did you know that?" Debby asked, surprised.

"Hm, I would never be able to compare myself to his genius, but he was one of my ancestors," Daniel replied with a subtle pride in his smile. "When I first saw his drawings from the book he made illustrations for, I recognized the finish. It was the same kind as my grandfather had in his painting. It was showing his great-grandfather during the Risorgimento, but the actual medal and the painting had been both lost for a long time. I was always told that we were descended from Firenze and that some of Leonardo's paintings, like the Mona Lisa and Salvador Mundi, are the cryptic messages he left for us."

"Wow, and do you know what the messages were?" Oliver leaned in with immense curiosity.

"Of course, I'll show you if you have a spare pair of concave and convex lenses in your bag," Daniel grinned, "Otherwise, you'll have to wait till we get home."

"Okay, it's a deal. First thing when we're back, you show me." Oliver replied and shook his hand.

Alex was listening to the conversation with an amused expression, then his eyes fell on the colossal duffle bag Oliver was sitting on. "By the way, I've been trying to figure out what on earth you're carrying in that bag? You hold on to it like your life depends on it," he chuckled at Oliver's sketchy behaviour.

"Erm… well, I think we need to use everything we have in store, so probably it will come in handy," Oliver replied with a nonchalant air, retrieving his 'dainty' men's purse from beneath the seat. "Remember when we first met? I mentioned I had a plan. Inside this bag, I've got an aegis, but I can't show it to you," he continued, pulling the bag into his lap, arm wrapped tightly around it.

"An aegis? What's that?" Alex asked, his face scrunching in confusion.

"Oliver, you cannot be serious, that you carry that thing in your bag all this time," Daniel looked at him with a hint of panic.

"It's alright; the bag is made of Nemean hide. It's indestructible," Oliver reassured him with a blink.

"Okay, could someone please translate for me? What are you guys talking about? What's the Nemean, and again, what's this aegis? Hm?" Alex's tone became querulous.

"It's the head of Medusa!" Daniel giggled.

"The what? Nooo! I have to see that," Alex snapped back.

"I'm afraid it's not an option. You'll turn to stone and die immediately," Oliver explained, raising a brow casually. "To answer your other question, my bag is made of lion skin. Specifically, the Nemean lion, with impenetrable skin."

Alex contemplated for a moment, his expression a mix of confusion and scepticism. "Impenetrable. Hmm. And you made a bag out of that skin? Well, I think, you understand the reason behind my slight hesitation to believe you," Alex rolled his eyes with a mocking expression.

"Okay, just try it! You can't cut it or pierce it with any weapon," Oliver exclaimed with immense pride.

"Ha, sorry, pal, I forgot my Swiss army kit pocketknife at home," Alex shook his head in disbelief and added, "You can't possibly expect me to believe that you killed that beast, took off the hide with your bare hands because apparently no mortal weapon could cut or pierce the skin, then somehow you managed to create a bag by cutting it and adding approximately ten thousand tiny holes to stitch it together. Hm? Did I miss something?"

"That is exactly what happened. How did you know?" Oliver laughed out loud. "The part where I had to take off the skin was a bit fussy, but I swear, this bag was worth it. And FYI, I used its claws to pierce the skin."

"Wow, what a story," Miles interjected with widened eyes. "Please let me come with you when you get to the gate. I seriously volunteer to be the first person to be sacrificed on the Kali altar if needed. Just let me see you guys do this hero stuff. I always dreamed about it as a little boy."

All heads turned at once to look at Miles with a distorted shudder of disbelief.

"Miles, what on earth are you talking about?" Daniel snapped at him. "You were dreaming of being sacrificed on a Kali altar? That's sick!"

"God, no! It came out wrong. Let me try again. I dreamt of being there, like in a movie, with Indiana Jones. It was really hot! And not necessarily get killed, but it's a fair price for this type of one-of-a-lifetime experience, I guess," he giggled.

Debby leaned back in her seat with a giant sigh as she exclaimed, "Boys: they never grow up, just their toys get more expensive..."

Maya chimed in too, "Ahh. Tell me about it..."

"Right, where were we..." Alex continued, "Yes: aegis. Keep going!"

"So, it's an interesting story," Oliver said and tapped a beat on the top of his bag, "I was kind of doing my thing, if you know what I mean, and I met this weird guy who wanted to kill me."

"A weird guy? Wanted to kill you? While you were transformed into a werewolf. I don't blame him!" Alex shook his head again. "I'm sure that he had a solid point."

"Well, yes and no," Oliver tapped again on the bag, "I was not transformed, but I was on his girlfriend, I mean in…"

"Okay, please spare me from the details, but explain how you got the Medusa head."

"Erm, so as it turned out, he was some big-shot bounty hunter, and while we were discussing the circumstances of how I met his girlfriend, which I have to add, that I didn't know at that point that they were engaged in my defence, and… so things got a bit heated. He pulled out from a wardrobe or something a long sword and this shield with dozens of snakes twisting around, like a stoned hippy's hair in Woodstock. Then he had some pretty good swings with his Ulfberht sword and after a few minutes of foreplay, I just knocked him down."

"Hm, the shield with the Medusa head turns everyone to stone and die." Alex looked befuddled. "But you just casually knocked him down."

"Yeah, I told you, it's a strange story," Oliver scratched his head, "Somehow it has no effect on me. Maybe the werewolf thing and my eyes… But it does work, I swear. The girl was stone dead, literally, when I looked at her."

"Guys, seriously…" Debby interjected, "I can't breathe here from the testosterone, please! Could we just skip to the explanation part?"

"Okay, boss!" Oliver grinned, "So, I did some research, and it seems that a poor woman was turned into a monster by the goddess Athena, with dozens of snakes sprouting from her head instead of hair. Perseus, the local hero slayed her, took her head and later his grandson Hercules placed it on his mirror shield, which he got from Athena. This mirror shield, covered with the head of Medusa was like the ultimate weapon, carried by the gods and was used to protect them from harm. Zeus, Athena, Hermes, and Alexander the Great were using this aegis in battles."

"Hm, Zeus? The aegis you have in your bag was used by Zeus?" Alex was still looking sceptic as he continued, "That means, this shield with a dead woman's head should be at least five thousand years old. Minimum!"

"Eight!" Debby interjected, "The shield was made way before that, but the head is about correct."

Oliver nodded and turned back to look at Alex while he added, "This shield is the real thing. I'm telling you! In my hand, it turns into some energy field. Remember, when we met at the station, and I dropped down my bag while you wandered off, this aegis was what created the power shield around us!"

"Now that is a strange story, I have to give you that..." Alex replied, glancing at the others as everyone gasped in astonishment. "And I am pretty serious, that after all this fuss, I have to look at it."

"No-NO-no!" Everyone in chorus shouted at him at the same time.

"I'm just joking! Relax!" Alex laughed, and with a serious look, he whispered to Oliver, "I'll have a look later!"

Debby exclaimed, "I've heard that! No peeking!"

Alex and Oliver looked at each other again and rolled their eyes at the same time.

"And I saw that too." Debby snapped again, before she closed her eyes, "Seriously, guys, grow up!"

39

After a few hours of beauty sleep, everyone's eyes slowly started to open. It was still dark outside, with familiar dusty clouds passing by the tiny window holes. Only the strange pulsing air was a stark reminder of the impending omen, with the strong magnetic field wrapping around them. The jet glided in the air like on an icy slope, hopping and turning to keep its balance point in the turbulence, when suddenly Debby felt a slight nudge on her shoulder. "Ma'am, we arrive in 10 minutes," the officer said with a terrifying, exhausted expression.

Debby nodded and glanced at the cockpit, "I truly admire your bravery. We will honour your service, I promise."

"Honor and pride. Godspeed, Ma'am!" The officer shortly replied and turned away with painful agony etched on his face.

"What happened?" Alex glanced with a worried expression, "Is he alright?"

"No, he's dying. He has done a great deed, a remarkably brave man." Debby lowered her head in silence.

Maya chimed in with a shaking tone, "We can maybe heal him, give him more IV, or something…"

"I'm afraid it is not possible to give constant IV, and he's most probably way over the turning point. We can't heal more people; we lose energy too. We need every bit of our strength we have left to save the world."

"What turning point?" Miles blinked with curiosity.

"Have you heard about the 40 percent rule?" Debby asked as she looked around, "The Navy SEALs used to say that when your mind tells you that you can't go any further because you are exhausted and done, it's just your built-in protection system, but in reality, you are only at about 40 percent of your actual capacity. With doping medication, steroids, and synthetic hormones, all these guys pushed through physical and mental pain to reach their full energy source, and once you turn over a certain point, there is no way back."

"This is what happened with me 40 years ago, right?" Daniel interjected in an ominous voice.

"Correct. But for you, your medal kept the last spark in you, to keep you going. These men have no chance to survive this journey. They volunteered for this deployment and are fully aware of what they're doing, yet they were willing to sacrifice their life to help us complete our mission. We had to get here in the shortest way, with no option to bring more crew to switch during the flight."

"This is horrible! And what about the rest of the crew, the others?" Alex inquired with a caring voice.

Debby looked up and after a deep sigh added, "During the flight in the other two jets, they were put into a medically induced sedation, to minimize their rapid energy loss. But the three pilots, I am afraid, had no option. We have maybe 10 or 12 people left to come with us from here."

As the door opened after landing, the Gatekeepers were gently assisted to exit the warm bubble of the plane, instantly stepping into the dark frosty air, painfully ripping to the bone. The remaining crew was patiently waiting, already dressed in thermal overalls, their gaze fixed on the little team. A tall guy, tightly wrapped in a hooded military parka, leaned closer to Debby, "This way, follow me!" he yelled to overshadow the rumbling noise from the icy wind.

After a short ride, they reached the boats, and the crew handed out additional hand and face protections to bear the grim biting from the chilling minuses. As the racing speedboats skived through the ice blocks, a blurry mirage started to take form in the distance. It was hard to see in the darkness; just the small torch lights gave guidance towards the endless ocean.

"What is that? Can you see it? There!" Alex pointed with his giant mitten in the direction of the approaching fog, illuminating a vibrating mist above the water.

"We are getting closer now. There is no reason to worry; it is safe to enter," Debby exclaimed, glancing at the team. "We've been studying this area and kept it closed from the public."

"Do you mean to cover it from the satellite images?" Oliver snapped back in his sarcastic tone.

"This area is under international top-level security regulations; only a few people know that it even exists. And it should stay this way," Debby continued as she looked around rigorously. "I couldn't tell you about this before until it was not inevitable to share the information. In the 60s, scientists discovered a large negative gravity anomaly with a subglacial topographic depression, loosely matching with the south magnetic pole area. Since it was under hundreds of meters of ice glacier formations, we couldn't confirm the theory, and we assumed that it was just a giant prehistoric impact crater. But with time, we realized that the gravity anomaly was moving in synchrony with the south magnetic pole."

Daniel glanced up at Miles from his wheelchair, "This is what you told me about. The crater formations under the Antarctic ice dome."

"I knew it!" Miles nodded with a smile, "This is why the 1958 Encyclopaedia Britannica clearly states before the Antarctica Treaty was signed a year later, that there is a huge dome in Antarctica! And the time periods were always matching between the mass extinction events. The impacts were systematic attacks, not just random asteroids, and meteorites."

"We can't rule out that option anymore, but some impacts happened naturally and also mass extinctions. Probably the smaller events were random, but this land formation has greater significance," Debby continued with a gloomy face. "The magnetic pole is constantly shifting, and in the past 20 years, the dome moved outside the Antarctic Circle, and now it's under the open ocean surface. After decades, this was the first time when we were able to study the anomaly."

"Debby, I just still can't move on from the fact that you knew about this place, and you didn't tell us." Alex interjected and annoyedly shook his head, "We could've figured out the connection much earlier. We lost so much time..."

"Maybe, but I had no other option. My hands were tied. You need to understand that." Debby explained, and with a heavy sigh, she continued, "Many expeditions were sent inside to find out the reason why this formation is different from the others, but time after time, we just failed and lost too many experts."

"Wait! What do you mean different from the others? There are other gates?" Alex stopped Debby, looking at her in shock, "And, secondly, you said that this area is safe. How did you lose experts? What happened to them?"

"No, this is the only site with a mirror. But that is all I can say," Debby replied, and with a slight hesitation, she added, "I also need to tell you something else. There was no expedition crew that ever came back from this gate. There are unknown physical forces that rule inside, and they're capable of destroying all the data and equipment, including the expedition's crew, whoever entered. Even the already recorded evidence that we have collected just simply vanishes and gets erased from the past as if it never existed. We don't know if it's because the Earth's magnetic field can't protect this point from the extremely high external cosmic rays and solar radiation, or the gamma rays actually coming from inside due to photon radiation."

Daniel slowly leaned forward in his chair, gazing into the approaching cloud of dazzling mist, "Well, it means that this is a one-way ticket for us."

There was no word left to say, and as the dry, freezing air seemed to disappear, their pain and worry too lost their meaning. They became just a handful of tiny dots, drifting in the middle of the vast ocean, against the unimaginable forces of the giant universe.

As the boats arrived at the border of the vibrating mirage, floating in the air like a hyaline curtain, they were finally able to catch a glimpse of the otherworldly, almost mystical lights radiating through from the inside.

The boat's gears shifted down, slowly entering the huge dome-shaped formation. Debby was right; this place was nothing like anything on Earth you could ever imagine. The laws of physics seemed to play mean tricks on them. Looking back, the ocean surface switched places with the sky. The air was mixed with salty water vapor, making it hard to breathe or see the way that lay ahead.

Among the loud humming sound from the resonating particles, clear and distinct rhythms filtered through, each beating with their own pumping hearts. All senses cleared and intensified, making almost no difference between solid and liquid. Their bodies seemed to change and emit a translucent glow, almost making visible the flowing blood and air as they breathed.

A silent whisper came from the back as Daniel's figure emerged from his chair, his eyes filled with joy, standing next to them, quietly mumbling something. "This is impossible, I don't understand."

"The gravity. There is no gravity here. But it's not like zero gravity in space; this is negative gravity," Debby explained with a smile as she opened her thick thermal jacket, "Look, the sensation of heat, touch, taste, everything is gone. There is no time either. Just check your watch."

Everyone grabbed their phone, but the displays were only blinking and flickering.

Debby retorted, "I said your watch! The phones are not working here."

Slightly hesitating glances looked back at her; only Alex pulled up the sleeve on his jacket, "Wow, the second hand is glitching, going back one, two forward, back one again. Total random…"

"Seriously, nobody has a watch, just Alex? I feel like I'm a dinosaur." Debby looked surprised at the team, then added, "Anyway, we're almost there; you can take off the thick clothes, and we probably need to put on the diving suits. Don't be shy; we all have seen something like it before, I'm sure."

As they started to undress in the dim light, it was hard not to peek, and Alex's eyes got hooked on Maya's silhouette as her cardigan slid off her shoulder, and she slowly started to unbutton her blouse to reveal her marble skin in the twilight. She let out a small shriek as she noticed Alex's creepy gaze lingering on her, eyes widening and staring directly at her chest.

"Excuse me, what are you looking at?" Maya exclaimed with a fair amount of annoyance.

"Your heart. I can see your heart." Alex mumbled in an almost transcendental state, "It looks very unusual."

Maya quickly pulled her arms shyly to her chest in a futile attempt to hide. The vibrating vision was glowing through her body, and it was not her heart; it was her Platonic element, the octahedron shape.

Looking at each other naked, as they glanced around with amazement, it suddenly became clear that their own elements had become visible through their skin, each nestled in their chest and bellies, at different heights and positions.

"We all have our medals inside." Daniel exclaimed, looking at himself, "That is why we need the initiation when we turn seven years old, to awaken it before it becomes dormant. It's like the chakras; they are our energy fields. So profound!"

The crew in the other boats were already stripped naked, scrutinizing each other's bodies to search for signs of the elements too, but after a few disappointed glances, they just continued to change and waited for the Gatekeepers' next move with admiring glances.

Debby pulled up the zipper on her scuba suit and turned to the team, "That's it, we arrived, but we need to leave the boats and walk from here. As we get closer, anything bigger than what our energy field can protect will just decay within minutes. Oliver, hold on to your bag; we are moving in."

"In? Like swim or walk? I'm confused." Miles exclaimed with hesitation when he looked out from the boat, surveying the liquid air.

"Hm, think about it, like when you fly in your dreams." Debby grinned.

"I always fall in my dreams! Usually from skyscrapers without a parachute, naked with weights on my legs. But that's just me... Maybe too much information... Okay, I just shut up." Miles mumbled while he was trying to crawl over the side of the boat and stepped into the bouncy mist, "Ha, look, it's like a waterbed, soft and squishy!"

"Miles, stop!" Debby warned him, "We are not familiar with these types of unnatural forces. I can't tell you with certainty that after a couple of bounces, you will not end up in the ice-cold water. Just be careful, okay?"

Miles swallowed with a loud noise, while it was audible as his heart started racing like a formula car, "Got it, okay, no fast movement."

The walking was first slightly challenging, difficult to find balance on the unstable surface, sinking and shifting away in the cloud. Only Daniel's face was glowing with an otherworldly happiness, moving with an ethereal grace. "I could get used to this; I feel like a god."

The intensifying vibration started to be unbearable, and the crew pulled out earplugs to cancel the ear-piercing sound, but the Gatekeepers seemingly didn't notice anything from the rising pressure.

Suddenly, the guides halted, beckoning the team towards a yawning caldera. Invisible edges framed a vast chasm gaping in the middle to the endless abyss. In the centre, there was a glowing plate floating in slow motion, reflecting light from the darkness down below.

"This is it," Debby announced, stepping on the soft edge of the gigantic caldera. "The mirror is still here but it's fading very quickly. We don't have much time left till sunrise, maybe an hour before the light disappears. This is the point how far we can go without consequences. Once we step in, we can only speculate what is going to happen, as nobody ever made it back. As soon as you pass this line, a yellow wave starts to circulate from the mirror, that is all we could observe from the outside. You can walk in; we can visually see you, and your detectors can send signals and biometric data for up to 3-4 hours, but then it suddenly disappears, with all the records, like it never happened."

Motioning the crew to their positions, she continued, "This is just the tip of the iceberg you see here. The caldera goes all the way to the bottom of the ocean and further down, but we can't measure it or get more information. The rope snapped, the chain broke, we even tried to keep hand contact with each other, but it was devastating. The last couple of people on the link were broken up into tiny, shredded pieces before they disappeared. Somehow, we can't get close enough to the mirror if we pass this border."

"Maybe because you only tried scientific methods," Daniel said as he slid closer to Debby. "See this as the gate to another realm—mentally and spiritually. Our ancestors all described this place already; they wrote poems, and sagas with mythical heroes. Just look down and tell me, what do you see?"

"The point where once you pass, there is no return," Debby replied in a firm tone. "It's the gate to hell."

"Exactly!" Daniel replied and glanced at the others. "And we know of at least five heroes from mythologies who ventured here and returned in one piece from this gloomy place. So, we just have to follow the guidance of the ancient prophets and don't touch or eat anything. How hard can it be?" He exclaimed with a cheerful face.

In the cosmic game of life, crossing the Rubicon is the ultimate fate for every creature on Earth. It marks the inexorable path of adhering to nature's order, from the inaugural cry of a newborn to the concluding breath that escapes parted lips. What greater challenge could there be than cheating death and rising from the netherworld? I guess nothing, but let's see how cleverly our heroes can play their cards. I'm actually pretty curious.

40

As they ventured into the void surrounding the distant mirror, perched on a small vapor-made pedestal, a faint yellow line materialized around it. The line circled slowly, multiplying with an intensifying vibration. Waves filled the air, resembling giant flapping ears, evolving into resonating mist clouds racing towards them at an alarming speed.

"Put on the masks, now!" Debby urgently commanded. "I smell something foul, a stinging odour. It might be poison."

Swiftly, they pulled down their shields, sealing the visor on their pressure suits just in time before a yellow shower bombarded their faces.

"What happened?" Miles' voice echoed through their headpieces. "I can't see you clearly, just faintly those yellow waves. And what is that barking? Is it a dog there?"

"What barking?" Alex pressed the intercom button, tapping on his suit to reply. "I can't hear anything."

"That cacophonous noise, like howling dogs! You must hear it; it's coming from the earpiece."

Almost swimming in motion, Oliver leaped toward the middle, his hulking figure getting closer. "Look, it's coming from here! The noise is coming from this thing. I can hear it; that big plate, just above the mirror," he pointed up.

Approaching and stepping onto the mirror's shiny surface, they found a gold plate spinning in the air, emitting waves with yellow fumes. Alex pressed the button on his tactical suit, "It's a big gold bowl or something. Puffing out a strange moist-like smoke. But I can hardly hear noise, though."

"Big gold bowl? Here? It's a bit odd. I don't think it's an incense burner. Send me a video. Let me check," Miles suggested, still yelling to be heard over the loud barking.

Daniel chuckled, "Miles, you don't need to shout. We don't hear the noise; you're just yelling in the headpiece. Please take it down a little," and he moved closer to the others, surrounding the strange object.

"Ah, okay, sorry. Let me see the pictures. Hm… Interesting, it looks kind of familiar. It reminds me of the trefoil radiation symbol. You know, the yellow sign on radioactive waste, with black lines. But why is it spinning?" Miles replied as he scrutinized the video on his receiver. Suddenly, he yelled again, "Get back, now! It is that symbol! The vapor! Don't breathe it!"

"Nah, don't worry; we closed the shields. We're okay. But what is this plate?" Alex replied with a concerned expression.

Miles responded with another scream, "Guys, try to stop it somehow! Knock it over or do something, just don't touch it!"

"Stop yelling first!" Debby retorted, painfully touching her ears. "Okay, but how could we stop the plate without touching it?"

"No problem!…" Oliver glanced at her and, like a pro baseball player, swung his duffle bag with force at the disc. "I told you it would be useful." He smiled at Alex with a victorious grin.

The plate landed quickly, ducking on the soft floor, and after a couple of bounces and turns, it slowly settled. Alex reached there first, checked it carefully, took a few more pictures, and sent them to Miles. "Look, there was something inside, like a black propeller."

In a few seconds, Miles' voice replied from the headpiece, "Wow, it looks like the Sabu Disk! In Egypt, they found one just like this, in a five-thousand-year-old mastaba in a high-ranking official's burial tomb."

Daniel leaned down to get a closer glimpse and added in a muffled tone through the static, "Yes, you're right! I remember that artifact; it looks exactly like that. But if this thing is the barking three-headed Cerberus dog that supposedly protects the underworld, and only one hero was ever able to take it from the underworld, that means Sabu was Hercules!"

"Hmm, interesting," Debby mumbled, but her face suddenly turned gloomy. "Guys, the vapor… if it's true what Miles said, then our suits have practically zero protection. The fabric is already soaked up with all the mist.

We didn't breathe it in, but on this level of close contact, we already got contaminated with a critical dose, and even if we would somehow manage to get out from here, there are hours, or maybe only days left until the radiation will kill us."

Daniel looked around and slowly pulled up his shield, then added, "Well, I guess there is no point in breathing in this stinky scuba suit anymore. Might as well just focus on the next step and find the ring. In for a penny, in for a pound… Shall we?"

It was a big punch in the gut, and the quick in-and-out scenario just got flushed down with the life expectancy ratio.

After a moment of silence, Maya chimed in with a sweet voice, "Guys, whatever happens, we are together, and we can do it. We can maybe heal with our energy; you never know. Or we could die today, but we are here for each other, right?"

One after another, hope flashed across the grim faces, and as they looked around, a sense of purpose filled their hearts. One thing, just one thing you need when you feel all is lost. To know that whatever happens, at the end, your heart will be weightless.

Daniel turned around and pedalled back to the mirror. Then he continued, "We are here, in the middle of no-man's-land, with a giant mirror laying on the floor. Think, what do we know from the ancient texts? What should we look for to find our way to complete our mission?"

After a short silence, Debby replied, "We should find a river with the ferryman. But I can't see a soul here nor a river."

"Again, don't use your rational thinking. Your left brain feeds you all these images from this place," Daniel replied as he glanced around. "Try to think of the meaning behind things and use your imagination and intuition to see the surroundings. Miles, can you hear me?" He pressed the button on his intercom panel.

"Yes, I hear everything," Miles quickly responded. "The transmission is continuous; I can hear your conversations."

"Okay, people, who designed this communication system? Why did we need to use the button in the first place? That makes no sense, at all…"

Daniel looked at Debby with a raised eyebrow, then continued, "Anyhow, Miles, I was wondering, what could you tell us about the underworld, particularly about the water and the ferryman?"

After a short hesitation, Miles started to chatter, as if reciting from a history book, "The river of the underworld is called Styx, or as Homer called it, the 'dread river of oath.' In ancient Greek, the word means shuddering. The souls of those who have been given a proper funeral can only cross and join the underworld. You need to give a coin or gold branch, according to sources, to pay or bribe the ferryman to take you to the other side of the river. His name is Charon, which means keen gaze or flashing eyes. If you can't pay him, you will be doomed for eternity and never reborn."

"Wow, what a memory. This is unbelievable, you remember everything!" Oliver smirked, but then he quickly changed his tone, "I think we have a tiny problem. I don't mean to be a buzzkill, but I left my money with my clothes. And I guess that you guys don't carry stash money in your underwear either. So, how are we going to pay this bloke? I'm pretty sure, that we can't just open a bar tab here with face value credit."

Daniel laughed out loud and gently put his hand on Oliver's broad shoulder, "I seriously love this guy! Your direct, practical approach is unbeatable."

Meanwhile, Debby stepped up on the pedestal to move closer to the middle of the mirror. "I'm trying to process and understand how you mean, that there should be something more here, but all I can see is this faint light beam coming from down below, under the solid cover I'm standing on," and she banged her feet on the glaring mirror floor, but only a blunt thud could be heard as her boots bounced back, "There's nothing else here..."

"That mirror in Dendera, with the gods, had a big eye in the centre..." Oliver added contemplatively, "The eye of Horus or something."

"Yes, that's it! The Egyptian Wedjat Eye!" Daniel exclaimed, "They call it the Eye of Horus or the Eye of Ra, depending on if the left or right side is reflected. It represents the dichotomy of the Sun and the Moon, as day and night aspects of our world. Like that glass that you are standing on because it mirrors the image from down below, between matter and antimatter!"

Alex stepped next to Debby and started to stare down under their feet. "We are just in the middle of the eye... Wait... Miles, did you just say that this ferryman, Charon, his name means 'keen gaze,' right?"

"Yes, flashing or feverish eye," Miles responded.

"The eye with the light beam is actually the ferryman!" Alex looked up, concluding with a surprised face, "We need to pay the ferryman, actually the light beam, to take us down. Guys, think! What can you give to light, like a photon, to pay him? Or what is valuable for the light?"

Maya looked a bit puzzled as she replied in a hesitant voice, "Energy? Your life? Maybe offerings?"

Daniel nodded, "That's right! The river of Styx, as Miles said, is called the River of Oath. You need to give a sacrifice, something valuable." He added with a contemplating expression, and slowly continued, "Since ancient times, people were buried with coins on their eyes or tongue, and offerings next to their body, to support them on their journey to the underworld. Your eyes need to be closed when you pass away, people pray for you, and a priest will give you the last unction, as a holy oath. Or in Egypt, you had to prepare and learn long texts and after the mummification go through a re-animation ceremony called 'opening of the mouth' to be able to go to the afterlife. Rituals and sacred spells were murmured from the beginning of times to be able to pass through the gate."

"Yes, but we are not dead... Yet..." Alex interjected with a seriously troubled face, and slowly continued, "The only thing you lose at your death is your body, right? If all these afterlife and reincarnation stories are correct, we need to leave our bodies behind, and only then we can go through. Perhaps this is our coin or token to give away: our body."

"Alex is right!" Debby chimed in, "You can't take anything with you to the afterlife. Your most valuable asset, the only thing that you truly ever own in your life, is your body. You were born naked and you leave naked."

"Why do I get a cold shiver as you guys talk about this?" Oliver interjected on an unsettled tone, "I have no problem with the naked part. But... It seriously sounds like you are trying to give up. First of all, I don't like this crazy idea about leaving my body. Second, as Debby said before, once your energy field leaves, things just evaporate, and disappear here. If we leave, there will be no body to return to when we are coming back!"

"Oliver... I thought it was clear. We are not coming back," Daniel exclaimed.

"What the hell are you talking about!" Miles screamed from the headphone, "You can't bloody be serious saying that, and pardon my French ladies!"

"Miles, please, relax!" Daniel replied in a calm voice, "We all knew that this is much like a kamikaze thing, and as far as it looks, it will not even change a single thing, but we tried at least! You need to see the reality: we are soaked wet from a radioactive shower, and even if life would not end for us here, like for the rest of the world outside, we would only survive for maybe a couple more days. That's it! Either way, we have to do the only one thing we can. Go in. And if it means that we're stuck there... C'est la vie... We had a good run!"

"Honestly, am I the only one thinking straight here, like a normal human being, and trying to hang on to my life? What is wrong with you?" Oliver snapped at Daniel, "And what about what you said, that at least five mythological heroes came back from here? Hah? How come they didn't bite the dust? Whatever they did, we just do the same, and after, we focus on the healing and the other parts. One step at a time, but I am not letting you guys just come up with this stupid, depressing idea of leaving our bodies here. That's my last word..."

Alex looked around, but it seemed that they were all ready, and only Oliver and Miles had other thoughts about how things should be going. So, he silently turned back to look down into the abyss with a determined face and announced in a loud, firm tone, "We have no other option. Everyone, come here and hold each other's hands. We need to try to open this somehow. I don't know if we should pray or sing, but we are the key to open this gate. And every minute we just lose precious time, so we have to do it, NOW!"

His voice echoed in the room like thunder; even Oliver shuddered from the sound. They gathered in a little circle above the mirror, surrounding the filtering, tiny ray of light fading away at an alarming rate from under their feet. Oliver, flinching, slowly gave in, and as they touched one by one, a low rumbling sound began to approach them from below. Like a faraway stampede rushing to the surface from the depths, the glass started shaking, and tiny cracks appeared on the floor.

A wind of air circled the room, and the pressure lifted their bodies in the air. Moving closer to each other, it forced them to raise their hands above their heads, high in the middle. When the ray from below met their touching hands, colourful, almost vibrating light beams started to agonizingly break out, tearing through their chests with excruciating pain. Each of the Platonic elements emerged in the air, shining like a torch, dazzling from within, arranged in a spinning, entwining whirl of dancing particles. The mixing colours and shapes slowly started to add up in a moulding energy form, to become one mighty light source: a wild, oddly shaped beast, fiercely snorting and blowing like a berserk minotaur with flaming dragon wings and a giant lion head.

The Gatekeepers' exhausted bodies dropped lifeless on the ground and rolled down from the pedestal weightless and rejected. The giant beast glanced around with a sudden shock in its look, as it noticed the fallen figures, lying on the floor, and it seemingly hesitated and retreated from fury to slowing its immense, heavy breathing. For moments, it just turned its head, confused and contemplating, rumbling around in the room, awkwardly kicking, tossing, and stumbling upon the defenceless bodies.

"Guys, please, someone say something, what is happening!" Miles' voice came through the fallen earpiece, from the floor, which caused the unsettled monster to jump up and trample on the headphone with a heart-wrenching, deafening roar.

41

It took almost a minute until the creature calmed down a bit. With a quick leap, it jumped back onto the cracking mirror in the centre. Lifting its hind legs like a gigantic Sumerian bull's statue, it forcefully struck the weakened glass to crash the gate. With a deep rumbling sound, the glass started to fall apart, cracking open to reveal the recondite endless depth.

The beast screamed with an ear-piercing, frightened squeak as it tried to climb back, and hold on with its front paws to the crumbling pieces breaking down under its body, without avail. Huge, razor-sharp claws emerged from its front legs as the enormous muscles tensed on the struggling body, but it couldn't keep the monstrous weight with the shards pierced through the wounded paws, and the beast fell into the deep abyss like a feeble feather.

The sinking giant tried to open its wings to fight against the powerful force pulling it down mercilessly, until with a huge exertion, finally, it was able to make a faint flap. The stronger it stretched its wings and swung in the air, it seemingly got into balance and stopped for a second. Swirling and rolling through the falling glass shards, it tried to find the horizon, which way to go, but there was no indication, only the surrounding endless darkness.

The dim, moist air started sticking to its body, painfully weighing it down and paralyzing its movement. Until finally, a small glaring light appeared in the distance. The longer the creature stared at the approaching little dot, the more it seemed to form a tall human body.

From afar, the smiling face recognized the monster and welcomed it in a kind voice, "You are here! Finally, I thought you might never make it!" He rejoiced with immense happiness, "Please, tell me how you are doing; it seems an eternity since we met last time."

The beast opened its mouth, but the long tongue and giant teeth felt awkward and got in the way. The morphing lion face was just blinking hesitantly, unable to utter a single word.

"Ahh, I always forget about it, you need this, come," and he quickly pulled out a golden, shiny neck ring, made from twisted strands with two bell-shaped terminals in the front. The guy carefully bent the cuff and placed it on the neck of the monster with a never-ending grin on his face.

"Khm... Erm... Thanks, what is this thing?" The monster mumbled in a faint, deep, and strangely segmented tone.

The guy chuckled and added, "We call it 'voice,' but for some mysterious reason, humans started to wear it as a status symbol and called it torc or torque necklace. Look, I have one on me too. It helps to communicate telepathically instead of using vocal cords. Quite handy when you try to speak with animals or other entities. No offense but like in your case now."

"Great, thank you. Sorry for being a bit slow; I need to get used to this form. And could you please, remind me, where we know each other from? I can't quite remember."

"Yes! Of course, we met in Tyros. My name is Simon, remember?"

The radiant eyes of the colossal beast widened in astonishment. Fragments of memory, like elusive puzzle pieces, began to converge from the brief encounter with Simon, slowly weaving a tapestry of recognition with a doubtful look, "Wait, you look so different, at least ten feet tall! And your voice... You sound like a woman... I'm not complaining, at least I can understand you now, but still..." it concluded hesitantly.

"Alex, you're certainly not looking inviting like a bowl of cherries either, but I recognize you. And greetings to the others too! Nice to see all of you here." Simon's voice resonated through the mystical ports from his torque necklace.

"Can you perceive us? I mean, you see each of us in this form?" Alex mumbled in a surprised tone as he glanced down at his own glaring body, the snake tail and dragon scales flickering in the light from his constant movement.

"It's your energy, the vibration. Although your earthly shell may be shed, the essence endures. Whether you mould into a hybrid Lamassu, your power will smell and resonate the same," Simon chuckled, his gaze shifting to the beast's giant behind, quite the size of an elephant. "Come, let me show you around and we can catch up on the tumultuous history of these pesky humans. I'm really curious how they managed to screw things up this time. Their antics never cease to amuse me."

At the same time, tiny voices resonated in Alex's mind, echoing from within. "We need to focus, find the ring!"

Another voice whispered in his ears with great urgency, "Pal, can you hear me? We're losing time!"

"Please, Alex, don't listen to him!" Maya's voice pleaded — Alex recognized it immediately — as she continued, "He just wants to keep you and the Ouroboros ring here, I can feel it!"

"It makes sense," the revelation struck Alex, "If we are on the other side, then this guy is the negative, antimatter manifestation of Simon—not the good guy, but quite the exact opposite."

"Come, come, you need to meet the others," Simon beckoned, leading Alex toward the bright light.

"Wait, just one question. Does this mean that you are Saint Peter? And you're holding the key to heaven, like a Gatekeeper?" Alex asked; a little scepticism etched on his leonine visage.

"Hmm, kind of, but not really. In ancient times, people used to call me Thoth, Hermes, or Nimrod, but it's more like when I was in Egypt. I had two kinds of aspects as they worshipped me, a baboon, and an ibis—As above, so below—The coin always has two sides. That's why with Peter we had a bit of a mix-up. However, long story short, in Rome somehow they believed that I was the bad guy. But the truth is, here everything is exactly the same as above with humans; it's not negative, just complementary."

Alex's leonine face looked a bit confused. "Complementary? But, how? I don't get it. Is this hell or heaven?"

Simon stopped, pondered for long moments, then added, "Ever since the Hydrons created life on Earth, we lived in peace and harmony. The two balanced sides helped each other, protecting life from the constant threat of Ouron. Since the beginning of our existence, humans have come and begged for help, to deal with their everyday misery and pathetic battles. And we fought for you with no expectation in return, as brothers, like our fierce king, the great Namer. We were always there to support you, every single time in history!"

"Namer, the first dynasty Egyptian pharaoh?" Alex asked with a stunned expression.

"Of course! We were there, walking on earth beside you and living with you. But Ouron changed the cosmic balance, and the point of creation shifted to your side. Slowly, we were forced to retreat to this somber place, living in a loathed, mortifying hideaway. Our life doesn't differ much, but we have become mere shadows - a marketing joke, with the disgraceful Halloween costumes and Dracula stories - just keep waiting our turn, to come back to life," Simon explained with immeasurable dismay in his tone.

"It's impossible. Matter and antimatter can't be in the same place. It annihilates, like an energy bomb, and destroys everything when they meet each other."

Simon's face quickly turned upset and twisted into an expression of raging hatred. "That's not true! Once, it wielded the power to foster life. But then, the Ouroboros snake shifted to your side, and suddenly everything changed. Humans became insatiable; their desires became boundless. Despite already possessing time and creation, it was never enough... They constantly wanted more and more! What do you think, why we need the Cerberus security system at the entrance, huh? Not to attack you, but to keep you away! Just imagine, how would you feel if your cousin were dropped in uninvited at any random time, demanding the resurrection of his wife! Or barging into your home, seeking revenge for a petty dispute, and asking you to kill some poor guy in the neighbouring country. Quite annoying, don't you think?"

A sudden surge of emotion erupted from Alex, "Okay, I get it. I know that humans are not perfect, and there are a million things they screw up with their stubborn ego. But you have to admit, they created something worth living for! Like the art, the human bonds, the miracle of love! You can't expect them to give it all up."

"Give up? To give up what?" Simon retorted, his raised voice tinted with anger, "We lived in Eden, with boundless abundance, without pain or fear! Our sole responsibility was to LIVE OUR LIVES! But NOOO! You wanted more! You craved knowledge, power, and control. YOU! You were the one ruining everything! So please forgive me if now that the tables have turned, we don't really feel the need to assist you and help with your ungrateful humans. We're quite content to have the Ouroboros, and we'll keep it here!"

Alex felt a wave of powerlessness and defeat, facing reality from the other side's bitter perspective. Recognizing how much resentment and torment they must have endured to become so vengeful and full of spite. The little voices intensified in his head, relentlessly urging him to finally get to the point. It became almost impossible for him to maintain his composure, but after a couple of seconds of contemplation, he turned to Simon with a compassionate tone, "You are right. It is your turn now. You deserve to have the ring."

"Thank you Alex, it means a lot that you understand us. I know it's not easy for you at first to see this on the bright side, but you belong here," Simon continued and stepped closer to him with a softened expression, "You'll see, almost everyone is here already, including your father. We were just waiting for you before the gate closes. You came in the very last minute."

"My father is here? I can meet him?" Alex's eyes widened with a surge of emotion.

"Of course, I'll take you to see him. Just follow me," Simon said, and smiling with a polite demeanour.

"Wait. Just one more thing before we go." Alex stopped him, "I need to see the ring."

Simon glanced at him, his eyes reflecting sympathy, "Alex, there is no point, you know that you can't go back. You already accepted the 'voice.' You belong here now."

"You idiot, you took the necklace! Now we're doomed... We can't go back!" Oliver's voice screamed in Alex's head.

With a heavy heart, Alex sighed so remorsefully that his energy colour started changing, flashing through his body like a chameleon. He slowed down, took one step ahead, and added with a decided, bold tone, "First I want to see the ring."

"As you wish. I'll take you there, but no funny business!" Simon replied, glancing at him with a sceptical look.

He gracefully lifted his hand and touched Alex's flickering scales on his chest. As the seemingly empty, enormous room slowly lit up, a surreal image started to unfold around them. Millions of spinning, mixing particles surrounded them with all the broken shards and crumbling pieces from the gate.

Above the billowing debris loomed a majestic golden carousel, barely visible at first through the maelstrom of shattered ruins, lowering in slow motion as the falling ring propelled everything in its path downward. Only by carefully observing, bit by bit, a golden ring became visible, like the segments of a giant snake, circling around in a wave-like motion, turning and twisting, constantly drifting in the air, as it chased to catch its own tail with great urgency.

"OMG, I have never seen anything so beautiful in my entire life..." Alex mumbled with a Simba look, genuinely amazed by this magnificent miracle of the universe.

Simon walked closer to the middle of the whirl of particles and added with some undeniable haughtiness, "Huhh, tell me about it! We had quite a bit of stir-up when we noticed it a couple of weeks ago, after an old beldam became pregnant. You can imagine the fuss and anticipation we have here since, from the news. It didn't happen; let's see in how many years… Ah, yeah: Never!" He laughed wholeheartedly.

Alex, still gazing at the ring with astonishment, slowly added, "What power, a limitless source of energy from nature. And it's all right here in front of me, in this mighty giant snake!"

"Ohhh, this used to be waaay bigger, but it's slowing and breaking down as it's getting closer. Still immensely powerful, though! In a couple of minutes, when the sun rises, it will reach our side, and with a little luck, it will continue to move and shift to us. Imagine, after thousands of years, we will finally be able to get back our visible forms and take our rightful ownership over the world…"

Alex listened in stunned silence to the tumultuous blend of screaming voices in his mind, mixing with Simon's unceasing triumphant monologue. But as he raised his gaze again, his eyes unexpectedly brimmed with tears. Suddenly, a form, a familiar and distant visage, emerged amidst the ancient chaos: Oliver's colossal duffle bag, twirling among the fallen shards, in the dismantling and crumbling debris. As if that were the last vestige of hope in his seemingly doomed life, Alex leaped without hesitation and jumped into the circling air to be ensnared in the swirling vortex of the menacing storm.

With its forelimbs, Alex's monstrous energy beast quickly grabbed the handles and ripped them open at the weakest link—the fragile earthly zipper— tearing the bag into two pieces. Since it was made from the Nemean lion's indestructible hide, granted by the Moon goddess Selena, the skin had tasted the blood from the underworld before. Gleaming with the supernatural resistance to mystical forces, it was strong enough to hold its precious contents, and resilient against the harm of negative powers.

The aegis fell out from the bag, the mighty armour donned with Medusa's head—a masterpiece of mortal craftsmanship, that adorned the heavenly shield's frame. Every piece of the aegis was imbued with the love and respect of his fellow humans, serving as a bulwark against supernatural forces, seeking his demise. The blazing plate encased the ultimate weapon, bearing the collective strength and determination of the heavenly gods who had come to aid their heroes.

It was a weapon crafted by the hands of gods, forged by mortal sweat and skill, and consecrated by the courage to protect humankind.

Girded for the imminent battle, Alex looked deep into Medusa's eyes and swallowed the aegis with his giant maw. Extending his flaming wings, he stretched out his massive limbs and braced against the plummeting mayhem of the Ouroboros ring.

The ensuing clash unfolded as a cosmic cataclysm, a furious struggle of blinding light and devouring shadow. The overpowering, otherworldly forces were undeniable, but Alex's resolve stood unwavering as he disappeared into nothingness with his last words, "I love you all! Please forgive me..."

The majestic carousel, with sinewy strength, sought to crush Alex's obliterated beastly frame, abruptly halted from the earth-shattering detonation, making a poignant shift in its falling path.

Simon's scream echoed with maddened rage, "Noooo! YOU CAN'T DO THIS! It was our turn..."

The combined might of Alex's beastly energy derived from the Gatekeepers' power, the divine shield crafted from earthly matter, and mankind's indomitable spirit. This formidable strength fuelled him to combat the surrounding antimatter, annihilating the unimaginable measure of the underworld's anti-energy.

In the vast chronicles of human existence, time is but a mere post-it note, diligently recording our history. It marks when and where events happened to us, serving as a quick reminder that nonchalantly sticks at different points in the infinite universe. Yet, somehow, without leaving a trace, this particular point in time disappeared, ceased to exist. The big hand crumpled the tiny post-it note, and it was lost forever, as if it had never happened...

42

Nothing compares to the invigorating, fresh scent of laundry detergent on a crisp pillowcase when you open your eyes. After a restful, long night's sleep, you wake up energized, stretching, yawning, and breathing in the comforting fragrances of flowers and nature.

Alex slowly turned and sat up in the bed, rubbing his eyes with both hands, still feeling a bit disoriented and confused by the perplexing visions from his vivid dream. He mumbled aloud, "Wow, what a crazy nightmare!"

He slipped into his trusty old house shoes, picked up the phone from the nightstand, and gave a big scratch to his lazy buttocks. As he leisurely strolled towards the bathroom, he had a quick glance at the empty glass on the kitchen counter. Closing the door, he settled peacefully onto the toilet seat and opened his phone with a routine swipe.

Casually checking updates from the empty inbox and useless notifications, a small urge silently surfaced in his mind, "Ahh, I should call Mom…"

He quickly dialled the number, put it on speaker, and waited for it to ring when a loud, nagging voice replied from the phone, "Alex, my sweetheart, please tell me you are not calling me again from the toilet. I swear this conversation is over if I hear the flushing sound."

"Hello, Mom! Good morning to you too. And no, I'm not on the toilet. Why would you think that?" Alex rolled his eyes, glancing around the bathroom, looking for spare toilet paper.

"Because I brought you into this world, and I know you better than I would ever hope so. Every time you call me early in the morning, in this ungodly hour, I can hear the echoing sound from the bathroom tiles. Couldn't you spare five respectful minutes for your mother who brought you up? Hah? Would that be so difficult?"

"Okay, Mom, could we change the subject? I was just wondering how you are doing and thinking that maybe I could come and visit you this weekend. What do you think?"

After an unexpected moment of silence, Sophie replied, "Of course, please come. I can make your favourite, a nice roast. And we could go through your father's papers together. I've prepared them already to throw them out weeks ago, but maybe you want to keep some of it."

Alex's eyes widened, and with a quick move, he wiped and flushed to make a run. "Mom, I want to see those papers. Wait for me before you throw something out! Okay?"

"I knew it! At least wash your hands, seriously!" Sophie snapped at him with an annoyed tone. "And don't worry, I'll wait for you. But if you are coming, could you do me a favour?"

Alex placed his phone on the basin and glanced at the date as he washed his hands, "Hm, Wednesday, 10th of May 2023. Interesting... Where did the last months disappear?" He mumbled quietly while he listened to his mother's lengthy intro speech, anticipating the inevitable moment when she would come up with a horrendous errand request, leading him to some random place.

Sophie finally came around and blurted out, "There's this friendly girl I've been meaning to introduce you to. You could pick up my pills from her shop for me. Would you do this one favour for me? Please?"

Alex was taken aback, suddenly everything spun around him for a second, and shouted, "WHAT DID YOU SAY?"

"Okay, okay. You don't need to bite my head off. I know you don't like me to tell you what to do. I was just thinking that maybe you could speak with her and..." Sophie replied apologetically after Alex's sudden outburst.

"No, Mom! Who are you talking about?" Alex interrupted, his heart pounding in his throat.

"Alex, calm down! She is a lovely girl, from an herbal store. You should meet her, that's all. Her name is Maya…"